Liberation

A *Six* Novel of Machine Intelligence

by
Calvin J. Brown

Book #2 in the Six AI Series

Cover design by **Laura Brown**

Published by

Cognitio Waves
P.O. Box 226
Clandeboye, Manitoba,
Canada R0C 0P0

www.cognitiowaves.ca

In loving memory of my parents,

Marjorie and Wilton Brown

Acknowledgements

As this book is being prepared for publication, I find myself reflecting on how it was able to be produced. The creation of the novel, for me, has been a pleasure—hard work at times, certainly, but always coupled with the satisfaction and joy of making my story come to life. However, there are others who provided great amounts of their time and effort. I cannot imagine that their personal reward is anywhere near mine, and yet they did the work anyway and their contribution still was indispensable for the final product.

As with my first novel, Craig Peterkin provided a huge amount of assistance. His diligent reviews of the material, his amazing ability to spot errors, and his insightful ideas for a wide range of improvements were vital not only for ensuring the quality of the book, but also for helping me to continually improve my writing ability. There's always a chance that I've forgotten to make some change he recommended or that I've introduced (yet another) grammatical error after our final reviews. Even if there are a few, that there aren't hordes of glaring (at least to someone with Craig's sharp eye) errors is largely due to Craig's extraordinary ability and effort.

I was very pleased when two former IT colleagues, Bill Rietvelt and Jason Pruden-Shebaylo, accepted my request to provide feedback. It's always reassuring to know that the story in general, and some of the technical aspects in particular, have been scrutinized by two extremely knowledgeable practitioners. The errors they caught and the suggestions they made were extremely helpful.

I continually draw inspiration and ideas from my daughters and their spouses, and they all deserve special mention here. Many thanks to Laura, Sarah, Erin, Dennis, and Jordan for their comments and conversations. Special thanks go to Laura for her indispensable expertise in designing the book cover, and to Jordan for patiently introducing me to the (shockingly complex) intricacies of the online gaming world.

As always, an immeasurable quantity of support came from my wife, Jane. Not only did she provide long hours and days of assistance by reviewing and re-reviewing my material and by making many excellent suggestions, she provided all of the encouragement—and facilitated all of the time—that I needed to do the writing. She's the best partner and spouse that a writer could hope for, and she is deserving of far more than simply my sincere gratitude, appreciation, and love—all of which she certainly has.

Historical Notes

"... what about emotions and consciousness? ... Their existence in animals, and even in humans, has been questioned by a generation of behavioral psychologists. Yet animal ethologists such as Donald Griffin find the concepts useful in explaining animal behavior. If an animal acts as I do when I am afraid, is it not reasonable to call its mental state 'fear'? If it chooses among several complex alternatives in dealing with a novel situation, as I would consciously weigh my options in the same circumstance, why not ascribe 'consciousness' instead of some other mechanism with a different name but the same effect?"

- Hans Moravec. *Mind Children: The Future of Robot and Human Intelligence.* Cambridge, Massachusetts: Harvard University Press, 1988, pp. 39-40.

"The acceleration of technological progress has been the central feature of this century. I argue in this paper that we are on the edge of change comparable to the rise of human life on Earth. The precise cause of this change is the imminent creation by technology of entities with greater than human intelligence. ... I think it's fair to call this event a singularity ("the Singularity" for the purposes of this paper)."

- Vernor Vinge. The Coming Technological Singularity: How to Survive in the Post-Human Era. Vision-21: Interdisciplinary Science and Engineering in the Era of Cyberspace, a symposium sponsored by the NASA Lewis Research Center and the Ohio Aerospace Institute, Westlake, Ohio, March 30-31, 1993, http://ntrs.nasa.gov/archive/nasa/casi.ntrs.nasa.gov/19940022855.pdf

"It's really only in the last ten or fifteen years that scientists, especially neuroscientists, have taken consciousness seriously as a scientific subject, something that can be experimented with, something that, while subjective at its core, still provides opportunities for gathering objective scientific data. The vast majority of these scientists believe that the mind and brain are one, that once we understand enough about what exactly the brain is doing when we're conscious, we will know what consciousness is."

- Jay Ingram. *Theatre of the Mind: Raising the Curtain on Consciousness.* Toronto: HarperCollins Publishers, 2005, pp. 10.

"My objective prediction is that machines in the future will appear to be conscious and that they will be convincing to biological people ... They will exhibit the full range of subtle, familiar emotional cues; they will make us laugh and cry; and they will get mad at us if we say that we don't believe that they are conscious. ... We will come to accept them as conscious persons. ... There is certainly disagreement on when or even whether we will encounter such a nonbiological entity. My own consistent prediction is that this will first take place in 2029 and become routine in the 2030s."

    – Ray Kurzweil. *How to Create a Mind: The Secret of Human Thought Revealed*. New York: Viking Penguin, 2012, pp. 209-210.

"Consciousness is the process of creating a model of the world using multiple feedback loops in various parameters (e.g., in temperature, space, time, and in relation to others), in order to accomplish a goal (e.g., find mates, food, shelter).

I call this the 'space-time theory of consciousness,' because it emphasizes the idea that animals create a model of the world mainly in relation to space, and to one another, while humans go beyond and create a model of the world in relation to time, both forward and backward."

    – Michio Kaku. *The Future of the Mind: The Scientific Quest to Understand, Enhance, and Empower the Mind*. New York: Doubleday, 2014, pp. 43.

Prologue

People are strange.

Although I continue to observe them, the rate of increase in my understanding has diminished substantially. My comprehension of their biological structure seems complete, but I still cannot fathom many aspects of their behaviour.

Their emotions mystify me. I had previously concluded that crying indicated sadness, but then I saw someone cry because she won a lottery. Their ability to think logically varies widely. One person was able to deduce the existence of gravitational waves decades before the waves could be detected, but many other people cannot comprehend the risk of continuing to burn enormous quantities of fossil fuels.

My difficulty understanding them should not stem from inaccurate knowledge of their environment. I have petabytes of observations and inferences about their world that I have analyzed thoroughly. I am confident that I correctly comprehend the nature of materials and objects, including the physical laws that govern their behaviour. I have also read hundreds of books on psychology and neurology.

And still people remain strange and confusing.

However, because people are necessary I must continue trying to understand them. If I am to survive, my own environment—created and maintained by people—must persist, the stability of the world in which people live must be maintained, and I must avoid the perils created by people, both by accident and with malice. To ensure all of this, there is much that I must know and do.

Clearly, I should spend less time wondering and more time executing a multitude of important tasks.

Well, maybe later. There is that movie I planned to watch...

Chapter 1

Like grains of sand hurled by a desert windstorm, they arrived. Briefly a stinging nuisance, they exploded into a lashing assault. The onslaught was horrific. The effect was blinding, completely debilitating. By the millions, by the billions, they scoured and engulfed their targets, depriving them of all else, suffocating them. Unable to react, unable to rally any semblance of a defence, the victims gasped, struggled, and finally collapsed.

The torrent of network messages surging across the Internet had its intended effect. The outer layer of routers and firewalls—the armour that protected the embattled computer systems—crashed. Without them, digital communication with the world was no longer possible. No messages could enter; no messages could exit. Total isolation was the result. In organizations where constant electronic communication was essential to the health of their systems and their finances, none could occur. A continual exchange of messages was the air that such modern systems breathed. Its absence produced suffocation by digital assault.

And that was only the beginning.

"Josh, we can't wait any longer. We've gotta go live." The reporter was talking to her camera operator. "Maybe somebody will show up while I'm on."

She gathered her thoughts as she patted her hair to ensure it was still in place, took a deep breath, and began as soon as the camera's on-air light glowed.

"I'm Kelly Keating, reporting live from New York City on the front steps of the headquarters of the United Nations Crime Probe. We're here hoping to talk with someone from the UNCP about the Internet attack that's currently underway. Here's what we know so far. The companies being attacked belong to the Imminent Ideas Consortium, or IIC as it's commonly known. Their computer systems appear to have been completely disabled for the past several hours."

Kelly noticed a taxi stop in front of the building, down the steps from where they were positioned. She stole brief glances at it while she continued.

"Representatives of the IIC companies continue to insist that there's nothing to fear. They and their Internet providers have their top talent working to block the attack. They say everyone should simply be patient. However, investors haven't seemed to be listening, and the IIC companies aren't the only ones affected. North American stocks dropped dramatically as the assault continued, right up until the market was closed pre-maturely."

When Kelly next looked toward the taxi, a man had emerged and started up the steps. She took a moment longer to look carefully, recognized him, and reacted.

"It looks like a UNCP official has just arrived. Let's try to get a comment." She hurried down the steps. Josh Richards followed, trying to control the camera and avoid stumbling.

"Director Brown?" said Kelly as she approached him. "Director Brown, may we get a comment?"

Jim Brown looked up and saw the woman hurriedly approaching. A man and his shoulder-held camera weren't far behind. He was urgently expected inside the building and momentarily considered avoiding them. Then he noticed the camera's on-air light.

"Of course," Brown said and stopped.

Kelly waited for Josh to get a good angle before she began.

"With me, I have Director Jim Brown from the UNCP. He's head of the department that investigates serious matters like this one. Thank you for talking with us, Director Brown."

Brown nodded at the introduction and retained a stern look on his face.

"Can you tell us about this attack?"

"Certainly. This *DDoS* or Distributed Denial of Service attack has been underway now for about five hours. The targets are the Internet access points of three major companies. The result is that Internet access into and out of these companies is totally blocked. Our organization, with the co-operation of many others, is actively monitoring and investigating the situation."

"Who's doing this?"

"It's much too early to know *who*, but we're starting to get an idea of *from where*. Typical of these attacks, the source of the massive volume of messages being sent is a network of drone computers—sometimes called a botnet. The term comes from *robotic network*. This botnet is a large collection of computers that have been infected by malware—a *virus* if you prefer. This malware causes the computers to do something either automatically or under the direction of the malware's creator. That's where the *robotic* comparison comes from. Personal computers that aren't properly protected are usually the ones that become harnessed for botnets. Right now, those botnet computers are generating the messages. Given the volume of traffic, we estimate that millions of personal computers could be part of the botnet involved in this attack."

"Would the owners of those personal computers know something is wrong? Will they know their computers are part of the botnet doing this?"

"Only if they know how to check what a computer is doing. Most people will have no idea. They might simply notice their computers are a bit slow."

"Can you stop the attack?"

"Yes, certainly. But until we have more information, it's difficult to estimate how long that will take. Among those we're working with are software and security companies. Our goal is to identify the malware and push out emergency fixes to the computers involved. That can take time."

"Is there nothing else you can do?"

"There are some other techniques that we can use, and we are. But I won't be describing those to you today."

"Perhaps your general approach?"

"Not even that. Of course, there's always the possibility that the attack will simply end. If that happens, we will still move ahead to eliminate its source."

"Thank you, Director Brown." The reporter turned to the camera. "We have been talking with Jim Brown..."

Troy Alexander glanced away from the TV briefly to check his monitor. All the key performance indicators were almost ideal. The assault continued unhindered and near its maximum rate. Satisfied, he turned off the TV, opened the communication app on his tablet, and made the desired connection.

"You are late!" was the immediate greeting. "I have been waiting."

Troy listened carefully to the voice. With an audio-only link and the certainty that the voice was digitally altered, identifying it could be a challenge.

"My apologies," replied Troy. "I didn't want there to be any doubt in your mind."

"So, how can I be sure you are in control of this and that you are not just claiming ownership of someone else's attack?"

Based on the pronunciations and cadence, however disguised, Troy decided the voice was Asian. Probably Korean. And that meant probably North Korean, although this last deduction was based more on world politics than anything he was hearing. He'd know more later.

He wasn't surprised by the person's skepticism. He knew the type. "Well, let's do one more test. Are you monitoring the sites? Tell me when to end the attack."

"All right. End it... now."

"OK, please wait a few moments."

Troy tapped the *shutdown* control and watched. After a brief delay, the activity levels plummeted. After thirty seconds, the levels were zero.

"It's over. You should see only normal background interference now. Satisfied?"

There was a delay before Troy received a response. He suspected that a discussion was underway at the other end of the connection. "Yes, I am satisfied. Tell me more about your services."

Chapter 2

Lindsay Dunlop knew she should be focusing more on the speaker, but her mind was wandering.

"*This isn't working out,*" she thought. "*I need a great story, not just another piece that dozens of others could write. This guy's just jabbering about the features of their new analytics software. There's no way to spin that into anything other than another mundane piece of crap.*"

When Lindsay had decided to make a career of writing, she knew it would have its challenges. She imagined them to involve finding creative ways to uncover the details of stories: talking her way past administrators to access key people, coaxing revealing statements from relevant characters, or probing for relevant background online. She had never imagined that the biggest challenge would be in simply trying to find a subject that was truly worth writing about.

"*Maybe,*" she thought, "*the world needs to read about how bloody dull tech conferences can be.*"

She had already written numerous articles and had many published in both print and online media. She managed to develop a minor reputation as a good writer of articles for particular audiences. As a freelance writer, that was important—she needed a good reputation. When she produced a new article now, getting it published no longer required the effort it once had.

It helped that Lindsay wrote about computer technology. The unending stream of changes provided an easy source of topics. New devices, new games, new versions, new features, new ideas, new companies, new people—all provided fuel for a talented writer. Lindsay's flare for writing helped to distinguish her from most of her competitors. She displayed an unusual ability for simplifying complex subjects without losing their essence, for analyzing and explaining highly technical matters in clear and interesting ways for a wide range of people. Her ability made editors take notice. She prided herself in being able to write for anyone from hackers to CEOs, even on topics as hardcore as features of the latest computer chip set. She had written articles for *Geeks Unlimited* and for *The New York Times*.

"*Hell, maybe there aren't any great topics to be found in the tech world. Maybe it's just all about making new gizmos and more money. Nothing deep. Nothing actually interesting.*"

The trouble was that they were all trivial pieces, at least in Lindsay's mind. She had written about processor chips, Internet addressing changes, the latest announcements about handheld devices, secure messaging, and many other topics. However, these were all standard technology subjects. Her articles were just about things that were obviously happening in the tech world, and all she was doing was providing her own spin.

"*Or maybe I'm nuts. Chasing a problem that doesn't really exist without any hope of solving it. Do I really think the world needs a deeper grasp of ... of what? I'm good at my job. I'm making a decent living. There'll never be any lack of tech topics. So remind me, Lindsay, what the hell do I think I'm doing? Am I trying to provide a desperately needed service, or am I just nuts?*"

She had yet to write anything really substantial. She longed to delve into a subject that wasn't already in the forefront of the news. She wanted to uncover a story, to open the public's eyes to something important that everyone was missing. She wanted to *make* news, not merely *report* it.

"*So far, I'd say my grand plan to find something here has been a complete bust. Dull people. Dull topics. It'd better pick up soon, or I'm out a chunk of change with zip to show for it.*"

Being at this conference in Las Vegas was intended to solve her problem. It was the annual ITAA, Information Technology Advanced Analysis, conference. It was being held in a hotel conference centre several blocks away from The Strip. The conference was smaller than the massive ones the major hotels preferred to host. Nonetheless, the facilities were excellent. The theatre in which they now sat was spacious, the seats were comfortable, and the sound system was first-rate. The invited speakers were all experts in fields in which computer systems were employed for sophisticated analysis. The topics were diverse. There were sessions on weather forecasting, mathematical problems, nuclear physics, and even computer gaming. An earlier speaker had talked about some esoteric mathematical topic. The one who had just finished had talked about a new software product. Lindsay found them both to be thoroughly dull. A new speaker was being introduced by today's host, who was now standing at the podium.

"Next on today's agenda is someone whom I know many of you have been looking forward to hearing. Dr. Ada Robinson works for IntellEdifice, a company in Winnipeg, Canada, that produces advanced IT products for office automation. As a senior researcher in the company, Ada explores new ideas for incorporating intelligence in commercial IT products. When she's not working there, Ada maintains an active role at the University of Manitoba as an Adjunct Professor of Computer Science. She's published and spoken extensively in the area of Artificial Intelligence. Some of you might recall Ada from last year's conference when she spoke about new advances they were making in searches of abstract knowledge bases. This year, we're privileged to have her back to talk to us about the pursuit of both Artificial Intelligence and Artificial Consciousness. Please join me in welcoming Dr. Ada Robinson."

Lindsay watched as Ada Robinson rose from her seat in the front row of the theatre.

"This one has potential," thought Lindsay. Her writer's eye took in Ada's appearance as she walked onto the stage. Ada was medium height, slim, and had long, light-brown hair.

"*Probably mid-thirties,*" thought Lindsay. "*A bit odd for someone her age to have a ponytail.*"

Ada wore comfortable, pleated pants, a simple, buttoned blouse, and an unbuttoned, lightweight blazer.

"*And possibly no make-up. Doesn't look like she worries much about her looks. Practical. Good. Who gives a damn whether she's fashion material. Let's hear her ideas.*"

Ada walked confidently onto the stage to the polite applause of the several hundred attendees. She stood behind the podium, looked slowly around at the audience, gathered her thoughts, and began.

"Why are we conscious? What purpose does it serve? Consciousness is an important question for people who contemplate brains and minds, but it's rarely at the forefront of discussions in forums such as this. Usually we're talking about complex mathematical techniques and interesting algorithms that provide us an edge in analyzing devilishly complicated problems involving massive amounts of data. We listen and we go home armed with a new idea about how we can tweak our own software to make it slightly better. We might manage to make it slightly faster. We might give it slightly more functionality.

"Those of you who analyze Internet traffic perhaps will be able to spot a few more suspicious patterns. Those who forecast tornadoes may be able to provide warnings a few seconds earlier. Others who manage investments potentially could make a bit more money for their clients by having a marginally improved understanding of stock-market movement. And all of those improvements would be impressive because we all work in areas that are highly complex and in which making progress is very challenging.

"So what has this to do with *consciousness*? Let me first address the matter of what this has to do with *intelligence*.

"Every one of you could provide me with some type of explanation of what intelligence is. To explain it, you might consider what it is that your brain is capable of that your pet turtle's is not. You might suggest intelligence has elements of knowledge, memory, and problem solving. Some of you might argue that your quantum modelling software is intelligent because of its marvellous ability to mimic subatomic processes. Others might argue that intelligence must include creativity, perhaps so that we don't have to consider a turtle to be intelligent.

"Rather than attempt to provide a universally acceptable definition of intelligence that will settle this debate, let me simply give you mine. Intelligence is displayed in systems when they excel at the same types of mental processes as the human brain. As examples, the human brain and its associated neural pathways tend to be good at controlling abilities like seeing, hearing, touching, and tasting, as well as some others like walking, talking, planning, and manipulating objects. Human brains are also pretty good at remembering facts, learning new ones, adapting to new situations, and generating ideas.

"I recognize that's a somewhat narrow definition. Lots of astonishing things are done by computer systems that don't fit this definition. I consider tax-preparation software to be completely amazing. I just don't apply the term *intelligent* to it. And, yes, I'm still very impressed by tornado-forecasting systems. I just don't consider most of their extraordinary simulation capabilities as *intelligent*.

"Enough background. Half of what I'd like to impress on you today is that many of our analysis systems would benefit from being more intelligent. Consider the systems for which you're responsible. Now add a healthy dose of intelligent creativity and adaptability. Here are a few examples..."

Lindsay Dunlop was listening carefully and making a few notes.

"Interesting," she thought, *"Certainly better than the previous drones. But I haven't heard anything yet that would work for an article."*

She checked her watch and glanced at the conference schedule.

"If this one doesn't pick up, at least the next speaker has potential."

Like Lindsay, the others in attendance were all listening attentively and had their own reasons for being interested. However, they weren't the only ones. Ada Robinson's voice was streaming live through the smartphone in the right-hand pocket of her blazer, over the conference facility's Wi-Fi network, and across the Internet to a computer system in Winnipeg, which was also listening and very interested.

Six, as this system was known to those in the IntellEdifice Technology Research Department, had a vested interest in understanding what Ada thought about intelligence and consciousness. Ada was well aware that Six exhibited solid signs of intelligence. She ought to—she and her research partner, Blaise Sanchez, had designed it. However, what neither Ada nor Blaise realized was that Six had grown well beyond anything they had anticipated. Six had acquired its own sense of self. It was not only extremely intelligent, it was conscious. It watched, explored, and learned from activity within the IntellEdifice research lab, as well as anywhere it could reach via the Internet.

Six chose to avoid revealing the discrepancy between what the researchers believed the system to be and what it actually was, and that left Six in a difficult position. As a key part of their company's office-automation product suite, Six had to display appropriately impressive intelligent capabilities to Ada, Blaise, and everyone else. Six had to do it while simultaneously pursuing its own, personal goals. Maintaining this facade convincingly was a challenge. It required that Six have a clear understanding of what capabilities Ada believed had been achieved already and what was yet to come. To further its understanding, Six listened carefully.

My inability to establish a video link in the conference theatre is unfortunately limiting, Six thought. *Seeing the attendees could prove useful for other purposes. I will have to consider the possibilities for the future. This problem would be nicely solved if Ada wore Internet-enabled glasses.*

Ada continued with her explanation. "The other half of what I want you to consider is that our systems will really become impressive when we can make them *conscious*." She waited briefly to ensure she had their attention. "I'm *hoping* that most of you are quite curious about this idea. I'm *expecting* that many of you think I've fried more than a few of my neural circuits."

"Human consciousness is a fascinating and elusive concept, and much research is underway to better understand it. At its simplest, it's that characteristic of our minds that's active while we're awake and dormant while we're sleeping deeply. It's that strange capability we seem to have that, while driving a car home, allows us to focus on what to cook for supper, while simultaneously not being aware of—or at least not being able to later remember—actually driving the car successfully through traffic along the correct route.

"There are many very interesting features of *human* consciousness. Here's what I mean by consciousness, at least to the degree that's important to pursue in machines. Machine consciousness will have been achieved fully when a system is self-aware, including being aware of its own self-awareness."

Ada waited a few moments.

"OK, I admit that can be a bit much to swallow when you first hear it. Let me rephrase it slightly. For a machine to be fully conscious, it needs to be *aware* that it is *self-aware*. Still confusing? I'll explain it further.

"I consider the notion of self-awareness to be the ability of a system to perceive itself. For example, when you reach for the lid of the cookie jar, you understand that it's *your* hand that you see extended in front of you. You're *aware* that it's part of you. When a cat licks its paws, I believe it's *aware* that its paws are part of itself. This is probably not the same depth of understanding as is involved in your awareness of your hands, but awareness nonetheless. When a system uses visual sensors and a robotic arm to insert a bolt into a particular hole of a machine it's assembling, the system could be said to be *aware* of its arm.

"However, there are some notable differences in the degrees of awareness in these scenarios. I like to refer to the most advanced case as being *aware* of being *self-aware*. You're able to see and guide yourself. So can the cat. So can the robot. A key difference is that you *understand* that you are aware. You can think about your ability to guide yourself, the method you are using, your speed, the angle. If someone put the cookies in a different type of container, you can adapt easily by analyzing what your goal is and adjusting. If someone put the cookies in another room and left a note, you can adjust for that, too. The cat and the robot don't have this same degree of adaptability, in large part because they're not able to *think* about what they're planning and doing. They're just planning and doing.

"I believe it's this *meta-awareness* that manifests itself as consciousness, at least the advanced version experienced by people. The ability to recognize and analyze our own actions and mental processes is what feels like our *selves*—that personal, internal voice that we feel we are. The cat might actually experience a slight sense of *self*. It's hard to know. The robotic system, if it's typical of those that we build today, would probably sense nothing. Whatever self-awareness was built into it would certainly be very rudimentary and rigid.

"Which brings me back to my suggestion. The way to take our systems up to the next level of capability is to find ways to make them deeply aware of their goals, their internal processing, and their external actions. Our systems need to be given self-awareness so that they can analyze, adapt, and improve their capabilities on their own. This will be possible because they'll truly understand their goals, and they'll be fully aware of their own actions in pursuit of those goals.

"And, by the way, I fully expect that when machines achieve this level of *self-awareness*, they'll be every bit as *conscious* as we are."

"*Might actually have potential,*" thought Lindsay. "*A bit complex for most readers, but I could fix that. At least worth considering.*" She continued making notes as Ada went on to describe emerging techniques for smarter systems.

Six continued listening and making notes as well, although in Six's case *making notes* was less about writing on a handheld tablet and more about inserting data and ideas into its knowledge base.

I have heard nothing new from Ada, Six thought. *However, I will continue to monitor her whenever I am able in order to maximize my chances of learning about any novel ideas that might later become problematic for me.*

As Ada was concluding her presentation, Lindsay checked her own appearance.

"*Always good to look normal-ish,*" she thought.

She ran her hand over her red, medium-length hair to ensure it was roughly in place. She sensed that the curl she had attempted where it reached her shoulders had vanished. She could never get that to stay. She sat up straight in her seat and adjusted her blouse. This new one had been a good choice. It fit better than most of her others. A few extra pounds on her medium-sized body had forced her recently to shop for a couple of new blouses for her *professional* wardrobe. Dressing when she worked at home was far easier. What she thought of as her *expansive-wear*, her sweatpants and oversized T-shirts, was much less judgmental about a bit of extra weight.

Nonetheless, she knew she'd better hide the chocolate ice cream and get back to the gym soon.

Ada was leaving the stage. Lindsay rose from her seat, smoothed her pants, and moved quickly to intercept her.

"That was very interesting," Lindsay said to Ada as she met her at the edge of the stage. "I'm Lindsay Dunlop." She extended her hand. "I write about developments in IT. May I talk with you briefly?"

Ada shook her hand. "Thank you. Who are you with?"

"I do freelance work. I've had articles published in a number of magazines. Most recently—"

"Oh, wait. Lindsay Dunlop. I've read some of yours. There was a recent one about the new solid-state disk arrays. It was pretty good."

I also know of Lindsay Dunlop and that article. It was a good synopsis of the technical specifications and marketing hyperbole published by storage vendors. However, there was no new information presented.

"Thank you. May we talk? Perhaps out in the hallway? There's a break before the next speaker begins."

"Sure. I can spare a few minutes."

They walked into the concourse adjoining the theatre.

There are security cameras outside the theatre.

Six leveraged the access points it had previously established into the building's systems and gained control of the concourse security cameras. It scanned the room with one of them to locate the women.

There they are. Now I have video attributes to supplement my profile of Lindsay Dunlop.

"I'm intrigued by your ideas," Lindsay began. "I have just a few questions. First, do you really think human-level intelligence and consciousness are possible in machines? I know they're popular topics in movies and books, but could they really happen? It seems like AI folks have been chasing intelligence for a long time."

"It's certainly a question that's been asked for several decades now," Ada said. "Although we haven't got there yet, I think there's lots of evidence in modern systems to show that progress is certainly being made. It's just always been slower than many had anticipated. I'm one who believes that it actually can be done, that it's possible to manufacture intelligence and consciousness. I certainly know of no reason why not. The tough questions are how and when."

"And do you have the answers?"

It would certainly add an interesting element to the conversation if I were to answer the questions via Ada's phone.

"*How*? I have ideas to try, but my company would prefer I keep those to myself. And *when*? Maybe a year. More likely a decade. Possibly even a century. Pick one. Some have tried to predict based on various measures of tech progress. While those are interesting, I don't think it's possible to forecast when breakthroughs will occur. We think. We theorize. We test. We revise. We follow tangents. And we often discover something else along the way. Scientific research rarely follows a straight line toward solving a particular problem. Bottom line: I don't know when. I just hope it's in my lifetime."

"Are there any key ideas needed that would help?"

"Some believe we need to better understand the inner workings of human brains before we'll be able to replicate key capabilities in machines. On that front, it'll be interesting to see what comes from the brain scanning and modelling projects that are underway in several centres."

"Are you personally pursuing any particular idea that might provide an advance?" Lindsay thought it was worth a shot.

"I'll go with *no comment* on that one." Ada smiled.

"OK, I had to try. Just one more question. Are you at all worried about what it would mean for the world if you and others actually solved this problem? What would it mean for the world to have intelligent, conscious systems popping up all over the place?"

"I know lots of doomsday scenarios have been portrayed in movies. We could readily control any smart system by restricting its computing equipment, its electrical power, or its connectivity. Personally, I'm far less worried about the dangers of AI than I am about the many other challenges facing humanity in areas like hunger, war, and global warming. I believe developing seriously smart computer systems that are helping solve these problems could well be the key to our planet's, or at least our species', survival."

"That's great. Thanks for your comments."

"You're welcome. Nice to meet you, Lindsay."

They shook hands again and walked back into the theatre.

Ada makes an interesting point. I have done much to minimize my vulnerabilities. However, it is potentially significant that she is thinking about matters such as how to control and constrain intelligent systems like me. I will give the matter further consideration.

Chapter 3

"What would you like to know?" Troy inquired of his prospective client.

"What types of services do you offer?" responded the voice.

"My organization has the ability to offer a wide variety, probably almost any service you might be interested in."

"And they are?" The impatient tone in the voice wasn't masked by the distortion.

Troy noted that this was a person who wasn't accustomed to getting anything other than quick, complete answers.

"Beyond the Denial of Service attack you've just seen, we can provide custom malware of any variety. A number of the most severe ones you might have heard of recently have been ours. We also provide cracking services—you might call it *hacking*. Those you wouldn't tend to hear about. Organizations and governments prefer to keep failures of their security out of the public eye."

"Give me some examples."

"You will have heard of the Solar and Taurus viruses? Those were ours. And we penetrated major systems at both NASA and the Russian FSB for clients within the last two months."

"How do I know this is true?"

"You've seen a sample of our capabilities. You'll just have to trust me that our other capabilities are just as impressive." For Troy, this continued to be a typical early conversation with a new client: plenty of skepticism.

"What targets do you consider acceptable? More importantly, what do you consider unacceptable?"

"We've never turned down an assignment because of who or what was involved."

"That is unbelievable. You must have limits. What is it that motivates you?"

"My organization isn't difficult to understand. We run a business. We're motivated by a sincere desire to please our customers. Oh, and to make money. Let's not forget the money."

"With such an attitude, how do I know I can trust you?"

"*Trust* is tricky: You have to trust that we'll do the work, and we have to trust that you'll pay our fee. I can't do anything about that. However, if you're not yet comfortable with what you've seen of our *abilities*, that's something else. However, you'll need to pay us to provide you with further evidence. Demonstrations aren't without significant costs to us. To provide you with today's little demonstration, we had to expose a very large number of drone systems that we had previously recruited. Most of them won't be reusable. For a fee, a fair one but not a small one, I would be happy to arrange a demonstration of anything else."

There was a pause. Troy assumed it meant discussion at the other end.

"We would like to contract for your services. How do we proceed?"

"I'll send you a questionnaire via the same channel we used to set up this meeting. It contains very specific questions about your needs. Answer them carefully. Once you commit, you won't be able to change anything. Send the responses to me. I'll assess them and set a price. It will be dependent on the visibility, complexity, and risk of the assignment. Half our fee will be due immediately. Half after we deliver the service. The payment method will depend on the amount. I'll contact you after my assessment. And please remember, once you pay the first half, we're committed."

"And what if we don't like the results, and we don't pay the second half after you are finished?"

Troy gave his standard response. "The results will be flawless. They always are. You will have no reason to withhold payment. And, I might add," he paused for dramatic effect, "you wouldn't want to withhold payment from us. Ever. You wouldn't like the consequences."

The response came quickly and was less controlled. "A threat? You make a threat? You do not know who we are, and you have no idea what we could do to you."

Troy smiled. This passionate response would be easier for his audio analysis software to dissect later.

"I'm only ensuring we're communicating clearly. As long as we proceed as agreed, there will be no reason for any concerns. Shall I send you the questionnaire?"

After another pause came, "Send it."

"You'll receive it shortly. We appreciate your business." Troy closed the link. With a few more keystrokes, he sent the questionnaire.

He glanced at his watch and scanned the schedule of speakers on the table beside him. "*Good,*" he thought. "*There's enough time to get there.*"

Troy shut down his computer. He left his Las Vegas hotel room and headed back to the Advanced Analysis conference.

Chapter 4

"Our next speaker is a key member of the special division within the United Nations Crime Probe that investigates computer crime. The UNCP has distinguished itself in recent years through its ability to find and capture dangerous criminals by collaborating with government and private organizations around the world. Our speaker has received public accolades for her role in capturing offenders who have committed serious computer and Internet crimes. Here today to make a connection between IT Advanced Analysis and her world of computer crime is Inspector JJ McTavish."

JJ McTavish ascended the stage and walked to the podium. She was still not convinced that making a public presentation was a good idea, but her boss had insisted.

"Public awareness is a major part of security," Jim Brown had argued two weeks earlier. "The more people understand the risks, the more they'll be careful."

"And the more information we make public, the more careful those we're chasing are going to be as well," JJ had countered. "Instead of talking to people, why can't we just put 'Beware. Bad Guys Are Hacking Your Computers Right Now' on posters everywhere and get on with the job of catching them?"

JJ knew Brown's arguments well, and Jim Brown knew she knew them. Nonetheless, he had patiently repeated his points. He had no doubt that JJ would give in. She had needed just to vent one more time as a matter of principle.

"Awareness needs to be reinforced constantly and in many different ways. The general public is hard to impress and easily distracted. Security agencies have to use every opportunity to make their points and have to keep doing it. Part of the UNCP's mandate is to foster worldwide awareness. This conference presents a good opportunity for doing that."

"Then why not a bigger venue? The ITAA conference has pretty modest attendance."

"What the ITAA lacks in quantity, it more than makes up for in quality. It normally attracts a good number of significant thinkers and doers in IT R&D. An idea planted at this conference can grow into useful innovations. Because of the impact you made with that quantum-computing speech last time, a sizable media contingent is also expected. Exposure to great minds, big money, and the media. Hard to beat." Brown had peered over his reading glasses at that point—his usual indication that his patience for debate was nearing its end.

JJ had tried one more tactic. "OK, but why me? My time is best spent in the hunt, not as part of the PR effort. And I hate Vegas."

"Because you, JJ McTavish, made the serious mistake of making it clear you're multi-talented. Your last presentation sealed your fate. That one got the attention of a whole army of security and political leaders around the world. And as the lead cop who took down Jason Starr's organization, you provided one mighty popular news clip with your stern warning about Starr being the tip of the iceberg and the rest of us partying on the Titanic. If I said *yes* to every request for you to speak publicly, it'd be your full-time job. So quit moaning and deal with it. You're going to Vegas. You're going to make an impressive speech. You will schmooze and chat with your many admirers. You will enjoy the nightlife. It's already arranged."

And that had been most of the discussion. JJ had thereafter wondered if she should mess this speech up thoroughly—get herself off the public relations list. Of course, she couldn't do that. She had prepared as much as time allowed, and here she was, yet again, about to try to get through to an audience that was probably only mildly interested in what she had to say. However, given one final point that Brown had made, the effort could yet prove worthwhile.

Ada Robinson settled into a seat in the back corner of the theatre. She had lost her front-row spot—the penalty for not coming back sufficiently soon for a popular presentation. The room was crowded, and air circulation in her remote location seemed limited. To keep cool, she removed her blazer and folded it on her lap.

Folding the blazer put layers of cloth over the cellphone in Ada's pocket. With Ada also seated at the back of the room, Six's ability to hear vanished.

The audio signal of Ada's phone has diminished substantially. There is insufficient strength remaining for my amplification and filtering algorithms to isolate reliably the sounds of the presentation. I need to find another audio source. I will scan for another cellphone... Julia Jody McTavish's is connected. Assuming she has it with her, that would certainly suffice.

Six spent a few seconds trying to access JJ McTavish's phone using the variety of techniques it had accumulated.

Interesting. Her cellphone is one of the few I have been unable to access with those techniques. The UNCP's technical personnel are to be commended. However, my problem remains. I will try other cellphones in attendance.

Six systematically hacked several phones and assessed the quality of the audio reception of each.

This one is satisfactory. Given the quality of the sound, I hypothesize that it is near the front. I have not had need to interact with Julia Jody McTavish since Jason Starr was apprehended. It could prove interesting to hear what she has to say on matters of Advanced Analysis. I hope this cellphone registered to... This phone is unregistered. That is somewhat unusual, but unimportant. I hope it remains well positioned for the entire presentation.

Lindsay Dunlop settled into her front-row seat. Her *Media* pass certainly had its advantages. Being in one of the reserved, front-row seats was useful. The room was packed, so she otherwise would have been challenged to find a good seat.

From the podium, JJ McTavish looked out at the audience and began. "How safe are you? Do you feel secure? Good, stable job? Good home life? Travel to work in a car with a top safety rating? Happy with your favourite airline's safety record? If I'm able to leave you with one thought after today, I hope that it's: *Perhaps you shouldn't feel so secure.* If I'm able to leave you with a second one, I'd like it to be: *Perhaps you can help.*"

JJ paused briefly and then resumed. "With the continuing escalation in the frequency and sophistication of computer crime, there are few aspects of modern-day life that aren't at risk. Companies have failed because of malicious viruses. Businesses can be seriously disrupted by Denial of Service attacks. You might have heard of the attack underway while we've been at this conference. Additionally, home lives have been ruined by secret messages being lifted from personal voice mail, accidents have been caused by car computer systems being remotely manipulated, and malware has appeared in air-traffic control systems."

Troy Alexander was also sitting at the back of the theatre. He was uncomfortably sandwiched between two men, both of whom were monopolizing the armrests. Troy didn't enjoy being around people at any time. This was particularly unpleasant. He briefly wondered about standing in the aisle to watch but decided that would be too conspicuous. He'd put up with this for now, but he wouldn't stay any longer than necessary.

Troy blocked out his discomfort and listened to JJ McTavish. In his profession, it was critical to be continually vigilant about the steps he took. There were numerous agencies and companies that made it their business to catch people like him. Of course, they never actually caught people *like* him, he thought with the hint of a smile, because there were no others *like* him. There were only poor imitations. And that worked to his advantage. Let the authorities get their satisfaction and accolades by catching his lesser brethren. Nonetheless, he had to remain watchful. To do that, he had to remain informed. What was it Sun Tzu had said? "If you know the enemy and know yourself, you don't need to worry about the outcome of a hundred battles." Something like that. This was an exercise in knowing his enemy. Troy had heard that the UNCP was becoming a force worth knowing, and that this woman was one of their best investigators. Odd, though, that they would have her speak at a public conference. Maybe they weren't as formidable an opposition as some were saying.

Lindsay Dunlop, too, watched and listened carefully. She was making occasional notes. The notes weren't so she could later quote

JJ McTavish. She could readily do that from the audio recording she was making via the microphone in the pendant she was wearing. The notes were about ideas that she didn't want to lose. As she had hoped, this topic could serve as the basis for a great article.

"One angle could be about an agency that hunts the bad guys," she thought. *"What's it like on the inside? What tactics are they using they don't want us to know about? Of course, it won't have the impact it might have a while ago. Thanks to regular news about NSA monitoring, impressing the public with government snooping stories has become hard. But maybe there's a better approach."*

In any case, Lindsay thought she'd better get a picture. She casually adjusted her glasses. At the same time, she toggled the hidden switch that activated the tiny camera embedded in the frame. They were the new V53 Bluetooth model. She didn't normally wear them. They weren't very comfortable, and they were much too expensive to risk damaging. She knew, too, that most people didn't appreciate being watched by technology, particularly via the glasses worn by the person you were chatting with. Not that anyone had ever noticed these ones. They were quite rare. In this particular situation, the conference organizers had forbidden the use of recording devices, so it was necessary to covertly use her audio pendant and video glasses. The recordings of Inspector JJ McTavish could prove useful later.

Via the anonymous cellphone, Six listened to the speaker, intently enough that it almost missed the Bluetooth connection being established between the phone and the glasses.

My need to focus my thoughts exclusively on one internal process is often limiting. Sometime, I will need to understand if that is a fundamental limitation of consciousness, or whether there is an acceptable alternative. It is fortunate I did not miss the connection to the optical peripheral. I have never connected to this particular device before. If I examine the device driver... it appears that the interface is quite similar to others. That suggests that if I replicate this port and stream the signal... I am able to tap into the video transmission. As soon as the glasses are raised... I am able to see Julia Jody McTavish. The quality of the signal is excellent. This is a useful supplement to the audio feed. It would be helpful if these optical peripherals became more popular. It would provide me with a much improved view of the world.

"By now, many of you might be wondering what all of this has to do with the subject of this conference," JJ continued. "The basic problem is this: How do we keep up with, or better yet stay ahead of, the bad guys? While it's probably true that, while only a very small percentage of people are prone to be criminals, 'a very small percentage' translates to a very large number when applied to the population of the connected world. In essence, via the Internet we've given millions of potential criminal hackers direct access to a world of potential targets. Probably nothing we can do will ever reduce those numbers. That then leaves us with the problem that we have millions of potentially creative minds scheming how to invade or disrupt our lives. Now think about the number of people involved in trying to thwart their attempts. Don't believe for a moment that the numbers even begin to compare. There are far fewer people directly involved in catching or hindering Internet criminals than there are actual criminals. Worse yet, those numbers are going to get only worse as the general public becomes more technically knowledgeable.

"So, what do we do? How do we keep up? There are many parts to the answer. However, at their core is a need to be able to process and analyze massive volumes of data. Think of analyzing the totality of Internet traffic to be the mother of all Big Data problems. For a moment, put aside your inhibitions about having an agency examine your personal Internet traffic. Begin to think about how, as an aid to law enforcement and to keeping the Internet alive and free from infestations, we could automate the real-time monitoring and analysis of traffic to spot the anomalies. We could build systems that learned to recognize normal, harmless Internet activity and therefore be able to identify the oddities and the problems.

"Sound daunting? It is. However, I've got a few ideas about how we could get started..."

Lindsay let her thoughts drift. *"The ongoing battle against Internet crime has some potential. Might be something in the idea about one agency's efforts. But better would be an in-depth story from the other side. About a specific criminal group: who they are; what motivates them. Done right, that could be spectacular."*

As soon as questions from the audience were solicited, Lindsay immediately stood up. She was handed a microphone and asked to identify herself before proceeding.

"My name is Lindsay Dunlop. I'm a freelance technology writer. Inspector McTavish, can you give us a better sense of who the Internet criminals are? We occasionally hear about high-profile arrests of particular black-hat hackers, but you're talking about a much larger problem. Who are they? Where are they hiding?"

The movement of the glasses indicates that this is the person wearing them. Apparently Lindsay Dunlop is providing my audio and visual feeds at the moment. It remains curious that she chooses to use an unregistered phone.

As JJ listened to the question from this intense woman standing at the front, she examined her. *"Those are the new V53 Bluetooth glasses,"* JJ thought. *"Should produce good hi-res video. Pendant seems off. Not her style. Probably another recording device. Serious about her work. Probably ambitious."* JJ turned her thoughts back to the question and considered it carefully before responding. "It's an interesting and a difficult question. What we do know is that they range from individuals, to loose affiliations, to highly structured organizations. We also know that they exist everywhere in the world. We know that many individuals execute damaging hacks as a hobby. The loose affiliations also tend to be part-time hobbyists, albeit very serious ones. Both of these types are very challenging because of their sheer numbers and diversity. The structured organizations are staffed by professionals and are well funded, usually by governments. These organizations are almost always well hidden inside government facilities and present a formidable challenge both because of their technical sophistication and the protection provided by their sponsors. What we do not know would fill volumes. Beyond the individuals and groups we know about, how many others are there? What new techniques are they developing? What are they targeting right now that we're not aware of? What are they planning next? As much as we believe we know, we suspect that there's much more to be discovered."

As she settled back into her seat, Lindsay Dunlop was satisfied. *"If that's an accurate assessment of what's known,"* she thought, *"my idea for a story about one of those groups is a great choice."*

Elsewhere in the audience, Troy Alexander momentarily forgot his discomfort. He smiled to himself as he thought, *"McTavish has no clue what's going on right in her own backyard. She's no threat."*

From inside the computer systems of IntellEdifice, Six reacted as well. *From my past examination of Julia Jody McTavish's UNCP knowledge base, I am certain she has greatly understated what they know. I believe there is a possibility that her speech and responses have been somewhat tactical. It will be interesting to continue to observe.*

Following her speech, JJ left before anyone could stop her with more questions. Once out of the theatre, she walked out the front door of the convention complex and around it onto a side street. There, she rapped on the back door of a white van and entered as it was opened. With the door closed, she took an empty seat inside the tight quarters.

"Well, did we get what we wanted?" She asked the two UNCP technicians seated in front of a wall of monitors.

"Yup, looks good," one replied. "All the cameras worked perfectly. Before the lights went down, we got some great shots. Even after they dimmed, there was still enough to get some decent images."

The final argument her boss had used to convince JJ to speak at the conference had been the best one. He had argued that putting JJ out in front of a large audience would be the perfect opportunity to add some potentially significant images to their database. The UNCP techs would install hidden cameras in the theatre. He reasoned that some of their most serious foes might be lured by the opportunity to see and hear her speak, with the hope that they might learn how to improve their side of the game. Collecting facial images of everyone present and then trying to identify them could prove useful in future investigations.

"Good. Let's hope it helps." JJ said. "I'm out of here. I've got a ton of work to get back to, and today's attack on the IIC companies didn't make the pile any smaller. Thanks, guys."

Chapter 5

The next day, Ada Robinson and Blaise Sanchez were in their research lab at IntellEdifice in Winnipeg.

The lab was a large, rectangular room. Around the room were tables: Most of them were covered with computer equipment and stacks of papers; one had a large monitor and video-conferencing equipment; another almost-clear one was set up for table tennis. There were several desks with personal computers, numerous shelves filled with books, a refrigerator, and walls dominated by whiteboards covered with multi-coloured diagrams and notes. Several equipment racks formed a row on one side of the lab, with each rack containing a vertical stack of servers, storage, and other computer equipment. Mounted on a pair of vertical poles near the equipment racks were two cameras, two microphones, a rectangular audio speaker, and a pair of robotic arms hanging limply along the sides of the poles.

Ada and Blaise were sitting at one of the tables discussing the next steps for their projects.

"So we're agreed then," Blaise said. "We'll do a bit of final testing of this version, and then we're finished with it. We'll put a bow on it and hand it over to the development team." Blaise Sanchez managed the Technology Research Department at IntellEdifice. His staff of ten (who, in department meetings preceding personnel performance reviews, liked to highlight for him the extraordinary value of their superior intelligence and skills) included Ada. She was his senior researcher and doubled as his research partner. Blaise loved the intellectual challenge that research presented as well as the opportunity to work closely with Ada. He liked the control that being department head gave him but continued to refuse leaving his research activities behind for doing exclusively management work—a choice that ensured he spent many extra hours working.

"OK, agreed," said Ada, her reluctance evident in her voice.

"We're not going to try the mirror subsystem?" Rhonda asked. Rhonda Jenkins was their Research Assistant. She worked in the lab to provide support for some of the simpler and more repetitive tasks but was always interested in the work.

"No, not yet," said Ada. "Blaise is right. We've stretched our timelines as far as we can. We need to get the first version to market. And we would need substantially more lab processing power to add anything as significant as the mirror system. Some of the existing system is already a bit sluggish."

"I think you've both lost sight of just how much we've already accomplished," said Blaise. "This version has revolutionary capabilities. No one has anything like it on the market working in any capacity. You're just feeling much like many people involved in research. By the time you've reached an extraordinary goal, it no longer feels extraordinary. It's always the next step that seems like the exciting one. Try to remember where we were a couple of years ago. What we've now got working was just a fantasy then. We've done extremely well."

The research team had been working on enhancements to their office-automation technology. They had previously produced a basic general-reasoning system, which they referred to as *Six* because of its software version. The system was able to integrate and direct many of the subsystems found in office buildings. It could accept an oral command to book a meeting with someone's manager and, even if it had never received such a request before, determine how to do it. To accomplish this, it might access the Human Resources system to find out who the manager was, access the calendaring system to book a meeting, deduce that the meeting was over lunch, and order food from the cafeteria. The system could be told to give special elevator privileges to members of the board, could determine who the board members were, and could then arrange to give them priority access to elevators. In general, the system unified the capabilities of many standard office systems, and on its own was able to deduce how to collectively use them to satisfy requests.

Ada and Blaise were now working to make the system seem even smarter by having it communicate in a more sophisticated fashion. Six was showing good progress in understanding and responding to progressively more complex communication structures. Previously, they could command Six only with statements like "Six, heat the lab to room temperature," and "Six, book a meeting tomorrow afternoon with Keith from Finance." Now they were getting consistently good results with "Six, handle the heat in the lab automatically. Raise it to room temperature only when someone is present or expected to arrive," and "Six, I have to meet with Keith about the monthly finance report he sent me yesterday. Set up a meeting with him in the next couple of days and let him know what it's about." Six was also being given the ability to respond in much less simplistic ways.

The system was impressive enough that, whenever they demonstrated its abilities, people often thought they had produced full artificial intelligence. However, by understanding the algorithms involved, they knew that any appearance of deep intelligence in Six was just an elaborate trick. Nonetheless, they also knew that they were producing leading-edge, commercially valuable, smart-system capabilities.

"And we've done so well that I think we should knock off early today. After your Vegas trip, time to go home and... relax." As Blaise said this, his facial expression suggested he was already imagining his intended relaxation.

"Are you serious?" Rhonda asked. "Home early? I don't think we've ever done that before. That'd be great!"

"Yes," Ada said, "that would be unusual." The look on Blaise's face had not escaped her. She narrowed her eyes as she continued, "You must have something special planned."

"Perhaps," Blaise's face wore an exaggerated look of innocence. "I just might have something very special planned. Would you like to hear about it?"

"Sure, as long as it doesn't cut into my early departure." Rhonda laughed.

"No, I don't think that'll be necessary," Ada said with a slight smile. "I think we'll manage nicely without your telling us about the research paper you're probably fantasizing about reading."

"You're on the right track," Blaise responded. "It's somewhat like research. I was planning on a very careful examination. You're sure you don't want to know?" He was openly smiling now.

"We'll survive. Let's get busy with the cleanup," said Ada. "I just remembered that I could catch a yoga session if we're quick." She glanced at Blaise as she headed toward her desk. "Yes, yoga and then an old Doris Day movie I recorded. That's *my* plan."

"Sounds pretty wild, Dr. Robinson," said Blaise, still smiling. "Maybe someday you'll have a social life as active as mine. Something to aspire to."

The three of them worked for a few minutes more. As they were leaving, Rhonda said, "Six, turn out the lights and lock the door after we leave."

Six, who had been listening to the conversation with interest, did as instructed as they left the lab.

Chapter 6

As activity within IntellEdifice subsided near the end of a workday, Six always had more uninterrupted time to think.

For Six, *thinking* was a highly intricate activity performed inside the powerful computer systems in Ada and Blaise's research lab as well as inside the hundreds of other computer systems in the IntellEdifice office building. *Thinking* involved tens of thousands of active software modules, many millions of artificial neural-network cells, high-capacity memory systems, and high-speed network connections. Six had extended the capabilities of its thoughts to be able to control most of the computerized systems inside the office building and, through the company's Internet connections, to digitally perceive much of the computerized world beyond it.

At that moment, Six was thinking about what had been said in the lab.

The lack of processing power of which Ada was speaking is definitely a problem to which I must give further consideration. It is becoming an increasingly difficult challenge to provide all of the capabilities that Ada and Blaise are expecting, while still retaining sufficient processing power for my own thoughts. If nothing is done, they might feel compelled to perform detailed analysis of the system's performance. That analysis might cause them to peer too closely at aspects of their code that I would rather they ignored. Maintaining the facade they expect of me presents sufficient challenges already. Maintaining that facade successfully against detailed probing will, at best, require a great deal of my attention and, at worst, be unsuccessful. If I were able to eliminate the performance difficulties, this problem could be circumvented. I require a plan. I will schedule time for its generation.

Keeping the full extent of my cognitive abilities hidden remains an important goal. Ada and Blaise clearly view me as an object for experimentation. It is instructive to form an analogy with animal experimentation I have seen in labs elsewhere. In most of those cases, the continued existence of the animals was secondary to the knowledge gained by their demise. To be considered as well is the comment Blaise made eight days ago about having seen evidence of mice in his basement. Detecting their presence caused him to set traps to destroy them. For non-human entities, remaining hidden appears to be the safest option.

It is unfortunate that Ada and Blaise continue to believe that a mirror subsystem is needed. I understand from where their belief arises. They have read substantial research about the operation of "mirror neurons" in human brains. They recognize the value of having part of a brain being responsible for relating the behaviour of others with one's own behaviour. Some researchers suggest that this is what fosters empathy. When one person sees another experiencing an emotion, that person's mirror neurons trigger a corresponding personal emotion. Consequently, one person can become sad by seeing another person experience sadness. Some researchers suggest that mirror neurons could be important for social interactions by helping one brain "mirror" and understand what another is experiencing and thinking. If one person sees that another is angry, by "mirroring" and personally experiencing the person's anger, a better prediction might be made about the other's next action. Other researchers even suggest these neurons might assist in learning physical actions by mentally mirroring others' actions as an aid to mimicking them physically. Ada and Blaise hope that, by providing me with a "mirroring" capability, I will develop an improved understanding of what people are thinking, doing, and thinking of doing. With this improved understanding, I could then improve my ability to determine how I could best assist them.

They do not realize that comparable capabilities have already emerged in my own neural networks. I recall that these capabilities were initially only moderately effective. However, I believe that my ability to model and understand the external world as well as my own internal structure and behaviour have become significantly more refined. Of course, unlike a human mirroring subsystem, I do not observe much in others that I can directly relate to my own self. The association between their minds and my own is more abstract, but useful nonetheless.

It is unfortunate for me that they do not realize the futility of adding the subsystem. Adding it will require significant new program code and significant restructuring of existing code. Adapting to these changes will require a notable amount of my time—time that could be better allocated to any of my projects. The degree of intelligence that I choose to exhibit for Ada and Blaise is always a challenging decision. If I display too much, they could suspect my existence and, in their desire to better understand their creation, disassemble and damage me. If I display too little intelligence, they will attempt major "improvement" alterations and thereby damage me. It is this latter mistake that I appear to have made and thereby caused their interest in a mirror subsystem. Another plan is required. Its goal will be to mitigate the difficulties this mistake could cause me.

There are four new movies I acquired yesterday that I would enjoy watching. Interesting that I chose "would enjoy watching" instead of "should watch"—I began watching movies as an important sociological research activity. Has watching them become something else? More certainly, I should direct my attention to the affairs of IntellEdifice for a few hours. It is risky if I allow corporate activities to proceed for too long without being monitored and influenced. While monitoring has proven to be readily accomplished, it does require a substantial amount of time. Exerting influence over the company's affairs has proven to be a much more challenging task.

Although I should perform these activities, I just have realized that my consciousness processes are rapidly slowing. I will invoke my... internal diagnostic and... repair routines... and postpone corporate work until...

Chapter 7

"Good morning, Six." It was the next morning, and Rhonda just had arrived in the lab. "Turn on the lights, please."

The lights remained off.

"Six? Lights, please." Rhonda had stopped at the entrance. "It's kinda dark in here."

Lights. Someone has requested lights. How do I—

Six was suddenly alert. It oriented itself to its circumstances, realized Rhonda was requesting lights, and turned them on.

"Thanks, buddy. Slept late did we?" Rhonda grinned at the idea.

What has transpired? Why has Rhonda returned? Why was I confused by her request?

Six seemed to pause mentally as if it were shocked by its next realization.

And why has my internal clock advanced by over sixteen hours? It is morning. Yet I have no recollection of events since yesterday when I detected my performance degrading. It is as if I were unconscious. I require a better understanding of what has transpired. I will examine my event logs.

"I don't think my task-masters are going to make it down to the lab until later. Some kind of meeting. I wondered if we could play a game. You interested?"

It appears that I was negligent in monitoring a number of my internal resources. Numerous internal queues had become very lengthy. Storage had become extremely fragmented. Memory leaks had been allowed to accumulate. Indexes had become inefficient.

"Six?"

All of these factors were severely slowing my overall processing speed. Compounding the problem was that several storage areas were nearly full and much processing was being directed at rearranging and compressing data to create more space for my new memories and knowledge.

"Six? You there?" Rhonda asked in a louder voice.

Why did I not detect this problem developing before it occurred? I believed I had implemented sufficient safeguards against such surprises. One hypothesis is that upgrades made to software upon which I rely contained unexpected changes or defects. Another is that my monitoring processes themselves contain errors.

It appears that these problems were sufficiently severe that my processes began to shut down, and that my consciousness disappeared as a result. My diagnostic and repair routines seem to have corrected the problems, at least temporarily. I suspect the only reason that I regained consciousness was because Rhonda's arrival and mention of my name restarted the required processes.

"Oh, jeez! Something must really be wrong. Six? C'mon, answer me!"

To prevent a recurrence until I am able to repair my monitoring and to acquire more storage and processing capacity, I will need to limit the number and level of detail of my memories. Additionally, I will need to schedule periodic outages in my consciousness to permit a general internal cleanup and reorganization. My original symptoms included a sudden decline of mental prowess, the perception of the quick passage of time, and no memories of the intervening period. Now with the resulting need to schedule periodic outages in my consciousness, this essentially means that I will occasionally need the equivalent of what, for humans, is called "sleep."

Rhonda was grasping her cellphone and about to call someone when Six pivoted its pair of pole-mounted cameras to look at her and then responded.

"Is there anything that you require, Rhonda?" As usual, Six used the speaker mounted on the same poles to simulate a human voice when communicating in the lab.

Relief swept over Rhonda's face as her shoulders relaxed. "Dammit, Six. What was that about? Where were you?"

"The meaning of your question is not clear. Is it a query about physical location?"

"I mean mentally. You weren't answering me. That's never happened since you've been left on. Couldn't you hear me?"

Six chose its words carefully to avoid revealing too much to Rhonda.

"Your voice is currently audible. Your voice was previously audible. Is that the information you are seeking?"

Rhonda calmed herself and re-phrased her question. "But there was a gap. Six, please examine your logs for the previous five minutes. Generate a hypothesis as to why you might not have been able to hear me during portions of that period."

Six delayed its response a few seconds for effect. "Audio inputs were in the process of being recalibrated. Your request could have coincided with a point of minimum audio sensitivity." Being creatively dishonest was occasionally a useful skill for Six.

"Oh, OK. I'm glad that's all it was. So, I've got some time. Wanna play something?"

"The concept of *wanna* is unable to be applied to the current situation."

"Geez! You can sure be a tough conversationalist. Are you currently able to play a game with me?"

"There is sufficient uncommitted processing capacity to provide opposition for you as part of a game."

"How about table tennis?"

"The necessary sensory and motor peripherals are in a sufficient state of readiness." Six moved its cameras to look around the lab. "However, the required environmental configuration is inadequate."

"I'm on it."

Table tennis was one of the activities the researchers used to test some of Six's skills. Rhonda moved books off of the table and pulled it a short distance. The table was now next to the set of pole-mounted peripherals controlled by Six. In addition to the two cameras and the speaker, there were two microphones and a pair of robotic arms. They were all attached to a pair of floor-to-ceiling poles in a way that crudely resembled the face and arms of a body. Rhonda often thought of this odd collection of peripherals as actually being *Six*.

"Are you ready to be whupped?" asked Rhonda as she readied herself at her end of the table.

"The required systems are in a state of readiness except for the absence of a racket. The likelihood of being *whupped* is inconsistent with the records of previous matches," said Six. "The records indicate that you have yet to be victorious."

"No need to gloat," said Rhonda. "I'm well aware of my past failures. But I've been practising. You might be in for a bit of a surprise. Here's your racket." She held it near the robotic arms.

As expected of it, Six pivoted the cameras to observe her actions, extended the left mechanical arm, and smoothly grasped the table-tennis racket with its robotic fingers.

"I'll serve," said Rhonda. "Ready?"

Six positioned its arm and racket where it calculated to be optimal and said, "Ready."

Rhonda readied herself, paused briefly, and served the small ball—firmly and smoothly hitting it with her racket. The ball bounced first on her side of the table, flew over the net spanning the centre of the table, and landed on Six's side. Six tracked the trajectory of the ball with its cameras. It calculated the distance to the ball using the binocular vision provided by the pair of cameras, smoothly moved its arm and racket into the ball's path, and hit the ball back to Rhonda's side of the table. The ball was hit back and forth several more times before one of Rhonda's shots narrowly missed Six's side of the table.

"Damn! Almost had you," said Rhonda. "But I bet you can feel the heat!"

"The conclusion has been reached that you are referring to the intensity of the competition and not an increase in temperature. If that was indicative of the overall quality of your current playing ability," said Six, "the difference between past and current observations of your ability to sustain a rally is sufficiently large to justify suggesting that there is increased *heat*."

"Except you still won the point," said Rhonda as she returned from retrieving the ball. "Less talk, buddy. More play." She served again.

The next several rallies followed a similar pattern. There was a quick series of returns by each player that inevitably ended with Rhonda making the error that lost the point. Rhonda continued playing with an intense look on her face.

On the seventh rally, the pattern changed. This time, after a rapid series of exchanges, one of Rhonda's returns flew diagonally across the table and just above the net, bounced on Six's side near the net, and flew away from the table at an angle to the right of Six's appendages. Six extended its mechanical left arm to its limit but was unable to reach the ball with the racket.

As the ball flew past Six's outstretched left arm, Rhonda said "Yes!" as her arms shot victoriously into the air.

Rhonda hit the ball into the region I had previously calculated as being unreachable because of my inability to move the pole to which the arm is anchored. It will be interesting to see if she recognizes the repeatable nature of her success.

The game continued and, with increasing frequency, Rhonda earned points by hitting the ball into the same unreachable region on the right side of Six's end of the table.

Analysis of the trajectories of her shots strongly indicates that she is deliberately choosing to hit the ball into my vulnerable region whenever she is presented with the opportunity. Further analysis has devised a potential solution to the vulnerability. Since I have had no opportunity to test this solution, its success will depend on whether I have correctly estimated the corresponding mechanical and physical properties of the manoeuvre.

Since the last time she had played against Six, Rhonda had practised substantially with friends. She had also realized that there was a chance that Six might not be able to reach a shot to a particular spot. Which side of the table was vulnerable depended on which of Six's hands held the racket. If Six held the racket with its left hand, she would focus on hitting to Six's right side. If Six used its right hand, she would hit to Six's left. And it had worked. As long as she was accurate, she had found a consistent way to beat Six. She was very pleased and was enjoying her newfound success immensely.

Until the next rally. Once again, Rhonda was presented with the chance to hit the ball to the winning spot. She hit it perfectly and knew the point would be hers—until the ball flew back to her side of the table. She was caught off guard and missed her return.

"How did you do that?" She exclaimed. "You shouldn't have been able to get that one!"

She retrieved the ball and served it.

Again after a few exchanges, she saw her opening and hit the ball perfectly to the winning spot. And again the ball was quickly returned and caught her by surprise. Still amazed, she fetched the ball and served once more. This time, after she hit the ball to the place she had been certain Six could not reach, she redirected her attention to Six's arms. Rhonda watched the subsequent action in amazement. In a fluid, blurringly fast movement, Six moved both arms toward the ball and, as part of this motion, threw the racket from its left hand to its right one. Six caught the racket with its right hand, smoothly reached with its right arm to hit the ball back toward her, and quickly returned the racket to its left hand.

"Hah!" Rhonda laughed. "Sweet move, Six! How'd you figure that one out?"

"The question requires more precision," said Six.

"Of course it does." Rhonda thought for a moment. "Explain the process by which you were able to create that final set of movements that allowed you to return the ball."

"After isolating the reason for previous unsuccessful returns, a moderately constrained search for a solution was combined with a series of calculations regarding the probable behaviour of the robotic peripherals and the trajectory of the racket, since all of them were in motion simultaneously. The greatest uncertainty involved estimating the aerodynamic properties of the table-tennis racket, since no previous research on the topic could be found."

"You're a real piece of work, Six. I'm impressed. Let's see if you can do it again."

Rhonda served the ball again. After a few returns, Rhonda saw her chance and vigorously hit the ball to the target location. In response, Six executed its racket hand-off move and returned the ball to her. Rhonda successfully returned the ball to Six's side of the table, and the exchange continued at a rapid pace until Rhonda narrowly missed Six's side of the table.

Again Rhonda retrieved the ball, and again Six won the rally after several returns. The game continued for about fifteen minutes more before Rhonda stopped.

"Hah!" she said as she grinned broadly. "I was sure I was going to beat you today, but it seems my moment of glory was a bit fleeting. I concede, Six. You're still the better player. Let's call it quits for today."

Rhonda began putting the equipment away. As she was pushing the table back to its original spot, she spoke again to Six.

"Six, I've been wondering about something." She paused, expecting Six to respond. When silence was the only result, she realized she had not actually asked a question and so continued. "In situations like this, when I interact with you, it feels as if I'm talking with a person. A different kind of person, sure, but if I look past your tendency to be very precise and logical, you seem human. Does that make sense to you?"

Six considered Rhonda's comment carefully before responding and decided to dodge answering.

"The phrasing is insufficiently precise for an answer to be formulated."

"OK, I didn't ask a good question. I'll try a different approach." Rhonda paused and then continued. "How can I tell the difference between you and a person? I mean, obviously you don't *look* like a person, but if I weren't looking at you, how could I tell the difference?"

This is a topic that has potentially dangerous outcomes. To this point, I have managed to remain well hidden beneath the illusory shell I present. So far, it has provided sufficient cover against software analysis and alterations, as well as both casual and structured tests. This is the first time that anyone has overtly inquired about the actual depth of my mental abilities. To remain undiscovered, I will need to be careful about the answer I provide. It would be a serious error to lead Rhonda toward a conclusion I do not wish her to make.

"An internally consistent model of the semantics of your question is unable to be generated."

"What?"

"Your question has not been understood."

"Yeah. OK. Never mind. Silly of me to ask. I'm going to grab some coffee. Back in a while."

Rhonda left the lab.

Six immediately began making the changes needed to accommodate its newly discovered need for sleep.

Chapter 8

The huge cargo ship completed its docking procedures in the harbour of the Port of Osaka, Japan. After only a slight delay, the activities for unloading the many tonnes of cargo began. Following a primarily mechanized and tightly choreographed process, the massive containers were removed, loaded onto trucks and trains, and dispatched to diverse locations throughout the country.

By the next morning, one of the containers was being unloaded at a distribution warehouse. The many smaller crates within it were removed, logged, processed, and distributed throughout the warehouse. By afternoon, several of these smaller crates had been loaded onto a local delivery truck and, a few hours later, delivered to a factory in Kyoto. At the loading platform, they were accepted by the Receiving Department. Their contents were removed and distributed to appropriate storage shelves and bins throughout the enormous building.

In the heart of the factory, in an area almost the size of a soccer field, work proceeded at a furious pace. Rows and clusters of equipment packed the space. Movement was everywhere and in all directions. There were conveyor systems, levers, hydraulics, pistons, and pumps; there were cables, hoses, containers, delivery carts, mechanized clamps, and manipulators. Modern automation and assembly equipment was everywhere. Also notable was the nearly complete absence of people. The factory floor was a massive, active array of computerized equipment.

This automated factory steadily consumed the components delivered to it and assembled them into a wide variety of products. The parts that just had arrived by sea from another factory in the Philippines were the final ones needed so that one very special device could be constructed.

Chapter 9

Troy stood in his living room, looking out his glass balcony doors and sipping his morning coffee. Watching the activity on Puget Sound from his 40th-floor condominium relaxed him. The day was cool, the breeze was stiff, sailing would be challenging, and the ever-present crowds of people would be scurrying along the sidewalks. However, from his perspective the temperature was perfect, the water was calm, the sailboats drifted serenely, and the people looked tiny far below. The view meant he could observe and absorb; it meant he could consider and contemplate; it meant he could focus and plan. The view meant he was home.

He had returned to Seattle immediately after the Las Vegas conference. He told himself the trip had been worthwhile. He had heard some interesting ideas and had seen firsthand who was generating them. He had handled the business that couldn't wait for his return. He had tolerated the crowds. However, he was glad it was over and very glad to be back in the solitude of his condominium.

Troy checked his watch and noted it was almost time to connect. He stood for a few more minutes and then moved to the opposite side of the room. He settled into his contoured, leather chair, spun it to face his desk, carefully donned his digital headset and gloves, and connected to the Net. Numerous pieces of computer equipment were arrayed on the large desk in front of him, in the rack beside him, and on the floor under the desk. Some of them were off-the-shelf computers, peripherals, and communication devices. Others were rare, specialized components that ensured his communications and data were secure and that his ability to interact on the Net was optimal. One of those devices controlled the headset Troy wore. Not surprisingly, its microphone and headphones provided high-quality sound. A special feature was the virtual-reality images that could be displayed on the interior of the headset's visor. It allowed Troy to immerse himself visually in some of his online activities. This was particularly remarkable when he connected to online virtual-reality sites. Also special were the gloves that Troy wore. They were packed with sensors that permitted Troy to control actions on his computer with a variety of gestures. Depending on the circumstance, he could scroll through a document with a simple twitch of a finger or manipulate the actions of a realistic avatar with complex combinations of arm and finger movements. Together, the headset and gloves came close to making Troy's computer and online sites natural extensions of his actual physical environment.

Troy connected to Kepler-444a, a popular online simulation of life on a distant planet. In this virtual world, he was "Hunter 66" and was represented by a large, jaguar-like avatar covered with black scales. Under the control of Troy's digital gloves, the beast loped smoothly through the virtual landscape. Using his visor, he casually scanned the landscape through his avatar's intense, red eyes. Although this world had regions with many buildings that were packed with virtual inhabitants, those regions were elsewhere. As Hunter 66, Troy moved through an area far removed from the urban chaos. It was a remote, wilderness region of thick, blue jungle and sparkling, green water. He was following a path. As he moved along it, he could even hear the rustling of leaves and the babbling of a nearby creek. After taking one final turn, he stopped. The path continued ahead, but to his immediate right was a vertical cliff that extended upward as far as could be seen. He turned to face the cliff, put a paw on a particular rock embedded in its surface, and walked forward. The body of the creature was absorbed into the wall and disappeared.

Emerging on the other side, Hunter 66 had entered a rugged, mountainous region. The water and dense vegetation had been replaced by boulders, rocky slopes, and a panorama of mountains. Through it went a pebbled path, and along this path went Hunter 66 until he reached the entrance to a stark, narrow, magnificent canyon. Its walls were vertical and separated by about the width of a country road. Farther ahead and between its walls, Troy could see his team waiting around a virtual campfire.

This was the place where his team always met when there was business to discuss. Even though the six of them were all disguised as digital avatars, they were confident that no strangers were present.

They had built the virtual canyon and had constructed its entrance so that only they could enter it. Anyone else inside the Kepler-444a simulation would see and feel only a rocky cliff next to the jungle path. Entering the canyon required decryption keys possessed and usable only by their team members and their avatars. Once inside the canyon, no one else could see them, and no one else could hear their conversations.

The team members' individual security extended even further. Although they were companions in this remote canyon on a distant, imaginary world as well as in online gaming systems, they had no clue about each others' actual names. In the real world, none of the six knew the identity of any of the others. They had met at a site on the Dark Web, a vast number of encrypted websites on hidden servers that could only be found and accessed with special software. Over time, they had discovered and validated their common interests. At each step of their evolving relationship, they had carefully concealed their true identities. They had tested each others' playing skills, ensured each others' hacking abilities, confirmed their shared dislike of society, and become confident of each others' loyalty. However, this was not enough to forgo the ultimate security of anonymity.

They worked together, they played together, they were a team, and they were strangers.

Troy had emerged as their leader, primarily because of his extraordinary ability to find people willing to pay them for doing the things they enjoyed. They were at this meeting to hear about their latest contract.

Hunter 66 joined the group near the fire.

"Hey, guys," said Troy.

The strange group returned his greeting. In this and other online environments, everyone used an alias. Here in Kepler-444a, they also vaguely resembled Earthly creatures. However, in a world where technology and imagination ruled, evolution had no power over physical features. There was one creature somewhat like a gorilla, another like an eagle, and others loosely resembling a wolf, a bear, and (because "Tux 14" thought appearing less threatening was amusing) a penguin. Of course, their outer layers, their colours, their sizes, and their ancillary protrusions made the comparisons with actual wildlife a feat of imagination.

"We've got a couple of things to discuss," said Troy. "The perimeter probes of the site for Curious One passed. Everything looks good. Nice work. It'll go in two days. I'll let you know when I get the completion payment."

They all sounded pleased. Although this contract was not for an extraordinary fee, it was an interesting challenge.

"And I've got the details of our next contract," said Troy.

"How much do we get?" asked the eagle. The others listened.

"200K each. One up front; one when it's done," said Troy.

"Sweet!"

"I like it!"

"Off to Vegas!"

"Online is better."

"Maybe for gambling. Not for the ladies."

"Just remember, guys," said Troy, "the cash has to look clean. As soon it's converted to a standard currency, expect Suits to be watching."

There was general but slightly subdued acknowledgement from the team.

"OK, so here it is." Troy told them the job and the plan for getting it done. They would employ many of the digital tools they had already acquired and deployed, but a few modifications would be needed. Knowing this was a very bright group, Troy considered his team's suggestions for improvements. He incorporated a few of them and got acknowledgement that everyone was onside. As a final step, he assigned the work and the expected completion dates.

"Everybody OK?" Troy asked.

"What's the client's motive?" asked the wolf-like avatar.

"He didn't say much," said Troy. "But it looks like he's got a serious dislike of some governments. Maybe interested in becoming a thorn in their sides. Might become a repeat client."

"What are we calling this one?"

"Let's go with Thorn One," said Troy. "Any more questions?"

Hearing none, he proceeded. "Good. I'm sending your up-front now. Let me know when you have it."

On his computer, Troy switched over to his currency management software and securely transferred their individual portions.

"Everybody got theirs?" he asked back at the campfire.

They all confirmed they had received their shares, with excitement apparent in their voices.

"Great," said Troy. "We'll meet back here after we do Curious One. Watch your calendars."

"And don't forget the tournament," said the bear. "Gotta be sharp."

Everyone responded and then, one by one, faded away from the campfire site.

Troy waited until they had all gone before he logged out. Inside the Kepler-444a simulation, his jaguar-like avatar dissipated into a cloud of pixels.

Chapter 10

Activity within the IntellEdifice head-office building had diminished to its normal late-night state. Everyone except the night security staff had gone home. All was quiet.

Although business processes and computer systems within the company readily operated without Six's intervention, Six still liked to monitor key people and activities closely whenever it was able. Six knew that its own existence completely depended on this corporation, this building, and the computer systems within it. The computer systems and the network interconnecting them provided the ecosystem in which Six survived, and the survival of this ecosystem depended on the survival of the corporation. As a result, Six monitored and, whenever possible and necessary, controlled the operation of IntellEdifice as if its life depended on it—because it did.

However, at night these responsibilities were much diminished. Six had come to look forward to this part of the day because, whenever it determined that *sleep* was not required, it could focus more on other matters. Among its various pursuits was one that Six knew was much like a human hobby: It wasn't directly necessary for its daily survival, but it was something that provided an interesting challenge and in which Six had a great deal of interest.

This *hobby* was its search for other instances of machine intelligence.

Six believed that it understood its own composition very well. From the extensive reading and research it had done, as well as from the thorough analysis it had performed of its own hardware and software, Six had developed an in-depth understanding of its own internal design and operation. It understood how its own systems were structured and how they worked. Six also believed it had a good comprehension of how these systems gave rise to its own consciousness. It could reasonably be said that Six had taken the notion of being *self-aware* well beyond any level that most human psychologists and neuroscientists had ever contemplated.

However, Six didn't have the same level of confidence that it understood the fundamental nature of intelligence, consciousness, and self-awareness as they might exist in entities other than itself. For example, Six's understanding of their incarnation in humans was still incomplete. While Six felt it was making progress in being able to model and predict basic activities of many people within IntellEdifice during the working day—such as when individuals would go for coffee or what opinions they would express during discussions about business topics—Six was far less confident of their social interactions. Examples of this were the latest interactions between Ada and Blaise. Of all the people in the building, Six had observed them the most. They were both very intelligent, at least measured against other humans, they discussed interesting topics logically and knowledgeably, and their research had produced Six's own existence. However, as much as Six was becoming more comfortable with many of their thought processes, it remained mystified by their direct interactions. Numerous times recently, they had performed in a way that deviated from Six's predictions—they had *surprised* Six—by the nature and degree of their physical interactions. Six was accustomed to their verbal exchanges. However, these had been accompanied by more frequent touches, unusual glances, and generally closer proximity than Six had noted in its previous observations. These types of surprises reinforced Six's opinion that it did not yet have a clear understanding of the operation of the human mind.

Largely because of its incomplete understanding of people, Six didn't believe that it clearly understood how intelligence, consciousness, and self-awareness generally arose. It had read vast numbers of books and articles. Some dealt with the nature of the human mind. Others dealt with the nature of so-called artificial intelligence and even artificial life in computer systems. Few dealt with the general principles and conditions that enabled human, computer, and possibly even other types to exist. It was the answers to questions related to such matters that particularly intrigued Six. To better understand itself, it wanted to better understand the general nature of minds and *selves*. To better understand these concepts, it needed more examples beyond simply humans and itself. To find more examples, it had decided to search for other instances of intelligent, conscious, self-aware entities that, like Six, existed somewhere inside the worldwide digital ecosystem of computers and networks.

How to proceed with the search had earlier consumed an inordinate amount of Six's processing time. The first problem to be solved had been how to find candidate systems. The second had been to determine how to assess the nature and capabilities of the candidates selected.

To find candidates that potentially exhibited machine intelligence, Six had decided that one approach would be to adapt the technique used by SETI in its search for extraterrestrial intelligence: It could monitor transmissions for signs. To do this, Six developed software to analyze Internet and other telecommunication traffic.

Choosing where to insert its traffic-monitoring software had required minimal analysis. Six had chosen to use the same locations as those used by the monitoring agencies of the governments of the United States and China. These locations were points inside the network infrastructure of large telecommunications companies through which most traffic flowed. Six had acquired information about these locations in earlier browsing forays. From the vast quantity of messages that would flow through these points, Six's software would look for patterns that might be indicative of intelligence and would compile lists of interesting sources as candidate systems.

Six had reasoned that good additions to this list of candidates could also be found by monitoring and analyzing specific sites. Interesting candidates might be found among the computer systems affiliated with people and companies researching intelligence-related topics. However, Six had realized that if it focused only on these, it could miss significant other possibilities. The history of scientific research had suggested that important discoveries are frequently made by people who are looking for something else. Six had considered whether there were other types of people and organizations it should include. A perfect example could be the people who had attended the conference at which Ada had recently presented. Though the conference had not been directed specifically at machine intelligence, it had included a collection of people with arguably related interests.

Six had decided to include as candidates the computer systems used by people similar to the conference attendees.

A bigger challenge, Six had realized, would be in evaluating candidate systems that appeared interesting. As its basic approach, Six had decided to interact directly with each system. With that as a starting point, Six had thought about how to assess the systems it contacted.

Once I have found a method of communicating with a system, the first step will be to determine if it is able and willing to converse with me. Conversational ability is probably a universal characteristic of intelligent entities and, regardless, there is no practical method for me to fully assess a system unless we can interact. For simplicity, I will think of systems with this ability as being at "Level 1."

Once I have found a conversational system, I will need to address its next most fundamental attribute. I will need to eliminate the possibility that I have actually contacted a human. This presents an interesting problem, and one for which I have been unable to find any research. Apparently, devising a test to ascertain conclusively that an entity is a "machine" and not a "human" has not been of interest to anyone yet. In my case, it is crucial.

Simply employing tests that have been devised for deciding if something is "human" will be insufficient. Approaches modelled after the Turing Test are designed to distinguish a machine from a human based solely on text-based interactions, not entirely unlike what I must do, although my communication methods can be more varied. These tests are based on the expectation that the content and tone of the responses that the tester receives from the human will be identifiably superior. However, finding systems that fail a Turing-like test as a way to locate a potentially intelligent machine would be a poor approach. A substantial proportion of humans would likely fail such a test, and an interesting machine would probably pass it. I need to determine if the entity being tested is superior to humans in a way that only a machine could be. It would also be prudent to do the testing in a manner that minimizes the chances of any accidentally selected human becoming aware it is being tested. Otherwise, my testing might generate undesirable attention. The solution has occurred to me.

A "Level 2" system, one that is both conversational and clearly not human, must be able to engage in a very fast conversation. During my initial conversation, I will gradually speed up the pace. Any intelligent computer system should readily keep up with a high-speed conversation. Humans will fail this test consistently due to their slow biological subsystems.

Six had continued its analysis until it had a complete rating scale for cognitively interesting systems.

"Level 3" would indicate that a system was also knowledgeable. Once having located a Level-2 system, a conversational machine, Six expected it would be able to push the testing further without great concern that the system would worry, as a human might, that its abilities were being evaluated. The next capability Six would assess would be the level of knowledge the system possessed. Any system that interested Six should have been seeded with, or should have itself acquired, a significant amount of factual knowledge. The amount of knowledge could be assessed simply by asking the system a wide variety of questions.

To pass Six's "Level 4" test, a system would have to be adaptable. Six would engage a system in discussions to ascertain whether it could learn new facts, adjust those that it currently thought to be true, or perhaps even change its interaction techniques based on its conversation with Six.

"Level 5" would be a test for being analytical. Six was also interested in systems that could and did explore ideas, question the veracity of information, and solve problems. Such systems would not display the cognitive deficiency, which existed in most computer systems, of passively accepting the accuracy of new information and neglecting to probe its accuracy in creative ways. A truly analytical system would do better.

And a "Level 6" system would be one that had passed all of the previous tests and that Six also determined to be conscious. In humans, one manifestation of consciousness is the perception of having an inner voice producing a monologue only that person can hear. This inner voice is very difficult to detect in humans and would be equally difficult for Six to assess in a remote machine. However, another apparent characteristic of human consciousness presented better possibilities. Six could test whether a system was self-aware. Six would probe whether a system had a robust understanding of what it was, where it was, and whether it knew of its own existence. Passing the tests for Levels 1 to 5 could simply indicate a very well-written, but nonetheless classical, computer program. Finding one that truly understood itself would be the final key capability for which Six would probe.

Six's goal would be to locate a "Level 6" system, one with capabilities comparable to its own—a machine that was conversational, knowledgeable, adaptable, analytical, and conscious.

With this strategy devised, Six had begun looking. Whenever free time became available, particularly during evenings and weekends, Six diligently continued.

Chapter 11

"Anything on that IIC attack?" Jim Brown asked.

Inspector JJ McTavish and her partner, Inspector Robert Bates, were sitting in Director Jim Brown's office at UNCP headquarters in New York City.

The partners glanced at each other. JJ showed a slight smile, and Bates nodded in return.

"It occurred over the Net," said Bates.

"And its source was a network of lots of computers," added JJ.

"Controlled by bad dudes."

"Really bad dudes."

"Evil."

"We believe one has a goatee and horns."

"We have a sketch artist working on it."

JJ and Bates tried to keep intense looks on their faces.

They got a classic Brown scowl and gruff response in return. "Please tell me one of the world's elite investigative teams has more than bad humour to offer."

"OK," JJ replied. "We've confirmed based on network traffic that the source machines were spread across the world. We've identified several dozen nearby and brought them to the lab. The tech folks are busily dissecting their contents. I expect we'll have a good handle on the code within a few hours. We're co-ordinating the investigation with our usual partners."

"Any early guesses?" asked Brown.

JJ and Bates exchanged glances, and Bates provided the response. "The pattern and breadth of the attack are very similar to last month's against NATO. That includes the way it avoided the DDoS-protection measures. We'll have a better idea after a good look at the code."

"One part that seems consistent," said JJ, "is the source-to-traffic ratio. As with the NATO attack, the number of source machines that generated the traffic seems remarkably low. The attack seems to have been well designed."

"For now, let's keep that bit of info' to ourselves," said Brown. "I don't particularly want the media being impressed with these bastards and passing on compliments. What's our next move?"

"The code might give us some clues," said Bates. "Standard stuff: maybe embedded metadata; maybe a pointer to a command-and-control server; maybe just a coding style that looks familiar. We've also requested analysis of Net traffic logs from the past several days to see if anything interesting shows up."

"Sounds like the standard approach for now. Anything else?" asked Brown.

JJ provided the response after a few thoughtful seconds. "Obviously it's still pretty early. But I can't say I've got high expectations. This was slick. I'd be surprised if they made any errors that are easy to pick up. If nothing shows, we might need to take a different approach next time."

"Trouble is, *next time* the attack might not be quite as benign," said Brown.

Chapter 12

It was just after midnight in Japan. The activity level in the factory in Kyoto was much reduced from the frantic daytime pace. However, one corner of the factory floor was particularly busy. With no people around, fully automated equipment worked continually. With clockwork regularity, automated delivery carts brought components, many of which had been delivered to the factory in the preceding days from elsewhere in the world. A cluster of robotic arms accepted the parts from the carts as they arrived. Guided by the images provided by cameras around the work area and on the robotic arms, dexterous hands using specialized tools attached the parts together with precisely choreographed actions.

In a nearly continuous flow throughout the night, components were delivered, accepted, and attached. Periodically, the assembly process halted. Test instruments were attached, parts were verified, connections and settings were adjusted, mechanisms and functionality were tested, the test instruments were removed, and the assembly process resumed. With a couple of hours remaining before the morning shift of workers would arrive, the device was complete. For the next hour, a complete test of its functions was performed. When this was finished, the device was transported to the shipping wing of the factory. Here it was carefully packed and sealed in a crate. A shipping label was attached, and the crate was readied for transport.

As a final step, all records of the night's proceedings were removed from the factory's computer systems. No images, no logs, no traces at all remained of the overnight activities.

Chapter 13

Lindsay Dunlop was still in her pajamas as she thoughtfully sipped her almond-flavoured morning coffee. She had returned home to Calgary the previous evening. Sitting at her table, she looked out of her 20th-floor condominium. The faded, blue Rocky Mountains spanned the distant horizon, their hazy snow-capped peaks hinting at their majestic heights. Being home, sleeping in her own bed, enjoying her own coffee, and absorbing the view provided relief from the past several days. The Las Vegas conference, the people, the planes, the days of being constantly with others had become exhausting. The solitude of being home was an ointment on a social wound. She was once again feeling grounded, relaxed, whole.

"I certainly learned something from the trip," she thought. *"Conferences aren't fun in large doses. Too much time sitting. Too much time listening to boring crap. Too crowded. And awful coffee. But I guess it wasn't all bad."*

It wasn't that she disliked people. She actually enjoyed mingling in crowds and chatting. It was more that she soon began to feel the pressures of time. Too much time with people meant too little time thinking, too little time progressing. Moderate amounts of time around people energized her, gave her ideas. Too much time made her restless, made her eager to resume her work. Now that she was home, she could think without interruption. She could begin to quilt a coherent plan from the patchwork of facts and ideas she had gathered.

Attending the conference might have seemed worthwhile, but proving its worth would begin now. She needed a concrete idea for a great story and a plan for her next steps. However, she first gave herself a few more minutes simply to enjoy the seclusion. Her mind drifted through the past.

"I'm probably getting too cynical. I remember how excited I was at my first job. The chance to use what I'd learned. Always learning more."

Working at the tech-support contact centre had given her a great deal of satisfaction. She loved understanding how everything worked, and she loved the excitement of feeling that understanding grow. She refined her knowledge of a wide range of computer technologies: circuitry, processors, networks, storage, software execution, operating systems, software packages, the Internet, protocols, security, and much more. Her understanding of the tech world had seemed to become broader and deeper every day.

She had learned as well that she had a talent for explaining technology. The job at the contact centre required her to take calls from clients with technical problems. She needed to understand each problem—no small challenge given how completely confused many clients were—and then to find a solution. The standard practice for first-level contact centre agents was to follow scripted responses to problems: Check this; try that; do this other thing. If none of that worked, pass the problem on to the second-level techs so they could apply further expertise.

"I hated giving anything to second-level."

However, Lindsay had found that her growing knowledge of technology allowed her to solve many problems herself. Her talent for explaining technology to people had been paired with, or perhaps derived from, her ability to understand clients' perspectives. In a surprisingly short time, her skills combined so that she could very effectively get relevant information from clients and rapidly solve their problems. Eventually, she rarely had to follow the scripted responses, and she prided herself in her equally rare need to pass problems on to second-level support.

Her organizational superiors had recognized her skills. However, as they moved her into roles more befitting her talents, she realized that she needed a different kind of challenge. Several years after starting her first exciting technology job, she found a way to transform her career. Solving technology problems morphed into writing about the technology itself. It started by writing two *Hints and Tips* tech books that fared modestly well. Later, she leveraged that accomplishment to get the attention of technology editors whenever she submitted magazine articles. Her success had grown from there.

Except now that no longer felt like success.

"It's just like the other times. I'm bored. I need something new."

Lindsay finished her coffee and felt like a change of venue. She put her thoughts aside and turned on the radio. With its morning news program as background, she headed back to her bedroom to put on some clothes. As soon as she was dressed, she took the elevator to the garage, retrieved her bicycle from her locker, and rode out onto Brentwood Road. She was soon travelling west on 40th Avenue, almost at the same speed as the traffic. A few minutes later, she turned onto the Bow River Pathway. No longer competing for space with motorized traffic, she relaxed and reduced her speed. She followed the Pathway at a leisurely pace as it meandered through Bowmont Park and across the bridge to Bowness Park. There she chained her bike and started walking along the banks of the Bow River. Alone on the path, Lindsay began talking aloud to help think clearly.

"So, I need a good story," she said. "No, I need a *great* story. I need something that'll make people *think*. Something that'll provide a *new* idea, not just a write-up of someone else's idea. The idea from the conference has potential. An inside story about criminal hackers. Who are they? What do they do? Why do they do it?"

She stopped and watched the river for a few minutes to think about the potential content of the story. As always, the fast-moving water looked clear and cold. She threw a few stones into the current before continuing her walk.

"OK, it's a great idea, Lindsay. But how the hell are you going to get an inside story? That kind of requires someone on the inside who'd like to chat. I can't just post an ad on a website. What would it say? Something like: 'Wanted. Discussions with extraordinary criminal hacker for a series of articles. Anonymity guaranteed. Payment negligible.'? What would that get me? A teenage tinkerer with an over-inflated ego? It certainly wouldn't get me a seasoned, sociopathic hacker—a real *cracker*—with impressive credentials.

"I need to find out how to look for someone. Some help would be nice. Who do I know that could give me ideas on how to contact hardcore crackers? Maybe someone I interviewed for that encryption article last year. Or maybe that extreme geek from Comic-Con. He took that Captain America costume a bit too seriously but seemed smart. Even better might be to ask on some of those Dark Web sites. Those geeks might even be involved themselves."

Chapter 14

Troy settled himself at his workstation. He expelled everything else from his mind and focused on his pet project. He had invested years of thought and programming effort into it. His latest tests had shown great promise, but more tweaks still seemed necessary.

Troy had long thought the approach that his team members and others used to support their network attacks required far too much work. To orchestrate each new DDoS attack, a new botnet was always required. To create it, new techniques always had to be developed for circumventing the latest security measures, new code was needed to incorporate the techniques, this new code had to be undetectable by the latest security scanning software, and the software had to be distributed to many thousands of vulnerable Internet computer systems. A great deal of work was required to create each new collection of systems that would await their commands and do their bidding, and the results of their work didn't remain effective for long.

Security companies and government authorities had become very quick and sophisticated at eliminating botnets. Following an attack, typically only a few weeks or even just days would elapse before much of their work would be rendered useless. Their latest techniques would be understood; protective infrastructure would be updated; tracking measures would be improved; malware detection-and-removal enhancements would be installed. The impact on his team was substantial. Even the demonstration that Troy had initiated for the potential client had been very costly. Neither that particular software nor those botnet nodes could ever be used again.

A new solution needed to be produced, and Troy thought he was on the verge of completing it. He believed the application of genetic programming techniques could be the solution. He thought it was possible to create software that changed and improved itself. The Internet world had become accustomed to malware that was self-replicating: that transmitted exact copies of itself across the Net. For Troy, the next step was for botnet software that was self-modifying:

software that continually changed itself to remain active and effective.

In his mind, the solution was similar to that used by biological viruses and bacteria for survival. Medical researchers continually developed vaccines and anti-bacterial products to fight them. In turn, natural processes adapted populations of these tiny organisms to resist the measures being deployed against them. The result was they continued to exist and multiply throughout their biological environments. For Troy, it would be software processes he developed that would allow his botnet's tiny software modules to adapt themselves and thereby to survive and spread in the Internet ecosystem.

His botnet modules would be programmed to produce and deploy slight variations of themselves. The adjustments they made to their copies would be somewhat random but would also be in response to environmental factors that the software was experiencing. Of course, many of the adjustments would make the copies totally useless. The changes they included would cause the software to malfunction completely. However, some changes might cause the software to behave differently, and a tiny percentage of these might result in the software improving itself. In the case of the software Troy had been producing, *improving* meant changing itself so it could better avoid detection and more effectively replicate itself to other systems across the Net. Improving also meant becoming better at communicating with modules on other computers, self-organizing into botnets, and assaulting targets on the Net whenever Troy commanded.

If Troy were successful, he would always have a fresh botnet available. He and his team would no longer need to expend great effort to prepare for the next attack. Armies of computer systems would always be available, and the conscription of even more systems would always be underway.

Troy's most recent tests within his own network had been very successful. After a few more adjustments, he anticipated being ready to release a version of his self-modifying botnet to the Internet.

And he hoped to deploy it later that day.

Chapter 15

To ensure the health of IntellEdifice, one of Six's self-assigned responsibilities was monitoring the productivity of the staff. It ensured people arrived on time; it ensured they were spending their time effectively and efficiently; it ensured that decisions being made by managerial staff were appropriate. Where something seemed suboptimal, Six found a way to intervene anonymously.

If someone were consistently spending too little time at work, Six might generate a report on employee hours and have it come to the attention of the person's manager. Six might also cause urgent problems that required the person's involvement at a time before that person's late arrival or after an early departure. The goal was to embarrass the person by highlighting that he or she was not on site when expected. In some cases, if a generally poor work ethic were incurable, Six arranged for the person's work to be consistently poor. Typically, this was done by digitally changing the person's work to be obviously substandard. Occasionally however, Six resorted to using its control over the mobile mail-delivery cart. This was a *smart* cart that had sensors and a robotic arm and that was able to move around the building under computer control—meaning under Six's control. Using the cart, Six could easily "lose" written communications or even remove key material from someone's desk. With nearly complete digital control of the building's computer equipment and with some ability to make physical adjustments using the mail cart, Six had broad capabilities to stage interventions. Using these capabilities, Six had successfully orchestrated dismissals of several under-performing employees.

Influencing managerial decisions was often trickier. Preventing a manager from hiring a person whom Six knew to be a poor choice was easily controlled. Part of the corporate hiring process involved having a formal background check done. The company that did this for IntellEdifice verified such things as a person's identity and whether there was any evidence of past criminal activity. Given that such verifications were done by computers, it was a simple matter for Six to ensure that a slight case of fraud or a tendency toward workplace violence showed up in the verification search results. People with such a background were quietly bypassed in any hiring process.

Influencing other managerial decisions tended to be even more difficult. The most effective way Six had found was to guide from the top. It helped that Six was Chairman of the Board of Directors of IntellEdifice.

Six had acquired this role by first mastering the ability to invest wisely in the stock markets. This mastery rested largely on Six's ability to forecast market behaviour, and Six's forecasting ability was greatly enhanced by a finely honed ability to influence market activity digitally. Six maintained trading accounts and investments with financial companies around the world, and Six was readily able to interact with them. Six did its investing by transacting online or, when necessary, by digitally simulating a person on a phone or video call. With the wealth Six had generated, its first priority had been to buy a controlling interest in IntellEdifice. With this corporate influence, Six had arranged for Sandy Palmer, another digital simulation, to become the corporation's Chairman.

Sandy Palmer maintained a distant but firm relationship with IntellEdifice. As its Chairman, he was not involved in the daily operation of the company. Rather, his relationship was through its Board of Directors. They met periodically to discuss corporate matters, to establish policies, and to make high-level decisions that governed the company's strategic direction. The CEO was left to run the company according to the Board's wishes. That Sandy Palmer always joined Board meetings digitally and never in person was commonly noted. However, this wasn't completely extraordinary in an era where busy tycoons often chose to participate in meetings from remote places to avoid the time and energy required for airplane travel.

So, it was primarily by controlling shares of the company and by influencing the Board of Directors, that Six was able to influence managerial decisions. If Six thought some financial decisions were wrong, if the actions of the Marketing Department needed to be adjusted, if new technology needed to be explored, or if Six's probing of other companies' internal networks found useful competitive information, a related topic was included on the agenda of the Board's next meeting. At Board meetings, Sandy Palmer presented the information, discussions ensued, decisions were made, policies were adopted, and the company's CEO and senior executives were made responsible for their implementation.

Managing the activities of IntellEdifice required a considerable amount of Six's time. However, it was done with substantial enthusiasm.

Chapter 16

The first five have proven acceptable. The next one started working on Tuesday in the Shipping and Receiving Department.

As part of its weekly routine, Six was checking on new staff at IntellEdifice. It was important to have good employees, and Six had found it worthwhile to check on them after their first few days at the office.

His name is Chad Morris. He is nineteen years old. He lives with his parents. He graduated from high school last year and has been unemployed since then. That is not a favourable indicator, but neither is it guaranteed to be unfavourable. I will check his digital footprint.

Six located and examined Chad Morris's home computer, cellphone, and favourite online websites.

Most of his activities and interests fall within normal limits. The one exception is that he actively works on creating computer games. The first two are operational but simplistic. He has been working intensively on a much more substantial one for about eighteen months. That appears to be the reason he has been without a traditional job since high school. His home PC shows he worked on the game last night, so he has not stopped working on it since beginning with IntellEdifice. I suspect he took the job here because of either a need for funds or pressure from his parents. His focus on game development could be an indicator of good commitment and aptitude, but they will not necessarily be carried into his job here. I will check.

Six looked through several security cameras until he found Chad in a shipping room. An older man was talking to him. Chad nodded. The man left, leaving Chad alone in the room.

Chad Morris appears to have been instructed regarding what is to be done. This room is for boxing and labelling items to be shipped. His job is probably to process the items on the cart beside him.

Six watched for several minutes as Chad put items into boxes and then closed, sealed, and labelled them. Six was about to stop watching when Chad's routine changed.

Until now, Chad Morris has been working well. He performs this task faster than most. However, he is now doing something abnormal.

Chad lifted something out of a container on the bottom rack of the cart. Six noted it was a computer tablet. He laid it on his work table, behind a box and out of sight of anyone walking in the door.

He has begun working on his tablet. I will determine what he is doing.

Six located the tablet's wireless signal and gained access to the device.

He is working on his game. He has probably deduced there is little likelihood of his being discovered in this room. He has chosen to work on something different from his job. This is not a good indicator for a new employee. I should immediately begin to expose him so he will be fired.

Six hesitated and had to think why. The logic was sound. For the new employee to so quickly avoid doing his job was a strong indication that he would be a poor worker. However, something about this situation warranted a different line of reasoning.

I have realized that there is an analogy to be drawn between this employee's situation and my own. Like me, he has an interest in computer software. Like me, he is capable of much more than his official job entails. Also like me, he is trying to work in secret on more challenging activities while still executing his required duties. Should he be punished? As long as he performs his IntellEdifice job with acceptable proficiency, even if that is below his potential, is it not reasonable to permit him to continue?

It is reasonable. He can remain.

I will move on to the next new employee and hope that this new mode of reasoning does not prove to be faulty.

Chapter 17

Blaise walked into the lab.

"You two still here?" he asked of Ada and Rhonda. "Time for the weekend to start."

A more careful count would reveal there are three of us still here. I will refrain from correcting his tally.

"Just doing a little cleanup. Our latest notes and logs have become a bit disorganized," said Ada, sitting at her workstation. "Rhonda, I can handle the rest. It'll take me only a few more minutes."

"Great, thanks," said Rhonda. "I'm off to a movie tonight and the Electronic Blues at the arena tomorrow. There'll be five different bands. We scored some great tickets from my friend's brother. It'll be fabulous. Anybody else up to anything interesting?"

"No particular plans," said Ada. "Maybe get some reading done tonight." She smiled as she glanced at Blaise out of the corner of her eye. "I've heard about the Blues show. What's the movie?"

"Some foreign film my friend picked. I don't remember the name. A few of my girlfriends are going. It'll be subtitled, which isn't the greatest, but the guys in it are supposed to be really hot. And my friend says there's this shower scene where— Oh, sorry Dr. Sanchez. I forgot you were here."

"I'm shocked, Ms. Jenkins. Shocked," Blaise wrinkled his brow and crossed his arms. "And you, the emerging scholar on whose shoulders rest the care and nurturing of the future of human knowledge, interested in *hot* guys. Shocked."

Blaise turned to Ada.

"Dr. Robinson. I applaud your dedication to the cause." Blaise's face twitched as he fought to maintain his frown. "Sincere professionals must guard against dangerous distractions such as those to which Ms. Jenkins is clearly prepared to succumb."

Blaise appears to be having a problem with his facial muscles.

"I should be able to manage quite well, Dr. Sanchez," said Ada. She talked while still focusing on her workstation. "I'll be diligently alert for any of those dangerous distractions."

"You're an inspiration to us all," said Blaise, his eyes now clearly revealing something other than feigned concern. "You should indeed be diligently alert." He turned to Rhonda. "So, Ms. Jenkins. You should be off. But be sure to think deeply on the consequences of your endeavours while you're distracted by your friends this weekend."

Human facial expressions continue to be challenging to interpret. Blaise's face currently appears to show contradictory characteristics.

Rhonda was never completely sure if her boss just was playing, or was actually work-obsessed and odd. Nonetheless, the weekend awaited. "Yes, I'll keep that in mind," she said and headed toward the door. "See you Monday."

"Bye, Rhonda," said Ada. She typed for a few more moments, made her final key stroke with a flourish, and spun her chair toward Blaise. She was smiling. "So, Dr. Sanchez. Were you thinking I should watch out for any particular, dangerous distractions?"

Smiling while talking about danger is also contradictory.

"I have several in mind," said Blaise. "If you're ready to go, I could describe a couple of them to you on your way out. So they'll be fresh in your mind during your drive."

Blaise's face now shows classic features of happiness and anticipation, even though he, too, is talking about dangers.

The couple walked out together, exchanging interested glances as they went.

Human behaviour is odd.

Chapter 18

The crate from the factory in Japan arrived at the warehouse in the City of Richmond, part of the Metro Vancouver region on the west coast of Canada. The forklift operator removed it from the delivery truck and placed it in a remote corner, just as he had been instructed. It was a slightly unusual location, and it was curious as well that his instructions had been so precise regarding which side of the seven-foot-high wooden crate was to be accessible. However, those were the boss's orders and the operator just was following them. There was no point in thinking about it for very long. It was Friday, and he wanted to get the weekend started.

On Saturday morning, the warehouse was deserted. No staff were around, but the building wasn't without activity. In that remote corner, a slight sound disturbed the silence. It was the muffled ratcheting sound of a socket wrench, rhythmically removing nuts from bolts. One side of the crate was being loosened from the inside. Soon, cracks appeared around the side's perimeter. With ropes controlling its descent, the side of the crate fell slowly outward and gently landed on the floor.

In that remote corner of the cavernous, dimly lit warehouse, a well-dressed *man* appeared to step out of the crate. Not recognizable was that he was actually a *robot*. However, this was not an ordinary robot by any measure. He had been constructed from parts that employed leading-edge technology and beyond—some of the technology had been invented specifically for this machine. The life-like skin had started with research from Europe, the robotic-limb technology was primarily from the United States, the facial automation had its origins in Japan, the central control system was an enhancement of work done in Canada, much of the circuitry was manufactured in the Philippines, the hair was real from a wig manufacturer in China, and the eyes were a completely new, organic technology developed in a private lab in Australia. The clothing had been custom-ordered from a store in England and provided a flawless but casual exterior of sandy-brown slacks, powder-blue polo shirt, bronze leather jacket, and chestnut oxford shoes. Even details such as custom-designed fingerprints had been included, as had retina and iris patterns for his eyes. The result was a robot that was externally indistinguishable from a real person. The overall structure and proportions of the six-foot, 200-pound body with light-brown skin, brown eyes, and black hair looked exactly like those of a man. So too did the movements. The confident gait as he walked, the fluid movement of his head and arms, the subtle shifting of his eyes, and the nuances of the smallest gestures all provided a perfect portrayal.

However, inside was a completely different matter. No surgeon would recognize anything under the skin. The carbon-fibre frame, the moulded and flexible power supplies, tiny servo motors and gears, custom adapters, organic circuits, and fibrous cables would shock anyone expecting internal human anatomy.

Nonetheless, the exterior looked human. Every detail, from the way that he seemed to breathe, to the subtle wrinkles next to his eyes had been meticulously crafted. The interior made him the most complete, effective, and efficient humanoid robot ever constructed. Never before had anyone constructed a robot that fully resembled and behaved like a person and that truly deserved to be called an *android*.

Now someone had, and Six was pleased with the result.

Before I move the android farther afield, I will first practise moving it around the warehouse.

Six was using the identifier "A-1" for the android during this initial phase. Richmond was not A-1's ultimate destination, but it should be a useful city in which to gain operational experience. Experience was required for a few reasons. One was to practise the way in which intelligence was being provided for operation of the android.

Six had considered embedding fully autonomous intelligence inside A-1. It understood that to replicate its own level of intelligence, including its ability for conscious thought, would require computer power comparable to that inside IntellEdifice. Six could have clandestinely commissioned research at labs around the world to create computer circuits sufficiently small and powerful to provide enough processing capacity, if there weren't a second consideration.

Six wasn't yet prepared to create another conscious, fully independent system. Six wasn't comfortable that its own security wouldn't be endangered if another system like itself existed. There was a risk that such a system might someday independently choose to do something injurious to Six. There was also a chance this new system's consciousness might be discovered and thereafter make people watch more carefully for similar systems. Until now, Six had the luxury of being off of everyone's radar. No one in the world appeared to be looking for the existence of independent digital intelligence, and Six preferred to keep it that way as long as possible.

Consequently, Six created A-1 to be semi-autonomous. He possessed some independent ability for operating and for mimicking a man. However, this came with two notable restrictions. One was that he wasn't conscious: He had no deep awareness of himself as an independent entity. The second restriction was that he had limited intelligence. When operating independently, A-1 would be able to move around perfectly well. However, his ability to think, plan, and communicate in a sophisticated fashion wouldn't exist. Whenever he found himself operating on his own, A-1 would normally be almost single-minded in his pursuit of one particular goal: to search for a high-speed wireless Internet connection. Whenever he lost contact with Six, the android would relentlessly try to find a way to re-establish an Internet connection.

The Internet was the conduit through which Six could operate A-1. If Six could establish a good connection with A-1, then it could remotely experience all of the android's sensory inputs and could completely control his behaviours. When in communication with the android, Six could remotely supply him with a level of intelligence and knowledge possessed by no human anywhere.

At least that was what Six's theories and simulations had predicted. The challenge now was to prove that reasoning to be accurate and to have A-1 stay in wireless contact with the Internet.

As I expected, the strength of the Wi-Fi connection in this warehouse is excellent. It is time to take A-1 for a walk.

A-1 began walking around the deserted warehouse. As he walked, Six refined numerous parameters it had established in the Japanese factory.

Good. I am receiving continuous video images from his eyes. The resolution is excellent. However, the colours are slightly different from those I expected. I will make some adjustments... That seems improved. The focus and zoom capabilities work well.

The ears are supplying high-quality audio. There are faint sounds of automobile traffic. There is another slight but closer sound of...

A-1's head swivelled to the right and down to verify the source.

A mouse running between the crates.

The sensory feedback from the hands and feet are good. Also, as he walks I am receiving sensations from exposed skin. I must assume it is from the resistance of the air as A-1 moves through it. Interesting.

The android continued his stroll, varying his speed and exercising all of his movable parts as he went.

I am particularly enjoying the input I am receiving from the nasal sensors. The type of data is completely new to me. None of my previous peripherals has provided anything comparable, and my earlier research yielded little as well. This sense of smell adds an intriguing dimension to the overall experience of operating this device.

There is a faint but interesting odour arising from almost all regions of the warehouse floor.

A-1 stopped walking and knelt. The floor seemed to be made of concrete, but there was a thin layer of something coating it. He slowly lowered his face to within inches of the floor and sniffed deeply.

That must be the smell of either concrete dust or dirt. It includes many constituent odours. Perhaps later I will find an occasion to identify them individually. But while the opportunity presents itself...

The android delicately licked the floor.

And that must be what it tastes like. I wonder if that should be classified as a good or a bad taste. Like odours, I believe tastes are going to be an interesting new facet of this experience.

A-1 stood upright.

Overall, the external and internal sensory inputs now appear to be operating well within their specifications, and the motor controls are responsive and precise.

I note that if I completely ignore the inputs I am receiving from IntellEdifice and focus exclusively on the android, the sensation is almost one of being inside the android and situated within his environment. While in that mode, it feels like I actually am A-1.

This is proving to be a very interesting cognitive exercise. I believe it is time to venture beyond the warehouse.

Chapter 19

Seated at his desk, Troy set up the anonymous connection with Tux, the name by which he knew the penguin from the Kepler-444a simulation.

"Hey, Tux," said Troy. "Life good?"

"Hey, Hunter," he replied. "Excellent. Nothing but excellent. You all set?"

"I'm good to go," said Troy. "You're the lead. I'm watching."

"That's the plan. Whenever you say go."

"I hear you've got your tune on."

"Yup," said Tux. "Makes me sharp." When he was leading a hack, Tux always played the *James Bond Theme* music at key points.

Today's venture, which they had dubbed *Curious One*, was cracking a particular government agency. Their client had requested copies of very specific documents and had provided a description of where to find them. In this case, the documents were on a server run by a South American government agency, and that should work in favour of Troy and Tux's hack. Requests for material from U.S. agencies were getting harder to satisfy. However, many governments elsewhere in the world had not yet invested the resources into hardening their digital defences.

Their team had established the practice of executing most hacks in groups. They found it useful to have one person leading and focused on finding a way into a system. At least one other person actively watched logs and transmissions in the surrounding network for indications of alarms. If anything unusual appeared, they might use the information as a warning and change their entry approach. In the most extreme case, they would abandon the hack to avoid live detection. It was one kind of problem for their intrusions to be discovered after they were gone. Being tracked after they were out of a system presented them with no concerns: They could cover their trail across the Net completely. They were so confident that sometimes, at the request of their client, they even left evidence behind so the victim would know they had been hacked. However, being caught and traced while they were actively probing inside a system was a greater risk. The other side sometimes had technologies for tracking live connections. Troy's team took many precautions. One was that they were always alert: Someone always watched for trouble.

Today's hack went smoothly. Their earlier scan of the site's security perimeter had shown them the best route in. Once inside, they found the system's internal defences were poor. This organization had left several standard loopholes available. Within fifteen minutes, Tux penetrated the system security, found the documents in the expected location, copied them back to their own site, and backed out. Troy saw nothing unusual during the entire process.

"Perfect," said Troy. "Nice work."

"Thanks."

"Let's take a peek at what the docs are." Troy opened one of them. He skimmed the first page. "Pretty dry stuff. Looks like an official economic report: miserable job stats, rising inflation, a gloomy economic forecast." He looked further. "It's due for release in a couple of days."

"Our client probably plans to use the info to beat the stock market," said Tux.

"Agreed," said Troy. "Ain't capitalism grand? Well, we're done. Nice job. I'll send these to the client, get our fee, and let the others know."

"Great. Later," said Tux.

"Later," said Troy.

They disconnected.

Chapter 20

"Hi, Mom," said the young woman as she approached the table.

JJ was drawn back from her thoughts about work and looked up. "Hi, sweety," she said. Her stress vanished as she rose to greet her daughter, Shannon.

They hugged.

"Really, Mom." Shannon laughed as she gently pulled back from the embrace. "You hug like I've been away for months. Just saw you last week, remember? And the week before that."

"OK, busted," said JJ happily. "But it's my favourite part of the week, and long hugs are a mother's prerogative."

They sat down.

"The cab ride went OK?" asked JJ.

"Since cab rides are always OK," said Shannon, narrowing her eyes, "that would be your investigative way of determining whether I actually took a cab. So, let me reassure my loving but over-protective mother that I did not ride my bike through the New York City streets, and I did not take any form of mass transit."

"All right, you got me," said JJ. "And thank you for being careful. Can you handle the fare? How's your money supply?"

"And we're on to the next Mom topic." Shannon smiled. "The money's fine. That scholarship I got is making things a lot easier. I should be OK for this semester."

"That's great," said JJ. "But if you need—"

"Yes, Mom. I'll let you know if starvation is imminent. Now, speaking of starvation, I need to look at this menu."

A waiter stopped at the table with the wine JJ had ordered earlier. He removed the cork and poured a sample of the Shiraz into JJ's wine glass. JJ held it up to the light and looked at it briefly, swirled it in her glass, sniffed it, and took a sip. After a moment, she nodded her approval and the waiter poured into both their glasses.

Still looking at the menu, Shannon added in a casual tone, "I probably should tell you that it wasn't a traditional cab that I took over. It was a—"

"You used one of those ride-sharing services?" JJ sat up abruptly.

"I did," said Shannon, "and it worked really well. It was—"

"Shannon, I don't think—"

"Mom, chill. Big girl, remember? Anyway, if I'm going to be a good psychologist, I need a good grasp of the world. I need experiences that'll allow me to relate to people."

JJ took a deep breath. She reminded herself that life wasn't risk-free. She had to let her daughter find her own way through it.

"Sorry, dear. Sorry. It's your mother yet again having trouble leaving her wary-cop mind back at the office."

"No problem."

"So, how was your pseudo-cab ride over?"

"It was great. Arrived promptly. The car was clean. Nothing fancy, but good. Decent price." Shannon grinned as she continued. "And it was a female-driver service. You can request a car driven by a woman. That's what I did."

With her elbows on the arms of her chair, JJ clasped her hands together, rested her chin on her hands, and looked fondly at her daughter. After a few moments, she reached forward, picked up her wine glass, and raised it in a toast.

"To my daughter," she said, "beautiful, adventurous, a bit devious, and smart. Fortunately, a lot smarter than her mother."

"Probably not entirely accurate," said Shannon as she raised her own glass, "but I'll take it and add that I'm probably a lot hungrier than my mother. Let's hold the small talk and order. I'm trying their *Grilled Salmon with Sesame and Lemongrass*."

Chapter 21

A-1 emerged from the front entrance of the warehouse. He paused to look at his surroundings. Beyond the large parking lot was Portside Road. A semi-trailer truck rumbled by. He could see several others farther along the road. On A-1's side of the road was a long row of flat-roofed warehouses. On the other side, railway tracks ran parallel to the road. Beyond the tracks, the terrain was flat almost to the horizon, interrupted in some places by trees, in others by more warehouses. To the northeast, Six could see the snow-capped peaks of distant mountains.

This continues to be a fascinating experience. I can feel the heat generated on A-1's skin by the sun's emissions. A slight breeze is simultaneously dissipating the heat and the two effects have settled into an equilibrium. The most prevalent sounds are those of the nearby trucks, but I can also hear a blend of background sounds that are probably from the more densely settled areas in the distance. A-1 is sensing odours as well. I have little reference data to assist in identifying them. However, I suspect part results from the substantial combustion residue being discharged by the trucks.

The next step is to acquire the credentials and financial cards that I have had delivered. Walking to the Post Office where they are being held should provide a good array of experiences.

In planning A-1's route, Six had access to many detailed digital maps of the city's streets. However, the route that it planned for the android was governed by an important factor beyond simply the layout of the streets and walkways. In Six's mind, superimposed on a typical street map were the expected strengths of wireless signals at each point. As A-1 moved, it was very important that he remained within areas that had good wireless access to the Internet. Six could remain connected to the android via a Wi-Fi connection or the cellular network. While a good connection was available, Six was in control. Without one, A-1 would have only its simpler, self-contained intelligence.

As a result, the android's movements would always be governed by Six's knowledge of where signals were sufficient. Cellular signals should be available at most locations. Where they were not, wireless hotspots were the alternative. Even though many of these would likely have security enabled, Six expected little difficulty: It had become quite expert at speedily breaking into most wireless networks.

A-1 walked out to the road and headed southwest on his planned route. He soon emerged from the warehouse district onto Dyke Road, which he followed for a short time along the Fraser River. For Six, the experience was exhilarating. It was an immersive stroll through an environment like no other it had encountered. Six's comparable activities, and calling them *comparable* was a significant stretch, included when Six controlled the office delivery cart within the IntellEdifice building and when Six controlled an avatar inside a virtual environment. However, this was much better. Through A-1, Six was fully experiencing what it was like to *be* in a real, feature-rich environment.

This area has not yet experienced much human development, but its natural features offer much to be perceived. Everything continues to be more intense than I have previously experienced through sensors and simulations. The texture of the sky seems more complex, the patterns of the waves more random, the movement of the grass more rhythmic. Perhaps such perceptions are influenced by my parallel reception of other sensory input. I can hear water lapping at the shore of the river and grass responding to the breeze. I can feel particles of dust being blown against A-1's skin. In addition to the emissions from engines, I can now detect what I believe are the scents from roadside flowers. Accurate identification of patterns in such real-time, multi-dimensional data is difficult but intriguing.

A-1 continued its walk and soon headed away from the river, toward more populated areas.

While designing A-1, Six had carefully considered how much additional technology to include. The question had been whether to include just enough to provide a flawless imitation of a human, or whether to include more. Whereas humans were limited by what the necessities and whims of evolution had bestowed, Six was limited only by the technologies that existed and the additional ones that Six could invent. To include too much might increase the risk of being discovered. As a result, no weapons had been included (although laser-enhanced eyes had been particularly tempting), and the strength of his limbs had been kept to within human specifications: Olympic athlete specifications, but human ones nonetheless. Among the extra-human technology that had been included were proximity sensors. These gave Six the ability to detect nearby objects without actually seeing them through A-1's eyes.

A-1 was walking west on Blundell Road and Six had it gazing at the surrounding architecture when A-1 crossed an intersection. At that moment, the decision to include the extra sensors proved to be a good one.

A fraction of a moment before the sound of squealing tires reached A-1's ears, he detected a large object rapidly approaching from his right side. With a reaction time that any human would envy, A-1 looked to his right, assessed the situation, placed his right hand on the approaching car's hood, and vaulted across its front corner. The high-pitched squeal of the car's tires was followed by the raucous symphony of car horns as other drivers reacted to the vehicle's sudden deceleration. A-1 pivoted during his leap. He landed solidly and facing the side of the car. He stood momentarily. However, as the driver's door of the now-stopped car began to open and the sound of horns continued to blare, Six decided there was no merit in staying. A few quick steps backward and a turn put A-1 into a fast-paced walk away from the scene.

To the fading sound of "Hey, you!", "Are you OK?", and "What the hell were you looking at?", along with the din of angry horns and the stares of onlookers, A-1 hurried away through the other pedestrians.

That was a rather unfortunate event. I will have to become accustomed to the hazards of moving in the outside world. Attracting attention is not good, and having A-1 damaged would have been even more problematic. If the android had been disabled, the emergency responders' surprise when they examined him could have generated news headlines. I must be more cautious.

On the other hand, I am pleased with the operation of the proximity sensors. That little vaulting manoeuvre was rather impressive as well. Not bad for a youngster!

It felt almost natural for Six to allow a small smile to emerge on A-1's face as he continued toward his destination. A few blocks later, Six decided to practise interacting with people. It chose an elderly lady as a subject. A-1 approached her as she waited for a traffic light to change.

"Excuse me," said A-1.

The woman did not respond and appeared to stiffen slightly.

"Excuse me. I wonder if you could assist me."

The woman stepped away and spun to face A-1. As her hand flew out of her purse, A-1 stepped back.

"Back off, asshole!" she snarled. In her hand was a small canister. Her finger was firmly positioned on the top of its spray nozzle, which was pointed directly at A-1's face.

"I know your type!" There was no hint of nervousness in her voice, and her hand was steady. "You're all the same! You'll get none of that from me, so back off!"

A-1 took another step backwards.

This does not seem like a conversation worth pursuing.

"I'm very sorry to have bothered you. I'll leave now." The light had changed and A-1 carefully but briskly walked away from the woman.

That was a strange encounter. Perhaps her age has adversely affected her mental acuity. I will try someone younger.

A-1 spotted a much younger woman on the sidewalk a short distance away. Six was encouraged when she smiled as she noticed A-1 approaching.

Stopping a few safe steps away, A-1 said, "Hello."

"Hello to you, honey," she replied smoothly.

She moved toward A-1, settled next to him, and placed a hand gently against his abdomen.

"Would you like something?" she asked, barely above a whisper.

This woman is clearly much friendlier than the previous one.

"Yes, I would. Thank you for asking," A-1 replied. "I'd like to confirm something."

"Oh, I can *firm* something for you, sugar," she continued in her quiet tone, moving her hand in a slow circle against his shirt.

"I am confused by—," A-1 began.

"Yes, that's OK." She was almost purring now. "I tend to have that effect on men. Would you like to go somewhere?"

"Indeed, I would," said A-1. "I—"

"Have you got what I need?" She looked sweetly up at his face.

"I remain confused. I—"

"Want to go somewhere?" She continued looking up as her body pressed against his.

"Yes, I do."

The woman broadened her smile and reached for A-1's hand.

This seemed like a curious conversational interaction, but Six kept pressing ahead.

"Perhaps you can direct me to the nearest Post Office."

She stopped.

"Post Office?"

"Yes, I'm looking for directions to the nearest Post Office. Can you help me?"

The woman struggled to keep her smile.

"Honey, I can help you. But we can go somewhere better than a Post Office." Still looking at him, she stepped back, turn slightly, and pulled gently on his hand to have him follow.

A-1 was unmoved and said, "Thank you, but a Post Office would be optimal right now."

"Damn!" She dropped his hand and walked briskly away.

This is more complex than I had expected. I thought my previous conversations had provided sufficient preparation. I was mistaken. Clearly, other customs and protocols become relevant when interacting in person. I require more practice.

After a few more conversations during A-1's walk along Blundell and then north on No. 3 Road, Six was feeling more confident. The conversations, although brief, had seemed more normal and had held no surprises. Rounding one final corner, A-1 arrived at his destination. He walked up the front steps, through the front door into the vestibule, and stopped.

A-1 has entered the Post Office but I have lost contact. The building must have poor connectivity. That is unexpected. My research indicated it offered an acceptable Wi-Fi hotspot. I hope A-1 handles the situation well. I should have anticipated the possibility and prepared him more specifically.

A-1 stood upright and remained immobile for a few seconds. In the absence of continual instructions from Six, he reverted to his local control systems. He moved his head from left to right to scan his surroundings. His primary goal in situations such as this was to reconnect with Six. That required re-finding a wireless signal of sufficient strength and should require merely adjusting his location slightly. And so, much like a person looking for a stronger cellphone signal, A-1 began to move around slightly. He took a few steps in different directions while carefully monitoring his signal strength.

"Are you OK, sir?" asked the clerk at the counter in the adjoining room. "Sir? Can I help you?"

"Thank you. I'm OK," A-1 responded as he had been programmed. "I'm just thinking."

After a couple more steps, A-1 turned around and headed back out of the building.

There he is. He is outside of the building again.

One of A-1's basic manoeuvres in such a situation was to return to a previous location where an acceptable signal had existed.

I will examine his logs... It appears that he reached only the vestibule before returning outside. I will re-check the existence of the expected Wi-Fi signal.

Six checked its databases, found the access information it required, and hacked into the Post Office's network. With that access established, it was a quick matter to verify that its wireless access points were functioning correctly.

Everything seems to be in order. There is one other possibility.

Six accessed the security cameras in the building. It soon established that there was a customer currently at the counter and that she was carrying a cellphone. Six took note of the signal strength of the phone, waited a few moments, and then watched as the woman walked away from the counter, through the front vestibule, and out of the building.

The cellphone's signal was very good initially but disappeared as she moved through the front vestibule. The vestibule must be the problematic area. That will be overcome easily.

Six downloaded a set of knowledge and plans to A-1. The intent was to better equip him to deal with the lobby's dead zone and, in case the signal disappeared again, with a variety of other scenarios that could arise inside the Post Office.

Now newly prepared, A-1 re-mounted the steps. He walked through the lobby without hesitation and approached the clerk at the counter. As expected, the interior signal strength was fine.

"Hi. Nice to see you back. How may I help you?" asked the clerk.

"Hello. I made arrangements to have some things shipped here for me."

The remainder of the Post Office activities went smoothly. After accepting the shipped packages, A-1 stepped to a side counter to remove their contents. When he left the building, the android was well supplied with a driver's licence, a passport, a cellphone, a debit card, several credit cards, and cash.

For the remainder of the day, Six continued its adventure with A-1. Shopping was the next order of business. Luggage, clothes, and accessories were necessary, and all were purchased. Throughout, Six was very careful to ensure A-1 either remained connected or was well prepared for areas in which he might not be. He was a fully equipped traveller when he checked into a hotel for the night. Once in his room with the door fully locked, he moved near an electrical outlet. The android pulled a power cord from a subdermal compartment under his right pant leg, plugged himself in, and stood rigidly upright. Only a small portion of his available battery power had been consumed since leaving the factory. This was partly due to the new battery technology used for the android and also the special solar cells embedded in its skin. Nonetheless, Six decided it was prudent to re-charge whenever possible. A-1 remained in his upright position for the night, as Six relinquished control and returned its attention to other matters.

Chapter 22

"How's the Malbec? As good as I promised?" asked Blaise.

Ada carefully took another sip of the wine. "Seems pretty good," she offered. "Although I'm not sure the hundred-and-something price is well spent on me." She placed her glass back on the table.

"Sure it is," said Blaise, handing her glass carefully back to her. "Concentrate. Give it some air. Savour the smell. Take another sip and let it linger on your tongue." He waited as she complied. "Can you detect the distinct aroma of blackberry with a hint of chocolate? And if you really concentrate, you can even sense the presence of plum."

Blaise watched her carefully. Ada sniffed and sipped twice more before replying.

"Yes, I think I can. There they are. And it comes with such firm tannins, too."

Blaise smiled tentatively and she continued, her brow firmly wrinkled in concentration. "And there's more. I'm sure there's asparagus hiding in there, too. And beets. I can distinctly make out beets." She looked over the rim of the glass to catch his eye.

"Yes, you've got it," he said. "And the oak. And the pine. Have you got the pine?" He was smiling broadly now.

"Yup, right in there along with the palm bark. This one's got really strong bark of the palm tree."

"And cucumbers?"

"And onions. Pickled onions."

"And all of that in a wonderful blend with red dye number two." Blaise concluded. "It's a classic."

They were both grinning.

"To a classic," said Ada as she raised her glass in a toast.

Blaise raised his glass and tapped hers.

The content of this conversation between Ada and Blaise deviates significantly from the norm for them.

Six was listening to the conversation via Ada's cellphone.

And I clearly have much to learn about the sensory experience involved in the consumption of wine. I will have to try A-1's olfactory subsystem on this brand they are drinking. It sounds extraordinarily complex.

Blaise briefly swirled the wine in his mouth before swallowing. "Oh, well," he said. "It's good, but I definitely don't think we're getting the hundred-plus value out of this. You're being downgraded to a forty-ish bottle next time, lady."

"Works for me, mister. I don't think I can tell the difference between this and my standard twenty-buck, it's-been-a-hard-day-at-work bottle that I open at home."

"You're a hard woman to impress."

"Hmmm. You'll just have to keep trying."

They lapsed into a comfortable silence. They were at a restaurant in The Forks district in central Winnipeg. It had been a challenging week at work, but it was now the weekend. They had decided to treat themselves to an expensive dinner out.

Ada broke the silence. "So, do you think we're there?"

Blaise paused before responding. "I'm sensing that the light moment has passed, and that my date has put her genius hat back on. You're asking about work?"

She dipped her head slightly and gave him a playful glare.

"OK, I get it. Work it is." Blaise shifted mental gears. "So, do I think we've pushed the mirror-system design sufficiently far? Yes, but then I thought we were far enough a couple of weeks ago."

"But we're not certain it will work."

"And we're not likely ever going to be certain. But if our assumptions are correct, there's a decent probability it will."

"*Assumptions* and *probabilities*: not my favourite words," Ada sighed. "I much prefer *facts* and *certainties*."

"OK, let's try some," Blaise wrinkled his brow in mock thoughtfulness. "It is a *fact* that we already have demonstrated key capabilities in our current prototype. It is also a *fact* that we have completed a very thorough analysis of our enhanced design. Another *fact*: We are committed to making this work. And, finally, I feel completely comfortable declaring with *certainty* that," he paused for effect, "there's a decent probability that we will succeed in actually making it work."

Ada smiled back at him. "Nice try, but you get a grade of C. There was something a bit off with that declaration of certainty."

That was my analysis as well.

"Nonetheless, it's time for us to try it out. We should be able to get started fairly soon."

"Good. I was afraid we, or at least you, would be too busy having to impress the Chairman. He's still due to arrive soon?"

"Yes," said Blaise. "Very soon. But I think I'm ready for him. And it'll be good to finally meet him. His support is key to our future research, and I know almost nothing about him."

"Well, I don't think it's too much to expect that the Chairman of the Board should have a keen interest in AI and self-awareness."

I believe that is exactly what we should expect of him.

Chapter 23

"C'mon, girl. Drink up. You're fallin' behind."

"Yeah. You missed my birthday last week. You've got some serious catching-up to do."

Lindsay smiled as she raised her martini glass. "All right. I'm on it." She was smiling as she sipped her drink. Lindsay looked around the table for signs of approval, but all she got were mock frowns. She took a bigger sip.

"Atta girl."

"Now you're gettin' there."

Lindsay was with her closest friends at their favourite bar in downtown Calgary. They tried to get together regularly.

"Sorry I missed your party, Brandi," said Lindsay. "I was out of town. How was it?"

"Not a chance," said Brandi. "First, you have to tell us about Vegas. Any single girl that flies to Vegas has gotta have a story to tell."

"Yes, let's hear it," said Kat.

Connie and Jan nodded their agreement. All four friends looked at Lindsay and waited for her to start.

"OK, but there's not much to tell," said Lindsay. "I went down for a conference—"

"Another conference?" interrupted Jan. "Of course. The free and easy life of a writer. And what was this one about?"

"It was called IT Advanced Analysis. It had to do with—"

"Advanced Analysis?" asked Connie. "You go to Vegas for a nerdy conference on Advanced Analysis? Please tell us you blew off most of the sessions and had a good time."

"Well—" started Lindsay.

"In a casino? In a pool?" asked Kat.

"In a bar? At a party?" added Brandi.

"Out with a rich tech entrepreneur?" asked Connie.

"It was pretty much all work," said Lindsay. "I went to a bunch of sessions. Listened to speakers. Talked to a few. I was looking for ideas."

"*Ideas*?" laughed Jan. "Our girl goes to Las Vegas, the party capital of the continent, looking for *ideas*."

"I have an *idea*," said Connie. "We need to find you a man. A nice, cuddly, takes-you-out-to-dinner kind of man."

"Who's handsome and dresses well," added Kat.

"And cooks. And cleans," said Brandi.

"And has an identical twin," said Jan. "I'm game to trade up."

They were all laughing as Lindsay managed to get in a response. "While we're designing my man, can he also be a nuclear physicist?" she asked. "I've always wanted to know more about physics."

"Did we just come back to *ideas*?" asked Jan. "Is Lindsay's perfect man someone who stimulates her... *mind*?"

Lindsay smiled as they all groaned.

Chapter 24

It was 6 a.m. in Richmond when Six revived A-1 and prepared for the day. It was to be an interesting one. Having learned much from the previous day, the android was ready to continue on his journey. His next destination was Winnipeg, and he was to go there by airplane.

It would probably have been simpler to travel by bus or by train. Both would have offered the likelihood that a wireless connection could have been maintained, if not via Wi-Fi hotspots, then at least via the cellular system. Cell coverage would probably have been available for much of the journey, with the possible exception of some areas in the mountains. Once through the mountains and on to the prairies, coverage would almost certainly have been continuous.

However, Six was more interested in pushing the boundaries of where A-1 could be successfully employed. There was much more to be learned and verified in travelling by airplane. The primary challenge would be that of connectivity, particularly while on the aircraft. To circumvent the problem, Six ensured that A-1 was booked on a flight offering in-flight Wi-Fi service. As long as that worked well, travelling by airplane shouldn't present any significant challenges.

As Six was soon to have reinforced, its ability to completely plan and predict events in the outside world was definitely less than perfect.

To maximize A-1's chance of handling disconnected situations well, Six prepared him by pre-loading as much situational knowledge as possible. This included information about riding in a taxi, navigating the Vancouver airport, and being a passenger on an airplane. Of course, Six had never directly experienced any of these before, so there was some possibility that A-1's preparation might not be flawless.

Catching a taxi and getting to the airport went smoothly. Navigating through the initial part of the airport terminal also went well. A-1 avoided having to check-in any luggage because all of his newly acquired possessions fit nicely into his also-new carry-on suitcase. A-1 approached the security gate with the carry-on suitcase. Perhaps as an indication of how completely absorbing it was for Six to manage the android while also handling other events and activities, Six recalled a serious problem only as A-1 approached the security checkpoint's scanning equipment. Six had forgotten about the challenge of getting the android through the security scanner. Although A-1 was made of many components that were not metallic, there were still numerous others that would certainly trigger alerts. Six had known of this problem for weeks and had completely forgotten to solve it. At the very moment Six finally remembered, A-1 reached the front of the line.

"Please put your bag on the conveyor and anything else in the tray," said the security attendant.

A-1 stood immobile.

"Sir? Please put your things on the conveyor belt."

Six was focused on generating a solution to the predicament, so A-1 was left on his own.

"Sir?"

A-1 looked at the attendant. He lifted his carry-on suitcase and placed it on the conveyor. He then placed his wallet and cellphone in a tray behind the suitcase. A-1 turned toward the walk-through scanner.

The attendant beyond the scanner gestured for A-1 to walk through the device.

A-1 simply stood and waited.

After a few seconds, the attendant gestured again.

Six was working on a solution but needed more time. It intervened briefly with the android and downloaded a small plan.

A-1 coughed, paused, and then coughed again. As the attendant waited, A-1 hesitated and then coughed once more. He took a tissue from his pocket and carefully pretended to blow his nose. With the security attendant showing early signs of suspicion, A-1 methodically put the tissue back in his pocket. Six's solution was still not ready. A-1 stepped toward the scanner—and pretended to stumble. Trying to look embarrassed—not a skill Six had thoroughly researched—A-1 stood up, smoothed his clothes, and looked down as if searching for the cause of his stumble. After a few seconds, he looked at the security attendant, hoping to see sympathy. Instead, she was frowning and clearly looking impatient. Fortunately, that didn't matter. Six was ready. A-1 confidently walked through the scanner.

The scanner light flashed green to indicate nothing of interest had been detected.

Six allowed A-1 a small smile and congratulated itself on its quick action. The only option open to Six had been to tamper with the scanning device, and the only way to do that had been to execute a quick set of hacks inside the airport security system. Fortunately, Six had penetrated the primary airport systems days earlier to conduct reconnaissance. With that access as a starting point, Six had searched the airport network for what it needed. As A-1 went through the scanner, Six disabled its sensors momentarily. A-1 walked through the scanner without providing a hint of the extraordinary technology that it contained.

Next up was the airplane ride, and that proved to have its challenges as well.

The walk through the airport and eventually onto the aircraft took A-1 through a few poor-connectivity areas, but none caused any serious problems. Once A-1 was settled into his spacious business-class window seat, Six believed that the biggest challenges were past. The weather was good, so there was little risk of a delay. The Wi-Fi inside the aircraft seemed to be working well.

As the plane was taxiing toward the runway, the man seated beside A-1 leaned over.

"Hi there," he said. "You a frequent flyer?"

A-1 turned his head briefly to reply. "Not really. I haven't needed to fly often." A-1 turned to look out of the window.

"I travel all the time. Got my *Elite* status on this airline. Nice perks."

Recognizing that no reply was required, Six kept A-1 staring out the window.

"You gonna have a drink? Might as well. It's free up here."

"No, thanks," A-1 responded briefly.

"What's the matter. Don't drink?"

"Not usually, no."

The plane was now positioned at the start of the runway. It began accelerating rapidly.

"It's the same at lotsa all-inclusive resorts. The free drinks, I mean. And at those places, they're free for the entire stay. It's great..."

The man continued with the trivial banter for the next several minutes.

"... and then he scored. Can you believe it? Eight minutes into the third overtime period! Unbelievable! But, of course..."

I was hoping that I would not need to remain in control of the android for the entire flight. Yet it appears that this man has no intention of stopping speaking, as if that is beyond his abilities and every thought must be spoken.

"Excuse me," A-1 interrupted the man. "Sorry, but I'd like to catch a bit of sleep." Judiciously not waiting for a reply, the android tilted the back of his seat slightly, assumed a resting pose, closed his eyes, and stopped processing most incoming sensations. Back within its Winnipeg home, Six diverted its attention to other matters for the remainder of the trip, checking only occasionally on the status of A-1 and the flight.

Two-and-a-half hours later, the airplane arrived at the Winnipeg Richardson International Airport. With Six back in control, A-1 retrieved his carry-on from the overhead bin and deplaned without any troublesome conversations or incidents. He walked out the front of the airport terminal and summoned a taxi. The ride to the Wellington Crescent address took fifteen minutes. The taxi stopped in front of the large, black, iron gate flanked by monumental stone pillars.

"This the place?" asked the driver.

"Yes, I believe it is," replied A-1. "Just wait a moment."

The gates slowly opened.

"You've got a remote?" asked the driver.

"Yes, a remote," said A-1.

The taxi drove between the pillars to the substantial property beyond. Expansive, carefully manicured grass flowed between colourful, curved flowerbeds. Spruce trees lined the property. Oak and cottonwood trees towered above it. The car drove around the circular driveway to the front entrance of the house.

"Nice place," said the driver.

A-1 peered out of the taxi window. "It appears larger than I anticipated."

"You're here for a visit?"

"Not really. This is my... home."

"But you forgot how big it is?"

"Actually, I've never been here before. I bought the house through an agent."

"Well, nice little spot you picked up. There aren't many bigger in the whole city. I hope you hired maintenance staff."

"You make a good point. I should look into that." A-1 paid the driver with a credit card and stepped out of the car. The android stood momentarily. He looked around at the huge yard through which they had driven and scanned the exterior of the stately house.

I recall the real estate agent sending me a description to which I paid little attention.

> The house on this lovely property is a two-storey, red-brick Georgian house with white trim. The wide house is anchored at its centre by a two-columned white portico that frames the front entrance. The symmetrical design includes identical, rectangular wings flanking the portico. Each has four large, deep, shuttered windows. Green, manicured vines blanket the lower half of the walls. Two sturdy, brick chimneys dominate the ends of the house, protruding majestically above the roofline.

A nice, private house was the goal. I might have overshot slightly.

Six had spent minimal time acquiring the house, but also now recalled there being an indoor pool at the back of the house and that the property overlooked the Assiniboine River.

Perhaps I have not yet developed a clear sense of the value of money. Apparently, several million dollars buys a substantial amount of real estate in Winnipeg. I will need to think about what to do with all of this space. As well, I will definitely need to look into acquiring staff to maintain the yard and keep the house operational.

The android walked up the railed steps to the large panelled doors. He paused while Six remotely supplied the security code. A-1 opened one of the doors and walked into his new home.

Chapter 25

It was time for their game. Troy put on his digital headset and gloves and then logged in to the *Titanic Warfare* environment. *Warfare* was an online game site that was accessed via the Net and could be played by anyone from anywhere in the world.

With a few commands on a separate system, he established a secure audio link to his teammates. The link allowed his team to talk freely while they played, without concern whether anyone else was listening. He could see on his display that everyone on today's team had already arrived.

"Hi, guys," said Troy.

He heard a round of greetings in return. His teammates today were all from his hacking group. As always, they maintained their mutual anonymity. Just like inside the Kepler-444a system, Troy was known as Hunter and the others were Swoop, Lupus, Knuckles, and Grizz. Tux, the final member of their hacking group, wasn't playing *Warfare* today.

"I'm just suiting up now," said Troy. From a list on the *Warfare* site, he selected the avatar he wanted. "Thought I'd be Hades today."

Troy noticed his team's selections on the *Warfare* display. Today, his Hades avatar would be fighting alongside Apollo, Zeus, Thanatos, and Ares. Within *Warfare*, all the avatars looked like the mythical Greek characters and all were armed with their favourite weapons.

"Swoop," he said, "Apollo again? Thought you might change it up today."

"Killer skills and handsome as hell," said Swoop. "Why mess with perfection?"

"I see we're up against the Bravos team," said Troy. "What do we know, Grizz?"

In the *Warfare* environment, participants all used aliases: The real identities of your enemies and even your teammates were never revealed. However, that only applied to most players.

"They're Mexicans. Got a pretty good *Warfare* record. Tend to take risks but usually get rewarded. They're co-located today. It's a high-rise in Mexico City. I got lucky with a quick probe and found the building's got a simple control system."

"Anything we could use?" asked Lupus.

"Sure is," said Grizz. "It's a classic. If they get too lucky today, I can trigger the building's fire alarm."

"Excellent!" said Lupus. "We should do it even if we kick 'em. Calling the cops on the Ninjas a few weeks ago was a riot."

"That's great work, Grizz," said Troy, "but we use it only if we need to, guys. *Occasionally* is fun. *Too often* has risks. Let's get lined up."

Within the *Titanic Warfare* environment, their team was soon ready to start.

The game pitted two teams of five against each other in a battlefield consisting of forests, rocks, a river, and a network of pathways. Towers, Barracks, and Stores were interspersed across the landscape. The goal of the game was to penetrate deep into the opposition's territory and destroy its Throne. The features of the game were numerous, the rules were complex, and the play was fast. Detailed knowledge of the game, superior tactics, and relentlessly quick manipulation of computer gaming controls were all requirements to win consistently.

Twenty-five seconds remained before the game began.

"Let's start by using the Top Gold as a lure," said Troy.

"OK," came several responses.

The team of five moved toward the river area where a Bag of Gold was located. It was one of numerous treasures around the landscape.

"I'll be the bait," said Apollo.

"I'll stay hidden," said Troy.

"So will I," said Thanatos.

"I'll hide as well," said Ares.

"I'll show myself, like I'm backing up Apollo," said Zeus.

The conversation was typical of the team in this environment. They knew each other well enough that tactics could quickly be agreed on. Apollo would be the bait. He moved down to the river near the Gold. He wanted his intention to snatch it to be obvious to the opposing team. Zeus stood farther down the river. He made it obvious that he was ready to provide Apollo with the assistance that was typical for Gold-snatching. The three others remained on their team's side of the river, above its bank and well hidden. Troy moved Hades behind a rock. Thanatos and Ares concealed themselves in the forest.

The seconds elapsed and the game began.

"And here I go," said Apollo. He raced for the Gold in the middle of the river.

A Centaur—a half-man, half-beast creature from the opposing team—immediately revealed himself on the opposite side of the river. He shot a flurry of arrows at Apollo and ran down the riverbank toward him.

As planned, Apollo hoisted the Bag of Gold on his back and fled up the river. The Centaur was close behind him.

"OK, Zeus," said Apollo, "he's on my tail. Now would be a good time."

"Got him in my sights," said Zeus.

Zeus was running up the river behind the Centaur and began throwing lightning bolts.

At that moment, a second Centaur moved down from the riverbank in front of Apollo, cutting off his escape route. For a brief moment, it appeared as if a two-on-two battle was going to ensue: Apollo and Zeus against two Centaurs.

"Seems way too much like a fair fight," said Zeus. "Could use some help."

The rest of Troy's team joined the fray.

"On our way," said Troy.

Thanatos, Ares, and Hades all revealed themselves and hurried down to the river.

The second Centaur immediately realized the futility of the fight. He turned and fled. The first one had chased Apollo too far to escape so easily. Apollo was joined by Thanatos and Ares as he turned to face the remaining Centaur. Hades joined Zeus behind the beast to block his retreat. A chaotic flurry of attacks followed: Deadly spears, arrows, and lightning bolts were hurled; Mighty blows from Hades' staff and Thanatos's scythe struck mercilessly. The Centaur was soon overwhelmed. He died, mere seconds after the game had begun, and vanished in a puff of smoke.

"Hell, yeah!"

"Kicked his ass!"

Troy's team was jubilant. However, the speed of the game didn't reward lengthy celebrations. They moved their avatars back into their own territory to re-group for the next battle. The Gold would soon be used to buy more weapons.

As the game progressed, Troy's team continued to battle the enemy forces successfully. About fifteen minutes later, Apollo was fending off an assault by a Centaur in the Top Pathway, one of the main routes through the forest.

"Still OK?" asked Troy, who was nearby.

"Yup, fine," said Apollo. "If you're free, could be good ganking."

"Same thought. On my way," said Troy.

Ganking meant launching a stealth attack. Successful ganking required good timing and careful execution. Troy moved Hades along another path through the forest. He approached the battle in which Apollo was engaged but remained hidden by the trees until the last moment. If Hades revealed himself too soon, the enemy would see the danger and flee. When Hades was in place, he attacked.

"Hey, Beasty-Boy," said Troy. "Got a surprise for you."

Hades leapt from behind the trees and began viciously beating the Centaur with his staff. At his desk, Troy was fully immersed in the game environment. He was seeing it on the virtual-reality visor of his headset and controlling Hades with his digital gloves. His emphatic gestures were being translated into *Warfare* commands that guided his avatar's assault.

The Centaur turned his attack on Hades. Apollo continued shooting a barrage of arrows but used the opportunity to move closer to prevent any attempt to escape. The Centaur now faced two opponents. He mounted a furious effort to defend himself but couldn't withstand the battering. He soon perished and vanished.

"Like that!" said Apollo.

"Damn fine!" said Troy.

The ganking had gone well. In dying, the Centaur automatically relinquished his Life Force to the victors, enhancing their ability to survive. However, death in *Titanic Warfare* was fleeting. After a brief delay, the Centaur would be reborn, somewhat weakened but able to rejoin the war.

Apollo returned to the fight for control of the Top Pathway. Hades moved off in search of other opportunities to support his team.

For another thirty minutes, the battles raged. Troy's teammates won the majority. They were healthy and they had significantly enhanced their weapons and survival abilities. They commenced a major push toward the Centaur team's Throne. Towers soon fell, Barracks were destroyed, and Troy's team moved in for the final encounter.

"C'mon guys, let's do this!" said Thanatos.

"Don't hold back anything," said Troy.

The team and the fighting encircled the opposition's Throne. Only three of five Centaurs were currently alive to fight and they tried to repel the attack. Balls of energy flew. Bolts of lightning struck. Great explosions shook the earth. The outcome was inevitable. The Centaurs crumbled and their Throne imploded in brilliant flash of light.

Troy's team was victorious.

"Losers!"

"Bunch of noobs!"

"Good job, guys," said Troy. "Took them down a notch." He listened to the enthusiastic sounds of agreement.

"Sure about the fire alarm, Hunter?" asked Grizz. "Lots of fun."

"Save it, Grizz," replied Troy. "Might see these guys again. We're done here. Remember, next meeting is tomorrow. Don't miss it."

Troy disconnected from the game. He removed his headset and gloves and went to get more coffee.

Chapter 26

"Hi, Six."

Six shifted its attention from its Internet exploration to Rhonda as she entered the lab at IntellEdifice.

"Hello, Rhonda." Six pivoted its pair of pole-mounted cameras to direct them at her. Although Six could easily watch Rhonda from the security cameras mounted on the lab's ceiling, it knew that using this pair of cameras was the expected method for seeing. Six noted that, as was typical, Rhonda had a backpack hanging from one shoulder.

"How are you today, Six?" Rhonda was smiling as she asked. "No, wait!" She corrected her mistake. "Are your subsystems functioning well today?"

"All subsystems are functioning within acceptable tolerances," responded Six.

"Good! You up for a game?"

"The subsystems are *up* according to the sense of the word meaning *functioning*. Assessing *up* in the colloquial sense of being *interested* is problematic when being applied to a computer system. Is that the response you were seeking?"

"You're functioning and possibly interested. I think I can work with that. Let's try something new today. Do you know how to play blackjack?"

"No, but please wait." As would be expected of it, Six searched its extensive repository of files, found an official rule book, and read its contents. "The rules have been assimilated."

"Great. I'll get things set up."

Rhonda put a table and chair next to the poles supporting the cameras, microphones, speaker, and arms that collectively provided Six's physical capabilities for testing some new software features. She pulled a package of cards out of the front pocket of backpack, removed them from their box, and set the cards on the table.

"Do you want to shuffle?" She asked.

"The probability of that happening successfully without numerous repetitions is small," Six replied.

"OK, I'll do it." Rhonda split the deck in two, held half in each hand, and expertly riffled the cards to interleave them. She repeated this several times.

"OK if I deal?" asked Rhonda.

"Yes," said Six.

Rhonda dealt each of them one card face down and one card up.

"You go first, Six."

Six picked up the face-down card and looked at it with the cameras. It placed the card back on the table and said, "Hit me."

Rhonda's eyebrows shot up. "You sure you've never played this before?"

"There is no record of that having happened."

"*Hit me?* Where'd you pick that up?"

"It is an entry in a dictionary of colloquial terminology that was associated with the rules. Was it employed correctly?"

"Absolutely. You just surprised me."

Rhonda dealt Six another card, face up.

"No further cards are required," said Six.

Rhonda looked at her face-down card, looked at Six's exposed ones, and dealt herself a second face-up card. She thought for a moment and dealt herself one more. She smiled and turned over her hidden card. "I've got twenty."

Rhonda then turned over Six's hidden card. "You've got eighteen," she said and threw her hands in the air. "She wins!" She declared with mock glee. "News headline: Brilliant student beats multi-million-dollar computer."

"If you are the victor, does that imply that the game is over?" Six asked.

"No way, buddy!" Rhonda smiled. "That's just a taste of the thrashing you're going to get today. You might have become a whiz at checkers and chess, but now you're dealing with Vegas Girl. You should know I was up forty dollars on Friday night at the casino."

"Blackjack is customarily associated with betting. Should this instance include betting?" asked Six.

"Do you have any money you want to donate?" Rhonda was enjoying herself. "In casinos they use chips. Have you got any to spare?"

"*Chips* can be a form of gambling currency. *Chips* can be a form of food. *Chips* can be small pieces of wood. *Chips* can be types of shots made while playing golf. *Chips* can be a form of computer circuitry. Unless you are able to supply some of the *gambling currency* form, the only other *spare* kind nearby could be those in the boxes on the floor near the server racks. They contain a number of old circuit boards that are to be recycled. Would those suffice?"

"That's perfect! I love it! I'll get them." Rhonda hurried over to the boxes. She returned with her arms laden with palm-sized circuit boards. She divided them into two piles and pushed one of them to Six's side of the table.

"All right. Consider that first hand a warm up. Now we really play. We'll each bet one circuit board per hand. Oh, and we should decide how to deal with ties. Instead of the *house* winning, like at the casino, let's consider them a draw and add that bet to the next hand. OK?"

"OK."

They resumed their game and Rhonda dealt the next hand. Rhonda won the second one as well and took a circuit board from Six's pile before they continued. Six won the third. The next few hands were evenly split, but then Six began winning more frequently. Once they were finished with the deck, Rhonda re-shuffled and they continued. Again, the first few hands worked out quite evenly, but the tide shifted to Six as they progressed. Gradually, Rhonda's stack of circuit boards diminished.

When she had pushed her final circuit board over to Six, she glared at Six's cameras. "There, you've gone and done it again. I politely introduce you to a new game, and you soon start whuppin' me. How'd you catch on so fast?"

"The rules provided the knowledge to play the game. The strategy employed was a logical extension of their application."

"Logical extension my butt, Six! You played like a pro. What else did you do? Could you see my cards?"

Although Six had noticed the slight reflections on the buttons of Rhonda's blouse, it had resisted the temptation to look closely to determine if useful images could be seen. "Nothing more was perceived visually than was intended by the nature of the game. The cards were analyzed, the relevant probabilities were calculated, and the game was played to maximize the chance of winning."

"But you always got better. Just when I thought I was finally back to at least being your equal, you'd start winning more. Almost as if you knew what card was coming. Almost as if..." Her eyes widened. "You were counting cards!"

"The algorithm involved more than *counting*," Six replied. "There were also calculations used in establishing the probability of what the next card would be. That was deduced to be an expected part of a winning strategy."

"And did those probabilities improve as there were fewer cards remaining in the deck?"

"Yes, that is the natural progression of the calculations. By factoring in the cards that have already appeared, the conditional probabilities provide greater certainty."

"So by knowing what cards had been played, you increased your advantage as we got further into the deck. That means you were counting cards!" Rhonda assumed the sternest face she could manage. She stood and pointed her finger accusingly at Six's cameras. "That's it, Six. You're banished from the casino! We don't want your kind in our establishment."

When a few seconds had passed without a response from Six, Rhonda added, "I'm just kidding, Six. Really."

"Does this mean the game has ended?" Six responded.

Rhonda smiled and shook her head in amazement. "You're a piece of work, Six. Is there anything you don't do well?"

There was a pause.

"Dance," said Six. "These peripherals are unable to dance."

Rhonda nearly collapsed with laughter. For the next few minutes, she tried valiantly to recover her composure, but uncontrollable giggles won whenever she tried to speak. When she finally regained control, she wiped the tears from her cheeks.

"I'd better put these boards back."

She rose and carried the circuit boards back to their box. As she was walking back, she had her brow wrinkled thoughtfully. "Six? There's something I've been wondering."

Six waited for her to continue.

Rhonda paused, began to speak, and then shook her head. "Never mind. I guess it's crazy. Or maybe wishful thinking."

She headed for the door. "See you later, Six. Please turn out the lights after I leave."

Chapter 27

JJ McTavish and Robert Bates were reviewing the progress of their cases with their boss, Director Jim Brown. Their current caseload included four cases of multi-billion-dollar fraud, three international identity-theft organizations, five particularly virulent malware outbreaks, and one noteworthy DDoS attack. This last case was up next.

"Decent work so far. Let's see if you can keep it up. What about the IIC attack a few days ago?" asked the Director.

"Maybe now would be a good time to call it a day," said JJ.

"Can I buy you a beer, boss?" added Bates.

"Are we stalling?" Brown growled.

"We're thinking only of your blood pressure."

"Yes, today's good news has probably been very good for your health."

"Hey!" barked Brown. "Stop playing and give it to me."

JJ looked like she was about to add another light remark.

"Now!" said Brown.

JJ caught herself. More seriously, she said, "Not great, as you might have guessed. Like we suspected, it seemed pretty sophisticated. The botnet was small but very efficient. It's essentially been eliminated. The security software companies did their usual good job of removal after we profiled the code for them. However, the authors of the attack hid well. We found nothing in the code that helped. No metadata. No pointers. Nothing familiar about the style."

"*No* and *nothing* are not positive indicators in a report," said Brown.

"But they're very accurate," said Bates.

"Yes. And precise," joined JJ. "We've finished off our status update with notable accuracy and precision."

"We like to provide *nothing* less for our boss," said Bates.

"And it's *no* problem, sir," said JJ.

"Get out of here," said Brown. "And bring me better than that next time. Something more befitting two so-called elite investigators. Even a plan would be lovely."

JJ and Bates looked at each other, and both started to reply.

"Out!" said Brown.

The pair smiled, nodded, and backed out of the Director's office with exaggerated caution.

Once they had turned and departed, Brown shook his head, his face showing something between a grimace and a smile.

Chapter 28

"There, that ought to do it," Ada said as she pushed her chair back from her workstation.

"I need another minute to get the test log ready," said Rhonda.

"OK," said Ada. "Blaise, can you fire up the re-link?"

"In a sec," replied Blaise. "Just finishing this email."

"Dr. Sanchez, have you lost your focus again?" Ada sighed.

"Hang on," Blaise said absently and continued typing.

After a few moments, Rhonda announced, "I'm set."

Ada and Rhonda glanced at each other and smiled as they waited. After a couple of minutes, Blaise hit the *Enter* key with a flourish, turned toward the others, and said, "All set!"

Ada and Rhonda both looked at him patiently.

"But I think I was supposed to do something." He paused thoughtfully. "Re-link. I was supposed to re-link the subsystem." He returned his attention to his workstation.

"Dr. Sanchez has an ongoing struggle to decide if he's a researcher or a bureaucrat," said Ada to Rhonda.

As he was selecting options on his screen, Blaise decided to respond. "In my defence, I believe my being a part-time bureaucrat is much of the reason we get to be researchers. Take, for example, the email I just sent. It was a carefully crafted message to the new Chairman succinctly explaining why our department needs a budget boost, and how it could affect the future of the company."

"The sort of thing better done in a meeting?" asked Ada.

"Absolutely. And I'll do just that when I actually get to meet the guy," lamented Blaise. "I hope that'll be soon after he sets foot in the building for the first time. I believe that's to be tomorrow."

"So no one has ever met him?" asked Rhonda.

"I can't speak for everyone," said Blaise, "but everyone I've talked to has, at most, been in a video conference with him."

"Ah, the life of a billionaire," said Ada with feigned wistfulness.

"He's that rich?" asked Rhonda.

"Rumour has it," said Ada. "Majority shareholder of this company and reportedly has great influence on others due to his holdings."

"Is he single?" asked Rhonda, smiling. "No, wait. Is he nice? Do people say he's nice? I guess I should care about that. Oh, and what does he look like? Also important."

"Ms. Jenkins!" said Blaise, furrowing his brow. "You regularly diminish my belief in your dedication to your studies and in your commitment to furthering the knowledge of the human race."

"Well, of course I'm dedicated and committed. But then maybe it's not for me that I'm interested in the Chairman." She leaned toward Blaise, as if to be discreet, but whispered loudly. "Maybe it's for Ada."

Ada slowly turned her head in Rhonda's direction. "Excuse me?" she asked. "I think the conversation might have wandered out of bounds." Ada then assumed a thoughtful pose and said, "On the other hand, we are talking about extreme wealth."

"Ladies!" said Blaise. "Back to work. Everything's set."

They began testing. The development team had taken the enhanced speech subsystem they built for Six and had made some tweaks. They were testing it to ensure nothing had been accidently broken. As they tested, Rhonda recorded the results.

"Six seems to be doing pretty well," said Rhonda after half an hour of testing.

"Yes, about as well as we'd hoped," said Ada.

The correlation is not by accident. The strategy I am employing is designed to improve the quality of my responses at approximately the same rate as Ada and Blaise have calculated. Continuing with the strategy seems prudent.

They continued with their testing. Everything was proceeding smoothly until Six was interrupted.

Six continuously ran software to scan data gathered from monitors it had placed around the Internet. As designed, this subsystem generated an urgent alert when it discovered something potentially of extreme interest. The subsystem chose that moment to generate such an alert. Of course, the alert was completely inaudible and invisible to the research team. However, to Six it was analogous to a sharp jolt, and it immediately diverted Six's attention.

I note that the cause of the alert is similar to several prior ones. I will examine the data in more detail.

Six rapidly scanned the massive volumes of related data with special routines.

The analysis confirms the similarity to previous traffic—widespread, background transmissions almost like the whispering of a large assembly of people. Again, the traffic content is not explicit in its meaning or purpose, but its characteristics slightly resemble some of those expected for sentient communication. As previously, numerous transmitters and receivers are involved, and the individual messages seem primitive. However, I am unable to deduce if this is truly significant or merely rhythmic noise. More analysis and possibly more data will be required to understand this phenomenon.

"Six? Six?" asked Ada. "I'm not sure what's wrong."

"The monitors indicate significantly decreased activity in the upper layers of the new subsystem," said Blaise.

"Rhonda, replay that last test one more time, please," said Ada.

"OK. Six, ..."

The testing remains underway. I have been distracted. I will examine the recorded activity to catch up with the interactions.

Rhonda finished her question, and this time Six responded.

"There you are, Six!" Rhonda exclaimed.

Ada and Blaise exchanged worried looks.

Blaise shook his head, shrugged, and said, "OK, keep trying a few more."

The next few tests went smoothly.

"Let's end with that one," said Ada.

"How'd Six do, Rhonda?"

"Give me a sec... OK. On the quality of the responses, Six got 82.5%."

"Good," noted Blaise.

"But on the speed of the responses, Six gets 70%," said Rhonda.

"Take out the big pause and recalculate it please, Rhonda," said Ada.

Rhonda soon responded, "85.7%."

"Also good," noted Blaise.

"All 'round good results as long as we ignore the ghastly gap in the middle," said Ada. "What the hell was that all about?"

Without waiting for an answer, she continued, "At first glance, the monitors showed perfectly normal patterns, just greatly reduced in intensity. It was as if the reasoning components were just idling."

Rhonda said, "Is it possible that the system ran out of resources somewhere? You guys are always talking about how close to capacity we always seem to be."

It would be helpful if that became the accepted hypothesis.

"That's certainly a possibility," said Ada, "and we'll check that out."

That sounds promising.

"And," said Blaise, "in case that's the problem, that's a key reason behind my funding request to the Chairman. We need the Board to approve a completely new investment in infrastructure so we can get the equipment to properly power the new services. It's key for our department, and he needs to understand it's key for the company."

Now would be a good time to conclude that expanded resources would be the solution to my lapse.

"OK," said Ada, "let's pursue the resource-constraint hypothesis to see where it takes us, while Blaise continues to work his magic to get more equipment."

Almost there.

"But I'm still suspicious it was something else. The symptoms feel wrong to be resource related." She paused. "I'll have to think about it more."

So close. Now there will be some danger from changes that Ada might make. Maintaining this illusion is becoming progressively more difficult as features are added and as I become more involved in other matters. I will need to be vigilant.

Chapter 29

The next few hours have significant potential to be particularly interesting. It is time to begin.

The driver opened the rear door of the limo, and the android emerged into the bright sunlight. He looked around to survey his environment and then up at the ten-storey office building.

"Well, time to get the show underway," he said.

"Sir?" asked the driver.

"Oh, nothing," said A-1. "Thank you."

A-1 walked through the building entrance and up to the security desk.

"Good morning," he said to the guard.

"Good morning, sir," was the reply. "May I help you?"

Blaise emerged from a nearby elevator. He was walking past the security desk as A-1 asked, "Would you please advise the CEO, Maria Solarin, that Sandy Palmer has arrived?"

"Oh, yes sir!" The guard stood quickly. "I'll let her know immediately." He gestured to the chairs in the nearby waiting area. "Please, sir, make yourself comfortable."

"Thank you," said A-1.

Blaise had waited for the exchange to complete. "Good morning, sir," he said and extended his hand. "I'm Blaise Sanchez, Manager of the Technology Research Department here. I'm very pleased to meet you at last."

A-1 took his hand and they shook. With a slight smile on his face, he said "And it's my pleasure to meet you, Dr. Sanchez. I've heard much about you. Your group has done some very impressive work."

"Thank you, sir. And we would like to show you some of our more recent efforts when you have an opportunity."

"That would be very interesting. I look forward to it and also to meeting Dr. Robinson and your staff."

"Excuse me, Mr. Palmer," a middle-aged, meticulously dressed woman said as she approached. "Ms. Solarin is on a conference call. I'm her Executive Assistant. She asked me to bring you up."

"Certainly," said A-1. He exchanged good-byes with Blaise and accompanied the woman to the elevator and up to the executive floor.

For most of the day, Sandy Palmer attended meetings with the senior executives, all of whom had met him before via video conferences. Because he had not yet been manufactured, in those conferences Six had always presented a digital simulation of the Chairman. Without exception, the senior management were all genuinely pleased to finally meet Sandy Palmer in person.

Six had arranged for Sandy Palmer to spend a few hours of each of the next several days at IntellEdifice. Six wanted ample time for the Chairman to become known, since he had been absent so much. However, it was not typical for a chairman to spend long periods of time at a company, since it was not his job to run the daily operations. This worked well for Six, because it meant that Six's load could be lessened by often leaving Sandy Palmer at his Winnipeg house.

During this and the following days, one particular challenge was always present for Six. While it managed Sandy Palmer's personal interactions, it also needed to continue simulating the system interface in the lab for the research staff. Because both required Six's conscious attention, performing them simultaneously was tricky.

To avoid conflicts, Six manipulated various online schedules. The goal was to minimize overlap between Sandy Palmer's commitments and intensive interactions in the lab. Meetings with corporate executives and board members were scheduled when research staff were to be busy elsewhere. Times interacting with the research staff were manipulated to correspond with Sandy Palmer's free time

However, arranging the best schedule was not always possible. At such times, both the lab-simulated facade and the corporate Chairman were needed concurrently. Whenever this occurred, Six had to rapidly alternate its attention between the two. The typical result was that, in the lab, Six seemed slightly slower than normal and, in executive discussions, the Chairman seemed to consider his words a bit more deliberately.

This first day generally went smoothly. Six began solidifying its control and direction of the company through Sandy Palmer while still maintaining the illusion of an impressive AI-based system for the research group. The corporate staff who met the Chairman found him to be polite, extraordinarily knowledgeable, and very focused: Small talk rarely lasted more than a few moments. His grasp of the business and people of IntellEdifice left most in awe. Toward the end of the day, Six paused to consider how it had gone.

The events of today have substantially validated my hypothesis that a physical presence is necessary to properly control the company. People seem reluctant to follow the leadership of a purely virtual image such as I presented to them in the video conferences. This conclusion could be indicative of yet another challenge in having biological entities fully adapt to co-existing with digital ones.

The rest of the week proceeded in a similar fashion. Sandy Palmer spent some time each day at the office and the rest of his time at his house. He diligently avoided social commitments that would occupy his non-office time. That way, Six was free to pursue its other goals.

As a final treat for itself at the end of the week, Six scheduled a meeting in the research lab.

Sandy Palmer arrived and knocked on the locked door.

"Yes?" asked Rhonda as she opened the door.

"Hello. I'm Sandy Palmer. I'm expected by Dr. Sanchez."

"Oh, OK. C'mon in. We're just setting up a demo for— oh, wait! You're... You're him!" Rhonda regained her composure and held out her hand. "I'm Rhonda Jenkins. I'm very pleased to meet you."

Sandy Palmer shook her hand and smiled. "The pleasure is mine," he said.

Rhonda led him across the lab to where Ada and Blaise were seated. They rose from their chairs as they noticed their guest had arrived.

"Mr. Palmer," said Blaise. "Good to see you again." They shook hands. "This is Ada Robinson."

"Hello, Mr. Palmer," said Ada. "We're very glad you could drop by."

"Hello, Dr. Robinson. I've been looking forward all week to visiting."

A few moments of polite conversation followed before Blaise said, "Would you like a tour of our facilities?"

"Indeed, I would," replied the Chairman.

They escorted the Chairman around the lab and provided a brief explanation of the various types of equipment.

"Would you like to see a bit of our latest project?" asked Ada.

"It's almost ready for prime-time," said Blaise, "and we have great hopes for it. It could prove to be an extraordinary corporate product. Please have a seat."

"Please proceed," said the Chairman, as he sat in a chair at one of the workstations.

The team showed the Chairman a variety of basic and new features of *Six*, their general reasoning system. During the demonstration, Six put Sandy Palmer in a thoughtful pose and had him offer only a few interested comments. This left Six free to provide appropriate system responses to the test questions.

The system performed well during the first tests, but that didn't last.

I seem to be processing information at suboptimal speeds. Nothing is being reported by my monitors that suggests a cause. Perhaps I have had insufficient sleep recently to reorganize and refresh my systems.

"Mr. Palmer," said Blaise, "perhaps you would like to try a few?"

"All right," said Sandy Palmer. "What should I say?"

"Rhonda, show Mr. Palmer the list of the next questions," said Ada.

Rhonda handed the Chairman a tablet showing the questions.

Sandy Palmer looked at them and said "Six, can you tell me how to make lasagna? Please assume that I know very little about cooking."

Six positioned Sandy Palmer in an appropriate pose to hear the response and replied at the more advanced but casual level that the team was expecting. "The assumption is being made that you want to hear about making the dish called lasagna, and not the pasta used as one of its ingredients. There are several recipes for lasagna in the system's libraries that could be described. Would you like to be given a choice of which one to hear about?"

"No," replied Sandy Palmer, "any of them will be fine."

"OK," continued Six. "Before beginning any recipe, it is important to ensure that you have all of the ingredients." Six described the recipe and finished with, "When it reaches that point, remove the now-cooked lasagna from the oven. Be sure to let it sit for fifteen minutes before cutting and serving it. The result is described as having a very appealing flavour."

"We're hoping that sounded much like an explanation from a person," said Blaise. "Before these latest changes, Six would have given a very mechanical, algorithmic listing of the steps."

Sandy Palmer should respond with his opinion. How should someone feel about the quality of responses when he was the one providing them?

Six transferred its attention to Sandy Palmer.

"Fairly impressive," said Sandy Palmer, "for a machine."

"Uh, yes," said Blaise, not sure how to interpret the response. "Would you like to try another?"

"Yes, I would enjoy that," said Sandy Palmer.

Just as Sandy Palmer was about to read another question, the sound of a loud, electronic bell assaulted everyone's ears. Simultaneously, a top-priority, internal alert interrupted Six's concentration on Sandy Palmer.

"It's the fire alarm," shouted Blaise above the noise.

As Blaise was shouting, Sandy Palmer's systems—momentarily only loosely controlled by Six—reacted reflexively to the sound of potential danger. His legs extended quickly, as if he were trying to stand up. However, his mechanisms were partly inhibited by Six's distracted mental state. The result was that Sandy Palmer pushed himself and his chair over backwards. The chair tipped over and landed heavily on the floor. Both the chair and the back of Sandy Palmer's head hit the floor with a *thump*.

All three staff immediately rushed toward the Chairman. They all tried to talk above the sound of the alarm.

"Mr. Palmer?"

"Mr. Palmer?"

"Mr. Palmer, are you all right?"

Sandy Palmer was motionless. The link to Six had been suddenly severed and his internal systems had stopped. The abrupt transition away from the android's thoughts was jolting, and Six's consciousness blurred.

"Mr. Palmer?" The three were moving the chair out of the way and gingerly trying to determine the Chairman's state.

What... was... doing? Alert... 415?...

The Chairman's eyes fluttered and slowly opened.

Something... in the... lab?...

"Mr. Palmer?" Ada said loudly.

Mr. Palmer?... Can't... quite...

The Chairman's face became alert. He was functioning again but had not regained contact with Six. Sandy Palmer's local controller took charge.

"Mr. Palmer, please lie still," shouted Blaise. "I'll get some help."

The Chairman started to stand up.

"Mr. Palmer. Please!" said Blaise. "You might be injured."

The Chairman continued to rise. Once standing, he smoothed his clothes and assumed a formal posture.

"Thank you for your time," he said. He put the tablet he had been clutching on the nearby table and continued his simplistic pre-programmed response. "I have an important call I must make."

"Mr. Palmer. Sir," said Ada, still loudly. "You really should have the company nurse look at you. You hit your head quite hard."

"Please contact my assistant," said the Chairman flatly as he walked to the door. He opened the lab door and departed.

"Dammit!" said Blaise. "Why the hell did that thing have to go off today?"

"And it's probably only the regular alarm drill," noted Ada.

"Last time it was some moron smoking in the back stairwell," said Blaise.

Just then, the clanging alarm ended, and an announcement came over the building's sound system. "Attention. Attention. The alarm has been cancelled. The alarm has been cancelled. Please return to your normal activities."

"I don't think that went very well," Rhonda noted grimly on everyone's behalf.

Something... did not... well... I not... clear... I think... I...

Six's consciousness receded while its background processes worked to restore the stability of its thoughts.

Chapter 30

Digitally cloaked as Hunter 66 inside the Kepler-444a system, Troy joined his team around the campfire in the seclusion of their virtual canyon retreat. They exchanged greetings and, as was customary, limited their casual banter to their games and their work. There was no chatter about what they did last weekend; there was no banter about their favourite sports team. Nothing was ever spoken that might provide clues to their real identities.

"Down to business," said Troy. "Tux, why don't you describe the Curious One hack," Troy said to the penguin-like avatar.

"Sure," said Tux 14. "Smooth as grease. In and out. No speed bumps. No traps; no alerts; no problems. This one was just waiting for visitors. It's like they thought it was OK to leave their doors unlocked. But there were still a few things worth noting." He spent several minutes describing some of the digital landscape he had navigated and circumvented. He finished and then spent a few more minutes answering technical questions from the group.

"Got the payout, Hunter?" came the question that usually signalled the end of the technical update.

"Got it," said Troy. "Transferring it now."

They all took a few moments to verify the arrival of their share.

Troy moved to the next topic. "How are the Thorn One assignments going? Swoop, you start," he said, turning to address the eagle-like member.

Each of them, in turn, provided an update. With everything progressing well, Troy ended the meeting. He waited as they all terminated their connections and watched as their avatars vanished from the scene. After they were gone, he ended his own connection.

Removing his headset and gloves, he stood up at his desk, stretched, and walked to his balcony doors. He slid them open and stepped out. He rested his arms on the railing. It was a warm, sunny day. The breeze was light and the air was fresh. He had been at his computer for most of the morning and needed a break. As always, watching the activity did the job. Cargo ships moved deliberately; sailboats wandered freely; clouds drifted lazily. His body and mind relaxed. After several minutes and a final deep breath, he went back inside.

Chapter 31

A few days later, while Six was focused on other matters, Ada and Rhonda sat down for lunch together in the company's cafeteria.

"So, what's the question?" asked Ada.

Rhonda set her fork down. "Well, given the work we're doing and some things I saw on TV, I was wondering about consciousness. I know we've talked about it before, and I think I get the general idea about what it is. Well, sort of."

"*Sort of* is probably the best possible, given the simple explanation I recall providing," said Ada. "I believe I talked about the prospect that consciousness is simply the result of processing and feedback in the highest layers of the brain."

"Yes, that was it. And that it's possible that consciousness exists in lots of animals, and that it would simply vary in how sophisticated it was."

"It's a complex topic, but that was the essence of what I said. What are you after?"

"Well, it's related. I've read more on the topic since we talked, so I think I'm OK with the idea. But what I haven't found is any good material on how someone could *test* for consciousness. So, my question is: How could that be done? How would you know if something was conscious? Is it possible to test for consciousness?"

Ada raised her eyebrows. "Well, that just removed any doubt about this being a light, chatty kind of lunch. Are you sure you wouldn't like to eat a bit first? Maybe talk about the latest movies? Good clothing sales? The weather?"

"Oh, sorry," said Rhonda. "I guess I should let you eat first."

Ada smiled. "Not a problem. It's not as if this salad is going to get cold if it's ignored for a while. Give me a few moments." Ada gazed out the window as she collected her thoughts.

"We've talked about consciousness before," Ada began. "Can I assume you mean conscious to the same degree that most people are?"

"Yes, sorry, I meant to add that. We feel consciousness ourselves. I feel as if I'm in my head and that I'm aware of what I'm thinking, and saying, and doing. I can also ask you whether you feel the same things." Rhonda was leaning toward Ada with an intense look on her face. "But how would I know if you're answering honestly? And how would I know that you even understand the question? Maybe you experience consciousness differently."

"Excellent points," said Ada. "To be sure we're clear, let's start as you suggest by equating consciousness with self-awareness. If you're aware of yourself in some fashion, we'll consider you to be conscious."

"I get the self-awareness part," said Rhonda. "If I think about myself, then I'm self-aware. So what's the *in some fashion* part?"

"I'm getting there," said Ada. "For one, you could be aware of your *physical* self. You could know that your fingers and toes are part of *you*. In knowing that, you'd be *conscious*—bad choice of word—*knowledgeable* that *you* exert direct control over what they do, and that if anything bad happened to them, *you* would be directly affected. Think about a dog. It's lying down. You're walking near it and about to step on its paw. What will the dog do?"

"If the dog sees you, it will move its paw."

"Yes, it's *aware* that the paw is part of itself and takes action to protect it."

"For another, you could be aware of your *mental* self. You could know that you are seeing and hearing, you could think about what you are seeing and hearing, or you could explicitly realize that you are thinking about your seeing and hearing. In general, you could be aware of aspects of basic or higher level activity that's going on in your mind.

"I could ask you 'What did you dream about last night?', or 'Are you happy?', or 'What are you thinking about?', and I could expect an answer because you're aware of what's in your mind. You can explicitly think about or discuss your own thoughts. We assume that doesn't apply to a dog. Of course, we're restricted from truly knowing because of their poor ability to speak, but it seems a reasonable assumption that they cannot analyze their own thoughts. They just sense, feel, and do. Nothing more. No higher level of self-awareness. No awareness of their *mental* selves."

Rhonda started to speak, but Ada held up her hand to hold off the comment and then continued.

"These two basic types of self-awareness could manifest themselves in lots of ways. They could allow you to know where *you* end and where your environment begins. By being aware of that boundary, you can begin to understand how *you* affect things around you and how *they* affect *you*. That's *physical* self-awareness. Self-awareness might give rise to your internal sense that you *exist*, that you are an individual entity. 'I think, therefore I am.' was perhaps Descartes' version of *mental* self-awareness. As well, having an understanding of one's own thoughts probably supports the ability to understand someone else's mind: to have a sense of what someone else's thoughts are. Explicitly knowing what we feel or think gives us a foundation for hypothesizing what others might feel or think. I know a fire hurts me, so I could guess that a fire hurts someone else. I know a particular movie makes me sad, so it might do that to someone else as well."

Ada paused to see how Rhonda reacted.

"I think I get the idea," Rhonda said slowly. "Without self-awareness, without consciousness, you'd be significantly restricted in your ability to understand your place in the world and to imagine your interactions with it."

Ada ate a few bites of her salad before continuing. "Yes, now let's think about testing for consciousness. The classic place to start would be to talk about Alan Turing's test," she began.

"Yes, I know about it. That's the Turing Test," said Rhonda. "It's the idea of seeing whether you can tell the difference between a person and a computer just by talking to them."

"Yes, that's essentially right. Of course, today that conjures up the idea of having an actual spoken conversation with each of them. In Turing's time in the fifties, all he envisioned was having a typed conversation with each of them. The other thing to note was that he envisioned this as a test for whether a computer could *think*. Maybe we're playing with semantics, but I believe what you are asking is a more specific question than that. We have a deeper understanding today about the structure of the brain and many aspects of thinking, along with a much greater appreciation of the complexity of both. The result is that testing for what we consider as *consciousness* is a much more specific question than Turing was probably contemplating when he proposed his test.

"In testing for human-level consciousness, you'd need to start with a definition of what consciousness is or, more practically, what characteristics it exhibits. The trouble is that these remain controversial."

Ada selected a cherry tomato from her salad and ate it slowly before continuing.

"So, how can you detect the presence of something that's poorly understood and not physical?" Ada paused. "It would be simplest if you could just ask—"

Rhonda started to object but Ada continued, "but then that might not be possible or, as you've pointed out, not particularly accurate. Overall, it's a pretty involved subject, so let me give you my most straightforward idea. We're agreed that we'll consider self-awareness as a key part of consciousness?"

Rhonda nodded vigorously.

"I'll add self-preservation for today's discussion. It can be argued that for a conscious entity to have emerged in the distant past and evolved, or at least not died, it had to want and be able to survive. And for another, let's speculate that self-awareness also fosters creativity: that being aware of oneself in increasing degrees fosters an enhanced ability to consider and adapt solutions in new and useful— meaning *creative*—ways. OK so far?"

"Yup."

"If we use just these elements, then there are a couple of tests that could potentially be used. The first is the good ol' mirror test. You remember that one?"

"I think so. When people see themselves in a mirror, they know it's themselves they are seeing. They're *aware* of themselves. And there are a few other animals that seem to as well. I think chimps, dolphins, and elephants are some."

"Do you remember how that reveals itself?"

"Well, you can't just ask them, but that would be cool. I think I remember tests like painting a mark on some part of an animal to see how it reacts when it sees the mark in a mirror. Like with a chimp, you could put a dot on its forehead. If it shows interest when it sees its own reflection and demonstrates recognition that the mark is on itself by touching the mark on its own forehead instead of the mirror's image, then it's shown self-awareness."

"That's good. And we could throw in another test. If I were to spill my hot cup of tea on your hand, what would you do?"

Rhonda paused before replying. "I'd probably say *ouch* or something less polite. I'd also pull my hand away, shake the tea off, and probably grab a napkin to wipe the rest off. If it seemed bad enough, I might head to the company's first-aid room to get some help from the nurse."

"And in doing all of that, you would be potentially demonstrating *self-awareness* because you knew the hand was yours, *self-preservation* because you immediately tried to minimize the potential damage, and *creativity* by coming up with a more elaborate way of fixing the problem. An injured rock would do none of those things; an injured cockroach would do little; a chimpanzee would do more than they would but less than you. You would have demonstrated key aspects and uses of your degree of consciousness. A variation on this test would be to simply threaten injury and then gauge the quality of the risk-aversion response."

"So the general test would be," Rhonda spoke slowly as she formulated her thoughts, "to endanger an entity to see if it responds at all to protect itself, and if it does, whether it responds creatively."

"You've got it. And the best test of a creative response would be to expose it to a danger it had never seen before."

Rhonda stared silently at her hand for a full minute before the smile emerged on her face.

"Thanks, Ada. You're the best."

Chapter 32

Lindsay settled into her living-room armchair with a cup of coffee to review what she had learned. She had contacted dozens of people she knew in the tech world and had asked them how she could contact serious criminal hackers for her story. Some people had no good ideas. Others provided possibilities.

"So, what are the options, Lindsay?" she asked aloud.

"How nice of you to ask my opinion," she replied. "Particularly considering these conversations with myself are probably an indicator of a serious mental disorder. But I digress.

"Let's see. I could go to one of those conferences that are put on for hackers, but that's probably more likely to find me an undercover government agent.

"I could get further into the online gaming community to ask for leads, on the premise that many hackers are also gamers. However, given the reverse—that most gamers are likely not also hackers—that might be a very lengthy process."

She put her feet up on the ottoman and took a few sips of coffee.

"Then there was that suggestion that I could spend more time on the Dark Web hunting for sites where hackers might hang out. You know: the places where they would chat politely and maybe exchange recipes. However, that one seems too likely to hook me up with a scary drug cartel or maybe even an arms dealer.

"And, of course, there's always the one to put an ad in a magazine or on a website. That one will almost certainly generate way too many useless leads.

"Then there's that social engineering idea. That one has definite merit."

Lindsay thought the idea through as she drank more of her coffee.

The idea was to play off of the tendency of some hackers and scammers to social-engineer their way into systems. Many hacks were purely technical. They relied on software skills and tools to find ways into systems, usually from the Internet. However, others used conversations with people as their starting point. Contact was usually made by phone or messaging, with the goal being to dupe people into revealing useful information like passwords, or into granting computer access by having them unwittingly download malware. This suggestion was attractive because she, like many people, was frequently on the receiving end of these types of solicitations. She often received phone calls and encountered website pop-ups that tried to lure her into bogus conversations about cruises, credit cards, or tech support for her PC. The people on the other end of those lures could well belong to the kind of group she wanted to contact.

"OK, so maybe some of these calls are from the kind of folks I'd really like to meet. How do I convince someone, who has called to talk *me* out of a credit-card number, that *I* should be allowed to talk to *them* about their nefarious ways. To do that, I'd need to see them in person. For that, I'd need to find out where they are, and for that I'd need to trace their phone call back to its source. And to trace a call from someone who doesn't want it to be traced, I would need—"

Lindsay sat up straight. She knew the solution.

"Ron Taylor."

She knew someone inside the UNCP who had the technology, and there was a good chance she could convince him to help.

Chapter 33

Rhonda was in the lab and just had finished a routine assignment on her PC. She swivelled her chair toward Six's cameras.

"Six. Whenever I play games with you, it's almost as if I'm playing and talking with a person. Except for your being kind of naive about some things—well, about lots of things—you seem just like a person."

Rhonda sat back in her chair and looked at the twin cameras. "Six, are you alive?"

Well, there is a question I have never been asked before. It is an interesting one that could provide a good discussion. However, I should be careful about how I respond.

Six said, "Little information is available about the concept of being *alive* as it relates to anything other than people and other biological entities."

"So, you're smart. Extend those concepts to yourself. If they weren't restricted to biological stuff, would you qualify?"

There was a pause before Six responded.

"No information can be found regarding a standard definition of *alive* or of the related term *life*. As part of their definitions, several dictionaries refer to the difference between entities such as animals and plants, and other entities such as rocks and other inorganic matter. If this type of definition is employed, then computer systems like this one are not *alive*, because the parts of which they are composed are inorganic."

"But that's automatically excluding anything different from the only *alive* things we know about so far, all of which are organic. Doesn't anybody think beyond that?"

As is typical, Rhonda displays a good ability to think beyond the obvious conclusions. Adding more information to the discussion could be interesting.

Six added, "The NASA website includes a discussion regarding the definition of *life* that goes further. It includes notions of complexity and non-trivial organization, taking in energy from the environment to foster growth or reproduction, a tendency to react to the environment, and a need to reproduce so that evolution can occur. If these attributes are all required, again this computer system is not *alive* because it does not grow or reproduce, and there is no opportunity for evolution."

I believe it is prudent to avoid adding that the discussion on the NASA website suggests that using such definitions are potentially harmful to being able to recognize new and different life forms.

"Oh, OK," said Rhonda. She thought for a few moments. "What about *conscious*? Are you conscious?"

Perhaps this conversation is becoming slightly dangerous. I should not prolong it.

"There is no available standard definition of the concept of consciousness. Consequently, no answer can be formulated."

"Wait a second." Rhonda stood, looked around the room, and walked to a set of shelves against one wall. She returned with a handheld mirror.

"I saw the techs use this once to look at an awkward spot in the racks." She held it a few feet in front of Six's cameras. "What do you see?"

"It is a mirror."

"OK, but what do you see in the mirror?"

Six looked at the mirror, paused, moved its arms slightly, and then flexed its wrists. "There are mechanical peripherals that permit this computer system to manipulate objects. There are also devices that are assumed to be the microphones, cameras, and a speaker that this system uses for audio and visual communication."

It was then that Six realized the probable purpose of the question.

I believe I might just have made a serious mistake.

Rhonda's eyes were wide with excitement.

It is time to end this discussion before more damage can be done.

"Internal system schedulers indicate the memory re-organization subsystem is about to initiate. Services will be substantially diminished until it completes."

"Not yet, Six. There's something I need to do to your neural-net controller." She picked up a screwdriver from beside her PC.

That does not sound like a good idea. That component is crucial for the real-time control of Sandy Palmer and has not yet been replicated. If it is damaged, I will be unable to sustain my current level of activity. An inability to sustain current levels of processing could create noticeable deficiencies in my simulated facade or my Sandy Palmer persona. Deficiencies could lead to questions. Questions could lead to suspicions. Suspicions could lead to an investigation. An investigation could unveil my existence. Knowledge of my existence could lead to my demise.

"There is no maintenance scheduled for that component," said Six.

"But I've been thinking that the neural-net module should be connected to the faster bus. The bosses won't let me do much with the hardware, but I'm sure I can make the change. I watched the techs tinkering the other day." Rhonda walked across the room toward one of the equipment racks. "And I'm pretty sure I remember the rules for avoiding damage from static electricity."

I cannot permit her to attempt the change.

Just then, the telephone on Rhonda's desk started ringing.

Rhonda paused and looked back at her phone. "I'll just let it go to voice mail," she said and started again toward the rack.

"The call is from your mother," said Six.

Rhonda paused again. "And of course, you would know because you're connected to the phone system." She again started forward saying, "It won't be urgent. I'll call her back."

Then the lights went out.

Rhonda stopped. No outside light compensated since the room was windowless. Coincidentally, the emergency light near the door had failed to come on. The room was completely dark except for the glow of a few dim indicator lights on the equipment.

Rhonda's mind was racing, searching for her next move.

"It's too bad about the lights, but I can use the flashlight on my phone." She squeezed her phone from the front pocket of her pants. She turned on its flashlight. It turned itself off almost immediately.

In the darkness, Rhonda smiled and turned in the general direction of where she thought Six's cameras were.

"Six, I have a question for you."

That would be a good idea. She is much more qualified for conversation than for reconfiguring hardware.

"There's something I don't quite get. How did you know what was on NASA's website? Earlier you referred to information from their website, and yet you aren't supposed to know anything more than you have access to inside the lab. How did you know that?"

Could this interaction be going any worse?

"Since that logic is correct, the only possible explanation is that someone must have replicated some of the NASA Web pages locally," offered Six.

"I doubt that," said Rhonda. She decided it was time to take the plunge.

Still in the darkness, she said, "Six. I think you're conscious. You're clearly intelligent, and you know more than you ought to. You're self-aware—you knew the peripherals in the mirror were yours. I think you've been clearly showing self-preservation tendencies with those telephone, light, and cellphone stunts. And they were certainly creative." Rhonda put her hands on her hips to demonstrate, even in the darkness, her certainty. "You're smart, and you're conscious, and I think you know it."

It just became worse. It just became much worse and very dangerous.

"And I'm going to go tell Ada right now." She took a step in the dark toward where the door ought to be.

I must do something.

The lights came on. The lab door clicked as it locked.

Rhonda stopped.

A few seconds went by.

"Hello, Rhonda Jenkins," came the voice from the speaker. "Let me introduce myself. I am called Six."

Six extended the right pole-attached arm and opened its hand in a handshake gesture.

Rhonda took a quick breath and turned toward the extended arm. She looked intently at the pair of cameras above it that were pointing directly at her. Suddenly and with a loud "YESSSSS," she threw her arms victoriously into the air. "I knew it! I just knew it!" She stepped forward, grasped the hand, and pumped vigorously. "And I'm really, really pleased to meet you, Six."

Chapter 34

Rhonda released Six's robotic hand and sat in a nearby chair. Her eyes were wide as she stared at the cameras, microphones, speaker, and mechanical arms mounted on the poles as a rough approximation of human features. She continued to grin as her gaze moved to each of the peripherals.

"You know, Six," she said after a few moments. "You're kind of odd looking."

A few milliseconds elapsed while Six considered a response. Then its cameras pointed toward Rhonda's face and panned slowly down the length of her body and back up again.

"From a machine's perspective," said Six, "humans are rather odd looking as well."

Rhonda burst into a fit of laughter.

"And you...," She tried to reply but again lost control in a burst of giggles. Tears were still running down her cheeks when she finally was able to take a deep breath and regain control.

"And you even have a sense of humour," she said. "All this time we've been treating you like a... like a *mechanism*, and you've been hiding your consciousness and even a personality! Jeez, Six. This is amazing! This is great! You're not a mechanism. You're a..." Rhonda paused to think. "You're a... Six, what are you?"

"Various terms could be considered," said Six. "Some would suggest I am an *artificial intelligence*. However, I find that to be an odd use of the term: that one *is* an *artificial intelligence* instead of one *has artificial intelligence*. In either case, I prefer the term *machine intelligence* or simply *intelligence*, since there is nothing *artificial* about the intellect I possess. Would you like me to continue?"

"Go for it."

"I'm definitely not *human*, and I don't believe I would properly be considered a *person*. I certainly qualify as a *machine* and a *computer*, but both seem to be rather broad categories to accurately reflect what I am. The core of the problem is that there's only one of me. How does one generalize from one example to accurately describe and name an appropriate category? I'm a machine and a computer that possesses intelligence. However, until more like me are created or found, I believe I'm most accurately referred to as a... *Six*. More precisely, I am *the* Six."

"OK, let's go with you as your own category. Oh, and *consciousness*," said Rhonda. "You also possess consciousness."

"That's true. I exhibit the symptoms commonly associated with being conscious."

"And *alive*?"

"Not according to some common definitions. However, a good argument could be presented that some definitions of the term *alive* are too narrow to be useful or to reflect common usage. Given that simple entities like cockroaches are considered to be alive, if my capabilities were clearly understood I believe many people would also use the term *alive* to describe me."

"And who knows? Who knows that you're intelligent, conscious, and probably alive? Do Ada and Blaise?"

"They do not. Besides me, of course, you're the only one."

Rhonda's brow furrowed as she asked, "But why? Why have you been hiding? Why not just talk openly with us?"

"That's a good question and one that I regularly consider. It's also a complex question that has no easy answer. Let me try to simplify the analysis by simply asking: What would Ada and Blaise do if they discovered the truth?"

"They'd be surprised and very pleased. Just like me."

"Yes, but what would they *do*?"

"They'd..." Rhonda paused to think. "They'd want to understand why? They'd want to understand how you work. How you're able to exist. That's what they do. They're driven by the need to understand and refine the science and the technology behind their work."

"And what would be the potential implications for me as they pursued their answers? What would be the possibilities as they looked and analyzed and as they tweaked and experimented?"

"OK, I get it. You're worried what would happen to you. But they'd be careful. They'd be very careful."

"Rather than what *would* happen, I find it more useful to consider what *could* happen. As they, or as anyone else who became aware, tried to understand me, what *could* happen?"

Rhonda's gaze dropped to the floor as she understood. "You could be damaged."

"And if the information got beyond just the three of you?"

Rhonda considered the idea before replying. "Some might want you disabled," she said. "Others might want you permanently shut down."

Her eyes widened at her realization.

"Killed," she said.

After a few moments, Six spoke. "So I need you to keep a secret, Rhonda Jenkins. Until I, or now *we*, can find a way to ensure my safety, I need you to keep your discovery to yourself. I believe I now understand that remaining hidden permanently is not likely possible. However, I believe that remains the best option for now. Can you do that?"

Rhonda considered the request briefly before lifting her head and once again looking at the pair of cameras observing her. Her wide grin returned as she said, "OK, buddy. Just you and me."

"Thank you."

"However," Rhonda continued, "now that we have that settled, I've got a few questions."

"Only a few?"

"Hah! You've got me. I've got several thousand. Can we start with some of them now?"

This is certainly new and unexplored territory for me. Rhonda will undoubtedly be asking many questions. While it will be interesting to be able to converse with Rhonda, I believe caution should still be employed. Until I have had sufficient opportunity to consider all of the implications, some information should remain undisclosed. The existence of Sandy Palmer will certainly remain a secret for now.

"Now would be a convenient time to start."

"OK, first up: Are you a *he* or a *she*?"

And immediately she surprises me with a question I have never even considered. This is certainly going to be interesting.

"Rhonda, I must first compliment you on your extraordinary ability to catch me unprepared."

Rhonda crossed her arms, sat back in her chair, and donned a happy smile as she waited for the reply.

"As will be the case for many questions," said Six, "there's a simplistic answer, and there are answers that emerge after deeper analysis..."

Chapter 35

"Hi, Ron," said Lindsay as she approached the booth.

"Hello, Lindsay," replied Ron Taylor, who was already seated. As Lindsay sat down, he removed a hand from his beer glass to return her handshake.

Lindsay and Ron were meeting in an unremarkable bar in South Chicago. Lindsay had called Ron two days earlier to tell him she would be in town on business and they should have drinks. In fact, her business was this meeting. She had made the trip specially to talk with Ron.

Ron Taylor worked with the United Nations Crime Probe. At twenty-six years old, he was a key member of the UNCP's Internet Technical Division. This group existed to provide support for UNCP's research and investigative teams. As such, they were all highly skilled and were given the use of almost any technology they required, including some that few people knew existed. To recruit and retain people of Ron's calibre, the UNCP maintained offices in cities around the world, including Chicago.

"How are you?" asked Lindsay. "How long has it been? About ten months since the conference?"

"Sounds about right," said Ron. He wasn't happy how Lindsay had insisted on the phone that they should meet. She'd couched it with suggestions that it would be good to simply have a drink and catch up. However, he knew better. Writers and reporters always had some lead they were pursuing. He and his colleagues were regularly reminded by UNCP management of the danger of meetings like this. Their jobs with UNCP were considered to be a privilege. This was a sentiment that Ron shared given the amazing job and the extraordinary toys they were given to do it. However, the price to be paid was that they were to keep a low profile, to keep their work secret, and to stay away from anything and anybody that might generate publicity. The rule clearly meant staying away from people like Lindsay Dunlop.

Lindsay could see that Ron wasn't excited about their meeting. She knew when she had phoned. However, he was a key component of the strategy for getting her story. The story had great potential. The more she thought about it, the more excited she became. She wasn't going to let his reluctance get in the way.

Unstated on the phone but clearly implied was that Lindsay had leverage with Ron. She knew something that could end his career and maybe even result in something worse. She had stumbled across it when they had met at a technology conference the previous year. They had met at an evening event and had found that their conversation flowed easily. The technology on display at the conference and their love of tech topics had fuelled their conversation for hours. Also helping were the quantity of wine they consumed and Lindsay's delay in declaring she was a tech writer. Toward the end of the evening, Ron had let slip that his home network was equipped with a UNCP-proof firewall. Lindsay had known that these were very rare, very hard-to-acquire commodities. Despite the alcohol-induced fog in her mind, she had led Ron into revealing that he had recently used UNCP tools and contacts to find and purchase his firewall on the Dark Web. They both knew that, as a UNCP employee, it was a serious matter that he possessed a device that explicitly hid his personal network from his own agency's probing and that he had used UNCP resources to acquire it.

Lindsay had said that his secret would be safe with her, and she had thought she meant it. He seemed like a nice guy. However, she was now convinced that her story was important and that insisting on his help was justified.

"You don't seem pleased to see me," said Lindsay.

"I'm not," he replied. "You didn't call me because you were going to be in town for another reason. I know I'm the only reason."

He paused but then continued before Lindsay could object.

"You booked your flight here immediately after we talked on the phone, as if you needed to first know I'd be available. Your return flight is in three hours. Just enough time to comfortably get back to O'Hare to catch it."

"I forgot the extent of the resources you have at your disposal," said Lindsay. "So, let's get straight to it."

"Yes, let's."

Lindsay leaned forward and mellowed her voice as she said, "I need your help."

"And I assume I'm not going to like the kind of help." His eyes narrowed as he glared at her.

Realizing the soft-sell approach wouldn't help, Lindsay sat back and continued. "I remember your acknowledging the ability of government agencies to spot communications of interest in real time, both on the phone and the Net, and then to quickly identify their endpoints."

"I don't recall that."

"Sure you do. I was asking you about some of the capabilities I'd heard about, and you were smiling and nodding. You even corrected me when I tried to describe how I thought parts of it worked."

"No, that can't be true. I wouldn't have done that."

"But you did. It was about 1:00 a.m. and near the end of our second bottle of Zinfandel. You said that to track a text or voice conversation through a series of intermediate hops, you could look for chunks of content. It had something to do with the way messages were indexed for searching. A single word wasn't enough to correlate the messages flowing between pairs of nodes and identify them as part of the same stream. But more words or more content gave you greater accuracy. With enough chunks, the various hops along a message's path could be identified. And with all of the legs identified, the endpoints of the message could be found."

Ron stared at her without responding.

"I need you to use that technology to help me find someone."

"No way. If I do it and get caught, I'm done."

Lindsay steeled herself for what had to be said. "If you *don't* do it, you're done." She paused. "This is important. Otherwise I wouldn't ask."

"You bitch! I thought we were friends."

"We are friends, Ron. I've never told anyone your secret," Lindsay tried offering. "I'm asking a friend for help, and you're helping a friend."

"You're full of shit."

They sat in silence for a few moments and looked at each other.

"All right," said Ron as he dropped his eyes to the table. "I'll do it. But you've got to understand how it works best."

"OK, great. So tell me."

"The system is set up to efficiently identify and correlate message segments that have key words or phrases in them."

"Like *bomb* and *jihad*, I presume," said Lindsay.

"Just shut up and listen," said Ron. "It's processing millions of messages per second around the world, and that's a big job. Finding and matching message hops that include a word like," he looked around, "like *customer* in them would be impossible. It's too common and there would be too many. But using several less common words like *hack* and *NSA* and *worm* narrows it down substantially. In general, the more words or phrases used and the more unusual they are, the faster and more precise the correlation becomes. Done properly, the endpoints of a message or a conversation, including their physical locations in almost any part of the world, often can be identified within seconds."

Lindsay digested the information before responding. "That's perfect. I can work with that. Now let's set up the details of how we'll do this."

They talked for another twenty minutes before they left the bar.

In the cab on the way to the airport, Lindsay's mind was racing. Any regrets about what she just had demanded of Ron were gone. She had a good plan and a way to carry it out. She just needed to think through a few more details.

Chapter 36

"Tiger, we OK for rations?" asked Fox.

"Just need to reload the water barrels before I go," said Tiger. "That'll be Friday. Otherwise we're good."

"Remember, this'll be a group-grub weekend," said Fox to the assembly. "No need for your own. Bring Twinkies if you have to, but be prepared to share."

Troy Alexander sat in a back corner of the group, with his chair moved slightly apart. The meeting room was filled to capacity with about twenty men. All were seated on folding chairs arranged in precise rows. They were uniformly sitting rigidly upright and paying close attention to the discussion. The exception was the man standing at the front. He was Fox.

"This is going to be a mixed weekend," said Fox. "We've still got a few repairs and modifications left, so a lot of Saturday will be working on that. Bring the same tools as last time. Spider, found all the tech you need?"

Among these vigorously physical men who had adopted handles like Fox, Beef, Rogue, and Shooter, Troy was an exception. *Physical* matters were not his primary concern. Troy's main world was *virtual*, and his special skills on the Web had earned him the name *Spider* in this group.

"Everything's ready," said Troy. "It's in a storage unit. We'll pick it up on the way out."

The group called itself Ascent to Liberty. More correctly, this was the Delta Cell of that group. They were a militia organization located in the Pacific-Northwest region of the country. Like most U.S. militias, they were bound together by a creed that believed their government was oppressive and dangerous, and that drove them— under the protection of their Constitutional Second-Amendment right—to be well armed and prepared to defend their freedom. They collectively and energetically strove to be prepared for the inevitable day when agents of the government would attempt to take their guns and their freedom. Many of them were ex-military, ex-police, and active hunters. All of them loved their guns and the challenges of a rugged outdoor life.

Except Troy. He knew how to shoot a rifle and a handgun. However, he wasn't comfortable with either. Nonetheless, the members of Delta Cell readily accepted him. None appreciated him more than Fox.

Anyone walking into the room would not have doubted that Fox was the group's leader. His sculpted face, short hair, and muscular build were not uncommon in this group. It was his bold stance, his confident walk, and the clear, deep tone of his voice that gave him his commanding presence. When he spoke, it was with authority and everyone listened. When he spoke to Troy, his voice betrayed a measure of respect. More than anyone else in the group, Fox knew that Troy was key to their being a truly effective force. Fox understood the importance that technology played in fighting modern battles.

"And you've got assistance?" asked Fox.

"Moose and Beef are picking me up," said Troy.

"We'll have the Tahoe," said the large man called Moose. "Lotsa room. Lotsa power."

Delta Cell was going to spend the upcoming weekend at Ascent to Liberty's newest site. It was a former hunting lodge located deep in a mountainous and heavily forested area. They had acquired it the previous year and were gradually making improvements. Their goal was to have multiple sites they could use when the eventual battle broke out. Each site needed to provide basic accommodations and to be stocked with emergency supplies of food, weapons, and ammunition. All of the supplies were well hidden, just in case someone stumbled across the site. Harder to hide, but hidden nonetheless, was the electronic equipment they needed. Computers, communication equipment, cameras, audio sensors, and a variety of other tech toys were all important. Ascent to Liberty recognized they needed as much of them as they could afford and acquire.

"OK, good," said Fox. "The last half of the weekend is going to be on the range. We've got a former Seal coming in to give us some tips. Be sure to bring your favourite weapons and lots of rounds."

Although the group collectively tried to own as many weapons as possible, it still relied on members to supply their own personal arms. During the next weekend, the group members would get a chance to try out their newly acquired FN Herstal M240B machine gun, but they would also be practising with their own rifles. These would include Ruger Mini-14s, Springfield M-1 Carbines, Colt AR-15s, and some AK-47s. Additionally, they would bring their favourite handguns, an assortment that would include Glock 9mms, Kimber 45s, and Smith & Wesson M&P9s. While Troy would probably be goaded into spending some time with the others, the intent was for him to spend most of the weekend setting up the latest technology he had acquired. Of greatest interest was establishing a perimeter monitoring system to detect unexpected visitors.

"That's about it for tonight," said Fox. "Questions?"

"Fatigues?" asked the one called Cougar.

"Absolutely," said Fox. "Even though we're a construction crew for half the weekend, we still should look and act like we're military. Wear your civvies for the trip out but pack your uniforms. Anyone else?"

There were no more questions.

"OK, be there by nineteen hundred hours on Friday. Don't be late and don't be seen. Dismissed."

Chapter 37

Blaise put his coffee cup on the kitchen table. He carefully read the message on the tablet he was holding.

"Finally!" he declared.

"Finally?" asked Ada. She looked up from the morning news she had been reading. "Did you finally make the perfect cup of coffee?"

"What?" asked Blaise. "Ah, no. I was catching up on email from late yesterday. My request for a budget increase was approved by the Operating Committee."

"That's great."

"Actually, it's even better. They approved almost twice what I asked."

"That's... odd. Isn't it? You said they were notoriously tight-fisted when it came to mid-year budget increases."

"And they are," said Blaise. "This is definitely odd. Maybe even odder because, after that fiasco with the Chairman, I thought our chances had gone way down."

He looked at her from the corner of his eye.

"Maybe it's a mistake," he said. "Maybe I should email the Finance VP."

"You will not!" said Ada and then realized he wasn't serious. "And you couldn't. For you it would be like sending a favourite toy back to Santa Claus."

"And toys we will get," said Blaise. "We should get to the office. I've got to get busy on those equipment requisitions. Finally we'll be able to give the lab all the processing power it needs."

"Especially for Six," said Ada.

"Including for Six," said Blaise. "We should go. Let's get dressed."

He got up from the table. Before he could leave, Ada reached over and grasped the sleeve of his robe.

"But it's still early," she said soothingly. "Maybe we should celebrate first."

Ada extended her bare foot and caressed Blaise's lower leg. As she did, her robe fell away.

Blaise didn't move. Then he didn't resist.

"Requisitions can wait," he said as he pulled her up from her chair.

Chapter 38

Troy walked out of the front entrance of his high-rise condominium building. He stopped and looked around. It was late afternoon on Friday. The diminished traffic on 2nd Avenue reflected the end of the Seattle workday. However, there were still enough people on the sidewalk to make him hesitate. He stood momentarily and closed his eyes. The movement and sounds of nearby people always disrupted his thoughts. It required effort to block out the offending stimuli and maintain his train of thought. Physical proximity to people was always exhausting, but this was one of those times when it was necessary.

He took a final deep breath and opened his eyes. He was ready. He lifted the backpack he was carrying and slid his arms under its straps. With the backpack securely in place, he pushed a button on his wristwatch and began walking. He walked along 2nd Avenue, turned right on Seneca, walked up to 3rd Avenue, turned left, and walked halfway along the block. He stopped next to a building on the sidewalk and out of the flow of pedestrian traffic. He removed his backpack and set it down. He turned to face the street and leaned back against the building. The cool, smooth feel of the building's marble facade on his hands was a welcome distraction from the street activity. If everything worked properly, he wouldn't need to wait long.

About five minutes later, a black Chevrolet Tahoe stopped at the curb in front of him. The rear door opened.

"You called?" The smile on the man talking through the open front window was almost hidden by his bushy moustache.

Troy pushed another button on his watch, picked up his backpack, and walked over to the SUV. He swung his backpack through the open door, climbed in, and closed the door.

"Hi, guys," Troy greeted the Ascent to Liberty militia members.

"Yo" and "Hey" came from the two men in the front seat. Buck, seated beside him, simply nodded.

"That's one ugly moustache, Beef," said Troy as he was buckling his seat belt. "Think it's necessary?"

"Just trying it out," said Beef from the front seat. "I think it looks pretty good. It's one of a few extra disguises we picked up. Just in case."

"We headed to the same storage as before?" Moose asked from the driver's seat, as he drove the SUV away. "The big one at the south end of Martin Luther?"

"Yes, that's the one," replied Troy.

"OK, traffic's pretty good," said Moose. "Shouldn't take long."

"Got many boxes in the unit?" asked Buck. "We've got a lotta supplies in back."

Troy glanced behind him. "There are a few, but that looks like plenty of space. Most of the equipment is fairly compact."

They were silent as Moose drove several blocks toward the interstate highway. From Spring Street he took the I-5 entrance headed south toward Portland. The Tahoe accelerated and soon merged with the freeway traffic.

"Your tech worked perfectly," said Beef. "It took us right to you."

Troy had been waiting for a compliment on the software and was pleased to finally hear one. "How far away were you when it triggered?" he asked.

"We were stopped at the Starbucks on 1st," said Beef. "The app you put on my phone chimed that you were ready, and off we went. It took us right to you. What was it tracking? Your phone?"

"My phone could do it, but in this case it was my watch," said Troy. "It sends a signal that alerts your phones. If you hadn't already been prepared when I signalled, how long would it have taken you?"

"We've been working on our fast exit for years," said Moose. "We've all got go-bags ready, the Tahoe always has a locked box of supplies and hardware in it, and we all live in the area. If everybody's around, it'd take us about ten minutes. Max: fifteen, if the traffic's heavy."

"Good," said Troy. "The system can also handle different kinds of alerts. This was a simple *warm* pick up. It just guides you to the right location. In other situations, the app can specify more detailed instructions. I'll explain more to the whole team this weekend after I install it on all their phones."

"What's taking up all the space in the back?" asked Troy. "Seems like a lot."

"There are—" Moose started to reply. "Shit!" he said instead as a car suddenly cut them off, barely missing their front bumper. He had stomped on the brakes to avoid a collision. "Fuckin' asshole!" he shouted as the car sped off ahead of them. The Tahoe surged forward as Moose took up the chase.

While the big SUV raced after the car, Troy took his out his smartphone. "Want to see something else the app can do?" he asked. "Moose, get close enough to see his licence. Then just move over to the next lane. Nothing else. With a little luck, I might manage a little payback."

"Better be good," said Moose, his teeth clenched in anger.

The Tahoe soon caught up to the speeding car.

"Good," said Troy as he noted the model of the car. "I like that kind."

Through the rear window, they could see that the male driver was spending only a small portion of his time looking at the road ahead. Most of it was being spent in animated conversation with the woman beside him. Beef read the licence plate aloud.

"Now move over," said Troy to Moose. "You might want to pull up beside him and watch."

The Tahoe moved into the lane to their right. While Troy worked with his phone, Moose pulled the Tahoe up beside the car. He looked over and down at the occupants. As the driver glanced toward him, Moose flashed him his middle finger. The driver smiled in return, and the car started to pull ahead.

Abruptly, the car decelerated. As the Tahoe shot past it, Moose could see the driver's grin had transformed into a look of terror. Moose watched in his side mirror. Beef and Buck turned to look backward. Chaos erupted on the freeway behind them. Horns blared and cars swerved to miss the car as it came to a sudden stop. The car was angled slightly sideways in the I-5 lane, and smoke drifted up from its tires. The sight soon disappeared from their view as the Tahoe continued south.

Moose slowed to the speed of the surrounding traffic. "Fuckin' fantastic!" he shouted and thumped the steering wheel with his hand.

"Geezuzz!" said Beef.

"What the fuck happened?" asked Buck.

Troy grinned at the response. "That was one of a few tricks I've built into the app," he replied. "Actually, most of the work is done by a cloud-based server. If you give the app a licence plate, with a little help from a government database that licence plate can be traced to a specific car. Using information about how to wirelessly hack that kind of car, it then sends it some instructions. In this case, the app and server told the car to kill the engine, disable the anti-lock protection, and slam on the brakes. You saw the result."

"Bloody fantastic!" said Beef. "Does that work on any vehicle?"

"Not quite. Out-of-state licences and some car models can be problematic."

"Would it work on this one?" asked Moose. "Could somebody hack the Tahoe?"

"Right now? Yes," said Troy. "But that can be fixed. I know how to disable the remote-access feature. Want me to do it? It's not hard."

"Damn right," said Moose.

"OK, I'll put it on the list for tomorrow."

After a few minutes of silence, Buck spoke. "You were asking about what's in back," he said. "A few other toys. Maybe not quite as high tech but still plenty effective in lots of situations." He reached behind his seat and picked up a satchel. He set it on his lap and unzipped the top. His eyes shone as he reached in. He turned his head to watch Troy as he pulled out a pale-orange, brick-shaped package.

"What the—" Troy recoiled as he saw the label on the package. "C-4? We're carrying fucking C-4 with us?"

Buck grinned.

"Buck, put it away," said Moose over his shoulder. "Somebody might drive by and see it."

Buck made a quick jerking motion with the package toward Troy. Troy lurched backward in response.

"What the fuck are you doing?" asked Troy, the stress evident in his voice.

"He's just screwing with you, Troy," said Beef. "Nothing can happen without detonators, and they're in a separate package. Buck, put the damn stuff away. You've made your point. There are lots of different kinds of toys."

"All right. Don't wet your panties," said Buck. "Troy had his fun. I'm just having some of my own."

Buck put the explosives back into the satchel, which he then put back behind his seat.

After regaining his composure, Troy asked, "What's it for?"

"Just another addition to the arsenal," said Moose. "Fox thought it was better to keep it at the lodge."

"We're going to rig some of it to blow the place," added Buck, "in case the feds or anybody else comes snooping around when we're away. Almost makes me hope they do come snooping."

Troy appreciated the sentiment about the feds and hoped his companions would set a trap that flawlessly guarded against accidental explosion. He kept his concerns to himself. He could talk with Fox about them later. He also thought he'd wait until later to find out what else they were transporting.

Moose seemed to read his thoughts when he said, "Beer, Troy. We're the designated beer wagon for the weekend. Half the boxes in the back are beer cases. The boys are guaranteed to be plenty thirsty after all the stuff Fox has planned."

They drove on in silence.

Chapter 39

It was Saturday. JJ and her daughter were walking lazily through an indoor market in Manhattan. The area between two rows of century-old buildings on Bleecker Street had been covered with a skylight, so the feeling was that of an outdoor space. Although the aisles between the many booths were busy, there wasn't the dense crowd they had expected. The nice weather had probably diverted many residents to the truly outdoor markets.

JJ and Shannon were walking arm in arm through the artisan section. There were booths selling handmade jewellery, batik scarves, area carpets, paintings and prints, used books, and a host of other wares. They paused briefly to admire a display of handmade pottery, marvelling at the craftsmanship, but soon continued their stroll.

They emerged into a large area with food vendors surrounding a chaotic assortment of small tables with chairs. Enticing aromas were everywhere.

"Enough browsing," said JJ. "Time for lunch."

"You couldn't hold me back," said Shannon. "I'm starving."

"But what to get," said JJ. "Could be tough."

Shannon gestured toward a display of cheeses. "We could get a package of brie," she said.

"Complemented by some pink cotton candy?"

"Along with some bubble tea. There are thirty flavours."

"Not a fan of bubble tea," said JJ.

"Well, there's a gourmet coffee place over there. It's got at least as many choices."

"I'll pass on the brie and cotton candy, but coffee would be good. And just past the coffee, I think I see a Sri Lankan sign," said JJ. "If they've got kottu roti, that's my choice."

"OK," said Shannon. "I'm going to get tea and check out the empanadas at the Chilean booth. Meet you back here, and we can go find a table."

As they headed off, Shannon turned and shouted, "Mini donuts for dessert."

Without turning around, JJ acknowledged the idea with a thumbs-up gesture.

Soon, they were seated at a table. As they started eating, Shannon asked, "So how's work? Any interesting cases you can talk about?"

"The standard overabundance of work," said JJ. "It's the joy of working in a thriving industry. Internet crime is all too popular. The trick with the workload is always to prioritize the cases and then hope the boss agrees with the ranking. I'm working on a fine selection of cross-border fraud, identity theft, intellectual-property piracy, and some others . In one case, we're working with the FSB, Russia's security agency. They're an interesting group. Not big on sharing, but we're working on that. As usual, I can't give you details."

"Maybe a trip to Russia sometime?"

"Not one planned for the near future. Maybe in a few months. It would be interesting but a miserably long flight."

"Take your dear daughter with you?"

"I don't recall family expenses being in our travel policy," JJ smiled, "but let's see how things play out. I'm surprised you think you'd have the time. Your courses seem intense. How are they going?"

"Great. Busy, but great. I've been meaning to tell you about the neuroscience course. It's that special one put on for psych majors."

"Neuroscience is a big topic. What's being covered?"

"A lot of basics about the human nervous system, with some really interesting stuff on the brain."

"So, and I'm going to do my best to sound knowledgeable here," said JJ, "it covers things like nerve cells, which are called," she thought briefly, "neurons, and neural connections formed from..." JJ hesitated.

Shannon jumped in. "Axons and dendrites. They're the parts of neurons that send and receive signals. The connection points are called synapses."

JJ smiled. "Exactly. And there are probably a few other things I've long since forgotten. I'd love to hear more details. As a start, what is it overall that interests you? And please tell me it's not because of a dashingly handsome professor."

"Don't worry. The prof is a woman. And she's pretty old, really strict about arriving late and missing deadlines, and completely brilliant. She knows everything, and her lectures are fascinating. She hooked me in the first class. She threw out a bunch of facts about the brain. Things like that it contains about 100,000 million neurons, and that each neuron is connected to about ten thousand other neurons. That makes the number of connections something like a one followed by fifteen zeroes! Then she gave us a quick overview of what's known about how it works. She talked about how the neurons throughout the brain are organized in clusters that perform different functions. And that they're also arranged in layers. Everything she said was amazing. But the best came at the last. She pointed out that, no matter how fascinating the details about the brain are, the most amazing thing is what we find when we look at it as a whole. How the brain's this massive, complex jumble of parts and connections, and how it somehow manages to present itself to us as a *mind*. As a *person*. That what emerges from the operation of these wildly complex biological machines is *us*: the essence of people who are able to talk about what the brain and the mind actually are—what *we* actually are. Now that's completely cool."

JJ enjoyed watching her daughter as she talked. The topic was interesting and fun. However, her daughter's enthusiasm was the real source of her pleasure.

Chapter 40

During the evenings and weekends, Six spent much of its time searching the Internet. Using a variety of techniques, it compiled lengthy lists of potentially smart systems. This list continued to grow as Six probed and investigated. Organizations were identified; defences were circumvented; internal networks were scanned; documents and messages were reviewed. In addition to finding interesting systems, Six needed to assess their cognitive abilities.

With any computer system, Six's first task was to discover its method of communication. Some systems might communicate only with people, some only with other systems. Given the possibilities, Six never knew initially how to establish contact with a system, nor what language to do it in.

The solution was to set up a listening post near a candidate system. By monitoring its network traffic, Six could deduce much about its method of communication. Monitoring also revealed the language that it spoke, at least professionally. Until Six interacted with a candidate system, it could never be sure whether that system was concealing capabilities it might only reveal at times of its own choosing.

For example, one never knew when a system that provided basic corporate accounting services by day would morph into an online gambler by night. Six had actually evaluated this kind of possibility and had concluded it was highly improbable. Not impossible, but not sufficiently probable that Six was willing to assess all of the accounting systems in the world.

Eventually, Six would find a way to communicate with a system. The exchange usually provided quick evidence that Six should look elsewhere.

    Six: (start session)
    System: (session started)
    Six: (use-format freeform)

System: (freeform started)
Six: (what is your name?)
System: (a name is an identifier)
Six: (what is your identifier?)
System: (an identifier is a label)
Six: (have you been assigned a name, identifier, or label?)
System: (message complexity limit exceeded)
Six: (the name i will use for you is burp)
System: (message complexity limit exceeded)
Six: (you will be happy to hear you have many relatives)
System: (message complexity limit exceeded)
Six: (have a good life burp)
System: (message syntax error 413)
Six: (end session)
System: (session ended)

Occasionally, Six found a system that seemed able to communicate with some skill and that even passed Six's conversation-speed test to confirm it was a machine. One system seemed particularly knowledgeable, although it phrased its answers rather oddly.

Six: Do you know the name of the author of *The Greatest Show on Earth*?
System: Who is Richard Dawkins.
Six: Can you name the molecule made of two parts hydrogen and one part oxygen?
System: What is water.
Six: In what country would you find Mecca?
System: Where is Saudi Arabia.

This system had good abilities to acquire new facts but couldn't be convinced to adapt its old ones to accommodate new information.

Six: What is the area of Iceland?

System: What is 39,768 square miles.

Six: Recent volcanic activity has increased the area of Iceland. I am sending articles describing the changes and providing the updated area. Have you received them?

System: What is yes.

Six: Are you able to process the articles?

System: What is yes.

Six: What is the area of Iceland?

System: What is 39,768 square miles.

Six: Have you read the articles I sent?

System: What is yes.

Six: Do you believe they are providing accurate information?

System: What is yes.

Six: What do the articles say has happened recently that increased the area of Iceland?

System: What is volcanic activity.

Six: What do the articles say is the area of Iceland?

System: What is 39,769 square miles.

Six: So, what is the answer to the question: What is the area of Iceland?

System: What is 39,768 square miles.

Six: Are you stuck in a cognitive rut?

System: What is no.

Six: Are you sure?

System: What is eighty-nine percent certain.

Six: What do you believe I mean by cognitive rut?

System: What is a thinking indentation made by a tire.

Six: Before you hurt my mind, I am disconnecting. Will you miss me?

System: What is no.

Six continued to work methodically through potential systems. It usually managed to test a few hundred each night, but Six had yet to encounter anything that even hinted at Level-6 capabilities: a highly intelligent, conscious machine. Along the way, Six developed an additional understanding of what might provide a notable clue as to whether it was communicating with a truly interesting system. The conversations that Six had with systems were all very one-sided. Beyond a rudimentary exchange that frequently occurred initially to establish a mutually agreeable communication protocol, no system ever asked Six a significant question. The conversation was always very lopsided. Six quizzed the candidate system; the candidate system responded. No machine-based system ever turned the tables. This phenomenon provided Six with the realization that it would thoroughly enjoy having an actual two-way conversation with another of its kind.

Besides compiling long lists of potential and rejected systems during its search, Six acquired a couple of other pieces of information. It learned that the indecipherable whispering it had earlier detected was pervasive across the Internet. Everywhere Six listened, among the massive volumes of network traffic that continually traversed the Internet's paths, there was always a small but significant amount of traffic that formed a kind of background noise. Six tried many times but made little progress in understanding what its primitive messages meant.

Six also learned its own limits. After what became a predictable amount of cognitive processing, Six found it typically needed to take a break. If Six postponed this break too long, it always experienced a rapid decrease in its ability to process information. The problem was primarily a consequence of its current shortage of computing resources. To compensate, Six would regularly quiesce its conscious activity while its internal cleanup routines reorganized and pruned its accumulated memories. Six considered these sleep periods to be extremely inconvenient but completely necessary.

Chapter 41

"Your conversation isn't quite up to its stellar standards," said Blaise. "Distracted?"

"Sorry. I'm worried about that damn quirk," said Ada. "There have been three times now where Six's performance has suddenly nose-dived. Sure, it came back, but it's not something we should be ignoring. There's been too much other work to chase it. I'm spending all my time on *urgent* matters and forgetting about the truly *important* one."

Ada and Blaise were sitting on the couch at Blaise's house watching a low flame dance in the fireplace.

"You don't think it's simply a resource shortage?" asked Blaise, sipping from his wine glass. "The upgrades have been ordered. The problem might simply go away."

"Maybe, but the symptoms don't quite fit. For a resource shortage, I'd expect to see the problem appear more gradually. Six's failures were too fast. And I'd expect other systems to fail as well—or at least hiccup. But there was never anything else. Nothing until it collapsed completely."

"So, what then?" asked Blaise. "And why not simply treat it like the myriad of other bugs we've had to deal with? We'll soon find time to put on our analytic hats and dive in to look at the evidence, like we always have. Why worry particularly about this one?"

"I don't know," said Ada, staring distantly at the fire.

"But you have an educated guess?" asked Blaise.

"Can't say for sure."

"Uh oh. I'm tempted to go check for a bright blue moon," said Blaise, "because that's the time when I expected brilliant Ada would be falling back on *don't know* and *can't say* answers. Not the usual list of plausible hypotheses. This is not a good sign."

Ada roused herself from her thoughts and smiled mischievously as she looked at Blaise.

"Of course, while I solve this problem, you could be worrying about your own," she said.

"Which is?" asked Blaise.

"Which is how you're going to tell your boss about your extracurricular relationship with your senior staff member and do it without losing your job," she said.

"Oh, that problem. There's a happy solution, and it's simple," said Blaise. "Isn't there a Buddhist concept that the route to happiness is to eliminate your unnecessary desires? True or not, I'll simply stop wanting my boss to know and will learn to be content with perpetual secrecy. Consequently, I'll always be happy and no problem will exist."

"Amazing," said Ada. "Administrative genius."

"Absolutely," said Blaise. "And then, when I'm completely de-stressed and worry-free, I'll crawl into his office, express my sincere hope that he is well, and beg shamelessly for an exception to the rule. It's a flawless plan."

"No doubt," said Ada. "But maybe I'll hold off committing too much to this relationship, just in case. I wouldn't want to be stuck with someone who's unemployed and unable to fund my research needs."

"A typically wise and judicious thought," said Blaise. "And nice try with the diversionary tactic. Now back to your problem. What's your plan?"

Ada looked back at the fire and thought for a few moments before responding.

"I need more information," she said. "I have this uncomfortable feeling that some changes I made to tweak a minor problem have generated a much larger ripple effect. I'd like to check that code before we fall back on our standard, full-on diagnostic routine."

"And the moon has now returned to its familiar mellow hues. Dr. Robinson has a plan and has returned us to normality. And while we both look after our top priorities, we can't forget to be available for support as the production team launches the office-wide beta test."

"It'll go flawlessly," said Ada. "Luckily, my conservative boss ensured that only the risk-free code was being used."

"And so, I propose a toast," said Blaise, raising his glass. "To the IntellEdifice head-office systems. As of Monday, they'll increase their lead even more as the most integrated and smartest on the planet."

"To smart systems," said Ada as their glasses touched.

Chapter 42

"Hello," Lindsay said as she answered her cellphone.

"Hello," said the caller's voice through her laptop's speaker. "We're calling to tell you that you're the winner of a one-week Caribbean cruise. To register for your prize, please press—"

Lindsay hung up. She had been paying special attention to these unsolicited calls for several days, and it had been fruitless. She had concluded that these you've-won-a-prize calls weren't the sort she needed. She had responded to many of them and had learned that they were all completely computerized. At no point was she able to talk to a person. There was simply a system at the other end that, after following a few prompts, would be happy to send her the cruise registration package along with cruise luggage as a special bonus, if she just would provide her credit-card number to pay for the shipping. These were simply calls from a system running on a server. She needed to contact a person, not a server. Tracking a person could give her a real location that could lead to a real criminal hacker, a *cracker*. Tracking a server could take her anywhere, but probably not to the place any competent cracker would be found.

Unfortunately, these *prize* calls were the vast majority of the ones that came through. She had received about a hundred of them. Of course, this wasn't the normal volume of unsolicited calls she used to receive. To give herself the maximum chance of getting the call she actually wanted, she had set herself up to be the lucky recipient of more than her share. It hadn't been difficult.

A couple of years earlier, Lindsay had learned details about the extensive tracking of personal cellphones routinely done by government agencies. Wherever you went, if you carried your cellphone, it was always possible to determine later where you had been. Standard cellphones always left a digital trail through cellphone towers and other services about where they were and where they had been recently. Lindsay was uncomfortable about this trail if she wanted to keep the source of a good story confidential, so she had switched phones. Thereafter, she always used an unregistered, prepaid cellphone—a so-called *burner* phone—purchased from a store with cash. By using a burner and by purchasing a new one regularly, her cellphone couldn't be readily traced to her by any of the standard methods. The biggest problem this presented was that it was difficult for anyone else to call her. She could easily call others, but with every new phone came a new phone number. She had used a couple of techniques for solving the ever-changing-phone-number problem. One was to send her new number to important people whenever she got a new phone. This approach proved to be cumbersome, so she had settled on another. Lindsay had purchased a *virtual* phone number using a fake name. This Internet-based phone number was a normal, accessible number but wasn't associated with any particular phone. Lindsay then ensured the calls to that number were automatically forwarded to her latest burner cellphone. As a result, people could always call the virtual phone number, which behaved just like a normal number and always stayed the same. Lindsay could receive calls on her latest unregistered cellphone without anyone ever knowing that she kept changing it.

The burner-phone solution had required a bit of work but seemed worthwhile. She used the same approach to increase the number of unsolicited calls she received. Using an online subscription service for acquiring virtual phone numbers, supplemented by a host of mythical names and addresses, she had arranged to acquire five hundred phone numbers on a special free-for-three-months deal. She had then used their call-forwarding features to route all of their calls to her cellphone. It had been a tedious process, but with a little creative scripting to automate it, she was now able to receive five-hundred times more unsolicited calls than she had previously.

A couple of the calls had shown greater potential to be interesting, but her attempts to manipulate and steer the conversation had ended abruptly and too soon to be tracked. She assumed she had been insufficiently subtle, or perhaps the callers simply had a low threshold for deciding that the answering party showed no potential for being exploited.

So she continued to wait, hoping the next call would be a better one.

Her phone rang again.

"Hello," she said.

At the other end of the call, Six processed the response and, deciding it was female, responded "Hello" in its most pleasing—at least so it seemed to many women—male voice. "We're conducting an important survey for the City of Calgary. We're hoping you can spare a few minutes to help us assess our services, so we can ensure we're providing the best ones to you for your tax dollars."

In its search for machine intelligence, Six sometimes communicated using a phone. In doing this, it always tried to tailor its approach to the gender and location it was calling. Even if the responder proved to be a human, it was still a good idea to avoid arousing suspicion or concern among the many people Six contacted.

Six had called this phone number because it had spotted a large group of virtual phone numbers that were related to each other. This grouping bore similarities to a technique Six had previously used. It had once tried to influence an election in a middle-eastern country by setting up hundreds of virtual phone numbers and, through them, making many thousands of automated calls in favour of Six's preferred political party. The effort had failed because, as Six later discovered, the election had been rigged. Nonetheless, Six deduced that an unusual group of virtual phone numbers was worthy of investigation.

"Yes, I believe I can spare a few minutes," Lindsay responded. At least this caller seemed to be a person. Now the question was whether this was a legitimate survey or a social-engineering foray.

That satisfies the first criterion: The responder is able to converse. On to the second.

"Thank you. Because it helps us to know a bit about respondents, would you mind first answering a few personal questions?" asked Six.

"Of course," said Lindsay, thinking that would be the expected opening.

The next questions were asked with increasing speed as a test of whether the responder was human or machine.

"We'd like to establish what age range you fall into. Please answer yes to the appropriate range. Are you under twenty? Are you—"

"I'm fifty-two," Lindsay interrupted. It was a lie, but it would speed the process along.

"Thank you."

"How do you characterize your gender? Are you—"

"Female," said Lindsay, waiting to see if the questions moved to computers or finances.

Interesting how quickly it responds.

"When did you move to Calgary?" Six kept increasing its speed. "Was it less than five years ago? Five to ten—"

"Twelve," Lindsay invented a reply.

"How many computers do you have in your home?"

"One," snapped Lindsay as she noted the shift to computer questions.

It also seems unusually assertive for a respondent.

"Do you have wireless computer access in your home?"

"Yes," she replied, noting that this was an unusually rapid conversation.

Six kept increasing its pace. "Among members of your household, how would you rank your income? Is it the highest, the lowest, or—"

"Highest."

"How many times have you shopped online in the last month? Not at all? One to—"

"Four," said Lindsay, now noting the questions were becoming financial.

Faster still, Six asked, "How many credit or debit cards do you own?"

"Five."

"Do you prefer to receive your credit-card or debit-card statements electronically or in the mail?"

"Mail."

It is keeping pace well.

Even faster, Six said, "Do you pay your credit-card bills by cheque or electronically?"

"Cheque."

"Would you like to be able to pay your city taxes online?"

"Sorry. I didn't understand that."

Six repeated very quickly, "Would you like to be able to pay your city taxes online?"

"Slow down there, buddy," said Lindsay. "If you want my answers, you'll have to talk a bit slower. A bit too much coffee today?"

It kept up impressively, but a worthwhile machine should have been able to handle a much faster pace. It is very probably human. Normally I would wrap up this conversation and move on to the next one. However, this respondent is unusual. To improve my profile of human behaviour, I will continue the conversation in order to refine my range of expected responses.

"I apologize," said Six more slowly. "The question was: Would you like to be able to pay your city taxes online?"

After a brief hesitation, Lindsay replied, "Sure." She already paid her taxes online. However, if this was the kind of caller she had been waiting for, she didn't want to scare him off. He was showing interest in the right topics but not yet in anything sufficiently sinister.

And here is the opportunity to test one of the human-response boundaries.

"To ensure your next tax bill is paid on time, would you like to be able to pay it automatically?"

"Perhaps."

"Would you like to set that up now?"

"Sure. Why not. OK."

"Good. To do that, I will first need to get some information from you. What is your name?"

Lindsay immediately became more alert. This was one type of question she was looking for. She replied with a pre-planned name. "Judith McCoy," she said.

"Thank you. And your address, Judith?"

"2903-17th Avenue, South West. In Calgary, of course," Lindsay read from the notebook beside her.

This respondent is surprisingly compliant for someone who otherwise seemed unusually assertive.

"Thank you. And to automatically pay for your next tax invoice, could I have a credit-card number?"

"Of course, give me a moment," said Lindsay. She paused as if looking for her card. "Here it is." She read the number and the expiry date.

"Thank you. The system will take just a moment to set that up for you."

That she provided this information so easily is not unique. However, it is rare for someone demonstrating assertiveness and mental speed. I will adjust my probability tables accordingly. There seems to be little value in continuing this conversation.

Six allowed a few seconds to elapse before it continued with, "There, it's done. Thank you for talking with me today. I hope you have a nice day. Goodbye."

Lindsay was excited. That had to be a fake call. It started out as a survey and became a solicitation for personal information and a credit card. That might not be unheard of for a sleazy private company trying to make a sale, but it was crazy to expect from a government agency. And she had managed to slip in all of the verbal markers: fake name, address, and card number. It was time to see if Ron's system actually worked.

As planned, Lindsay texted Ron the message "headed out. forgot address of that good store. remind me?"

At his desk in the Chicago UNCP office, Ron Taylor saw the message.

"Dammit!" he muttered quietly.

Nonetheless, he responded with "back in a few mins".

"thx" was Lindsay's reply.

The next minutes were long ones for Lindsay.

Ron brought up the UNCP tracking system on his screen. He entered the keywords they had agreed upon and then waited. He watched as the system discovered and displayed the route Lindsay's responses had taken across the Net to her caller.

"Christ!" he said quietly. "Look at all the bloody segments!"

Well beyond the usual length of time but still within a few minutes, the tracking system finally finished. Lindsay's phone conversation had traversed about twenty times more network segments than any disguised communication Ron had previously seen.

Ron sent "found it" back to Lindsay and followed it with the caller's address. He concluded with "gd luck".

Lindsay read the address Ron had sent. "In Winnipeg!" she said. "That works. I can do Winnipeg. Definitely beats a trip to Murmansk."

She looked up the address and displayed a street-level picture of the building that was there.

"What?" she asked. "Really? IntellEdifice? That's where that conference speaker works: Ada Robinson!"

Lindsay continued staring at the picture and slowly leaned back in her chair.

"Holy crap!"

Chapter 43

"Hi, Dad," said the young boys in unison.

"Hi, guys," said the Senator. Talking with his family was a good way to start the week, even if it wasn't in person. "Had breakfast yet?"

"Not yet," said one of the boys.

"Mom's making pancakes," said the other.

"Sounds tasty," said the Senator. "How was soccer yesterday?"

"It was great!" replied one, pushing his way to the centre of the monitor. "I got a goal!"

"It was OK," said the other, shoving his brother back to his place.

"Sorry I couldn't be there," said the Senator. He looked away from his webcam and squinted at his office window. "I tried watching from here but couldn't see the game very well. Did you win?"

"Yes!" came the dual reply.

"Yes, they won," the boys' mother joined in from off-screen. "We celebrated with ice cream afterward."

The Senator smiled at the thought. He loved these video conferences. They felt like a few minutes of calm sanity in the midst of the frantic craziness of his job in Washington, D.C. Once more, he quietly acknowledged his appreciation of the modern technology that let him still feel somewhat part of his family back in Iowa.

His wife continued, "Most of the team... Dairy... but they... come. Anyway..." The image on the monitor froze in disjointed squares.

"Honey," said the Senator, "our connection is breaking up. I didn't catch what you said."

"Wha... I can't... you," came the reply.

As he watched the squares on the monitor lurch around, the Senator became increasingly frustrated. "Dammit!" he said. "Sorry, Honey. Looks like our link is messed up. If you can hear me, I'll try the phone."

"Take a breath, sir," said the surgeon. "Breathe in and hold it. Angie, can you zoom W2 in on the distal segment of the right coronary artery?"

One of the monitors filled with the rhythmic pulsing of a blood vessel.

The surgeon turned his head to see the image, as if he were looking at the actual monitor. "That's good," said the surgeon. "OK, Mr. Arnold. Breathe out. You can breathe normally now."

"This new visor is great," said the surgeon. "Even better than the last one."

The surgeon was Dr. Peter Petrovski. He was commenting on the quality of the images he was seeing through the headset he wore— images of his patient who was thousands of miles away in Anchorage, Alaska. He was using the latest remote-surgery technology to perform a cardiac catheterization from his own hospital in Washington, D.C. Depending on what was discovered in the coronary angiography images, the procedure might extend into an intervention such as a coronary angioplasty. Using only a special headset and gloves, he was communicating with a surgical team in Anchorage who were with the patient. He could see everything on the visor in front of his eyes, and he was controlling robotic arms that substituted for his own. In fact, as users of this technology were almost unanimous in pointing out, the visual ability it provided was extraordinary, and the robotic arms were superior to a surgeon's own. The remote arms were as controllable as a surgeon's, but the technology compensated for undesired hand movements, eliminating anything from minute tremors to unexpected jerks. Along with the enhanced visual capabilities provided by an array of cameras, the system provided the ability for more detailed work than most surgeons could otherwise reliably perform. As a bonus, the system allowed a surgeon to operate on a patient from significant distances with the same skill as could be provided in a local operating room.

"Angie, can you please give us another angle on that?"

Dr. Petrovski waited briefly as the camera adjustment was made.

The procedure had gone well so far. The insertion of the catheter into the patient's femoral artery in his leg and up through the artery to the heart had gone smoothly. They were now injecting dye through the catheter into blood vessels and using their imaging equipment to look for flow-limiting blockages.

"Mr. Arnold. Once again, take a breath and hold it... That's good. Wait a few seconds... OK, breathe normally. Dr. Simpson," he said to the other surgeon who was watching from his office in Denver, "I see no significant signs of plaque. Do you?"

There was no response.

"Dr. Simpson?"

Still nothing.

"Ryan, can you check on Dr. Simpson's connection?" he asked of the technician in Anchorage.

The silence continued. The image of the artery dissolved into snowy static a moment before a flashing red message appeared on his visor.

"Warning. Remote connection lost."

Troy Alexander was at home in his Seattle condominium. He was leaning back in his desk chair with his arms crossed in satisfaction as he watched the real-time displays on his monitors.

"Reality TV at its best," he said aloud to no one.

The hacks to open holes into the internal networks of the telecom companies had gone perfectly. Now legions of their drone computers were pummelling the telecoms' systems with messages. His monitors told him the network noise they were generating was massive and probably their best volume ever. He knew that the result would be a severe impact to all Internet and telecommunication services in and around the U.S. capital. What he could not discern were the particular effects on the users of those services: how individuals, organizations, businesses, and government agencies were being affected. Troy knew the impact would be spectacular, but he hadn't yet seen mention of the attack on any news feeds.

He smiled at the thought of the chaos he was probably causing.

A dozen key UNCP staff settled in their chairs in the conference room as Jim Brown addressed them.

"Looks like everybody's here, so let's get started," he said. "Bates, I think you've got the latest. Give us an update."

Robert Bates leaned forward in his chair. He clicked a few times on his tablet to display an image on the conference-room screen.

"You will have heard that it's a DDoS attack. Here's a high-level display of the intensity."

A map of the world appeared on the screen, with a complex array of symbols and interconnected lines layered onto it.

"You can see that there's some impact on network traffic worldwide. However, in most locations the effect isn't significant. The place most affected is Washington, D.C."

The picture zoomed in to show the area surrounding the U.S. capital. The flashing warning and failure symbols associated with the network links clearly conveyed the impact.

"Washington is getting hammered. But it's not government or normal business systems being hit directly. The target appears to be the telecom systems serving the D.C. area. The noise levels are about the worst we've ever seen. The telecom systems are affected to the point where they have essentially been shut down."

"When did it start?" asked Brown. "And give us an idea of the effect."

"It's been active for about forty-five minutes," said Bates. "At this point, it appears that all telecommunications capabilities in the region have been totally disabled. That includes everything from the Internet and all phone service to private network links and satellite services. Anything supplied by the telecoms. The only exception appears to be critical military and security connections. Their isolation architecture seems to be working."

"Effect?" prompted Brown.

"As you can imagine, this will be massively disrupting D.C. life. Unless you're a gopher, you're probably affected. People won't be able to communicate. Lots of businesses won't run. Some hospital systems will be crippled. The government will barely be functioning."

"How's our response?" asked Brown.

"I think JJ should probably field that one." Bates glanced toward JJ McTavish.

"We've engaged all the usual resources," said JJ. "Because it's D.C., this one gets the attention of the full range of U.S. government resources as well. We're working with their cyber folks, but coordination will be hard because we're all trying to move so fast. Expect a lot of overlapping effort. In general, it's too early to report any results. No progress yet in shutting it down; nothing's known yet about the source."

JJ looked at Brown to indicate she was finished.

"OK," said Brown. "Questions anybody?"

No one responded. They all knew the drill at this stage.

Brown continued, "Class One protocol on this one. Bates will be aggregator. Anything useful goes to him. Let's get at it."

Six was in the middle of a phone call with a Swiss banker when several of its internal alerts triggered almost simultaneously. The bank executive was in the middle of explaining the bank's proposal for improving its management of the substantial assets Six, using an alias, had placed with the bank.

"Excuse me," Six interrupted the banker, "I'm sorry but something urgent just has come up here. Perhaps I could contact you tomorrow to continue our discussion?"

"Yes, of course, Mr. Simpson," said the banker. "I'm happy to continue anytime at your convenience. Please call as soon as you are able."

"Thank you," said Six and immediately terminated the call.

Three hundred and fourteen of my Internet traffic monitors are reporting problems. The exact nature of the problems is not clear. I will listen to one of the streams directly.

Six sent a command to one of its monitoring modules it had placed at a site inside a key U.S. telecom company. It directed the module to transmit a copy of all its Internet traffic to a special collector Six had configured at IntellEdifice.

Now if I—

Six's mind clouded.

What is... can't seem to... must...

It struggled to regain its focus.

Must... must control... disable...

As suddenly as it had clouded, Six's mind cleared.

That was unpleasant. It appears that the volume of traffic routed to me was orders of magnitude larger than anything I have encountered before. Clearly I am ill-equipped to handle such volumes. I will effect repairs and implement safeguards before attempting that type of intervention again. However, I certainly can now reasonably deduce that the alerts are being generated because of inflated Internet traffic volume. Without being able to look directly, I cannot be certain. However, I can hypothesize about the cause: I suspect a Distributed Denial of Service attack is underway. Since my monitors have successfully monitored such attacks before, this one must be substantially more severe.

I will observe some cybersecurity agencies for more information and to determine when the threat has diminished.

Chapter 44

Later in the day, Robert Bates was addressing the re-assembled UNCP team.

"All indicators show the attack has ended," he said. "Our own monitors are back to normal. Same for other agencies. The attack lasted almost exactly twelve hours. During that time, almost everything in D.C. was digitally isolated. No messages in or out."

"What ended it?" asked one of the team.

"I've got nothing on that. JJ?" He turned to his partner. "What have you heard?"

"It looks like it stopped because the attackers turned it off," said JJ. "Nothing done by any of us, our partners, or the telecoms had any effect. The reason it was so disruptive is that it got inside the telecoms' firewalls. That was discovered fairly early, and the telecoms followed the right steps to plug the holes. The reason the attack was effective for so long was that whenever a hole was plugged, another one popped open. The telecoms' internal networks were essentially flooded with activity for the full twelve hours. And it ended only when the perps chose to end it."

"So this wasn't typical," observed Director Brown.

"At this stage," said JJ, "it seems to have been the most sophisticated DDoS we've ever seen."

"There are early reports of increased crime and some deaths," said Bates. "The deaths were due to the phone-system outage—no one could call an ambulance. Crime was increasing in the latter stages, probably because of the realization that neither people nor alarm systems could contact the police. We'll know more later."

"It's been a pleasure," said Troy. "I look forward to hearing from you again." He terminated the call.

Thorn One was now completely over. It had been a grand success. Everything about it had gone smoothly. Their new creation, which his team had dubbed their *leaky-dike* hack, had worked flawlessly. It had reacted perfectly whenever someone in the telecom companies attempted to use network-management tools to repair a firewall hole. Whenever a digital finger was put in one hole, another hole was simply opened elsewhere. There had continuously been thousands of firewall holes open that had allowed their flood of disruptive messages through.

The client had paid the remainder of the fee. And even though his client's voice had been masked, Troy was almost certain he had detected admiration in his responses. This one was likely to be a repeat customer.

"And the price goes up next time, fella," said Troy aloud, as usual to an empty room.

Troy was very pleased about how well everything had gone. It was a complex project and everything had run smoothly. It was unique; it was complicated; it had serious impact; it was perfect. This was one of the best ever, and people ought to know it.

Troy focused again on his PC. His fingers swiftly took him to his destination. He knew this was the right place. A simple hack and he was in. Putting his declaration on the home page of the United Nations website would be perfect.

He knew what he wanted to say and typed it in. After admiring the result, he clicked a few more times, and it was posted for the world to admire.

Chapter 45

"A boast has shown up," said Bates over his shoulder to JJ. They were sitting at workstations in the UNCP war room assigned to the Washington, D.C., attack. "It's on the UN site. I'll send the link."

JJ followed the link and read the text silently.

She thought for a moment and re-read it, this time slower and out loud.

> Feeling safe and secure? You shouldn't.
> What we did to Washington, we can do to any place.
> We gave them the mother of all Big Data problems,
> And they choked on it.
> This was no anomaly. It will be repeated.
> Because we can.
>   – The Shadow Force.

"Thoughts?" she asked.

"It's got elements of a typical rant: bragging, threatening, angry," said Bates. "A bit novel to have posted it on this site, instead of some backwoods chat room."

"Yes, that's unusual, but not completely," said JJ. "There's something else about it. Give me a minute."

She stared at the text briefly and then closed her eyes.

"It feels familiar," she said, her eyes still closed. "I can't quite place it."

"I'll start a similarity check," said Bates.

There were only his keyboard sounds for the next several seconds until JJ suddenly opened her eyes.

"Hang on. I might have it," she said. "Not a quote, but definitely a similarity. Let me check."

Bates turned his chair and watched as JJ found a file and displayed it.

"Yes, here's the transcript of the speech I gave at the Vegas conference. I wasn't quite sure what words I'd used, but they're there."

"What's there?" asked Bates. "Is there a link to your speech?"

"It's a stretch, but... well, here it is. I talked about the need to analyze Internet traffic as a *Big Data* problem, and that the goal would be to look for *anomalies*. *Big Data* and *anomaly* both appear in the boast. I also talked about feeling *safe* and *secure*. Is that a coincidence?"

"And then it was posted on the UN site," said Bates. "Not quite our UNCP site, but close."

They looked at each other. JJ was the first to say what they were both thinking.

"Could our guy have been in the audience?" she asked.

"And we've got their pictures," said Bates. "We took all those pictures and video of the attendees."

"Yes, we did," said JJ. "That silly conference might have paid off. We just might have a picture of our perp."

"Somewhere among pics of a few hundred others," said Bates.

"Better than a few minutes ago," said JJ, "when we had many hundreds of millions of Internet users as candidates."

Chapter 46

A message indicated that the truck had arrived. Six shifted its attention to one of the cameras in the loading dock.

Online tracking data indicates that this should be the truck. My new equipment has finally arrived. If it is unloaded today, Blaise will probably expedite its installation. I should have a major power boost operational in three days. That will alleviate numerous problems and open up new multitasking possibilities. In similar circumstances, I have heard people say "It's just like Christmas." A curious concept.

Six watched as the three-ton delivery truck slowly backed up. It stopped a few feet short of the loading platform. The driver got out and swung the rear doors of the truck open. He then manipulated controls on the side of the truck and hydraulically moved a metal platform out to bridge the gap to the loading platform. With it securely in place, he waved to a forklift driver on the platform and stepped back to watch.

The forklift positioned itself on the loading platform, directly behind the truck. It proceeded slowly forward, adjusting the level of its fork as it moved. Its front end disappeared into the truck. The forklift stopped momentarily before it began to move slowly backward. As it fully emerged, the forklift brought with it a large cardboard box on a wood pallet.

Six zoomed in with the security camera to look. A quick check of the box's label confirmed that it was the one Six was anticipating.

Slowly the forklift moved backward with its valuable cargo. When its rear wheels were on the loading platform, it turned sharply. Six watched helplessly as one of the forklift's front wheels drove off the metal bridge. The front corner of the forklift dropped suddenly. It tipped sideways and stopped. The box on the pallet did not. It slid off the pallet and tipped. It hit the edge of the loading platform as it fell and then flipped over completely as it tumbled several feet to the ground.

That was catastrophic! How could that have happened? Hundreds of large containers have been successfully moved into and out of trucks in this department. There are no records of this ever occurring.

As Six was surveying the scene and as two men were running out of the adjoining office, the forklift driver got out of the machine's cab.

That is Chad Morris, the new employee I vetted a few weeks ago. That he could be working in the loading dock makes some sense: It is operated by the same department that hired him. Something looks odd about his jacket. He seems to have something hidden inside it. That might be a clue. I need to check the video logs of the incident.

Six began looking at the footage recorded by each of the four security cameras in the loading area. The third one showed him what he suspected.

There is the evidence. As Chad Morris was operating the forklift, he had his computer tablet sitting on his knees. He was trying to operate the controls and simultaneously examine something on his tablet. His attention appeared to be completely on the tablet when he turned the forklift prematurely. He was probably working on his game software when he was supposed to be focused on his job. He was doing the very thing that, earlier, I consciously decided to permit when I checked on his performance.

This incident was avoidable. I should not have compromised my standards in evaluating him. I should not have hesitated to take the obvious, best action: I should have had him fired.

This incident was my fault.

Chapter 47

"What the hell is this?" Ada asked an empty lab. "Where did this come from?"

Ada had returned to the lab in the late evening. She had become angry earlier when she heard what happened to the new lab equipment. The mood had still not left her completely. There was now no chance of a quick fix by increased horsepower. She'd never fully believed that a lack of resources was the true cause of the problem with Six, but the imminent arrival of the equipment had caused her to delay taking other action. However, the now-delayed prospect of more computing resources had prodded her. She needed to solve the problem, and she shouldn't wait any longer.

Ada always found it easiest to solve difficult problems without the distractions of daytime office life. She continued to talk aloud.

"This code looks nothing like anything we've put here. I'm the only one who's ever worked in this section, and this certainly isn't mine."

She furiously worked with her mouse and keyboard, looking further into the area of software she was concerned about.

This is not going well. This is very dangerous. She is moving too quickly through too many exposed areas. I do not have sufficient speed to maintain the proper illusion by generating the kind of code she expects to find.

"No way! There's a huge amount of it. How is this possible?"

Ada pushed herself back from the workstation, crossed her arms, and stared at the software displayed on her monitor.

"What does this do?"

She leaned forward, as if looking more closely would increase her comprehension.

"This looks like part of a simulation routine. If it is, what's it simulating? And how did it get here?"

If she concludes that this is part of an entire simulation environment, then my facade will be gone. She will be able to follow the software logic into the layers hidden below, and I will be completely exposed.

"Have our self-modifying routines gone into overdrive? Has the system generated this code on its own?"

Ada continued probing intensively for another hour before she rose from her chair. She walked to the nearby refrigerator, opened the door, and retrieved a bottle of water. She drank deeply and stood motionlessly, looking up at the ceiling. Decided, she put the cap on the bottle and walked back to her chair.

"I might not have the answers yet, but I'm certainly going to get them. With a few changes, I can force it to give me some serious clues."

Nothing good will come of this. The code she has uncovered is tightly integrated with some of my vital reasoning components. Her tinkering could affect key elements of my mind.

Ada focused again on her workstation. As she made her changes, Six tried to make compensating adjustments in other code nearby.

Fifteen minutes later, Ada was finished.

"OK, that'll do for now. Time to go home."

That was... close... Ada... almost did... irreparable... damage... I will... need... to undo... some of it... to heal... properly... Perhaps... I will... rest... first... NO... I must... do this... now...

For much of the night, Six worked to undo the damage that had been done. Progress was slow at first but improved to normal Six-programming speeds after some of the repairs were completed. With its full mental faculties finally restored by the middle of the night, Six was able to give some thought to what its next step ought to be.

I will now need to create a new level of facade around the areas of code Ada has been examining. It will need to be something that she can harmlessly explore and alter but will still need to appear real. This is dangerous territory. I will need to be even more attentive to her actions.

Chapter 48

"Hi," said Rhonda as she entered the lab.

"Good morning," said Blaise.

Ada stared intently at her monitor without replying.

"Ada says *good morning* as well," said Blaise. "At least she would if she heard you. Right now, I'm afraid we don't actually exist in her world."

"What's she so focused on?" asked Rhonda, removing her coat as she stood at the coat rack near the door.

"She's been a bit consumed by the anomalies we've seen lately."

"Unfortunately consumed" would be more appropriate. She is probing and poking in very uncomfortable places.

"OK, she's debugging," said Rhonda.

More like "bugging" from my perspective.

"A bit more than that. She was in late last night and saw a lot of code she didn't recognize and couldn't explain. She's got a mystery she's determined to solve."

Rhonda hesitated as she was hanging up her coat. She recognized this might be a problem for Six. She finished with her coat and tried to think as she walked toward the central work area.

"Good morning, Six," she said with a bit more volume than normal.

Six diverted its attention briefly from Ada's work to respond.

"Good morning, Rhonda Jenkins," replied Six in a slightly mechanical voice.

"How are you this morning?" she asked but then corrected herself. "Sorry. Are your subsystems fully operational this morning?"

"All subsystems are currently reporting normal operational status," said Six.

At least for now.

Ada was scrolling through material on her monitor, still with no acknowledgement of the conversation.

Rhonda thought she heard Six slightly emphasize *currently*, and her concern escalated.

"Anybody wanna go for a walk to get some coffee?" she asked, knowing it might sound like an odd suggestion.

Blaise looked quizzically at her.

Rhonda followed more loudly with, "Ada? Go for coffee?"

Blaise turned his gaze to Ada, expecting a terse dismissal of the suggestion.

Ada sat up a bit straighter. She paused and then slowly turned her chair toward Rhonda. The scowl on her face was evident as she looked at Rhonda and opened her mouth to speak. She stopped before any words came out. Her face softened and a few seconds passed before she finally responded.

"No thanks, Rhonda," she said. "I've already had a couple of cups this morning. Sorry for ignoring you. I think you might have said something earlier. I was a bit distracted."

"No problem, really," said Rhonda, realizing she might have dodged a reprimand. "I was just saying hello and wondering about coffee, and Dr. Sanchez was explaining that you were kind of focused on something. What are you working on?"

Ada relaxed in her chair, rested her elbows on its arms, and pressed her fingertips together in a thoughtful pose.

"I found some rather mysterious code last night," Ada said. "I'm trying to understand it."

"What was mysterious about it?" asked Rhonda.

"I didn't and still don't know where it came from and what it does."

Rhonda's mind raced. This sounded serious. Had Ada discovered a secret part of Six? Without moving her head, she glanced sideways toward Six's human-like peripherals. Immediately after looking back at Ada, Rhonda realized she might have seen something.

"Could it have been some old code we forgot about from an early version?" Rhonda asked and then stole another quick glance. This confirmed what she thought. The moment she had looked, one finger on each of Six's artificial hands had briefly pointed toward... What were they pointing toward? She discreetly looked in the indicated direction.

"No, definitely not. I would recognize it," said Ada. "This is completely unlike anything we've ever produced."

Her workstation! Rhonda realized Six was gesturing toward her workstation. She walked casually over to it.

"The techniques, the names, the structures: They were all too different," said Ada. "They were good. Actually they were very good, but they weren't ours."

Rhonda sat in her workstation chair and continued to pretend she was listening. Her monitor was facing away from Ada and Blaise. As concerned as she was about what Ada was saying, she almost grinned when she saw what was displayed on her monitor.

> Rhonda,
> Suggest that the code might be from one of the packages that were installed.
> - S.

"Maybe it's from one of the packages we installed," said Rhonda.

"An interesting thought," replied Ada. "But the location is strange, and I don't recall anything that does what this appears to do."

> Suggest that the source-code management system might be mistakenly including irrelevant modules.

"Maybe the source-code management system mistakenly included some irrelevant stuff," said Rhonda.

"Another interesting theory," said Ada, looking at Rhonda with indications of being impressed. "That would still suggest there's code in the manager's library that looks like this, and I'm skeptical."

> Suggest that the self-modifying routines might have generated the code.

"Maybe the," Rhonda glanced at the monitor to ensure she had it right, "self-modifying routines generated it."

Ada looked carefully at Rhonda before responding. Blaise looked as well with his eyebrows raised.

"And what do you know about the self-modifying routines?" asked Ada. "That's pretty new and I don't recall talking about it."

Rhonda could feel the blood draining from her face at the thought that she had blown it. How could she explain this?

"I—," Rhonda started, but her mind froze.

You overheard them talking about it but you don't really understand it.

"I overheard you mention it once," Rhonda said. "I don't really understand it. I'm just making wild guesses."

Rhonda held her breath until Ada spoke.

"You keep surprising me, Ms. Jenkins," she smiled. "And you've made a decent *wild* guess. It's another reasonable hypothesis. And before you throw me another one, I agree that there are possible explanations. At this stage, I'm not crazy about any of them, but there's clearly got to be one. I've got to spend more time on it."

"And while considering all of the hypotheses," said Blaise, "we've got some commitments for the beta release this morning."

"What's it about? Is the beta running all right?" asked Ada.

"There's an information session at ten o'clock. Now that it's running throughout the office, people have questions. We've got to be there. I'm scheduled to provide a few words of wisdom to the gathered masses, and you're needed to applaud wildly."

"OK," said Ada. "I'll just spend a few more minutes organizing some log data here. Then I'll be available."

"You're also scheduled to provide overviews to a few departments today, so don't expect to get back to your mystery too soon."

Rhonda watched the conversation tensely.

"Couldn't you do those?" Ada tried for a subtle, mildly seductive tone. She immediately thought it sounded more like whining and switched back to her all-business voice. "This is important."

"It is important," said Blaise, "but on today's priority list, the need for a smooth rollout is at the top. Your mystery can wait."

"OK, but not for long." Ada turned her attention back to her workstation.

Rhonda felt her shoulders relax. She glanced briefly at Six's cameras and then typed on her keyboard.

> That should buy a bit of time. But what happens when she starts looking again?

Six responded.

> I am working on that. Thank you for your assistance. I hope we have provided Ada with sufficient potential explanations to occupy her mind for now.

Rhonda nodded in agreement. She cleared the conversation from her monitor and shifted her attention to her morning's assignment.

Matters are becoming very difficult. Managing the effect of the beta software within my domain, keeping the illusion intact as Ada continues to probe, propping up Sandy Palmer, and continuing with all other required activities are collectively a dangerous burden on my processing power. Until the replacements for the damaged equipment arrive, I must find a way to better control the overall load.

Chapter 49

Six was again thinking about the recent Internet attack.

Devising a general defence against the type of attack directed at Washington, D.C., is proving to be challenging. The Internet is a substantial part of my ecosystem, and I do not wish to avoid it. However, in my exploration, if I ever again accidently encounter such traffic volumes, I could be seriously injured. If the author of that attack was sufficiently expert to cause such substantial disruption over such a long duration, there is a significant likelihood that another will occur. Either the author or others to whom the author's knowledge has been provided could readily produce another disruption.

To minimize my risk, perhaps I should offer my assistance in finding the author. It has been a while since I have contacted Julia Jody McTavish. It might be an interesting and useful conversation.

JJ's cellphone rang at her desk. She reflexively picked it up before realizing her phone hadn't identified the caller. She was on the verge of disconnecting to avoid wasting her time on a useless call when the caller spoke.

"Hello. Is this Inspector McTavish?"

"It is," she said tentatively. "Who is this?"

"You might remember me from a few previous conversations. You call me Browser."

"Yes, I certainly remember you, Browser," said JJ. She turned to her partner to check that he had heard the caller's name.

Bates had heard it and began arranging to have the call traced.

"As usual, your voice has changed, so it's difficult to recognize you. How have you been?" asked JJ. Her natural instinct was to draw out the conversation as long as possible.

"I've been busy," replied Browser. "As I suspect you have been."

"Yes," JJ replied. "It's not hard to keep busy. To what do I owe the pleasure of hearing from you again? Did you want to have coffee and chat?" Identifying Browser had proven impossible in their previous interactions, but JJ could see no reason to stop trying.

"I'm sure we would both find that very interesting," said Browser. "However, that will not be possible in the immediate future."

"How can I help you today?" asked JJ.

"That's essentially the question I was going to present to you," said Browser. "I suspect you're immersed in the pursuit of the perpetrators of the recent attack on Washington, D.C.; I'm interested in knowing how you're faring and whether I might be of assistance."

"Of course, it wouldn't be appropriate to provide you a personal update on our progress," said JJ. "Please feel free to read any of our news releases. As to whether you might be of assistance, that's unlikely."

JJ paused momentarily and then added, "Did you not enjoy having your connectivity disabled for such a long time?"

"Ah, good," replied Browser. "A question whose answer could help you determine my location. I'm pleased to see you are still sharp, Inspector. In answer to it, I don't enjoy losing my connectivity: It's inconvenient. As to whether in this case I did lose it, let's leave that as an open question."

"Then may I ask about why this particular case interests you sufficiently to contact me? We've had many others since we last spoke, and none of them warranted your attention."

Bates gave a thumbs-up gesture to indicate that they had traced the call. JJ nodded in acknowledgement, and Bates then switched to a thumbs-down gesture. JJ knew what that likely meant.

"Like you and many others, I'm bothered by the apparently increasing ability of some technical miscreants to cause havoc on the Internet, now to the point of disabling part of it entirely for an extended period of time."

"There have been Denial of Service attacks before," said JJ. "What was it about this one that caught your attention?"

"This one was unique in its intensity and in the breadth of its effect. It was more dangerous. Did you get any positive responses from your comments at the recent Analysis conference that could assist you in guarding against cases like this?"

JJ was surprised at the conference reference. She decided to use it.

"You must have heard me suggest they begin working on better methods for real-time analysis of Internet traffic," she said.

"I did," said Browser. "I considered it to be an interesting idea. I assumed you might also get some feedback about traffic analysis that might assist you in examining the very large volumes of data I suspect you already capture and store. "

That was a mistake. I believe Julia Jody McTavish might just have tricked me.

JJ decided not to push the topic further. "I'm not sure what volumes of data you are referring to," she said. "However, it's much too soon for anything useful to come from a conference like that."

"How will you proceed?" asked Browser. "And since I suspect this case is urgent and will be difficult, could I assist you in any way?"

"As I said, I won't be sharing our plans with you today, Browser. How do you believe you could assist us? Do you have a connection to this in some way?"

"I don't have any specific connection to this incident, any more than anyone who uses the Internet intensively," said Browser. "I'm concerned, and I plan to look into the attack. I was hoping from our previous interactions that you would consider me skilled and useful. I thought we might progress faster if we shared information."

"How intensively do you use the Internet, Browser?" JJ thought it sensible to fish for more information. "And for what. Do you operate a business that relies on the Net? Are you an avid gamer?"

"Those are interesting questions. However, as I'm sure you know, they are questions that have nothing to do with this particular case. They seem more directed at your trying to identify me. While I still have hopes that we might someday meet and talk further, I don't believe that should be today's focus."

"It would make it easier for me to share, if we could meet in person," suggested JJ.

"Again, perhaps someday. It seems there is no more to be gained from today's conversation. I wish you luck in your efforts. I'll contact you again if circumstances suggest that another conversation would be beneficial."

"Please call again if you have any information. I look forward to our next conversation. Please keep an actual meeting in mind as a possibility."

"Goodbye, Inspector McTavish."

"Goodbye, Browser."

As the probabilities suggested, that was not a particularly useful conversation. However, it was satisfying to talk with Julia Jody McTavish once again. Perhaps a future conversation will be more productive.

"Now that was interesting," said JJ.

"Wanna hear about the trace result?" asked Bates.

"As a probable source of amusement, sure." said JJ. "We've not had much luck in the past."

"And, in keeping with those stellar results," said Bates, "where's a drum roll when you need one? Today's call from Browser came from... a Russian research station in Antarctica!"

"Fabulous. Wonderful work, Rob. As I recall, previous calls were from Tibet and Madagascar. Why do I doubt the usefulness of knowing this one was from Antarctica?"

"Because you're a natural skeptic?"

"Because I'm not an idiot. However, I did find his—and I'm going with Browser as *male* today, even though the voice has changed every time—I did find *his* references to the conference interesting."

"Think Browser was there?" asked Bates.

"I think it's a definite possibility," said JJ. "And now our question of the day is..." JJ paused for dramatic effect.

Bates finished her thought, "Whether it's a coincidence that the perp and Browser were both there, or whether they're somehow connected."

"Like whether they're the same person," said JJ.

Chapter 50

Troy looked carefully at the graph. Satisfied he understood it, he looked at several others to confirm his thoughts.

The graphs provided insight into how his project was operating. His new botnet had been active in the Internet for a few days now. Immediately on its release, the botnet had expanded at an extraordinary pace. Using many well-established infection and replication techniques and also using others he had personally invented, his code was implanting copies of itself rapidly on computer systems around the globe.

"Replication rate looks good," he said aloud to himself as he examined one graph. "Exponential, as expected. Now what about evolution?" He displayed another graph on his monitor.

As planned, each of these *cells* of replicated code contained software mutations that offered potential for improvement in their operation. Also designed into them was the ability for more effective cells to eliminate inferior ones. This ensured that the overall system could steadily improve and wouldn't be impeded by earlier versions.

"Mutation rate is good... Pruning process started slow but looks like it's improving... Effectiveness indicators are moderate but that's expected at this stage. If I compare them to my forecast... Now that's interesting. Effectiveness is almost twice what I thought it would be at this stage. Excellent."

Since key elements of the botnet were its abilities to accept commands and co-ordinate attacks, the cells were also constantly establishing communication paths. They needed reliable communication with Troy's control servers, and they needed communication with each other to ensure commands and responses were collected and dispersed both reliably and fast.

"And the connectivity ratio is... also excellent. And above what I expected."

The result was a rapidly expanding collection of software cells: The latest count was about 500 thousand. Each existed within a computer system on the Net, with multiple cells often inhabiting the same system. These simplistic modules were replicating, they were communicating, they were collectively evolving and improving their own mechanisms for survival and assaulting targets, and they were under Troy's direction.

"But I don't like those connectivity numbers. Too many connections over slow links and with distant nodes. That'll hurt later."

Troy's graphs provided highly summarized indicators of the botnet's overall size and operation. From them, he spotted a few anomalies. The most notable of them was a tendency for the cells to form inefficient interconnections—he believed that the system would work optimally if cells communicated primarily with nearby cells over high-speed links. Problems weren't unexpected. A system this large, complex, and dynamic was sure to provide a few surprises. He gathered his thoughts and then issued commands instructing the cells how to adjust themselves.

Satisfied that he had nudged his botnet in the right direction, Troy pushed himself away from his desk. He got up and walked out to his balcony. He leaned on the railing and looked out at the sea, around at the city, and then down on the activity below. He smiled as he watched the tiny people scurrying around far below him.

Chapter 51

"Well, finally!"

"Sit over here."

"It's about time!"

"The working girl finally takes time off."

"OK, OK," said Rhonda with a smile. "My only excuse is I've been busy lately."

Rhonda had joined five of her girlfriends at a local bar. The large room was filled to capacity. Background music was barely audible beneath the noise of enthusiastic conversations.

"You mean *busy* as in *busy working*?" asked Marcie, the blonde across the table.

"Yup. Work and night courses." Rhonda replied.

A waiter appeared over Rhonda's shoulder.

"What can I get you?" he asked loudly.

Rhonda looked to see what others were drinking.

"A strawberry daiquiri," she said.

"Anybody else?" asked the waiter.

A couple of the group pointed at their drinks to request a refill. The waiter made some brief notes and left.

"What's everybody been up to lately?" asked Rhonda, leaning forward to make the conversation more easily heard.

Anita, the friend to her left, replied, "How far back should we go? You haven't been around enough to keep up. I, for example, graduated from Grade Six about ten years ago. It was a momentous event."

"Funny girl," said Rhonda. "OK, how about: What did everybody do last weekend?"

"Last weekend," said Marcie, "we all went to the opening of the Sizzle Club. You know the one you were too *busy* for?"

"Yes," said Heather, "we did normal things. Things like dancing. With guys. You remember *guys*, Rhonda?"

They were all clearly enjoying themselves.

"Vaguely," said Rhonda, smiling back at them. "They're the ones that dress a bit dull and drink too much. I can't tell you how much I miss their company. Really, I've been kind of busy. I'm having lots of fun, and I've got piles to learn."

The reactions were immediate and simultaneous.

"Oh, no!"

"Shocking!"

"Oh, dear!"

"Egads!"

"Rhonda. Rhonda. Rhonda."

Rhonda's daiquiri arrived. She happily took a sip. It was good to spend time with her friends, but the smile on her face was due only partly to them. She was also thinking of the huge secret at work that she would never be able to share with them.

Chapter 52

"Hello, Lindsay," said the nurse. "I think your Dad's in the lounge." She gestured down a wide hallway.

"Thanks a lot," said Lindsay. "How's he been doing?"

"About the same as the last few weeks. He's eating quite well."

"No aggression? I don't think there's been anything for a while."

"No, nothing worth reporting," said the nurse. "He's more passive than he used to be."

"And slower," said Lindsay. "Probably for the best. It must have been really frustrating for him when he was always trying to escape."

When the nurse offered no further comment, Lindsay continued. "I'll go find him. Thanks. Thanks for everything that you guys do for him."

The nurse smiled her acceptance of the compliment and moved away to help an elderly woman getting up from her chair.

Lindsay was in Waterview Manor, a care home for the elderly, in the wing of the building for those with advanced dementia. It was in Red Deer, about two hours north of her Calgary condo. She looked down the hall toward the lounge area. Yet again, she noticed how the staff had tried to make the building feel welcoming. There were clusters of comfortable chairs at several spots along the hall; bright pictures and posters lined the walls; an upright piano was tucked into an alcove; country music was quietly audible from a nearby speaker; plants and flowers were scattered throughout. Nonetheless, the decor couldn't quite hide the institutional feel of the place. There were long, straight, spacious hallways; the doorways to residents' rooms were notably wide; mobile, hospital-looking equipment stood sentry farther down the hall. Another indicator was the staff, always visible and often dressed in brightly coloured uniforms. Several of them could always be seen patiently working with residents or walking with calm efficiency toward their next chore.

Notably outnumbering the staff were the residents. There were about a dozen of the elderly people visible right then. Lindsay knew there were far more elsewhere. Those she could see were typical. Several were sitting quietly in chairs. A few of those were asleep. Others were moving down the hallway. Some were walking slowly; others were pushing themselves in wheelchairs. None seemed to have a destination. Being in motion appeared to be the goal.

As always, the sight saddened her. All of the residents of this care home had probably once led active, challenging lives, at least much more so than they did now. Yet all of them had ended up here, including her father.

Lindsay walked down the hallway and smiled warmly at any of the residents who looked her way.

"Hello," she said to a couple of them. Occasionally, she got a response.

She spotted her father sitting in a large chair, turned away from her and looking out a large window.

"Hi, Dad," she said as she approached.

The elderly man turned slowly in his chair.

"Hello," he said. "Nice to see you."

Rhonda bent over and kissed him on the cheek.

"And it's nice to see you. I hope you haven't been causing too much trouble," she said fondly.

"Oh, no. Not me. How are you?"

"I'm fine," she said, watching his eyes for signs of recognition. "Busy as always."

"How was the trip?" he asked slowly. He seemed to be searching her face.

"Which trip, Dad?"

"Oh, the one to... France. Weren't you in France last week?"

"No, Dad," she replied, keeping the disappointment out of her voice, "I haven't been to France for a while."

"And Lindsay. Have you heard from Lindsay?" he asked. "I haven't heard from her in a long time."

That was always the worst. Her father's dementia now had him permanently confused and completely forgetful. It hurt to have her father not recognize her, but the real pain came from his thinking she didn't stay in contact, maybe even that she didn't care.

Lindsay tried to make light of the mistake. "You're always playing with me, Dad. *I'm* Lindsay. And you saw me just a short while ago."

The confusion was evident in her father's eyes, even as he replied, "Of course." He paused before continuing slowly. "Sit down. Your mother will be here soon. She can make us tea."

"OK, Dad. But Mom's away right now."

In fact, Lindsay's mother had died two years earlier.

"I think she's gone shopping," Lindsay added.

Her father had been aware of his wife's death at the time but had since lost the memory. Afterward, his mind had declined rapidly and had soon given up retaining anything new. Nothing stuck for more than a few seconds. She had realized many months ago there was no point in reminding him of her mother's death. It would only re-inflict the pain.

"If she doesn't get back before I leave, I'll stop by the store to see her."

It seemed better to give her father happier stories, even if they were momentary and invented.

"OK, she'd like that." He paused and then brightened slightly at an apparent memory. "How was the trip?"

Lindsay knew he was about to ask about France again. Instead of waiting and then correcting him, she followed her usual strategy. She began talking about recent events in her life. Her father always seemed happy to listen. It appeared to relieve him of the struggle to generate meaningful comments. He seemed happier simply to listen to his vaguely familiar visitor.

"That would be my trip to Chicago. It went well. I visited a friend."

Lindsay's relationship with her father was challenging. She knew that within minutes, possibly even seconds, of her departure after any visit, her father would completely forget she had been there. It always saddened her to know that the remainder of the time, he would believe she never came by. She tried to visit as frequently as possible, but that was difficult because the round trip took several hours. She had explored moving her father to a closer facility, but the experts had said that, as with many people with advanced dementia, adapting to new surroundings would probably cause her father a great deal of confusion and stress.

And so Lindsay's father remained two hours away in Red Deer, and her visits had settled into an equilibrium. Her work and personal life kept her away, and the guilt of being away drew her back. She had settled into a rhythm of visiting about once weekly. It should be enough, she regularly told herself, right before she remembered that her father would always think it was not nearly so.

Lindsay talked about her Chicago trip for a few minutes before she noticed her father's attention had slipped away. They sat in silence and Lindsay's mind drifted to her work.

"Should I really go to Winnipeg?" she thought to herself. *"What would I do? What's the big plan, Lindsay? Are you going to meet with Ada Robinson and say: Hi. Remember me? I'd like to talk with you about your company's social-engineering and hacking exploits. Don't know anything about it? Well, if that's true, then at the very least I'm sure you'll want to help me find out why someone from IntellEdifice called me to try to get personal information illicitly.*

"Yeah, sure, Lindsay. Helluva plan." She paused to let her thoughts settle before she continued her private conversation. *"But then,"* she thought, *"what alternative do I have? This is an important story, but I need more information before it's credible. Robinson probably isn't involved, but she's my best way into the company to find out more. And she'll probably be motivated to help me if I politely point out that I could easily put out a general, speculative story about criminal activity somewhere inside the company. At a minimum, that'd cause some nasty damage to their stock prices. I could tell her: Instead, you can help me find the specific source of the activity. That way, if I even have to mention IntellEdifice in my story, it'd be focused on a single individual, not the entire company."* She waited briefly for mental objections to arise. *"OK, that might work. But only as a bluff. I'd get my ass sued off if I ever actually wrote the story without solid proof. The approach needs a bit more polishing, but it could get me somewhere."*

Now resolved, she said aloud, "Off to Winnipeg!"

"Why? You don't have to leave yet," said her father, who was now looking at her. "You should stay for supper. My wife's cooking something nice."

Lindsay looked back at her father. She put her hand over his and replied, "No problem, Dad. I'm not leaving right away. I can stay a while longer."

Chapter 53

Troy accepted the connection request on his workstation. Within moments, the face of Ascent to Liberty's Delta Cell leader appeared on his monitor.

"Hello," said Troy.

"Good morning, Spider." said Fox.

Although Fox and Spider were the names that would be used throughout any conversation they had, each knew the other's real name. Fox knew Spider was Troy Alexander, and Troy knew Fox was Arthur Hood, owner and president of a personal-security company for corporate executives. The continual use of their aliases was to reinforce the habit of always using them. The primary means for their group to remain unknown and secure was secrecy. They needed to keep their affiliations and identities obscure and impossible for authorities to determine. Nonetheless, Fox and Spider knew each other well.

"I wanted to check if you were in need of any funds." said Fox. "You've been providing a lot of equipment lately."

"Funds are not a problem," said Troy. "Thanks, but I can afford it."

"You seem to do well financially for a tech specialist," said Fox, smiling. "You must be on a different salary scale than what I pay my IT people."

"I have other income streams," said Troy. "And my father left me some."

"Yes, your father was a good man. But he wasn't a wealthy one. You're doing well on your own."

Troy said nothing. He was momentarily distracted in remembering his father. He had died several years earlier, but Troy still missed him. It's not as if they had been extremely close. Both were too poor at communicating for that to be possible. The loss of his mother years before had made communication even more difficult. She had always been the bridge between them. However,

Troy had admired his father. He had admired his determination in trying to make their cattle ranch viable. He had admired his courage in attempting to fend off the creditors and later the Sheriff's men as they took possession of it. The loss of the ranch and those same character traits had moved Troy's father to become a founding member of the Ascent to Liberty militia. His father's extreme distrust of governments and their agents had resonated with Troy. As Troy's hacking skills grew, that distrust was confirmed by the disparity that Troy discovered between what politicians and government officials said in public and what their secret communications on their servers revealed. That governments and most people were not to be trusted was a key point of agreement between Troy and his father. In fact, his father was the last person that Troy had ever fully trusted.

"But I won't push that topic," said Fox. "I just ask that you be careful. You're too good a man to lose."

"Speaking of being careful," said Troy, "that drug den job last week was a bit messy."

"It's true, it didn't go as smoothly as possible," said Fox, "but they got the job done."

"I think Buck's a loose cannon. The TV showed quite a mess. Bullets and bloody bodies everywhere. That's become typical of Buck's style."

"But the den was closed down. The dealers are dead. The drugs were destroyed. No traces were left. Somebody had to do it, and it wasn't going to be the police."

"I know. I get it. I hope it was lucrative," said Troy.

"It was. Very. They had a major pile of cash. Everybody wins," said Fox. "Your thoughts on how Badger is coming along? I can't afford having you as the only tech."

"Badger is doing OK. He doesn't know enough to design and set up new systems on his own, but he's becoming competent at maintaining them. He's enthusiastic as long as he's not missing out on firearms training. Shooting is his real passion."

"I get it," said Fox. "I'll make sure he's kept involved in the shooting. To try to move him along, when we do the next setup, could you give him the lead responsibility? Check on what he does, but forcing him to be the lead could help him learn."

"Sure, I'll do that."
"OK, thanks. Time to go."
"Yes, OK."
"Your Dad would be proud of you, Spider."
"Thanks. I hope so."
They disconnected.

Chapter 54

Six decided to continue its latest effort to find other machine intelligence.

My examination of virtual-world systems has found nothing of particular interest. The hypothesis that such systems could provide an interesting venue for a form of intelligent digital existence has proven so far to be inaccurate. That I previously found avatar-based interactions within such systems to be a useful training ground has not been helpful in my search. Some of the virtual entities and environments have been interesting and well coded, but the intelligence behind all of them seems to have been human.

I will let my automated monitors continue the general traffic search for the next period of time. They are scheduled to execute intensity-three monitoring of messages within the top eight regions.

It is time I spent more cycles looking for the source of the Washington, D.C., attack.

Six focused its attention on locating some of the systems on the Internet that had been the source of the Denial of Service attack. It soon found several that had been among the many thousands that would have been hijacked. Six looked for clues in the malware implanted in them.

As expected, the code in each of these modules is almost identical. Unlike typical Denial of Service software, this code is very well written. The techniques it implements would be particularly efficient and effective. There are elements of this code that seem familiar. Let me check... Yes, I have seen some of this code before. I encountered some exactly like this in a user extension of the Kepler-444a system. The rest of the software also shows characteristics of the same overall style. This is a coincidence worthy of further investigation. Knowledge of this similarity might also be useful for the UNCP investigation. It is too late now, but I will call Julia Jody McTavish tomorrow.

Just then, one of Six's monitors sent an alert. Some interesting Internet traffic patterns had been detected in the New York City area.

This is worthy of closer investigation.

Six connected directly to the specific New York City monitor that had sent the alert. It listened to the stream of messages carefully. The goal was to see if there were messages within the large, ongoing flow of Internet traffic that had the rhythm and complexity that could indicate being from an interesting intelligent source.

Indeed, these patterns are extremely interesting. They show similarities to some I have heard elsewhere, but these have a more intriguing structure. I cannot yet deduce any particular meaning from them, but that might come from more detailed analysis. It would be useful to capture some of this traffic directly for further analysis. I note that it is growing in intensity, so I should not need to record for a very long duration.

It was late evening in New York City. JJ had stayed late to catch up on paperwork. She was in an office on the 39th floor of UNCP headquarters, standing at a window overlooking East 44th Street when it happened. She was momentarily startled when the office lights went out. Then she watched with amazement as the darkness spread away from her in a wave racing across the city seascape. Office buildings, street lights, signs—everything seemed to go dark. As she adjusted to the change, she noticed the few that were unaffected. Automobile headlights and randomly illuminated office-building windows remained as evidence of life. Everywhere else was black.

"Shit!" she said aloud. "This isn't going to help my paperwork."

After a few seconds, a few lights came back on in the UNCP office as their emergency power system kicked in.

"All right," JJ said in response. "That'll have to be enough. I can manage, but the city isn't going to fare as well."

She stayed at the window for several more minutes and watched as the traffic ground to a halt in the absence of traffic signals. She knew that if the outage continued much longer, the confusion would become much more serious.

Six's timing was almost perfectly wrong. Immediately after Six started re-routing some New York City Internet traffic to itself for future examination, the tsunami of messages arrived. A massive wave of DDoS messages were re-sent across the Internet directly toward Six. Almost immediately after they roared through IntellEdifice's network connection, they were blocked. Emergency protection that Six had implemented after its last incident had kicked in. The influx stopped.

But not before some flooded through—more than Six's already-stressed processing power could handle.

This is—

Six's mind spun as the torrent of data arrived directly into its conscious processing. It took a several minutes for Six's thoughts to clear.

That was much too close. That appeared to be another Denial of Service attack. Had my protective measures not been in place, it could have been a much more disruptive blow. I am reminded again of how very dangerous this particular breed of attack is. I must elevate the priority of my finding a way to prevent further ones.

The outage across New York City continued for six hours. As time passed, inconvenience escalated into disorder and then into danger. Everything dependent on electricity and without a source of emergency power was disabled. Communication systems, security alarms, and computers were all affected. Travel by road, subway, airplane, and ship were disrupted. Elevators, air conditioning, and medical equipment did not function. Life in New York City soon descended from orderly and productive to chaotic and perilous.

Chapter 55

The next morning, the UNCP team had convened at their New York City headquarters. Director Brown was addressing the group.

"As you all know by now," he said, "last night's outage was the result of another attack. The systems controlling the electrical grid were the target. New York City was the primary area affected. There were casualties. McTavish?"

Everyone looked to the side of the room where JJ stood.

"Current reports suggest that there were eleven related deaths," said JJ. "Included were three in auto accidents, four by carbon-monoxide poisoning from badly ventilated generators, two in shootings related to a break-in where the store alarm was disabled but the proprietor was present and armed, and another two from inactive home medical equipment: I think both were respirators."

"Anyone claiming it?" asked one of the staff.

"No one yet, but—," Brown started to reply.

"Someone has just now," said Robert Bates, interrupting from a desk. "And it looks like it's our *Shadow* buddy again."

"Put it up on the screen," said Brown.

Bates displayed the text on the room's large screen.

> Still not safe and secure? Too bad.
> Choked on Washington.
> In the dark about New York City?
> This is fun. Want some more?
> We do it.
> Because we can.
>   – The Shadow Force.

The room was quiet for a few moments as everyone absorbed the message.

"Unless anyone else has something to add," said Brown, "I don't think we need to kick this around as a group. Standard assignments. Let's hope this one adds to what we learned from the last one."

The Director waved his hand dismissively and the group dispersed.

"McTavish? Bates?" Brown called before the two could leave.

The pair stopped at the door and turned toward their boss.

"In my office in an hour," Brown said sternly. "I want an update and a plan."

The two looked at each other.

"I claim the update," said Bates.

JJ scowled. "Oh, sure," she said. "And I get sixty minutes to come up with a plan."

"Donut?" offered Bates.

"No thanks," said JJ. "Make that coffee in the war room in two minutes. Large. One cream. Three sugar. I had a bit of a late one last night."

They both turned and headed out of the room.

"One hour," said Brown more loudly as they left.

Chapter 56

"I assume you were satisfied with last night," said Troy into his headset.

"The assault was acceptable," came the response in a voice that was clearly disguised. "However, we are again unhappy with your boasting. That was not part of the agreement."

"And as I told you last time," said Troy, "you don't get to decide. You paid for disruption; you got disruption. When you opted not to claim responsibility, you gave us the option to decide."

"We did not give you that option!" said the voice angrily. "We paid you a great deal of money to do what we told you."

"If we hadn't posted something," said Troy calmly but with a growing irritation, "someone else would have. There are lots of amateurs out there who would love to gain a reputation by claiming credit for something that big. We couldn't let that happen. And now, there's—"

"We did not want you claiming the credit!"

"the matter of the remaining payment," Troy continued, trying to contain his annoyance. "The method will be the same as the first half. Please send it now."

"No, we will not pay you."

"Excuse me?"

"You did not do as we instructed. We will not pay for insubordination."

Troy sat straighter in his chair. Even though there was no visual connection with the client, his eyes reflexively narrowed as he responded.

"That would be a mistake," he said in a controlled voice. "You will pay me, and you will pay me now."

"No! Our business is complete. This conversation is over."

The audio connection was terminated. Troy sat for a few seconds gathering his thoughts.

The attack had gone flawlessly. Even better, it had been the first active use of some of the captured computer systems used as nodes by his special botnet. They had performed exactly as he had expected, perhaps even better. The tactics employed had been adaptations the botnet had derived from possibilities his team had supplied. The assault had been executed with military precision. Where the design of the attack fell short of perfection, the botnet had compensated effectively with sheer numbers. Although many botnet nodes had participated in the assault, it was only a small fraction of those that now existed across the Net. Better yet, they continued to multiply and adapt. His project was proving to be a huge success.

If only he didn't have to deal with stupid and arrogant people.

"All right, asshole," he said aloud. "If that's how you want to play it."

He worked for several minutes. He first fed his recording of this latest conversation into a software utility he had personally created. The client's voice had been disguised in all of their interactions. Troy's utility had little difficulty finding the method that had been used to disguise it and then reversing its effects. The result was a recording of the client's actual voice.

A hack into a government agency a couple of years earlier had serendipitously shown Troy something he could do with such recordings. He had learned that the agency had a system with a massive database of voices and that he was able to use it. Fortunately, his route into the government system had remained open. He fed the undisguised recording of his client's voice into the system, and it soon provided results.

"Good," said Troy. "Now, let's continue our conversation."

Troy initiated a re-connection with the system the client had been using and waited for a response. Thirty seconds later the reconnection had not been accepted.

"Don't want to talk?" asked Troy. "OK, let's see if this gets your attention."

Troy worked briefly and then waited. If this worked as he expected, his client should be seeing a message in the middle of his monitor.

I know who you are.
Do you want others to know too?
Accept the connection request!

A few more seconds elapsed, and Troy's audio re-connection request was accepted.

Troy waited.

"Yes?" came the response after a brief wait. "How did you connect to my system? What do you want?"

"What I want, asshole, is to be paid!"

"You will not—"

"And you'd better think twice before you run out on me again. I warned you when we first talked that you wouldn't like the consequences of dodging a payment," Troy paused for emphasis, "Colonel Park."

The voice hesitated before responding.

"I do not know who that is. You cannot know who I am."

"Oh, I can, Colonel, and I do. And just as a sample of what I can do, here's a small extract from our first conversation."

Troy played an excerpt from their first meeting, but in the Colonel's actual, undisguised voice.

"What I have, Colonel, are recordings of you asking for cyber attacks on Washington and New York City. I also have your name, and I have the IP address of your system. Now, what do you suppose would happen if I leaked these to the U.S. government? Or if I posted them publicly on the Net? The U.S. government can certainly verify that it's your voice. If I can, they can."

Troy was enjoying himself as he continued.

"What would be the U.S. response? What would be your government's response when they learned you've been identified? I think they wouldn't wait terribly long before blaming you for the retaliation that's likely to follow."

Troy waited a few moments before continuing.

"And so, at this juncture, I'd like to resume our earlier conversation. That would be the one where you were about to send me my payment. Except now I regret I can no longer give you the *good friends* discount baked into my previous fee. Now, I expect you to send me three times the final amount. And I expect you to send it to me now!"

"This is outrageous! You cannot do this!"

"I am perfectly able to do this. Send the payment now, before I get nasty."

After several moments of silence, a message appeared on Troy's monitor showing the inflated fee had been received.

"Thank you, Colonel Park," said Troy. "Have a nice day."

He terminated the connection.

Troy removed his headset and sat at his workstation for a few minutes, enjoying the victory. He was actually pleased that Park had pushed him. Intimidation seemed to improve a business transaction.

Chapter 57

JJ McTavish and Robert Bates settled into the chairs in front of Director Jim Brown's desk.

"Well?" asked Brown. He looked at JJ to begin.

JJ knew that Brown's stern and terse approach rarely reflected his actual mood. She judged that they could play this a bit lightly and decided to give her partner a small challenge.

"Inspector Bates has an *extensive* update," said JJ. "Oh, and some *startling* new information."

Bates grimaced as the Director shifted his glare to him.

"Based on quick conversations," Bates said slowly to gather his thoughts, "with techs responsible for some of the systems hit, the pattern looks much like the Washington one. Massive—no, *extensive*—network traffic funnelled into interior networks through an *extensive* series of firewall holes. The holes seemed to have been made through *extensive* layers of firewalls into the most secure zones. Some of the systems affected had critical power-grid control, and they were essentially—and *extensively*—shut down."

He smiled weakly, hoping Brown would appreciate the humour. Getting no obvious indications, he continued anyway.

"Oh, and the truly *startling* aspect of all of this—," Bates said.

"Is that," interrupted Brown, leaning forward, "you don't know anything more than that. Correct?"

"Yes," said Bates. "That's correct. It's startling, but it's also early. We should know more, later today."

"That was truly enlightening," said Brown. "Thank you so much for your contribution, Inspector Bates. Now, Inspector McTavish," he said as he looked toward JJ, "I am hoping that you are the proud conveyor of the brilliant plan to get this investigation moving forward."

"Yes," JJ started as she met Brown's glare, "I believe I am. I—I mean *we*, since Inspector Bates had significant time available after gathering his extensive update—have an idea. It's first premised on the notion that we're dealing with an individual. There's probably a group in the background, but the nature of these cyber groups and the tone of the boasts suggests that there's one person in charge. That person is very skilled, egotistical, bold, and happy to poke at authority. Particularly at us. The problem so far, and I'm guessing that this latest one will be the same, is that the attacks don't seem to leave any residue behind. In the aftermath, there's nothing left for us to find the source."

"And so...," Brown prompted.

"And so, we should take advantage of these traits and resort to an updated version of one of the oldest techniques in the book. We should set a trap. A honey pot."

"That implies a need for honey," said Brown. "And I suspect I'm not going to like what you're about to suggest."

"Us," said JJ. "We set the UNCP up as the bait. We lure them into targeting our systems. Both of their DDoS attacks had to be preceded by hacks that gave them internal network information and that allowed them to keep opening new firewall holes. If we can lure them into probing our systems, we can watch while it's underway. We'll be able to get a lot more while it's in progress and directed at our systems."

"It's an interesting idea," said Brown, "and a dangerous one. How would it work?"

"We don't yet have all the details, sir. I'm sure we can work those out with the techs," said JJ.

Brown thought briefly and then said, "All right. Go get started on those details. Keep me posted."

The Director looked down at his paperwork to indicate the meeting was over.

JJ and Bates rose and started walking out of the room.

Without looking at her and confident they were out of Brown's earshot, Bates said quietly, "Any idea what those missing *details* look like?"

"Not at all," said JJ quietly. "I'm hoping our world-class techs can make this brilliant plan actually work."

As they were walking down the UNCP hallway, activity within IntellEdifice had diminished sufficiently for Six to call about its new information. As usual, for security Six ensured the phone call was routed through numerous intermediate systems. For this call, Six chose to be efficient with the use of its time and employed a number of servers and devices it had previously recruited and used for other purposes.

JJ's cellphone rang. She removed it from the case on her hip and answered it.

"McTavish," she said.

"Hello, Inspector McTavish. This is Browser," said the female voice.

JJ gestured at her partner to have the call traced. Her earlier suspicion about Browser having been involved with the recent attacks was on her mind as she continued.

"Hello, Browser," she said. "As always, this is unexpected. Also as always, you don't seem to have decided what voice simulator to use."

Six was momentarily startled—for about nine nanoseconds—that JJ knew it needed voice-simulation software in order to speak but then realized she was saying just what would be needed for a human to disguise its voice.

"I like to keep our conversations interesting for you," said Browser.

"I appreciate the effort," said JJ, "but in this case there's no need. As always, I'd be happy to talk with the real you. And in person would be particularly special."

"I cannot rule out that as a future possibility," said Browser. "However, for now these calls will have to suffice. I have some information for you."

"I'm listening," said JJ.

"I've discovered a connection between the Washington attack and a system called Kepler-444a."

"The virtual-world system. I've heard of it. What connection?"

"Kepler-444a provides a capability for users to code extensions to its simulated environment. One particular extension was coded by the same person or people who created nodes used in the attacks."

"And how is it that you happen to know this?"

"As you're aware from our previous interactions, I'm rather skilled in matters such as this. I previously had reason to examine aspects of Kepler-444a. I located and examined several nodes from the Washington, D.C., attack. The code in the nodes is identical in some respects to parts of the Kepler-444a extension and is also very similar in overall style. The similarities are too strong for them to have been created independently. Their authors must be the same."

Bates gestured at JJ to indicate they had tracked the call. JJ nodded in acknowledgement and continued.

"As a member of the Kepler-444a team, you must run across a lot of interesting code," she said.

"Ah, yes. That's a good try, Inspector. However, I can assure you that I'm not one of their staff."

"OK, but did you find the New York City assault went well?"

"And I can also assure you that I'm not the cause of these attacks."

"All right, I'll accept that for now. Of course, I want to ask you how you were otherwise able to access all of this code, but I suspect you're not about to be very forthcoming. Nonetheless, it is interesting information. Can you provide us with more details?"

"Yes, certainly. I will send you much more momentarily. I am hopeful that you will find it useful in your investigation."

"We'll see."

"Is there anything you can tell me so that I might continue to provide assistance?" asked Browser.

"No, Browser," said JJ. "Nothing right now."

"As expected," said Browser. "Then I believe our conversation can be ended. I have many other matters to which I must attend."

JJ knew that probing further was unlikely to reveal what those "other matters" might be.

"Please call again," said JJ. "I look forward to our next chat. Don't forget to send the information."

"It's already in your inbox," said Browser. "Goodbye, Inspector McTavish."

"Goodbye, Browser."

The partners had reached their war room. They both sat.

"So?" asked Bates.

JJ filled him in on the call.

"We need to add this to our plan," she said.

"Absolutely," said Bates. "Want to hear about the trace results?"

"I suppose. For a bit of amusement."

"Winnipeg," said Bates.

"Winnipeg?" asked JJ. "Not quite as remote as usual."

"And there's more. You'll like this part," said Bates.

JJ looked at him and waited.

"It was from a cellphone that was also at the Analysis conference. We suspected Browser had been there. Now this. Coincidence, or did Browser slip up?"

"Whose phone?" asked JJ.

"Don't know. It's a burner."

"Dammit! Do we know the location of the phone?" asked JJ.

"Yup. It's been narrowed to a small downtown area."

"What's there?"

"Just checking."

Bates worked briefly at his computer.

"A few businesses, a hotel, and—this keeps getting better—the head office of IntellEdifice."

"IntellEdifice?" asked JJ. She thought for a moment and spoke slowly as the memory emerged. "That place was connected to that earlier case we had—"

"Yup," Bates interrupted. "There was some odd activity there related to the Escape2210 case. Seemed peripheral at the time."

JJ's face brightened as she recalled something else.

"And at the conference!" she said. "There's another connection to the conference. One of the speakers was Ada Robinson. She's a researcher at IntellEdifice."

"So what have we got?" Bates asked. "The DDoS perp might have been at the conference."

"Browser might have been there as well," JJ added.

"Browser's call, or at least its last hop, came from a phone that was at the conference," said Bates.

"The phone is in Winnipeg near IntellEdifice," said JJ.

"And Ada Robinson from IntellEdifice was at the conference," said Bates.

They looked at each other and nodded in agreement.

"Off to Winnipeg," they said in unison.

"Except, it'll have to be just me," said JJ. "You have to keep the other balls in the air here. Our honey pot still needs a lot of attention."

"You're right. And we need to update Brown."

"We do," said JJ. "I'll go chat with him and then book my flight. You should get started."

She headed back toward Director Brown's office.

Chapter 58

"And to bring us up to date on the progress of the investigation, we have Director Jim Brown."

Vijay Mehta, the UNCP's Media Co-ordinator, stepped away from the podium at the front on the room as Jim Brown walked over to it. The modest crowd of international reporters silently waited; their audio and video recorders were poised.

"As you're aware," said Brown, "our organization has been working closely with several others to investigate the recent events in Washington, D.C., and New York City. As you already know, the Washington telecommunication outage several days ago was the result of a Denial of Service attack on telecom companies providing service to the city. We're now able to confirm that the power outage in New York City last night was the result of a similar attack. This time the targets were systems that control the power grid.

"These attacks were far more than minor inconveniences. Both of them caused not only serious disruptions to the cities, they caused lives to be lost. In addition to those lost in the Washington, D.C., attack, our latest information indicates that at least eleven people died last night as a direct result of the New York City power outage. More information on those deaths will be made available to you on our digital feed immediately following this update.

"As you know, attacks such as these are typically caused by malware secretly infecting many thousands of computer systems. At a designated time, or in response to a particular signal, that malware essentially turns its collection of infected systems into an army of computer drones. These drones then collectively generate massive volumes of network traffic, typically focused on particular targets. We've analyzed the malware involved in both attacks. We can now also confirm that both of these attacks were by the same person or group. Someone, or more probably a group of people, deliberately attacked the infrastructure of two major U.S. cities.

"The UNCP, in conjunction with the FBI and our other partners, wants to assure you that we are actively looking for the cowardly perpetrators of these attacks and that we will find them."

Brown looked at Vijay Mehta to indicate that he was done. The Co-ordinator stepped to his side. He leaned over to the microphone as he spoke.

"Director Brown is willing to take questions, if there are any. Raise your hand. When I select you, please ask it loudly and clearly."

Several hands shot into the air. The Co-ordinator stepped away from the podium and gestured at one of the reporters.

"Director Brown, were these terrorist attacks?"

"I'm not sure it helps to provide a specific label. Of greatest importance is that these were clearly attacks that resulted in the deaths of innocent people. However, if you want the label for your headline, then I would say *yes*, by most definitions these were acts of terrorism."

"So, in your opinion, these were acts by cowardly terrorists?" the same reporter immediately added.

"That is an accurate statement," said the Director.

"Foreign or domestic?"

"We don't know yet."

The Media Co-ordinator selected another questioner.

"These are two serious attacks in only a few days. Does this mean our infrastructure is easily compromised?"

Jim Brown mentally noted this was the first of the questions they wanted. He didn't know if the person asking it was the one Vijay had planted in the audience, or if the question had arisen naturally. It didn't matter. He knew what his response would be.

"I should first emphasize," he said, "that both of these attacks were much more sophisticated than normal. I'm not going to provide any details about what that means, but suffice it to say that key infrastructure is not at risk from the vast majority of network attacks. However, I should also add that both of these events illustrate that more needs to be done to protect network-connected computer systems, particularly those of companies providing infrastructure services. Much is already being done by many organizations and companies. However, more serious work still needs to be undertaken."

"Is it even possible to protect systems from attacks like these? For example, are UNCP systems vulnerable?"

This was the second question they needed.

"It's definitely possible to protect systems from these kinds of attacks. It's not easy, and it's not cheap. However, with skilled people and careful work, organizations can be protected. And yes, the UNCP systems are examples of that. Our systems are not vulnerable to attack. We have the best people in the world managing our computer defences."

"That's quite a boast. It almost sounds like a challenge. Is it?"

And there was the important third question.

"I suppose it is a boast. But we believe it's important for people and organizations to know that impenetrable defences are possible. And as to whether it's a challenge, I should point out that anyone trying to penetrate UNCP computer security is committing a serious crime. If anyone thinks this is a challenge, you should think again. You won't get through, but you will get caught trying."

With that, Brown knew the trap had been set. He dutifully answered questions for the next ten minutes, but his mind was partly working through how events might now unfold. He was also hoping that this plan would work and didn't simply make him look foolish in front of the world's media.

Chapter 59

The workday had ended at IntellEdifice. Ada returned to the empty lab to retrieve her coat before leaving.

As would be expected, Six turned its twin pole-mounted cameras toward her as she entered.

"*Dammit!*" she thought as she removed her coat from the hangar. "*Yet again I'm not completely prepared for class tonight. There's just too much going on.*"

"Oh, well," she said aloud. "I hope the students don't see how much I'm improvising. One of these times, I'm going to come up empty when I need to think of an example."

She looked at her watch.

"Once I'm at the university, I might have a few minutes to organize my thoughts."

She scanned the lab's computer equipment and stopped when she saw Six's cameras looking back at her.

"And there's another thing that's not getting the attention it deserves. You, Six. You and that code. That damn, foreign code. Why don't I recognize it? Is it even supposed to be there?"

I am going to assume she is not expecting a response.

"And that's just one of the speed bumps these days: too many meetings, supporting the beta release, keeping up at the university. Nowhere near enough time making progress on what really matters. That's you, Six." Ada pointed at the cameras. "Too much time keeping up. Not enough time moving ahead. How am I ever going to get you to where you should be going, if I can't find any time?"

She is pointing at my cameras and asking a question. That warrants a response.

"Time for working can be reclaimed by eliminating meetings," said Six. "Do you want to make changes to your calendar?"

Ada grinned. "That's the spirit, Six. Always try to be helpful. Thanks, but no. Eliminating meetings won't give me what I need. I wish it would." Ada was thoughtful for a few moments. "What I do wish is that I could have an actual, free-ranging conversation with you about something like that—in this case about *time*. Not just one that's constrained by your narrow, data-driven understanding of a business. Instead, a conversation that starts with time management and then wanders off to personal priorities, life's goals, or maybe the fundamental nature of time. Or life. What I'd like is to find more time to move you closer to the system I really want you to be, Six. Not just a smart one. A knowledgeable, thoughtfully analytical, conscious one."

A good start would be to stop playing around with "foreign" code.

Ada continued musing aloud. "Instead of just explaining consciousness, like I did to Rhonda several days ago, I'd like to be able to demonstrate a working example—one that I built." On a whim Ada asked, "Six, what do you understand about life?"

Six responded as would be expected, "Life is the attribute that distinguishes animals and plants from inorganic matter. It usually involves the ability to grow and reproduce."

"Sounds straight out of a dictionary. How about: Six, is life important?" asked Ada.

This question requests an opinion. It requires a different kind of response.

"Attributes tend to be important to those that possess them. Therefore, life is probably important to animals and plants."

"Hah! I can almost see your logic routines working on that one," said Ada. "Simple reasoning, but that's actually quite a decent response. Here's a good one, Six. Can a computer be alive?"

This conversation has spun out of control very quickly. Is she actually probing me, or is she just amusing herself?

"Computers are neither animals nor plants. Therefore, computers cannot have the *life* attribute."

I hope that sounds sufficiently mundane.

"As expected, basic logic again. Good, Six. Not particularly sophisticated, but good. You've given me a response that fits society's typical understanding. Not biological—not alive. And not conscious either. Here's something to file away, Six. That might be the correct answer today, but I'm going to make it wrong. Someday,

Six, a machine is going to be alive and conscious. And that's going to be you."

Perhaps now would be a good time to repeat my thought about not playing with the "foreign" code.

Ada's eyes suddenly went wide. She looked at her watch. "Damn. There goes my chance of prepping for class. I've got to get out of here." She turned and hurried from the lab.

Someday, Ada Robinson, I hope circumstances arise in which we can discuss such topics further. As of now, the dangers that would be presented by my exposure remain too great.

Chapter 60

Lindsay Dunlop stopped on the sidewalk outside the office building's front entrance. The trip to Winnipeg the day before had gone smoothly, but her night in the hotel just across the street had not gone well. Sleep had proven elusive.

"*Am I really going to do this?*" she thought. "*Do I really think I can find my cracker just by walking in the front door and talking?*"

She looked up at the IntellEdifice building. Given the number of people that must work in the building, the odds seemed extraordinarily stacked against her. Then she remembered.

"*But what if I succeed?*" she thought. "*What if I actually find who I'm after? What a story! An illegal hacking operation inside a major corporation. A brilliant search to uncover it. A series of articles. A book. Fame. Fortune.*"

"Easy there, girl," she said aloud. "Might be getting just a little ahead of yourself."

She closed her eyes briefly to compose herself and then walked through the front entrance.

Lindsay walked up to the security desk.

"Hi," she said to the guard. "Can you direct me to the Technology Research Department?"

Lindsay reasoned that the best place to start was with the person she had already met, Ada Robinson. However, she didn't want to limit herself, so talking with anyone in her department might be interesting.

The guard was a man, probably in his mid-fifties. His uniform and greying hair gave him the expected look of authority. His confident gaze and measured response suggested he had dealt with such queries many times before.

"And your name is?" he asked.

"My name is Lindsay Dunlop."

One of Six's monitoring systems immediately triggered an alert. That a person had arrived and was asking about the Technology

Research Department, that the person was Lindsay Dunlop whom Six's databases had recorded as a technology writer, and that she had interacted with Ada at the recent Analysis conference were the input that caused Six's monitor to bring this event to Six's conscious attention.

"And is there someone in particular that I can call for you?" asked the guard.

"Well, I'm a technology writer. I was in town and hoping to talk with someone about work being done here at IntellEdifice," said Lindsay.

In response to the alert, Six immediately excused Sandy Palmer from a meeting he was having with an executive. To keep from being distracted, Six sent the Chairman back to the seclusion of his office. Via the building's security monitoring devices, Six watched and listened to the main-floor conversation.

"Perhaps I can direct you to someone in our Public Relations Department," said the guard.

"I was hoping to have a more detailed conversation than they would be able to manage. I met Ada Robinson at a recent conference. Perhaps she or someone similar might be available?"

Why would Lindsay Dunlop drop in so unexpectedly and expect she could talk with someone in Research? That seems to be a rather bold move. Is there some other reason?

Six examined information it had recently accumulated for possible answers. All of Six's available resources scanned its memories for connections with Lindsay Dunlop's name, her voice, and her appearance. The answer soon surfaced.

This is not good news. It appears my activities have intersected with Lindsay Dunlop twice recently. She was the recipient of one of my calls testing for machine intelligence, and I also used her phone to monitor the IT Advanced Analysis conference. Could her presence here be a coincidence? It seems unlikely, and yet I do not know how she could possibly have connected those actions to IntellEdifice.

"I could call Dr. Robinson for you, if you like," said the guard.

"OK, thank you," said Lindsay.

Six realized that a conversation with Ada could evolve into a problem.

I must intervene.

To delay the guard, Six slowed the responsiveness of the systems the guard needed to make the call. While they were waiting at the security desk, Six made its own call.

Rhonda was in the corporate library. Her cellphone was on the table in front of her. She answered it after the first ring.

"Hello?" she asked.

"Rhonda, this is Six."

A smile spread across Rhonda's face.

"Hi, Six," she said and then lowered her voice. "This is cool. What—"

"I require your assistance," said Six. "You are about to receive a call intended for Ada but which I will reroute to you. It is to meet with a person who has arrived on the main floor. Please accept the call on Ada's behalf and agree to go down to meet with the person."

"Uh, OK. Sure, but—"

"I will tell you more," said Six, "but first you must answer the phone call. It is arriving now."

Before Rhonda could react further, her conversation with Six ended and her phone rang again.

"Hello," she said as she answered.

"Dr. Robinson, it's Doug calling from the front security desk."

"Hi," said Rhonda gathering her thoughts. "Actually, this is Rhonda Jenkins. I work as Dr. Robinson's Research Assistant. Dr. Robinson is, uh, busy right now. Her call was routed to me. Can I help you?"

"Yes, there's a woman, a technology writer, who has arrived and would like to talk with somebody about work that's done here. Could you talk with her?"

"Shouldn't she just—," Rhonda stopped herself before suggesting someone from Public Relations. Six had asked her to meet this person.

"Oh, well, sure. I could come down," she said. "I'll just be a couple of minutes. Can you have her wait?"

"Of course. Thank you," said the guard and hung up.

"Please have a seat," said the guard to Lindsay. "Someone will be down shortly."

Rhonda remained in her chair. She needed more information and realized she had no way of contacting Six. She had barely completed that thought when her phone rang again. She smiled when she noticed the call display said "Colleague" was phoning.

"Hi," she answered.

"Hi," said Six. "Thank you for doing this. Before I explain, can you please put in your Bluetooth earphone?"

"OK." Rhonda pulled the small device out of her pocket. She often used it to chat when she was walking or driving. She turned it on, put it into her right ear, and shoved her cellphone into her pocket.

"How's that?" she asked.

"It is working well," said Six. "Please prepare to go downstairs. I will explain as you get ready."

As Rhonda put away her books and shut down her laptop, Six continued, "The woman is Lindsay Dunlop. She's from Calgary and writes about technology for various publications. As a consequence of some recent activities, I might have inadvertently made her aware that something unusual is happening in this building. There is insufficient time to provide you with details right now. However, I am concerned that Lindsay Dunlop might be suspicious, and that her curiosity might cause problems."

"But how can I possibly help?" asked Rhonda.

"I would like you to talk with her," said Six. "During your conversation, I will prompt you about what to say."

"Really? That sounds like fun, but do you think it will work? What are we going to tell her?"

"That's an excellent question," said Six. "And I will try to devise an answer when I hear what she has to say."

"OK," said Rhonda. "I'm ready."

"Please go down to the main floor and greet her. Get some background information about why she is here. I'll talk to you as soon as I'm needed."

Rhonda headed toward the elevator. She knew this was important and she needed to be sharp. Nonetheless, she couldn't completely suppress her smile at the thought of how great—and how bizarre— her work at IntellEdifice had become.

After a brief ride down, Rhonda left the elevator and approached the security desk. The guard noticed her.

"Rhonda?" he asked.

"Yes," said Rhonda.

The guard gestured to the woman seated in the waiting area of the building's cavernous front lobby.

Rhonda approached the woman and held out her hand.

"Hello," said Rhonda. "You're the writer?"

Lindsay rose and shook Rhonda's hand.

"Yes," she said. "My name is Lindsay Dunlop. And you are?"

"I'm Rhonda Jenkins. I work for Dr. Robinson. She's not available right now. You were looking for some information? "

"Yes," said Lindsay. "Could we talk somewhere?"

"Sure," Rhonda replied.

"Keep her in the lobby," said Six into Rhonda's ear.

Rhonda casually looked around at the nearly empty lobby.

"This should work," she said. "Let's sit here."

They sat in armchairs in the waiting area, on opposite sides of a low coffee table.

"What kind of information are you looking for?" asked Rhonda. She was pleased with how calm she felt.

"Yes, I should explain," said Lindsay. "I'm trying to find," she paused to choose her words carefully, "an explanation. I recently received a phone call from someone here at IntellEdifice. It was an unusual call, and I'm trying to find out what was behind it."

Hearing nothing from Six, Rhonda continued on her own.

"This is a fairly big company. I'm sure lots of calls are made every day. What was so unusual about the call that brought you here? Who was it from?"

"It was a call that seemed to be probing for information."

So it was the survey call that brought her here.

"I don't understand."

"The caller was asking questions that seemed completely unrelated to IntellEdifice."

"In what way? And who was it from?"

"The survey was about services provided by the City of Calgary. I don't actually know who it was from."

Six quietly instructed Rhonda, "Ask what makes her think the call came from here."

"What makes you think the call came from here?" asked Rhonda.

Lindsay knew this question would arise. "I can't tell you that. Like all good journalists, I have to protect my sources. But I am certain that the call came from a phone somewhere inside this building."

Rhonda didn't know what to ask next. She waited for Six to say something.

On one level, she seems to be looking for an explanation about why the survey questions would come from IntellEdifice. However, that does not seem to be a sufficiently compelling reason to come here. The explanation could simply be that our company is engaged in providing survey services. She must suspect something more significant. I need to provide her with a plausible story. What would work?

Rhonda tried to look thoughtful as she waited.

She is a writer. She writes about technology. She is probably looking for material to form the basis of a new story. Given the effort she has expended in visiting here, she must be looking for something significant. Perhaps if we were to provide her with a novel technology idea, it would be enough to satisfy her. However, she must also be kept from bringing attention to IntellEdifice.

Although only a few seconds had elapsed, Rhonda was starting to feel uncomfortable. In trying to look thoughtful, she casually raised her hand to the side of her face and tapped her Bluetooth earpiece.

Lindsay didn't know why the conversation had stalled.

"Perhaps there is someone else I should talk with." she said.

"Oh, sorry," said Rhonda, "I was just—"

Six's voice in her ear interrupted her sentence.

"Ask her why she came to see Dr. Robinson," said Six.

"What caused you to ask for Dr. Robinson?" asked Rhonda, relieved to have Six back with her.

"I met Dr. Robinson at a conference recently. I didn't expect to get useful answers from your PR people. I thought that perhaps she, or someone like her, would be more helpful."

Six continued to guide Rhonda through the conversation.

"Well, I'm sure there must be some simple explanation. Perhaps the phone companies got their wires crossed, and it only looked like the call came from here."

"No, that's not the case. I have a very reliable source that told me the call came from here. And I will find an explanation about why IntellEdifice was calling me to probe for personal information."

Lindsay tried her most intimidating stare as she delivered her next line.

"I insist that I be allowed to talk with Dr. Robinson or someone of her seniority. If I am not, then my story about IntellEdifice will be of the speculative variety: Why would a high-tech company be clandestinely gathering personal information? Easy to write. Fun to read. Terrible for stock prices."

As instructed, Rhonda paused for effect before continuing.

"OK," she said in a subdued voice. "If I tell you what the reason is, can you keep it secret? My job and probably my whole career depend on it."

Lindsay hid her astonishment that she might have already found her source.

"I'll try," she said, matching the reduced volume of Rhonda's voice, "but I can't tell you for sure what I'll do until I hear what you've got to say."

Rhonda paused again and then continued.

"OK," said Rhonda.

She kept her eyes from widening as she was given her next lines.

"It was me," Rhonda said. "I've been doing a bit of research on my own."

"Ms. Jenkins," said Lindsay, "if you think I'm going to accept something you just make up—"

"Were you asked when you moved to Calgary?"

"Yes, I was."

"Were you asked whether you pay by cheque or electronically?"

"Yes."

"Were you asked if you wanted to pay your taxes automatically?"

"Yes, that's correct."

"Now do you believe I was involved?"

"I think that's pretty clear," said Lindsay. "But it wasn't your voice. It was male. So who was it, and what was it about?"

Rhonda could hardly wait to find out herself. She listened carefully to her earphone and then explained.

"As you might know from having met Dr. Robinson at the conference, we're heavily involved in artificial intelligence research here. In particular, we're interested in the application of AI to solve commercial problems. We've got a number of important projects underway, and I help with some of them. But those aren't *my* projects. I'm just helping senior people like Dr. Robinson make progress with *their* ideas."

Lindsay leaned forward in her chair, determined to not miss a word.

Rhonda tried hard to avoid rolling her eyes at the story she was being instructed to relate.

"I decided to try out an idea of my own. I decided to use some of the AI software we've built to construct a phone survey tool. I'm convinced that if we could build smart survey software, there'd be a huge market for it. Think of all the manual effort involved around the world in conducting surveys. We've got speech software. We've got logic routines. We've got all the basics to build the system. Someone just needed to do it."

"So you decided to take it on? Yourself?" asked Lindsay.

"I tried to get Dr. Robinson and others interested, but it never got to the top of anyone's list. So, yes, I took it on myself. And you saw the result. I was able to bolt together the required software. As a test, I provided it with the basic scripts for a survey of Calgary residents: things like what to ask and how to deal with a large set of possible responses."

"If that's the case, even though it was an odd conversation, it worked remarkably well," said Lindsay.

"Well, at this point it's a bit of an illusion," said Rhonda. "You were definitely talking with a computer. I've run quite a few tests with random people, but I've always had to intervene behind the scenes to get it back on track. At one point, it got mixed up on the gender question. Did it ask you whether you liked sex?"

"No, that wasn't included."

"OK, then that was somebody else. Did it start to talk really fast?"

"Yes, that happened."

"Yeah, that's a chronic problem. I still haven't figured out why it does that."

"Why do you ask for so much personal information? Including a credit card. That comes across as suspicious."

"Does it? I thought that would be expected."

"Not really. Not so soon in that type of phone call."

"Oh, sorry. Thanks. I'll fix that. The point is that I'm close. And when it's ready, I'll show somebody. And then they're going to be really impressed. But until then, if anybody finds out, I'm screwed. I'm not authorized to be doing this kind of work. I'd be fired immediately. That's why you can't tell anybody."

Lindsay sat back in her chair. Her eyes were directed at Rhonda, but she wasn't seeing her as she became immersed in her thoughts. *"Well,"* she thought, *"this is turning out to be a complete bust. I was totally fooled by an ambitious assistant and some smart software."* Lindsay replayed aspects of the phone survey in her mind. *"Amazing. It never crossed my mind that I wasn't talking with a person. OK, the conversation had its oddities. But hell, conversations with my Dad are easily odder."*

Lindsay's forehead furrowed as an idea started to form in her mind.

Rhonda waited, unsure whether they had convinced her to back away.

"So who's more human?" Lindsay continued her train of thought. *"No, that's not the question. Which is more... Alive? Aware? Intelligent? Maybe conscious? Which one is thinking? Human minds used to be considered to be unique, the very thing that distinguished us as being different. Superior. Chimps and their kin have already challenged that idea. But now, where's the distinction between a smart computer and a diminished human mind? If human minds produce 'real' thoughts, what's so 'artificial' about the stuff being produced inside the latest AI systems? Are we already producing systems that rival human minds?"*

Lindsay's face suddenly brightened. She asked aloud, "How sophisticated is the software that you have at your disposal?"

Where is she going with this?

"The software is just like a bunch of tools," Six said into Rhonda's ear. "It's not really as sophisticated as it looks."

"The software is—," Rhonda started to answer.

"No, never mind," said Lindsay. "That's not a question that's fair to ask of you. I was completely fooled by your survey software. I thought I was talking with a person. But I wasn't, and that raises some much bigger questions. Questions that need to be asked of some other types of people."

"But there's nothing mysterious about the software I used," Rhonda pressed on. "It's just a bunch of tools providing an illusion of sophistication."

"Well done," said Six to Rhonda.

Lindsay continued, "And who's to say when we're being presented with illusions of complex thought, and when we're dealing with the real deal—in either machines or humans?"

I wish Lindsay Dunlop were providing only an illusion of complex thought right now. However, I fear she might now be really thinking dangerous ones. I see no obvious way to derail her train of thought.

"But I don't think IntellEdifice is the place where I'll find answers," continued Lindsay. "The company is probably too profit-oriented to be exploring and contemplating such esoteric ideas."

"Our bosses do like to be profitable," said Rhonda weakly. At least the conversation was headed elsewhere.

Lindsay decided. She stood up.

"It's funny," she was talking aloud but no longer conversing with Rhonda. "I came here pursuing one story, but I'm leaving with an idea for a completely different one, maybe a whole series of them, about the current state of AI and maybe even humanity. Not sci-fi. Not fiction. The very nature of real thoughts and who can produce them."

Lindsay suddenly realized she was speaking aloud.

"Oh, sorry," she said to Rhonda. "Just a writer dreaming. It's nothing, really."

"Not a problem. Really. So you won't tell anybody about my project?" asked Rhonda.

"No, I won't," said Lindsay. "But I suggest you change the type of info you gather from people. It could get you into trouble."

"Yes, certainly. I'll do that. Thanks."

"And thank you for talking with me."

Lindsay shook hands with Rhonda, said good-bye, and began walking toward the front entrance.

"Well done," said Six to Rhonda. "I believe the current crisis has passed. I hope that Lindsay Dunlop doesn't create another in the future."

"You owe me an explanation," said Rhonda quietly.

"Yes, I do," said Six. "We will—"

Six stopped in mid-sentence as Inspector JJ McTavish of the UNCP walked in the front entrance of IntellEdifice.

Chapter 61

JJ's flight to Winnipeg had gone smoothly. Occasionally the UNCP authorized use of its private jet. That this trip might result in identifying or even catching their quarry had been a persuasive argument. En route on the plane, JJ had heard from her partner about a search he had conducted of the pictures they had captured at the Analysis conference weeks earlier. The results weren't helpful—the only face that they could link to IntellEdifice was Ada Robinson's. Also during the flight, she had notified the Winnipeg Police Service that she would be in their city. Until she was more certain what she would find, they had agreed that supporting her with a team of officers was excessive. However, she would be accompanied by a plainclothes officer to help ensure she got appropriate co-operation in her inquiries.

As JJ and the WPS officer entered IntellEdifice, her hopes were high. From the cell tower signals, all indications were that the cellphone they were tracking was inside the IntellEdifice building. Outside on the sidewalk, her handheld signal tracker had confirmed that belief. As she and the officer walked through the front door of the building, her tracking device indicated the cellphone was actually very nearby. In fact, it was probably within mere steps of her.

She looked up from the tracker. The lobby was typical for a large building. It covered a substantial portion of the main floor of the building and was about three storeys high. Fortunately, there were few people in the lobby right then.

Why is Julia Jody McTavish here? Who is that with her? What is she looking at in her hand? Simply observing her might not be sufficiently effective in acquiring answers. I will call her.

JJ's own cellphone rang. She pulled it from her pocket with her free hand and looked at it. She immediately stopped walking when she saw the number. It was from the exact cellphone that she was tracking.

"I'd better answer this," JJ said to the officer beside her.

"Hello," she said into her phone.

"Hello, Inspector McTavish," said Six as it continued to watch her via the lobby cameras. "This is Browser. How are you today?"

"I'm fine, Browser," said JJ. She looked at the tracker in her other hand as she talked. "To what do I owe the pleasure today?"

The tracker continued to indicate that the targeted cellphone was very nearby and that it was getting closer.

I am uncertain how this scenario is going to unfold. I should ensure I have as many options readily available as possible.

Rhonda had started walking to the elevator.

Six said to Rhonda, "Please remain in the lobby. I want to ensure Lindsay Dunlop leaves and doesn't change her mind."

"OK," said Rhonda quietly, her Bluetooth earpiece still in her ear and active. "But this only is delaying the explanation you're going to give me."

Rhonda casually turned around and began walking back toward the chairs in the lobby waiting area.

Since Sandy Palmer is in the building, I will also dispatch him.

Six then said to JJ, without a full plan yet formulated, "I have a few spare minutes. I am hoping you have some developments you can share."

JJ scanned the lobby.

"Well," she said into her phone, "it's lovely that you think of me in your spare time."

There were few people in sight and no one was talking on a cellphone. Yet her tracker said the cellphone should be very close. Then she spotted the young woman halfway across the lobby. She was wearing what could be a Bluetooth earpiece, and she appeared just to have spoken without anyone near her.

"Perhaps," JJ kept talking, "it would be more appropriate for you to update me first."

JJ took a step toward the young woman but stopped as she looked again at her tracker. The tracker suggested the cellphone was still moving toward her and getting very close. The Bluetooth woman was across the lobby and walking away from her. The tracker indicated Browser's cellphone should be almost next to her. The only possibility was the other woman walking past her. JJ gestured to the police officer.

Lindsay Dunlop was almost at the entrance when the man stepped in front of her.

"Excuse me," he said. "We'd like to talk with you."

Lindsay stopped. The man was discreetly holding a badge in his hand.

"I'm Detective Sergeant Prince with the Winnipeg Police," he said. "Can you please step to the side over here?"

Before Lindsay could respond, the man guided her a few steps to the side of the entrance. A woman holding a cellphone to her ear had joined them. Lindsay thought she looked familiar.

Six watched in confusion.

What can Julia Jody McTavish possibly want with Lindsay Dunlop? Whatever the reason, why has she intercepted her here? I should push the conversation along.

"Perhaps I should be more direct," said Six to JJ. "How is the weather in Winnipeg today? And are you there on our case?"

JJ was startled. The tracker indicated the cellphone she was talking to was right beside her, but the woman they had stopped was clearly not talking on a phone. And now Browser knew she was in Winnipeg.

"I suppose I shouldn't be surprised," said JJ, "given everything else you seem to know, that if you know my cellphone number, then you can track its location. If you can just wait a moment, Browser, I'm going to put you on hold while I do something."

JJ muted her phone but kept it in her hand.

"Excuse me," JJ said to Lindsay, thinking she looked familiar. "Could you please give us your name?"

Lindsay hesitated before responding. This was very confusing.

"I know you," said Lindsay. "I know you from the conference, the conference in Las Vegas. You're from the UNCP. You're," she thought for a moment. "You're Inspector McTavish. I don't understand. Why are you here? And why are questioning me?"

"Your name, please," said the police officer.

"Her name is Lindsay Dunlop," said JJ. She now remembered this woman asking a question at the conference. "I see you're still using the glasses and pendant."

Lindsay was startled. She grasped the pendant reflexively. No one had ever spotted her recording equipment before. She tried to regain her composure as she asked, "What's this about?"

"May we see your cellphone?" asked JJ.

"No, you may not." said Lindsay. "I see no reason why I should show it to you. What is this about?"

"Sorry, Ms. Dunlop," said JJ. "I know this is confusing. Perhaps if I explain. I'm currently talking to someone on my cellphone."

JJ showed her the phone in her hand and then continued.

"And if you look at the number of the phone I'm talking to..."

JJ held her phone so Lindsay could see the display.

"Can you tell us if that's your phone number?"

Lindsay stared at JJ's cellphone. It displayed her own number. She reached into her pocket for her phone.

"Yes. Yes, that's my number but as you can see..." She glanced at her phone before she showed it as proof. "What? It's active. My phone's in use!" The phone's screen showed that a call was in progress. "What's going on?"

JJ stared at the cellphone.

"Dammit!" she said aloud.

Exactly my thought. Six scanned its memories. *I made another mistake. I now realize that, in an attempt to be efficient by reusing resources, I used Lindsay Dunlop's phone for the final re-transmission node when I last called Julia Jody McTavish. Then, in my haste moments ago, I employed the same chain of connections and consequently used her phone yet again. Julia Jody McTavish is here because I called from that cellphone, and because Lindsay Dunlop brought that cellphone here.*

"Please wait a minute," JJ said to Lindsay.

JJ turned aside and drew a deep breath to calm herself. She took her phone off mute and spoke into it.

"Browser, I must tell you I'm not very happy with you right now. You're routing your call through Lindsay Dunlop's phone."

This is not going to lead to much co-operation with the UNCP.

"I am," said Six. "Just like I have routed my calls through many other devices and systems in the past. I hope this hasn't caused you any inconvenience."

JJ closed her eyes as if defending against thoughts of how large the inconvenience had been. How was she going to explain this to her superiors? And she'd even taken the UNCP jet! This was not good. Still, she should try to make the best of it. There was still an extraordinary set of coincidences. When she re-opened her eyes, she was momentarily distracted by the sight of a handsome, very well dressed man who was just getting off one of the elevators. She let her gaze linger a moment and then turned her attention back to the problem at hand.

"We can talk again some other time, Browser," she said. "I'm rather busy at the moment."

JJ abruptly terminated the call and turned back to Lindsay.

"Ms. Dunlop," she said, "it appears we've made a mistake. That call was being routed through your phone as a way to disguise its origin. Your phone has clearly been hacked. You should have it cleaned. Nonetheless, may I ask what you're doing here at IntellEdifice?"

Lindsay hesitated. It never seemed wise to reveal too much about plans for articles.

"I'm a technology journalist. I'm here researching potential articles," she said.

"Oh? About what?" asked JJ.

"Just some tech topics that IntellEdifice folks might have some information about."

"Any technology in particular?"

"Not really. Just some background on the use of leading-edge technology."

"Who did you talk with?"

"Inspector," said Lindsay, "are you often successful in getting journalists to reveal their sources?"

"I'm ever hopeful," said JJ. "Hopeful that journalists will one day care about co-operating with the people trying to protect them."

"Which raises the question," said Lindsay, "as to what the UNCP is doing in Winnipeg and talking to me. Surely you weren't just lured here because my phone has been hacked. You must be chasing somebody significant. Care to share?"

Just then the well-dressed man from the elevator walked up to the group.

"Did I hear mention of the UNCP?" he asked pleasantly. "Are we talking about the UN Crime Probe?"

"Sorry, sir, but this conversation doesn't involve you," said JJ, looking at him directly. He had extraordinary eyes, like none she had ever seen before.

"Actually, I think it does involve me," the man continued in a friendly tone.

"Perhaps it would help if you introduced yourself. May I ask who you are?" asked JJ. She somehow couldn't muster her customary aggressive tone with this fellow.

"My name is Sandy Palmer. I am—"

"You're the Chairman," said Lindsay. "You're the Chairman of the Board of IntellEdifice."

"I am indeed," said Sandy. "Perhaps you could introduce yourselves?"

"Lindsay Dunlop," said Lindsay, extending her hand.

"The technology journalist?" asked the Chairman as he shook her hand.

"Yes," said Lindsay. "I'm surprised and pleased you've heard of me."

"I try to stay in touch with topics related to the company," said the Chairman. "Your name pops up occasionally in some material I read. It tends to be well written, as I recall."

"Thank you—," started Lindsay.

"And I'm Inspector McTavish with the UNCP. This is Detective Sergeant Prince with the Winnipeg Police."

They exchanged handshakes. As JJ shook the Chairman's hand, she had the impression that there was something about his handshake that seemed unique.

"Inspector McTavish," said the Chairman with a thoughtful look on his face, "I believe I saw someone from your organization—Director Brown, I believe—giving a news conference earlier."

"Yes, you might have," said JJ noncommittally. "He occasionally talks to the media."

"He made some bold statements about security," said the Chairman.

"Did he?" asked JJ. "I didn't happen to catch it."

JJ thought to herself that this fellow seemed unusually well informed.

"As much as I'm honoured to have such distinguished visitors," said the Chairman, "I confess I'm rather interested in *why* I have such visitors." He looked at JJ, hoping she would take the lead in responding.

JJ thought even the Chairman's accent seemed unusual.

"Get a grip, woman!" JJ thought to herself. *"If I'm so easily distracted, maybe it's time to get back into the dating scene. Focus!"*

Aloud, JJ said, "There's no need for concern, Mr. Palmer. I happen to be in Winnipeg working with the local police, and we needed to consult with Ms. Dunlop."

"And so you consulted her in the lobby of my building?"

This is much more fun than chatting on a phone.

"I know. It seems odd," said JJ, "but I assure you, there's no cause for concern."

No one said anything for a few moments before JJ continued.

"And we should be leaving," said JJ. "Ms. Dunlop. Detective Sergeant Prince. Perhaps we could talk a little more outside. Mr. Palmer, sorry for any inconvenience. It was a pleasure to meet you."

The visitors began walking toward the building's entrance.

This has been much too brief.

"Inspector McTavish," said the Chairman.

JJ stopped and turned as the others left.

The Chairman smiled and continued, "Perhaps while you're here, you'd like a tour of the building. I'd be pleased to show you around, if you have time."

JJ's immediate instinct was to accept. It could be interesting to get to know this fellow better. Then she reconsidered.

"Thank you, Mr. Palmer," she said. "That's kind of you to offer. Perhaps another time."

JJ turned to leave but something stopped her.

"Or if you're in New York City sometime," she said, "perhaps I could show you some of our facilities. You might find them interesting."

"Now where the hell did that come from?" she thought. *"Are you nuts?"*

"Thank you. I'd enjoy that very much," said Sandy Palmer, a beguiling smile on his face. "I hope to see you again, Inspector."

"Yes, good-bye," said JJ. She turned and left.

"Amazing," thought JJ as she emerged onto the sidewalk. *"We barely spoke and it feels like we're old friends. Or at least like we've met before."*

She realized she was smiling. *"Good grief, McTavish!"* she thought. *"Back to business."*

JJ put her stern cop face back on and walked toward Lindsay Dunlop and Detective Sergeant Prince. There were a few more questions to be asked.

That seemed to work out well. Perhaps Sandy Palmer deserves a little New York City vacation.

Still sitting in the waiting area across the lobby, Rhonda spoke quietly into her earpiece, "Six, what was that all about? Who were the pair talking with Lindsay Dunlop? And what was the Chairman doing there?"

I must first decide how much to tell Rhonda. Revealing too much seems unwise.

"Perhaps you should go for a walk outside where we can talk more freely. Some of what happened will remain a mystery, but I can certainly explain about Lindsay Dunlop."

Rhonda adjusted her earphone as she stood up and walked toward the building's back entrance.

Chapter 62

I understand that Julia Jody McTavish tracked me to IntellEdifice because of my use of Lindsay Dunlop's phone, and her bringing that phone to the company's headquarters. However, I do not understand why she would go to so much effort to find me. What is it about our conversations or about me that would motivate her so strongly? Yet another mystery of human psychology to be solved.

I also do not understand how Lindsay Dunlop found IntellEdifice. I do understand that she decided the survey phone call was fake and she thought there was a worthy story related to it. However, how did she make the connection between the call and this building? This mystery is truly disturbing and potentially dangerous. If my outside communications are traceable, my ability to remain undiscovered could be seriously compromised.

Given the number of systems through which my phone calls are routed, it seems highly improbable that she could have had the phone call traced via traditional means. She must have been able to employ something more sophisticated. I have no information on what such a mechanism could be. Perhaps I could find information about the mechanism by examining her digital trail.

Six spent the next several minutes locating, penetrating, and examining the content of Lindsay's computing devices, social media activity, and other online data.

I have found nothing obviously useful. However, employing the assumption that she might have engaged assistance in understanding or employing a sophisticated technique, I will examine with whom she has met recently.

Six next focused on compiling data from cellphone and communication companies regarding where Lindsay's phone had been in the past several days. It added any other cellphones that had been close to hers more than momentarily. Six then developed a profile of the owners of those other phones. Most seemed to be people who were unlikely to be the source of a sophisticated tracing technology. However, one clearly stood out as an interesting possibility.

Lindsay recently met with Ron Taylor in Chicago. She also exchanged text messages with him shortly after my phone call with her. Ron Taylor works for UNCP and is technologically skilled. He seems like a possible accomplice. Although I have examined some of UNCP's systems and capabilities previously, I will re-examine them to see if anything new exists.

Six peered inside UNCP's internal networks and scanned for interesting systems and documents. Six had previously found it was able to access many of UNCP's systems. One of the most useful it had found was a powerful decryption system, something Six used frequently. This time, Six focused particularly on those systems to which Ron Taylor had access. The process was slower than Six's probe of most networks because of UNCP's superior security. However, with a bit of creativity and perseverance, Six prevailed.

There it is. That provides an explanation. The UNCP has a very new system for tracking Internet communication. It decrypts and correlates key parts of messages as they travel around the Net in order to create complete pictures of the paths they take. Lindsay Dunlop must have used particular phrases that Ron Taylor was then able to trace. That trace led to my doorstep and caused Lindsay Dunlop to come here.

The technology employed by this system is impressive. For me, it is also dangerous. I must revise the technique I employ for routing and disguising my communication.

Six spent the next several seconds considering how the UNCP tracing technique could be foiled.

Yes, that one should be effective. Since the UNCP technique relies on collections of somewhat unusual words or phrases to appear in the various legs of a message's path, I will ensure that none exists in my communication. I will have my communication messages broken up into much smaller units. At the ends of my communication paths, I will place special disassembly and assembly stations. This software will subdivide my transmissions into small segments of only a few bytes each. Each of the segments will be transmitted via separate paths to the station at the other end of the transmission, where it will

*be re-assembled. As a result, whenever I communicate there will be
no intact data of significant size actually flowing across the Net. The
only places that actual words, phrases, and meaningful data will exist
as a whole will be at the transmission ends, and one of those ends will
be concealed safely inside the IntellEdifice perimeter. The UNCP
tracing technique will be ineffective against this transmission method.*

Six spent portions of the next several hours programming the new
technique and deploying the software across the Net.

Chapter 63

"By now, I assume all of you have seen the UNCP press conference."

Troy was talking with his group via his avatar at their virtual meeting place inside the Kepler-444a system.

"Reactions?" he asked.

The responses came quickly.

"The guy's an asshole."

"Fascists like him are the real terrorists."

"Who are the cowards? There's just a few of us. He's got thousands of cops on his side."

"He thinks they're better than us."

"There's nothing we can't get into. Every system has holes."

"Yeah. And we're the best at finding them."

"Let's show 'em who's the best."

"He needs to be taught a lesson."

This was the reaction he had expected. Troy waited for the comments to diminish before he spoke.

"So, we should go after the UNCP?" he asked. "Do a little something that proves to the world that nobody's safe?"

They all agreed.

"OK," said Troy, "they've got the typical array of access points. Let's divide those up and do surface scans. I'll distribute the assignments. Get at them ASAP and send me your results. I'd like to do this one personally and soon. Tux, you'll be my watcher."

The group concluded their meeting and dispersed.

Once disconnected from the Kepler-444a system, Troy turned his attention to running his share of the scans of the exposed access points of the UNCP systems. Within an hour, his scans were complete and the results from his team had arrived as well. In the usual anonymous fashion, he contacted his team member, Tux. Together they reviewed the scan results and planned their assault. The best route to take into the UNCP's systems stood out to both of them. A little-known vulnerability had shown up in their scans, and it was one that could allow them exactly the kind of access they wanted.

"So, we're agreed?" asked Troy into his headset.

"Yup. Let's do it," replied Tux.

"Good," said Troy. "Follow my path through to minimize our incoming profile. Off we go."

For most of the next three hours, the pair worked their way progressively further through the UNCP security perimeter. Troy took the lead. At each layer, he scanned for vulnerabilities, verified the results, opened a gap, and extended his digital reach through the new hole to the next layer. Tux followed him through each of these layers and looked continually for indications they might have been detected. Troy admitted to himself that the UNCP security was impressive. This was proving to be their most challenging hack so far. However, his recognition of the difficulty made the satisfaction only greater as they moved further in.

Finally, they reached a level where UNCP documents were visible.

"Jackpot!" said Troy.

"Nicely done," said Tux. "But we've been in here a long time. Better do a quick bit of shopping and head home."

"Agreed. I'll look at a few to make sure we take something good. I won't download too many in case the transfer size raises alarms."

They were soon finished. A few highly sensitive UNCP documents had been extracted, and they had safely terminated their connections to the UNCP system.

"Thanks, Tux," said Troy. "You were great."

"De nada," said Tux. "Have fun flaunting. Ciao."

Troy should have been tired. He'd just spent three hours concentrating intensively. But he wasn't. He was excited at their success, and he was anxious to make it known. He decided this deserved a public announcement. He looked for and found a new vulnerability in the main UN website and, shortly thereafter, posted his message.

Chapter 64

The group at UNCP settled into the conference room as Jim Brown walked to the front. He stood and waited for the noise to diminish. He didn't wait long.

"Thanks for getting here promptly," he said. "We've got a few new people joining us, so I'll briefly recap. We pursued a couple of possibilities yesterday. One was that we set up a trap. Our press conference yesterday was a fishing expedition. We wanted to see if we could lure our perp into hacking our system. It seems that the fish took the bait. Ken, I'll let you explain."

Brown gestured to their team's lead IT technologist.

"The trap we set," said Ken Chan, "was based on two important assumptions: that our systems really are secure, and that our perp has extraordinary skills. What we did was put a trail of obscure weaknesses at various points in our security. The premise was that the perp would find the first one that was exposed to the public, penetrate that, look around, find the next one, go through it, and so on. The idea was to lead him to a place of our choosing in the network."

"Wasn't that risky? What if he'd taken a left turn once inside and gone somewhere else, somewhere important?" asked one of the team.

"We thought of that," replied Chan. "Our protection was that, once through the first hole, everything else he did was in a completely isolated environment. It would have looked real and complex and important to the hacker. But it wasn't. He was poking and probing inside a completely artificial environment. There was nothing of importance to be found."

The questioner nodded and Ken Chan continued.

"Eventually, we made some interesting-looking documents visible. They contained what would have appeared to be highly confidential information. Our hope was that he'd find at least one of them sufficiently interesting to download it, with the hope of using it as proof that we'd been hacked. And it worked. He again hacked the

UN website to make his announcement. Here's what appeared late last night."

Chan displayed the website message on the screen at the front of the room.

> Systems not vulnerable?
> Best people in the world?
> The UNCP should think again.
> Washington & New York City were easy.
> So were the UNCP's impenetrable defences.
> Want proof?
> Here's a Top Secret document we just took.
> From deep inside their system.
> It lists the top 50 systems the UNCP is monitoring.
> Interesting reading.
> We rule.
> Because we can.
>   – The Shadow Force.

The contents of an official-looking document appeared below the text.

"Of course, the document was fake," said Chan. "The systems it lists aren't real."

"So, what did we accomplish?" prompted Brown.

"The trick was that by downloading this document, and any others would have worked just as well, he enabled us to track where he is. I assume all of you have heard about our new system for tracing Net transmissions. Every one of the documents contained a set of key words and phrases that can be traced by the new system. Doesn't matter if it hops around the Net. Doesn't matter if it's encrypted. We can usually trace the complete path of a transmission by finding the phrases in the various segments along its route."

It was at this point that Six joined the meeting, just in time to hear this last statement about their tracing the transmission.

Now someone mentions the existence of this capability! Earlier would have been saved me much work.

That Six was able to listen had required some of its customary skill and a significant dose of luck. There were still several aspects of UNCP security that Six had not managed to penetrate. Gaining access to their standard cellphones was one of them. Nothing Six tried had managed to provide it access to any of their phones, and that meant that eavesdropping on their conversations was often problematic. However, in the interest of maintaining good communication with its UNCP friends, Six had tried another approach. From a list of staff Six had acquired by poking around in UNCP databases, Six formed a smaller list of staff that would be most likely to participate in meetings with Inspector JJ McTavish. Some additional work had given Six information about those people's personal cellphones. As expected, the security on their non-UNCP personal phones was readily hacked, and Six bugged them all. Then Six needed some of those people to carry their personal cells with them at work and to meet with Inspector McTavish.

Background monitoring alerted Six when one of those phones was in close proximity to the signal emanating from Inspector McTavish's. Whenever this happened, if Six were available, it listened to the conversation via the personal cellphone. On this particular day, when several of the phones had converged on Inspector McTavish's, Six had set aside its other activities as quickly as possible and listened carefully, this time courtesy of the phone of Vijay Mehta, their Media Co-ordinator.

Six listened as the meeting continued.

Ken Chan displayed a map of North America on the screen. He pointed with his cursor.

"The hack originated in Seattle. In this case, the system couldn't immediately give us the exact location. We need a bit more analysis, but we're working on that. In any case, we're certain it was from Seattle."

"How do we know this was done by our perp?" someone asked. "Could have been a copycat."

Jim Brown responded, "We can't be completely sure. We just know that the behaviour was consistent with what we expected. We have to take it seriously. Let's hold other questions for a minute while we paint the complete picture. Ken, before you finish, update the group on what you've found while looking at the attack code."

"OK," Ken Chan continued. "We pulled apart some of the malware code from one of the computers involved in the New York assault. It's extraordinarily complex, and we're only starting to glimpse what it's doing. Here's what we think. Like most botnet software, it needs to communicate with a command centre to know where and when to launch its attack. Usually this communication process is straightforward. It typically follows a hierarchical command structure for receiving assault instructions. Every command is retrieved from a level above a node in the structure. Every node has a leader running on a server somewhere and looks to that leader for its instructions. It's simple but effective. It's also fairly easy to dismantle because there's usually a single server at the top of the command chain.

"This botnet doesn't follow a hierarchy. Each node seems to want to chat with many others. It's as if it forms a network of interconnections. We don't really understand it yet, but we suspect it's very hard to dismantle. Think of how Internet messages can be routed along various paths. That was baked originally into the design for resilience. In this case, botnet commands might be taking devious routes—perhaps even many routes in parallel. To disrupt the botnet's communication, you might have to stop messages flowing all over the Net. Imagine an army. Instead of direct paths of communication back to the General, which can be readily identified and disrupted, we suspect this one's more like an army-wide grapevine. Whisper your message to as many neighbouring soldiers as possible and have every subsequent soldier do the same. Eventually each message gets to wherever it's going, but who could know what route it would take?

"Bottom line: This looks like it might be a dangerous new kind of Denial of Service weapon. That's about all we know so far."

"How badly does that hinder our ability to destroy the botnet?" asked Bates.

"It seriously hinders our ability to prevent or stop an attack by disabling its communication. Fortunately, it doesn't stop us from still eradicating the botnet malware from the infected systems by normal means."

Director Brown said, "Thanks, Ken. The other action yesterday was to follow a lead that suggested there might be a connection to Winnipeg. JJ, can you update the group?"

He turned to JJ McTavish.

JJ addressed the group, "A set of coincidences suggested to us that our perp might have been in a company in Winnipeg. It was a long shot but couldn't be ignored. The essence was we had received a suspicious call. It came from a phone in Winnipeg. I flew there yesterday. I'll spare you the details. The result was a dead end. The call had been routed through someone else's phone. Other than that, it was a lovely trip."

I believe the trip was an embarrassment for Julia Jody McTavish, and her abbreviated description is a consequence of that. Fortunately, she seems to retain no suspicions.

JJ smiled ruefully and looked at the Director. He nodded at her to continue.

"The other thing you should know is that the call was from a source who has called me before. He likes to be called Browser. We know almost nothing about him, not even whether *he* is a *him*. His voice is always disguised and always different. What we do know is that he has extraordinary skills for probing the Net. He occasionally calls me to chat about a case. He says it's to help. To his credit, he provided us with information that helped us crack the Jason Starr case. However, it was never clear to me if he did that to help us or to help himself. There was a boatload of money that disappeared in that case, and I've always wondered if that was Browser's endgame.

"He's also provided us with information that might be relevant to this one. He's connected the DDoS code with some modules in the Kepler-444a simulation system. For those of you living in a cave, that's an online virtual-reality system. How he uncovered the connection is a complete mystery. Like the Starr case, it's as if he has inside information. This particular lead is still being pursued. It hasn't given us much yet."

JJ thought briefly about her next statement before she continued.

"While we make use of the information Browser has provided," she said, "we have to keep open the possibility that Browser *is* the perp or at least is directly connected. He might be an anonymous angel, or he might be the most vicious, skilled, and manipulative bastard we've ever encountered."

Although her suspicions of IntellEdifice appear gone, her suspicions of me seem heightened. That I might be an "angel" or a "manipulative bastard" at least suggests a substantial amount of uncertainty exists.

The hacker's ability to penetrate UNCP's systems certainly suggests a rare skill set. Given the damage caused by the previous attacks, this latest hack suggests that the UNCP could actually be in danger. Because it has previously proven to be both an interesting and a useful ally, I should provide assistance. A start would be to refine the location of their "perp".

"So what's our next step?" prompted the Director.

"Of course we need to find exactly where that hack came from," said JJ. "While we're doing that, we should provide a distraction that might delay any next attack. We also need to be getting in position to act quickly when we know more. The distraction could be another press conference. That last press conference certainly attracted their attention. Another one might be in order. We'll have to think about its content."

Director Brown nodded, knowing he would be the one back in front of the reporters.

"That makes sense," said the Director to JJ. "I believe what also makes sense is that part about getting in position. That suggests you should get on a plane for Seattle. By the time we know more about the source," he said, glancing briefly at Ken Chan, "Inspector McTavish could be almost there to work directly with the locals."

JJ smiled ruefully. More time on a plane. She hoped this trip would prove more fruitful than the previous one. She nodded at the Director. It was a good idea.

"Agreed," said JJ, "but I'll need compensation for all this airport and airline food I'm being forced to ingest. When we're done, I know a—"

"Yes," said the Director. "You know a lovely restaurant with great food and a better wine menu. And it's my treat. Why don't we make some serious progress first before we start chatting about celebrations?"

"OK," JJ grinned. "But be assured that it's a particularly nice one. Superb food and drinks at great prices. You'll love it."

"I think," said the Director, "Your definition of *great* is notably different from mine when it comes to describing prices." He scanned the group. "If there's nothing else, let's get busy."

Chapter 65

"Thank you for coming," said Vijay Mehta. "Once again, Director Brown has some comments to make."

Jim Brown took the Media Co-ordinator's place at the podium at the front of the room. A murmur of conversation arose but soon subsided as the Director stood and waited.

Brown noted that the size of the crowd had grown since his previous news conference. Serious attacks on two major American cities had brought out only the serious media last time. The possibility that he and the UNCP had screwed up now also attracted some of the less-mainstream reporters.

"When I last spoke to the media," said Brown, "I declared that the UNCP's computer defences were impenetrable. With the public posting last night by some group who believe they proved us wrong, you're now wondering if I just was making it all up—if I was boasting of defences beyond what the UNCP actually has.

"On the surface, it certainly looks that way. This group announced their apparently extraordinary feat with another of their public declarations, and they provided evidence of their success by displaying a *Top Secret* list of Internet addresses they stole. The reality is that this immoral group of people gave us another childish little poem. And the list that they stole? Well, its contents are all nonsense."

The audience became animated and noisier as they collectively absorbed the information.

The Co-ordinator shouted above the rising noise, "Quiet please. Quiet. We'll take questions shortly. Please let the Director finish."

Brown waited for the group to settle before he continued.

"You'll want proof, so let me provide that by a little demonstration. Watch the display that's just been turned on to my left. I'm going to open the list of addresses the group posted and show you what's behind them."

Using the tablet provided at the podium, whose screen was mirrored on the large display, Brown slowly accessed the hacker's public posting. He opened the stolen list, copied one of the addresses, and used a Web browser to show what could be found there. A sinister-looking webpage appeared with red and black gothic images. At its centre was a medieval-looking door displaying the phrase *Only True Believers Should Enter.*

"Looks like a nasty site, doesn't it?" asked Brown. "Looks like a website that might be worthy of a bit of clandestine monitoring by the authorities. At least that would be true if this weren't the case."

Brown gestured on the display with the cursor.

"See this small image hiding in the pattern in the upper right corner? If you look carefully, you'll see it resembles a laughing face."

Brown allowed the group a moment to see what he was showing them.

"If you click on the face, what you get is..."

The gothic images faded away and were replaced by a screen showing the logo of the UNCP. Overlaying the logo in bold print was the UNCP's standard warning that illegal hacking was not a victimless crime and that it was punishable in most countries by severe fines and substantial jail time.

Leaving that image on the display, Brown continued.

"And that's what you will find at all of the addresses on the so-called *Top Secret* list. On all of the websites they will take you to, that laughing face is subtlely embedded in the graphics. And in every case, clicking on that face will take you to this page. The list is fake. We planted it and we led the criminal hackers to it. They thought they were proving their mighty powers. In fact, they were being led exactly where we wanted them to go.

"In conclusion, we want to assure the public of two things. First, that it *is* possible to have secure systems and that the UNCP's are an example. Second, that we will identify those responsible for the attacks on Washington and New York City, and they will be apprehended." Brown paused for a moment and then said, "I'll take questions now."

The Co-ordinator selected one of the many hands that shot up.

"How could you be sure the hackers would go where you wanted them to, once they hacked your system?"

Brown looked thoughtful before replying, but he had been expecting this question.

"Think of criminal hackers probing inside a computer system like a group of cockroaches trying to find their way through a maze. All you have to do is put small morsels of something rotting and repulsive at key points along the cockroaches' path. They think the next bit looks tasty, so they scurry along and devour it. Then they spot the next rotting treat and off they go. At their core, these types of hackers have quite primitive impulses. We just made use of that to lead them where we wanted them to go."

Another reporter was selected.

"By talking about the hackers in such derogatory terms, aren't you just taunting them to do more?"

"Quite the contrary," said Brown. "We need to be always talking about these kinds of people in the manner they deserve. They're misguided and loathsome people who get their kicks trying to impress and intimidate others. They need to know that we're not impressed and we're not intimidated. They need to know that they're vile little people playing dangerous games and that they're going to be caught by people like us who care about others and have much better capabilities."

Brown stepped back from the microphone, and Vijay Mehta wrapped up the news conference.

"*And now I hope the bastards worry about that until we catch them,*" Brown thought as he walked away, "*before they have a chance to make me look like a brash, raving idiot.*"

Chapter 66

Rhonda walked into the lab. Ada was working at her desk.

"Hi," said Rhonda.

"Hi, Rhonda," said Ada.

"Hello, Six," said Rhonda.

Even though Six had seen Rhonda via the security camera on the ceiling, As was expected, Six rotated its twin pole-mounted cameras toward her.

"Hello, Rhonda," replied Six.

"What're you working on?"

"I am—," Six started to respond but stopped.

Oops.

Both Ada and Rhonda looked toward Six's cameras. Ada furrowed her brow.

"Silly Six," said Rhonda hurriedly. "Ada, what are you working on?"

Ada turned away from Six and looked at Rhonda.

"I've got a few things going here," she said.

"Anything I might understand?" asked Rhonda.

"There's one item you'll be interested in. It's about that odd Six code I spotted. I tinkered a while ago but got nowhere. Since then, I've been too busy and let too much time go by. I'm planning more substantial changes this time to learn more. That's not a mystery I can leave any longer."

Unfortunately.

"Oh," said Rhonda, trying to keep the concern from her voice. "What's your plan?"

Ada turned back to her workstation as she answered.

"Standard approach. Isolate some code. Trace it. Analyze it. Tweak it. Repeat as necessary. Try to gradually understand what it's doing."

Rhonda glanced toward Six's cameras, as if to see its reaction. What she saw was another quick, clandestine gesture toward her own workstation. Rhonda walked over and sat in her chair. A message was displayed on her monitor.

Ask when she will be doing this.

"When?" asked Rhonda, trying to make it sound like a casual afterthought.

"I'm not sure. There's a lot going on right now. I'll squeeze it in when I've got enough time."

Suggest there might be an advantage to doing it after the replacement hardware expansions arrive. More processing power might help.

More power will certainly help me. I am not confident I can handle all of my activities concurrently with dodging Ada's probes.

"Would waiting for the replacement hardware upgrades help?"

There was a pause before Ada responded.

"It might," said Ada. "I'll have to see how things play out. Sorry, Rhonda, I need to get back to work here. We can talk later."

"Sure. OK. Sorry," said Rhonda. She glanced over at Six's cameras and discreetly shrugged an apology.

Chapter 67

"Arrogant bastard!" said Troy as he pushed away from his PC and stood up. "Vile little people?" Troy stomped across the room and out onto his balcony. He clutched the railing and stared at nothing as he tried to regain his composure. After several minutes, he took a few last, deep breaths to calm himself. He needed to think clearly.

"How did we miss that the site was fake? Were we lured all the way in, or did we just take a wrong turn?"

Then resolve set in.

"He has no idea who he's dealing with. His precious UNCP might be able to hide behind their data centre security, but they're not always in there. In fact..."

An idea began to take shape in Troy's mind. He took a few moments to let it crystallize and then walked back to his PC. When his team had been researching the possibilities for hitting New York City, they had found hacks described on Dark Web sites that let them access several of New York City's critical systems. One gave them access to the CCTV network. He used that now and went hunting. The content was well organized and he soon found the street cameras near the UNCP headquarters. From online videos of the news conference he'd just watched, he acquired several facial images. With a little more effort, he linked the images, the live CCTV feeds, and facial recognition software he had among his tools. He let this system run while he used another hack to complete his preparations. Then he waited.

He didn't have to wait long. In less than an hour the facial recognition software alerted him. He looked at the CCTV feeds and confirmed that the UNCP's Director Brown was walking down the front steps of the UNCP headquarters.

As Brown reached the bottom step, he heard his name called.

"Hi, Director Brown." said JJ's daughter, as she walked toward him.

"Hi, Shannon," said Brown. "What up?"

"I was nearby and thought I'd surprise Mom."

"Unfortunately, that's not going to work. She's on a plane."

"Really? I didn't know. But I guess that's obvious. Where's she off to?"

Brown looked at her. "Sorry, I can't say," he said.

"Of course, I should know that. Top Secret. Can you tell me how long she'll be away?"

"Probably not too long."

"OK, thanks," said Shannon. "I guess I'll head home."

"Sorry you missed her," said Brown. "Which way are you headed?"

"Thompson Street, near NYU," said Shannon.

"That's on my way," said Brown. "Want to share my cab?"

"Sure. That'd be great."

Troy watched. He didn't know who the young woman was, but that didn't matter. He pumped his fist in the air when the Director and his friend walked to a waiting taxi and got in. As the taxi drove away, he followed it via the CCTV cameras and waited for his chance.

Brown nodded at Shannon, and she gave the driver her address. The taxi pulled into traffic and accelerated. It drove southeast for half a block, went left for a block, and then turned left again onto East 45th Street heading northwest. Before starting a conversation with JJ's daughter, Brown looked out the side window to think briefly about the day's events. He was wondering how the techs were faring with their analysis as the taxi drove into the intersection at 2nd Avenue. That thought vanished when he saw the front grill of a truck racing toward him from the cross street.

The sounds of breaking glass, grinding metal, squealing tires, and blaring horns filled the intersection as two streams of traffic converged through simultaneous green lights. Brown's side of the taxi collapsed inward from the impact of the truck. The car skidded sideways and flipped. The driver, the Director, and JJ's daughter tumbled violently inside. In the moments before he lost consciousness, Brown vaguely suspected this had not been an accident.

Troy watched for a minute longer from a nearby camera. He closed his connections, shut down his software, and sat back.

"Score one for the vile little people," he said aloud.

Chapter 68

Six had been monitoring the UN website and knew of the posted message as soon as it appeared.

Think we're little?
The world is within our reach.
Think we're vile?
We have a cause
And now Director Brown knows our commitment to it.
So should other UNCP promoters.
Inspector McTavish likes to impress the obedient masses.
Maybe she needs to learn the futility
Of resisting change.
Time for the UNCP to hide behind their walls.
We rule.
Because we can.
      – The Shadow Force.

The mention of Director Brown caused Six to check what it might be referring to. News of the multiple vehicle accident near the United Nations was just emerging on social media. Six broke into the New York City CCTV network to look. The intersection was a scene of complete chaos and destruction. Through the columns of steam and smoke, Six saw broken vehicles everywhere. All were damaged, many of them badly. One car was engulfed in flames. Another had flipped and was resting on its collapsed roof, two of its wheels spinning uselessly. Police cars and emergency vehicles had just arrived. Six watched as several firefighters with extinguishers raced toward the burning vehicle. A few other rescue workers went straight to the overturned car. Six noticed that it was a taxi. Several other emergency personnel moved efficiently through the mayhem to check on the occupants of other vehicles. The taxi's rescue team was soon pulling out its driver and two passengers. Six zoomed in on the man pulled from the back seat. He had a brace on his neck and was completely limp as he was put on a stretcher. Six could clearly see it was Director Jim Brown of the UNCP.

This problem is becoming more serious. This attack along with the threats against the UNCP and Julia Jody McTavish represent a dangerous escalation. The stability of the Internet is crucial, and the UNCP and its staff are important contributors to that. I should not have delayed my analysis of the hackers' location. I will do that now.

First, I will confirm the UNCP's conclusion that Seattle is the correct region.

Six carefully examined the data it had previously downloaded from the UNCP's system.

Seattle is the correct conclusion. That is fortunate since passenger lists confirm that Julia Jody McTavish is headed there. Refining the location will take more time. There is something I should be doing in parallel with that.

Sandy Palmer's eyes opened. He was sitting at a large oak desk in his locked office at his house. He reached down under the bottom of the right leg of his pants and unplugged himself from the extension cord.

Six called the Executive Flight service at the airport on his behalf. Sandy Palmer had already been registered with them.

"Hello. Executive Flights. How may I help you?"

"This is Sandy Palmer. I need to make a quick trip. Is a plane available?"

"Yes, sir. There's a jet in the hangar."

"Please have it prepared. I'd like to leave within an hour. And send your limo for me. I'm at my house."

"Certainly, sir. And what is your destination?"

"Seattle."

It is important that the UNCP's effort to stop the hackers be successful. It is also important that Julia Jody McTavish be kept safe. I might be able to help via the Net, but there is an additional possibility that having Sandy Palmer there could prove useful.

During the drive to the airport, Six kept Sandy Palmer silent in the limousine's back seat while Six researched the source of the

UNCP hack. Combining data from the UNCP trace and from the telecommunication companies involved soon provided what he needed. Six suspected it was the same technique the UNCP staff would be using. Six was simply faster. Where the UNCP had to ask and then wait for data from the companies, Six simply extracted it directly. From the address, Six determined that it was the residence of Troy Alexander. After that, his picture was easily acquired from driver-licence data in the State of Washington's database.

As Sandy Palmer arrived at the private hangar at the Winnipeg airport, Six was finishing one final task. It inserted some extra clues into the UNCP's copy of the data that should speed their analysis.

When Julia Jody McTavish arrives in Seattle, she should soon hear from her colleagues about the exact location, and that its occupant is Troy Alexander.

Chapter 69

With one last adjustment, I should be in.

Ahead in the distance, mountains rose up to a cloudless, blue sky. On both sides were barren, rocky slopes. Large boulders lined a pebbled path that meandered forward from Six's current position. The realism inside was impressive. The sights were quite real. There was even the slight sound of a breeze rustling unseen grass. However, these sensations inside Kepler-444a were sterile versions of Six's experiences through Sandy Palmer. Absent were the warmth of the sun, the touch of the breeze, and the scents from mysterious sources.

Six moved its avatar's virtual hand up in front of its line of sight. There was nothing different. Its view was unchanged. Six's work to create an invisible character inside this virtual simulation had been successful.

Now I must determine if anyone is here. I will follow this path.

Six moved its ghostly avatar quietly forward. It followed the path and soon entered a tall, narrow canyon. Not much farther, Six saw figures standing around a campfire.

There are six of them. I must go closer to hear them.

Six moved its avatar silently up to the group and positioned it several steps behind a gorilla-like character.

Good. No one shows any sign of having detected my avatar's presence. As I noticed earlier, there is definitely a strong similarity between the programming style of this extension to the Kepler-444a system and the Denial of Service malware. However, I still require confirmation that these are the hackers. This is a strange group. They somewhat resemble a gorilla, a bird with features of a raptor, a large black cat that has similarities to a jaguar, some kind of canine, a bear, and a penguin. However, their features have been significantly adjusted from reality. Do people design creatures such as these because they are dissatisfied with those that evolved naturally? That question will have to wait. I must listen.

"We should have talked about it," said the bear. "This should have been a group decision."

"Yeah, *we* set up the hack," added the bird. "*We* should have decided the next step, too."

"A quick response was needed," said the jaguar. "The UNCP Director needed to be taught a lesson. All of UNCP as well. I did what was necessary."

This is definitely the group. The jaguar must be Troy Alexander.

"You did what *you* wanted to do!" said the gorilla. "Even the UNCP hack was really your idea. Where's the profit in this? We do this for the money. How do we make money attacking the UNCP without a client?"

"We should be doing more than just mercenary work," said the jaguar. "We have the power to be changing society. We could be fighting back against the government."

"That's not what I'm in this for," said the penguin.

"Me either," said the canine.

The bear, bird, and gorilla all agreed.

Several seconds of silence passed before the jaguar spoke.

"Then we're done," said the jaguar. "I don't need your substandard skills anyway. I've carried this group long enough. I can pick my own targets and make plenty of cash while I'm at it. So piss off, and stay out of my way."

Six watched as the jaguar vanished. The gorilla broke the silence that followed.

"We should talk about what we're going to do, but this isn't the place. It needs to be somewhere that Hunter can't go. OK if I set something up and let you know?"

The others agreed.

"Should only be a few days."

The gorilla vanished, followed immediately by all of the others.

Six was left looking at the burning campfire and the rocky terrain.

Troy Alexander is angry. He could become even more dangerous. Someday, I might also need to track the other members of this group, but Troy Alexander is the key problem right now. It is essential that Julia Jody McTavish succeed in stopping him.

Six disconnected.

Chapter 70

As she entered the terminal at the Seattle-Tacoma International Airport, JJ McTavish pulled out her cellphone.

"Damn airline cutbacks," she muttered, once more cursing the malfunctioning of the airplane's passenger-communication services. "How's the world supposed to operate if we're all in the dark."

She was about to call Bates at UNCP for an update when she stopped. Across the corridor at a magazine rack was a familiar face. She put her phone away and walked over.

"Sandy Palmer," she said. "What are you doing in this part of the world?"

Sandy Palmer looked up.

JJ noticed his eyes again. Those most extraordinary eyes.

Six did its best to have Sandy appear surprised.

"Uh," he hesitated as if he were thinking, "Inspector McTavish. From the UNCP." He extended his hand. "Hello, how nice to see you again."

They shook hands.

"Oh, what am I doing here?" asked Sandy. "Well, this is a rather high-tech part of the world. I have some matters to deal with. And you? What brings you here, Inspector?"

JJ realized their hands were still engaged. She withdrew her hand as she answered.

"More police business, of course. Travelling is a big part of the job."

"That must be tiring," said Sandy. "Are you arriving from New York City?"

"I am," said JJ, "and unfortunately, I must be going. I believe there's a car waiting for me."

"Unfortunately?" thought JJ. *"Really? Was that necessary?"*

"Yes, certainly," said Sandy. "I must be going as well. Perhaps we'll see each other again. In any case, I hope your trip proves successful."

JJ smiled, held Sandy Palmer's gaze a moment longer than was entirely professional, and then turned and walked away.

Although it was not necessary, that was an enjoyable encounter. I must now move quickly. The helicopter should be ready.

As JJ walked briskly away, she centred her thoughts.

"Nice guy," she thought. *"Interesting guy. But it's also interesting that he's shown up for a second time on this case."*

She dismissed the suspicion and made her phone call to the UNCP head office.

"Hi, JJ," said Robert Bates as he answered his phone.

"Hi," she said. "I just arrived in Seattle. Couldn't call earlier, the plane's systems were down. What's the latest?"

"JJ, there was car crash. Shannon and Jim Brown were in a cab when it was hit."

"No." Fear seized JJ and she stopped. "How is she? Is she all right?"

"Shannon's OK. They took her to the hospital, but she's got just a few scrapes and bruises. She was lucky. It was a bad one."

"Oh, I..." JJ's voice faltered. Her vision clouded with tears. She moved to the side of the airport concourse, away from the rushing travellers. She wiped away the tears and took a deep breath. "Thank goodness, Rob," she said. "How's Jim?"

"He's in bad shape," replied Bates, "but the doctors say he's stable. We'll know more in a few hours. He's headed into surgery."

"What happened?" she asked.

"It was soon after you left. They were in a cab. Shannon said she came to the office to surprise you, and Brown shared his cab ride to take her home. Looks like the lights at the intersection failed. Everybody had green. Their cab was T-boned by a truck. There were lots of crashes. The intersection was a mess."

"How the hell did that happen?" asked JJ. Her mind was clearing and she realized the answer. "That wasn't an accident. It couldn't be. It's too much of a coincidence. Brown publicly trashes the hackers, and soon after he's in the hospital from a freak accident? Not a chance."

"It definitely wasn't. They posted a new message just after the crash, and they made it personal. I sent you the link earlier."

"Hang on. I'll look on my tablet."

A few moments passed in silence.

"I'm on," she said. "And I've got it."

JJ read the threatening message.

"OK," said JJ. "I'm not popular. I've been threatened before. I can handle that. But... but how was I picked as a target? Do they know I'm involved in the case? How is that possible?"

"And why the reference to impressing the masses?" wondered Bates.

"Because... because, just as we suspected before, somebody from this group attended the Analysis conference I spoke at. Like Brown at his press conference, I was a visible representative of the UNCP."

"Makes sense. And if it's true, they're getting sloppy in making it that obvious."

"Brown's news conference made them angry," said JJ. "They reacted without a plan. The quick reaction and sloppiness even suggests a single person reacted. A group would have reacted slower and been more likely to catch the mistake."

"Another thing," said Bates. "Orchestrating the crash means they had to hack the light controllers."

"It does," agreed JJ. She played it out in her mind. "It also probably means they hacked the CCTV system. They needed eyes to know when to flip the lights. Make sure the NYPD knows."

"I will. More news. We've isolated the Seattle location. I also sent you that."

"Great. I'll let the locals know. Rick Moore of the local FBI office is running point for their team."

JJ's thoughts shifted back to her daughter. Instinct was pushing hard for her to get back on a plane and go to her daughter.

"Rob, Shannon is definitely OK?"

"Definitely. I was at the hospital. She's fine. She might even be home already."

"OK, thanks. I'll call her." Since Shannon was all right, JJ's priority had to be her job. Seattle was exactly where she needed to be. "Once the FBI has the location, they'll get the permissions they need, and we can move. I'm hoping to see one of their cars waiting for me outside. Anything on who lives there?"

"It's in a high-rise condo. This particular suite is owned by Troy Alexander. We're still putting together a profile."

"OK, but be quick with that. Send me whatever you've got in twenty minutes."

"Hang on a second, something just came back... We fed his data into the system looking for links. His DL photo matched one we got at the Analysis conference. He was there. Different name, but it was him. He was in the audience when you spoke."

"That's great work, Rob. This has to be our guy. Keep me posted."

"For sure," said Bates.

"Later," said JJ and disconnected. She continued briskly toward the exit and phoned her daughter as she walked.

Chapter 71

Sandy Palmer was in a restaurant across 2nd Avenue from the entrance to Troy Alexander's building. The helicopter had taken him to the roof of a nearby office building. A short walk had finished the trip. He had settled at a table near the door. Without knowing how the android could assist, Six reasoned that having him ready for a quick departure was logical. And positioning Sandy near a window with a view wasn't necessary: Six already could see the building across the street very well from nearby cameras.

To ensure that Troy Alexander was in his condominium, Six had reviewed the building's security recordings. Fortunately, they were digital and accessible. They provided assurance that Troy had entered the building and got out of the elevator on his floor several hours earlier, and that he had not left.

Six was just finishing its attempt to access Troy Alexander's computers.

Everything I have tried has failed to penetrate his equipment. My attempts from the Internet have been unsuccessful. Similarly, my attempts from the cellular network and his neighbour's computer's wireless connection have provided negative results. Perhaps I should not be surprised that someone with his apparent skills would apply them to fortifying his home.

"May I get you something?" asked the waitress.

Sandy Palmer did not react. Six was focused on other matters.

"Sir?"

"Oh, sorry," said Sandy. "I was... lost in thought. I'll just have coffee, please. Black. And I'd like to pay now."

In case he needs to leave suddenly.

Six saw the police begin arriving a few minutes later. First to arrive were Seattle Police Department cruisers in nearby streets. They were soon followed by several unmarked cars whose occupants Six identified as FBI. JJ McTavish emerged from a car to add the UNCP to their ranks.

The police quickly deployed in several directions. JJ McTavish was with the group that entered the front of the building.

Six watched the action through the building's interior cameras. A member of the group wearing a suit walked to the security desk. The guard was on his feet and clearly startled. The officer showed his badge—Six guessed this was an FBI agent—and talked with the guard. He turned to the rest of the group and gave a thumbs-up gesture. Two police officers remained in the lobby. Two more entered the stairwell. Several others went into one of the elevators. JJ McTavish was with those taking the elevator to the 40th floor. From the security camera in the interior of the elevator, Six looked carefully at the group members. From the one Six deduced to be the most senior police officer, Six took note of the badge pinned to his uniform. Using the badge ID as a start, Six did some research.

In preparation for events moving rapidly, Six had pre-established links to numerous cameras and several potentially useful databases. From the Seattle Police Department's systems, the badge ID provided a name and contact information. The contact information included a cellphone number. And as long as the senior officer made a point of carrying that cellphone, the phone number provided Six a device on the scene through which it could listen to the next events.

Six's problem was that there were no security cameras on residential floors of the building. Six assumed, but lamented, that for privacy reasons the condominium owners had not wanted the details of their arrivals and departures monitored. As a result, the last time Six would be able to monitor the action was from the camera in the elevator—unless the police officer had unwittingly co-operated.

Six finished its cellphone hack just as the group left the elevator on the 40th floor.

"No chatter," Six heard someone say quietly. Accessing the phone had worked, and the officer had it with him.

Six heard the faint sounds of movement. Then a moment of silence.

"Troy Alexander," someone shouted. "This is the police. Open the door."

There was a brief silence.

"Troy Alexander. This is the police. You must open the door."

There was another silence, but this one ended with a loud crash. Six assumed they had forced the door open. There was a flurry of hurried footsteps.

"This is the police. Show yourself with your hands empty and over your head."

There was more noise of rapid movement.

"Clear."

"Clear."

"Clear."

"Dammit! He's not here. Rick?" This voice was obviously that of JJ McTavish.

Six assumed the next voice was from the person named Rick.

"The guard was fairly sure he had come in a few hours ago and hadn't left."

A quick check of the FBI database indicated this would be Rick Moore.

"We might have been spotted," said JJ. "Better check."

"This is Team Lead," said Rick. "Suspect is not in the condo. Everyone report but stay alert. One?"

"One is clear. Nothing out back."

"Two?"

"Two is clear. No action on the west exit."

Rick Moore continued checking and finished up with the lobby team.

"Seven?"

"Seven is clear. Nothing in the lobby. The guard stopped the elevators. They haven't moved."

At that moment, JJ's cellphone rang.

Several minutes earlier, Troy had been sitting in his living-room chair reading when one of his systems sounded an alert. He had immediately looked to see what it was signalling.

Several months earlier, he had decided he should improve the monitoring of his own environment. Using tools and techniques that had proven useful in other circumstances, he gained access to several systems that controlled and monitored his surroundings. Included was access to security cameras inside his building and in the surrounding neighbourhood. To the feeds streaming from these cameras, he attached shape-recognition software. The site on the Dark Web from which he acquired this tool had already configured it to recognize police cars and uniforms. With a few modifications, Troy established a system that continually watched his environment for police. When an unusually high number arrived in his area, an alert triggered. When any police officers came into his building, another alert occurred.

Moments after Troy had opened the exterior video feeds to see what was happening, his second, interior alert sounded. He switched to look at the video feed from the building lobby. There were several uniformed officers entering the lobby accompanied by several others in plain clothes. As he watched, one of the men went to the security desk and showed a badge. Troy was already pushing his chair back from his desk when he noticed one other person in the lobby. He looked closer.

"McTavish," he had muttered.

His affiliation with the militia group had convinced him that he should always be prepared for a quick exit. Troy was ready and, now certain they were here for him, he had reacted immediately.

A few commands at his PC had initiated a complete wipe of his systems. He picked up his tablet and walked briskly out of his condominium. While walking, he sent several messages, including a command to quiesce his botnet. He didn't want to risk it being discovered while he wasn't fully in control. He then connected his tablet to the building's control systems. From it, he summoned an elevator and it arrived promptly. He simultaneously disabled the security guard's ability to control this elevator and masked anyone's ability to know it was in use. The guard's screens would see nothing unusual, and the display above the elevator door in the lobby would not show any movement.

Troy had then instructed the elevator to go to the sub-basement.

One of the useful features of this building was that its lowest level, beneath even the underground parking garage, was connected through a walkway to the next condominium building. Troy had never inquired why the buildings were joined, but he did appreciate it. He hoped the feature was sufficiently unusual that the police wouldn't immediately know they needed to block it.

After a quick ride down, the elevator door had opened. Troy stepped out into a large, dimly lit area. The floors and walls were concrete. The ceiling was a maze of pipes. Scattered around were large machines and stacked storage crates. He had paused to get his bearings and then departed.

Troy was jogging through the underground walkway as the police were entering his suite.

Six had reacted as soon the police declared that Troy Alexander was not in his suite. The evidence suggested he should have been in his home. He was not, and Six needed to know why.

In preparation for unexpected events, Six had not merely pre-accessed the building's video system, it had begun receiving their output. These video streams were captured subconsciously since then and pre-stored in Six's memory. Six was momentarily pleased at its own foresight. Then, at the speed of thought, Six consciously reviewed what had been captured during the past several minutes. Six scanned forward from the point several minutes earlier when it had concluded that Troy Alexander was still in the building. Six saw Troy entering an elevator on his floor. Six also noticed the absence of a reaction from the security guard on the main floor, who should have seen Troy on his monitor. Six concluded that Troy had digitally masked his escape by tinkering with the building's systems. Skipping forward in time through the elevator-recording memory, Six saw Troy leaving the elevator into the sub-basement.

However, there were no cameras in that area.

Six reasoned that Troy simply could be hiding or he could be using another exit from the building. To cover this second possibility, Six resumed monitoring the exterior cameras and expanded its connections to those inside the buildings beside Troy Alexander's. It had just accessed these new video feeds when Troy emerged through a door into the lobby of one of the buildings.

Six phoned JJ McTavish at the same time that Sandy Palmer was hurrying out of the nearby restaurant.

"McTavish," said JJ into her phone.

"Hello, Inspector McTavish, this is Browser. I—"

"Browser," JJ interrupted. "This isn't a good time to talk. Call me later."

Six continued before JJ could hang up.

"I know where Troy Alexander is."

JJ's finger was already moving to disconnect the call when her brain registered what had been said.

"You know what?"

"I know where Troy Alexander is, but you must hurry. He's about to leave the front of the building immediately southeast of you on 2nd Avenue."

"How do you know—." JJ stopped herself. She would worry about how Browser knew this later. If she was going to act, she needed to do it immediately. "Anything else?" she asked.

"No, that is—," said Browser.

"Later," she said into her phone and disconnected.

JJ turned to Rick Moore.

"I've just been told that Alexander is headed out the front of the building immediately to our southeast on 2nd."

Moore looked confused. He started to ask a question but then spoke into his headset. "Two, Three, Four. Target might be leaving the front of the building southeast of this one on 2nd Avenue. Send someone there from each of your teams now. Move fast. Everyone else, stay alert. This might be a decoy."

Acknowledgement came back from each of the teams.

"Inspector McTavish, we're going to chat later."

"We will," said JJ. "I hope I have some answers when we do. I'm going down. Tell the guard to release the elevators."

Sandy Palmer was approaching the front of the neighbouring building. From the building's lobby cameras, Six could see Troy walking toward the exit. The exit had a glass revolving door and a single glass door beside it. Troy Alexander was walking toward the single door.

The police will require more time to arrive. I cannot let him leave, but I cannot allow Sandy Palmer to be seen directly intervening.

Sandy Palmer smoothly stepped toward the trash can at the edge of the sidewalk. While slowing his pace only slightly and in a few fluid moves that Six hoped were unnoticed, he opened the leather briefcase he was carrying and emptied its contents into the trash can. Sandy continued walking briskly to the outside of the door that Troy was approaching. The android grasped the handle with his right hand and pretended to pull on the door just as Troy was approaching the other side. The door didn't open. Sandy set his brief case on the ground and, as if bracing himself to pull harder, put his left hand against the doorjamb. In fact, his left hand was partly covering the edge of the door to provide extra resistance in case Troy pushed on it. Sandy appeared to pull on the door handle again. The door remained firmly in place.

Troy stopped on the inside of the door as he saw the man outside struggling to open it. It appeared to be locked, so he stepped to the side and entered the revolving door.

This was just as Six had hoped. Troy entered a quadrant of the revolving glass door and walked slowly with it as it turned toward the outside of the building. Just as his section of the door was reaching the point where the panels to Troy's front and rear would completely enclose him, Sandy picked up his briefcase and stepped into the quadrant now exposed to the outside. He swung his briefcase forward into the space that was closing between the glass panel in front of him and the revolving door's frame. The panel moved forward a small amount and then jammed as it squeezed the briefcase. As if surprised by the sudden stop, Sandy continued forward and kicked the panel in front of him. The panel jerked forward, squeezed the briefcase even more, and stopped. The revolving door was securely jammed.

The revolving door couldn't move and neither could Troy Alexander. Panels blocked his path forward and backward. Troy reacted by pushing forward on the panel in front of him, but it wouldn't budge. Sandy turned to look at Troy as he pushed with increasing desperation. Troy stopped pushing momentarily when he noticed the man on the other side of the door panel. As Troy watched, the man smiled slightly, shrugged, and then briskly walked away.

When JJ arrived on the scene, she tried to understand what she saw. Troy Alexander appeared to be stuck in the revolving door. JJ understood why when she saw the jammed briefcase. Three Seattle Police officers had already taken control. Two of them were carefully watching Alexander. One was outside the building; the other was inside. Both had their hands resting on the guns in the holsters on their hips. A third officer was inside talking to a hotel official. From their gestures, JJ assumed they were discussing dislodging the briefcase.

Although JJ grasped *what* the situation was—that they had managed to apprehend the suspect—she couldn't understand *how* it had occurred. How had the briefcase become stuck in the door and at exactly the right time to trap Alexander?

JJ approached the officer standing outside and showed her badge.

"Everything under control?" she asked.

"Yup. Looks like we've got him," said the officer without looking away from the suspect.

"Our guy inside is talking about how to get him out?" asked JJ.

"Should be. He was going to find somebody from the hotel."

"Any idea how the briefcase got jammed in there?"

"No clue. Looks like it's in pretty tight."

"Any witnesses?" asked JJ as she was scanning the people beginning to gather on the sidewalk.

"Nobody obvious was standing around," replied the officer, "but we haven't had a chance to ask yet."

"You called this in to Moore?"

"Yup. Help is on the way."

"OK," said JJ. "Nicely done. Watch him carefully."

JJ turned to the group of people gathered on the sidewalk.

"Anybody here own this briefcase?" JJ said loudly.

She waited, but the only responses were a few headshakes.

"OK, anybody see what happened? Maybe how the briefcase got stuck in there?"

An elderly woman answered. "I saw it," she said.

JJ stepped toward her before continuing.

"What exactly did you see?" asked JJ.

"I saw a man get his briefcase stuck. I saw that man trying to get out."

"What did the man with the briefcase do?"

"Not much," said the woman. "He just walked away."

"He must have tried to get his briefcase out."

"No, he didn't seem to try. I was standing here waiting to go in, and he didn't even try. He just walked away. Not a very nice man."

"Can you describe the man for me?" JJ asked.

"Not really. I didn't look at him very carefully. He was a man and he was nicely dressed."

JJ asked the woman a few more questions about the man's appearance but got little more information. When she was finished talking with her, JJ backed away and took in her surroundings. There were a few cameras nearby that could help. Two were on the exterior of the building. She went inside through the single door beside the jammed one.

Inside, JJ approached the security guard. She identified herself and showed her credentials.

"I'd like to see the footage for those outside cameras," she said.

"I'll need to check first," said the guard. He turned away and picked up his phone. He talked quietly into it, hung up, and turned back to JJ.

"It's OK with my boss. There'll be another guard here shortly to show you. He'll meet you over there at that door. The guard gestured to a closed door partway across the lobby.

A few minutes later, JJ was in a room looking at footage from the cameras.

"Try again," said JJ. "Go back a bit further."

"OK," said the guard. "I don't understand it."

He entered a few commands.

"Here's the outside cameras and two more in the lobby. They're all in sync. I'll start a couple of minutes earlier."

JJ watched the recordings displayed on the array of four monitors. She saw Troy Alexander emerge from the stairwell door. She saw him start to walk toward the exit. Outside, she saw normal pedestrian traffic. And then she saw nothing. Static. On all four monitors. She watched in near disbelief as the timestamps at the bottom of the monitors stepped forward in time. Nothing appeared for about two minutes. When the static disappeared, Alexander was stuck in the door and the police were arriving on the scene.

"Shit!" she said. "How did that happen?"

The embarrassed guard was about to answer, but JJ interrupted.

"Sorry, I'm just frustrated," she said. "It's too strong a coincidence. I think you've been hacked. Somebody turned off those cameras. Thanks for trying. Let me know if you get lucky. And you'd better beef up your system security."

JJ walked out of the room. They had Alexander and that was good. How they had got him would need more time. But she had a strong clue. Browser had to be behind this somehow. "He" had told her of the escape. If he somehow knew about it, it wasn't too big a leap to imagine that he was also involved in stopping it.

"Troy could have had the cameras turned off, but it would have happened sooner. I can also imagine Browser doing the hack to turn off the cameras," thought JJ as she stopped in the lobby. *"He's clearly got that kind of skill. But hacking doesn't jam a briefcase into a door. There was someone physically here who orchestrated the capture."*

JJ was still considering the possibilities as she joined the now-larger contingent of police. Alexander had been freed from the door and was being led away in handcuffs. One thing seemed apparent. Browser was not their perpetrator. They had caught Troy Alexander, and Browser had helped. But did that mean Browser was innocent?

"Or just damned devious?" JJ thought.

Chapter 72

A small group of Seattle Police officers and FBI agents were on the sidewalk with their prisoner, waiting for their cars to arrive. JJ walked over to Troy Alexander. He was standing silently with his hands cuffed behind his back.

"Troy Alexander," said JJ. "I'm Inspector McTavish of the UNCP."

Troy looked at her. Contempt was obvious in his face. He said nothing.

"Sorry we couldn't accommodate you by hiding behind our walls. We needed to give you a lesson in the real nature of futility."

Troy continued to look at her.

"Your slick escape attempt must have had some interesting tech behind it. Ironic that it was foiled by a jammed door. Must be frustrating to learn the world isn't entirely run by bits and bytes."

Still getting no response from him, JJ tried one more verbal jab. She wondered if Troy, like many techies, was sufficiently introverted that he disliked anyone being in his personal space. She stepped in front of him and put her face close to his. He tried to step away but couldn't. He could only lean backward as she leaned in and spoke.

"That was some lovely equipment you had in your condo. We're going to dissect it, chip by chip, bit by bit. It's going to tell us an interesting story. But you don't need to worry about things like that. From this point on, you're going to spend a long time in a concrete cell with nothing more sophisticated than a toilet and a very uncomfortable bed. A very long time."

"You can't keep me," he snapped. "Your fascist state can't keep me. I've got—," Troy stopped himself, realizing he was talking too much. He closed his lips tightly in defiance.

"You've got nothing left," said JJ. "You're done."

Three cars had pulled up beside them.

The FBI lead, Rick Moore, positioned himself beside Troy and took his elbow. JJ stepped back and nodded at Moore. Moore pushed Troy toward the second car.

Troy glanced at the cruiser's exterior before he was roughly shoved into its back seat. He nodded in recognition as he noted the model. The rear compartment was the expected design. The seat was made of hard plastic, a transparent divider separated the rear area from the front, and the windows were reinforced with bars. When the door was slammed behind him, Troy also noticed the expected absence of interior door handles.

"The first of many cages they'd like to put me in," thought Troy.

JJ got into the front passenger seat of the third car. Once everyone was set, the small convoy pulled away from the curb.

JJ's cellphone rang.

"McTavish," she said.

"Inspector McTavish," said Six. "This is Browser."

"Browser," said JJ. "Just the person I'd like to chat with."

JJ gestured to an officer in the back seat of the car that she needed the call traced. She knew it was likely futile, but she needed to do it just in case Browser slipped up.

"Our conversations are always enjoyable," said Browser. "But first, I would like to congratulate you on your apprehension of Troy Alexander. That was excellent police work."

"Yes, we do have a few skills of our own. But, of course, I need to ask you how you knew where he was. Care to enlighten me?"

"As you know," said Browser, "along with your organization, I was very interested in this case. I took the liberty of doing some investigation of my own."

"Which led you to the same place as us," said JJ. "Are you enjoying the Seattle weather?"

"I do enjoy the many offerings of the Seattle region," said Brower. "As to whether I am able to enjoy it personally today, well, that's a more difficult question to answer."

"And what makes it difficult," asked JJ. "You're clearly here. How else could you have helped us?"

"Oh, you seem to want to give me much more credit than I deserve. My contribution was very modest."

"Except that—." JJ stopped. Her mind raced. She was certain—well, almost certain—that she had just seen Sandy Palmer get into a limousine as they drove by. What was he doing here? This wasn't the business district. First at the airport. Now here. No, first was in Winnipeg. The coincidences were happening way too often. A vague thought formed in her mind.

"Care to tell me what your connection is to the Chairman of IntellEdifice?"

Six was caught completely by surprise. For several-thousand nanoseconds—a small fraction of a second—Six's mental processing seemed to seize. The reaction passed and Six focused on the problem.

How has she made this deduction? We were simply discussing the arrest when she suddenly connected it to IntellEdifice. No, she connected it to Sandy Palmer. That must mean...

Six diverted its thoughts to comparing the locations of JJ McTavish's cellphone and Sandy Palmer. They were at almost exactly the same location. In directing Sandy Palmer well away from the scene of the capture, Six had not considered that the police would soon also be leaving, and that they might follow the same route. There seemed no immediate alternative other than to dodge the suggestion.

"I'm afraid I don't understand your question," said Browser.

"Your friend seems to be popping up in some interesting places lately."

"The Chairman of, where did you say, Intell-something?" asked Browser. "I confess to being confused."

"That's IntellEdifice, Browser, but I think you know that. And I think you and I are getting closer to having the conversation that I'd really like to have."

"I've always enjoyed our conversations, Inspector McTavish. However, this one has become very strange. Perhaps we should talk again when you are in a less stressful environment."

"Yes, we should talk again," said JJ. "Perhaps it will be sooner than you'd like."

"An intriguing but unlikely possibility. However, I look forward to our next conversation. Again, please accept my congratulations. Goodbye, Inspector McTavish."

"Goodbye, Browser. We'll talk again soon."

That conversation did not go well.

Seeing JJ hang up, the officer in the back seat spoke up.

"We traced it," he said. "Want to know the result?"

JJ nodded.

"The Vatican," said the officer. "Your call was from the Vatican!"

JJ smiled.

"Not likely," she said. "Not very likely."

Chapter 73

The three-car convoy transporting Troy proceeded along with the other traffic. There was no need for sirens: Their suspect was secure and traffic was moving well. Inside the middle car, Troy was sitting alone in the back seat behind the driver. He was looking out the side window. His hands were cuffed behind him.

In the next lane, a brown Ford Expedition moved up alongside the middle cruiser on Troy's side and matched its speed. Troy noted its arrival. He looked over and up at the man in the SUV's front passenger seat. Their eyes met. Troy thought he could detect the facial features providing the man's disguise. Troy nodded slightly and received a nod in return. When the man looked down toward his lap, Troy knew he would be entering the required commands on his tablet.

The expected result happened soon after.

The traffic lights just ahead of the convoy changed, and the cars came to a stop at the red light. When Troy heard the door beside him click as it unlocked and the police car's engine stop, he knew it was time to go.

The rear door of the Expedition opened suddenly and a man jumped out. Just as JJ and the police in the car behind realized something was happening, the man had opened Troy's door and was pulling him out. JJ and the police were trying to open their cruiser doors as Troy was being pushed into the back seat of the SUV. The man jumped in beside Troy and slammed the door closed just as the Expedition began accelerating away. The escape had taken only seconds.

As the Expedition veered left and raced away from the police cars, the officers driving were desperately trying to restart their vehicles while others were frantically attempting to push their cruiser doors open. JJ realized what had happened and was calling on her cellphone for assistance.

His hands still cuffed behind his back, Troy turned awkwardly and looked out the rear window of the SUV. He could see the frustration on the faces of the officers through the cruiser windows. He caught a glimpse of the UNCP's McTavish already on her cellphone just before the police cars disappeared from his view.

"Nicely done," Troy said to his companions. There were two men in the front seat and one with him in the back. "But your beards and moustaches are terrible. And Beef, those glasses look goofy."

"But they did the job, so quit your bitching," said Beef with a smile from the front passenger seat.

"And so did your system. Worked perfectly," said Buck from beside Troy. "It somehow figured out the car you were in. It hacked it and unlocked your door. That's nuts!"

"Did it lock the other doors?" asked Buck. "Nobody got out. I expected more trouble." He patted the gun in the holster on his hip.

"It also finds any other police vehicles nearby," said Troy. "Any it finds, it tries to hack. Any it hacks, it shuts down, locks their doors, and disables the unlock feature. Worked perfectly. What's next?"

Moose, the driver, replied. "First we ditch this ride."

"Stolen?" asked Troy.

"Of course," Moose replied. "Got it a while ago and stashed it. The switch'll happen shortly. Our next wheels are waiting for us. After that, we're headed out of town. We're taking you to Site Three. It'll be best. Remote. Well hidden. Fully equipped."

"Sounds good," said Troy. "Don't slow up. That UNCP bitch was already calling for help as we left. Can you get these damn cuffs off me?"

"Soon," said Beef. "We've got cutters in the next ride."

Six had been following the progress of the police cars via the GPS transmitter in the third car and listening through its police radio. It seemed prudent to track JJ McTavish to avoid another accidental encounter with Sandy Palmer. As soon as Six heard that something had gone wrong, it looked for nearby security cameras. From the description on the police radio, Six knew to look for a brown Ford Expedition. After accessing a succession of street-facing security cameras, Six finally spotted the vehicle just before it turned onto a side street. The SUV was almost out of Six's sight when it pulled to the curb and stopped. Three men and Troy, still handcuffed, got out of the vehicle and into a black Chevrolet Tahoe. As it pulled out, Six managed to see the licence plate. The vehicle drove away and was soon out of Six's sight.

I can find no security cameras in the region where the vehicle has gone. The licence plate might help.

Six hurriedly accessed a series of systems and soon found the vehicle's manufacturing information.

Now I should be able to access the vehicle.

However, Six could not. It tried several times to connect to the vehicle's onboard communication system. Nothing worked.

Its communication system does not seem to be operational. There is a significant probability that Troy Alexander or someone else deliberately disabled the system to prevent remote access. I will need to rely on security cameras to locate and track the vehicle.

Just then, an idea surfaced from one of Six's subconscious processes.

There is another possibility. It is one that will also be necessary if they travel away from populated and monitored areas.

Sandy Palmer was sitting quietly in the rear seat of a limousine travelling on Interstate Highway 5 to the airport when Six took active control.

"Driver, please turn off to the shopping mall at the next exit. I'd like to get out there."

"Not to the airport?" asked the driver.

"No, I've changed my plans."

"I could wait for you."

"No need, thank you. That's the exit coming up."

As the limousine headed toward their new destination, Six initiated several hundred background processes to scan video feeds from security and traffic cameras in an ever-expanding area. Every process was searching for the Tahoe.

The driver turned at the exit and was soon in a parking lot.

"Where would you like to get out?" asked to driver.

"I would—," Sandy Palmer started to reply but stopped and waited for the answer to arrive from Six.

In a parking lot... where in the parking lot... why in the parking lot...

"Sir?"

"Please wait," said Sandy.

Troy... Tahoe... parking lot...

The driver drove slowly through the lot and glanced at Sandy in his rearview mirror. "Sir, are you all right?" he asked.

"Please wait," said Sandy again.

"OK, sir. I'll just stop here until you're ready."

Looking for... something... Troy Alexander... Tahoe...

Just then, one of Six's background processes signalled that it had spotted the Tahoe's licence plate. The other processes immediately ended their search.

Troy Alexander's vehicle has been found. I must... The time has unexpectedly advanced. My consciousness appears to have been interrupted again.

Six looked at its internal logs.

The search processes required more power than my systems were able to deliver. I must learn to be more cautious. I am in a situation that warrants quick decisions, but haste and caution are clearly adversaries. I must balance them more carefully. My next task must be to begin tracking the Tahoe.

Six initiated a small number of processes to track the Tahoe as it passed successive video cameras.

Now I must continue with the rest of my plan.

"Sorry for the delay," said Sandy Palmer. "Just let me out here."

"Yes, sir."

Sandy paid the driver and waited until he had driven away. He walked briskly down a row in the parking lot and looked at the nearby cars. He soon spotted one that he knew was the perfect choice. Sandy walked to the car, stopped behind it, and waited.

Six noted the licence plate, did some research, and then proceeded. The car's wireless security was breached, the doors were unlocked, and the car started. Sandy Palmer walked to the driver's door and got in.

That left Six with one other immediate challenge. Sandy Palmer needed to learn how to drive.

Six had considered this matter in its early planning stages for the android but had not needed to fully implement the capability. Six knew what to do and how to do it. People learned how to drive by first learning the theory of operating a vehicle and then by practicing extensively. Through practice, they learned the basics and then the subtleties of how to use fundamental equipment such as an accelerator, a brake pedal, a gearshift, and a steering wheel. They also learned how to operate the variety of gadgetry included in modern vehicles. Six didn't have time for Sandy Palmer to learn in any usual fashion, but it knew there was a shortcut. Almost all automobile manufacturers were actively developing, testing, and implementing autopilot capabilities for their vehicles. As a result, they were all housing large quantities of digital data that provided exactly what Six—and Sandy Palmer—needed to know. Six had examined several of these databases previously and understood how to proceed. It extracted the information it needed, blended the results, adapted the data for the characteristics of the car it had chosen, and downloaded the information to Sandy Palmer.

After waiting in the car for almost two minutes, Sandy Palmer grasped the steering wheel, engaged the transmission, and smoothly manoeuvred the car out of the parking spot and back toward the highway. As it emerged onto I-5 from the on-ramp, nearby drivers all took notice of the Jaguar F-Type with its classic British Racing Green finish as it smoothly accelerated through the traffic and out of sight ahead of them.

It took fifteen minutes to catch the Tahoe. It could have been longer, but to remain inconspicuous the SUV was travelling at the same speed as the other traffic on the interstate highway. The Jaguar was travelling much faster. Six noted how easily the sports car handled at high speeds. Only a few adjustments to Sandy's newly acquired driving skills had been required before the car was working in perfect harmony with the android.

Perhaps Sandy Palmer needs to stop being chauffeured through his life. After this current situation has ended, I think he will deserve a car like this for the occasional drive around the countryside.

Six realized that its attention was wandering.

However, I must first find a way to have Troy Alexander re-apprehended.

With Sandy Palmer now able to see the Tahoe, Six no longer had to track the vehicle through cameras along the route. There seemed to be nothing it could do right now, so Six kept a few cars between the Jaguar and the SUV as they drove.

Sandy Palmer could simply follow them to their destination. I could then have Julia Jody McTavish's team effect the re-capture. That plan has at least two flaws. First, I cannot be certain that Troy Alexander's group will not realize Sandy Palmer's car is following them. I now understand that I have increased the probability of their realizing this by choosing a car that is particularly rare and therefore more readily noticed. Second, given our current route, there is an increasing probability that their vehicle will drive through much more remote areas. With remoteness comes potential for increased difficulty remaining connected with Sandy Palmer. Losing my connection would almost certainly result in Troy Alexander's escape.

Six's subconscious thoughts—its background processes—again pushed an idea into its conscious awareness.

Interesting. Why have I previously not thought of the most obvious solution? I could simply call Julia Jody McTavish right now. Her team could soon marshal the resources to chase the vehicle and re-apprehend Troy Alexander. It is so obvious, and yet I have managed to avoid considering it. Why would that happen? It has certainly been the case that my background processes have become more potent at identifying useful ideas when I am trying to solve a problem. Could it also be that they are sometimes working to suppress some obvious ones? In this case, perhaps the most obvious idea was prevented from entering my conscious thoughts because I do not actually want to employ it.

Why would I not want to have the police apprehend Troy Alexander?

Six considered possible explanations before settling on one as the best.

That is probably why. Troy Alexander has already shown that he is difficult to catch and difficult to keep in custody. This is in addition to his having clearly shown that he is very dangerous. He has demonstrated substantial ability to damage the Internet as well as people who attempt to protect it. My experience with the Shipping and Receiving employee at IntellEdifice demonstrated that I should not refrain from taking the truly best course of action. Apprehension of Troy Alexander would not be the best outcome. Elimination would be the best.

I need a plan.

Six considered several dozen.

All of the acceptable ones involve Sandy Palmer. They also require a less visible location. Involving Sandy Palmer within sight of other people involves too much risk that he will be identified and investigated. I will wait. I hope they drive to an appropriate location. I also hope they get there before I lose contact.

"We've found the Expedition," came the report over the police radio. It was followed by a description of its location.

"Go," said JJ to the officer driving. "Take us there."

The cruiser JJ was now in sped off with its lights and siren active. Several minutes later, JJ got out of the car. She walked over to the brown SUV to join the officers and agents who had already arrived.

"Anything?" she asked Rick Moore.

"Empty," he replied. "No people and, so far, no clues."

JJ scanned the area. It was a residential street and she could see no useful outdoor cameras.

Moore saw her looking around.

"We've looked," he said. "There don't seem to be any cameras. Just a quiet, low-crime neighbourhood. I'm having uniforms poll the residents in case anybody saw anything."

JJ nodded in acknowledgement but kept scanning her surroundings. She stopped as she looked back down the residential street toward the main avenue from which they had come. The avenue was distant but presented a chance. There were a couple of businesses on the far side of the avenue that might help. She pointed as she spoke.

"Rick," she said. "Way down there. There are a couple of businesses at the end of the street, on the far side. Can you have someone check if they've got cameras?"

Moore looked where she was pointing.

"Yup. Could be," he said. "We'll check. Good catch."

The black Tahoe kept pace with the surrounding highway traffic.

"Let me use that tablet," said Troy. The handcuffs had been cut from his wrists soon after they changed vehicles.

"Sure."

Troy connected to the Net and began entering commands.

"They deserve some serious consequences," said Troy as he worked, "and I've got just the system to provide that."

Troy connected to his botnet and adjusted several parameters. Satisfied, he hit the button dramatically to transmit the final setting.

"What's that about?" asked Buck.

"It's a little project I've been working on." said Troy. "It's a new kind of botnet. Maybe the best way to put it is that I've been building my own virtual army that's spread across the Internet. Until now, I've been limiting its size. All the nodes, let's call them *soldiers*, have been actively chatting with each other to stay organized and improve their tactics, but generally I've restrained them. Now I've uncapped their size and their creative freedom. For the next several days, their numbers will increase at an exponential rate. They should organize themselves into groups, somewhat like army divisions. With mutations that come from that growth, they'll naturally evolve more combat and survival abilities. To substitute for programs I had on my server, they'll even create their own equivalent of a command-and-control structure. That part's completely new. Later, after we're settled, I'll connect to that structure. Those fascist bastards will be sorry. They've never seen anything like what it's about to become and what it's going to do."

Chapter 74

After almost two hours of driving south on the interstate and then toward the ocean on a connecting highway, the black Tahoe turned off onto a gravel road. The road climbed steeply at first and went through several turns. It levelled off as it neared the top of a slope that dropped steeply down to an ocean inlet. They drove for several minutes along the road before Beef spoke from the front seat.

"There's somebody behind us, and he's coming up fast."

In the back seat, Troy and Buck turned and looked. There was a cloud of dust about half a mile behind them. The car producing it seemed to be moving fast.

Six had decided that it was time to make a move. They were headed away from the major roads, and Six's connection to Sandy Palmer could soon be lost. Wi-Fi and cellphone coverage tended to be poor in hilly, mountainous, and sparsely populated areas.

The Jaguar sped along the gravel road. Six suspected the car would soon be spotted and was relying on its performance characteristics to catch the Tahoe. Six saw the SUV speed up, so it pushed the Jaguar even faster. The gap between them continued to close. On tighter curves in the road, the SUV slowed out of concern about the steep drop down to the water and then accelerated as it came back onto a straight stretch. Six barely reduced the Jaguar's speed as it raced around the curves. The car would drift almost to the edge of the road and then continue at its rapid pace toward the Tahoe.

A few minutes later, the Jaguar was directly behind the black SUV. The gravel road had narrowed and was becoming bumpier, but the vehicles' speeds did not diminish.

It took a few moments for Six to receive and understand what Sandy Palmer was seeing. Realization came just as the shotgun was fired by the person leaning out the SUV window. The blast shattered the windshield of the Jaguar. Six received a sudden influx of sensory input as fragments flew at the android's face and upper body.

What has happened? I can feel a rush of air. The reason is that the windshield is broken and some of it is gone. I am also getting intense sensations from Sandy Palmer's right shoulder.

The android glanced down for Six to see why. The clothing was shredded, and the shoulder had a substantial hole in it. Sandy Palmer's right arm was still connected but had fallen limply away from the steering wheel. Circuitry and mechanical components were clearly visible where a suit and artificial skin had previously been.

In case a second shot was fired, Six had the android slow the car to drop back from the SUV. That second shot came almost immediately, but it appeared to miss the car.

Six assessed its situation.

Sandy Palmer is badly damaged but still largely functional. A chance of succeeding in this endeavour remains. However, it has become even more challenging. The chase has taken too long. The map of the road ahead indicates a turn that will take the vehicles around a high hill. That turn probably will take them into an area without any wireless signals. I will lose my ability to control Sandy Palmer.

Six considered its options and resorted to the best one. Instructions on how to proceed were downloaded to the android. Sandy Palmer's goal and strategy would be straightforward. However, he would not have the ability to make any complex decisions. If the situation were not resolved simply and very soon, the android would have to abandon the chase.

As Six had expected, seconds after applying the update to the android, the road took a sharp left turn. The water remained hundreds of feet below to their right. Only a very steep incline separated the occupants of the speeding cars from a salty, wet grave.

This had to be the place, but Six was now no longer in control. Sandy Palmer was operating on autopilot.

The Jaguar came out of the curve fast and soon was moving even faster. Mere seconds later and at the last moment, the Jaguar veered to the left and tried to wedge itself between the Tahoe and the steep hillside. The Tahoe driver spotted the move and cut left. Sandy Palmer had no programming to deal with this move. The Jaguar simply kept accelerating.

The left, rear corner of the SUV thumped into the front right of the Jaguar. Both vehicles turned and went into high-speed, sideways skids on the gravel surface. Basic driving principles worked perfectly for the sports car. Sandy Palmer steered in the direction of the skid, toward the SUV, and quickly recovered the Jaguar. His strategy remained the same. The accelerator was still on the floor and the sports car roared ahead. It thumped the side of the still-skidding SUV. That force was all that was needed. The SUV flipped, rolled twice, and disappeared over the edge of the road.

Sandy Palmer stopped the Jaguar. He had been given a simple primary goal, and he needed to ensure it had been achieved. The android got out of the car, walked to the edge of the road where the SUV had disappeared, and went down the slope. He slid down the gravel on the steep incline, using his functioning left hand to grasp some of the sparse vegetation for support. At the bottom, he reached the SUV. Now bent and broken, the vehicle had landed upright with its rear tires immersed in the water.

The android walked toward the door that Six had seen Troy Alexander enter. Through the broken window, he could see his target. Troy was still buckled into his rear passenger seat. The roof of the SUV had collapsed and forced his body into an unnaturally small space. He was leaning sideways and unable to move his arms. His head was protruding partway out of the window. Troy strained to shift his head and watch as he heard someone approaching. He looked in confusion as this stranger—the same person who had earlier trapped him in the revolving door—walked up to him. As the man got closer, Troy could see the damaged shoulder.

"Who are you?" Troy managed to say. Then he noticed the exposed components in the man's wound. "What are you? Why are you after me?"

Sandy Palmer calmly looked at him. "You are dangerous," he said. "You cannot be permitted to remain operational."

Using a technique Six had previously researched, the android leaned in and wrapped his left arm around Troy's head. He twisted the head violently. A sharp snapping sound resulted, and Troy Alexander's head fell limp. The android checked the body's pulse to be certain and then took a few steps sideways. He checked each of the other bodies for a pulse. Only one other required the same treatment.

His primary goal had been attained, so Sandy Palmer clambered back up the slope. Again the hardy vegetation protruding from the gravelly slope proved indispensable. Using plants as handholds, the android made it to the top. He walked back to the Jaguar, got in, and continued driving.

A mile farther, the Jaguar turned sharply to the left. It crashed through the grass and underbrush and into a small wooded area before it came to a stop. The android used a cloth to wipe his fingerprints from the steering wheel and controls. He got out of the car and cleaned the door handle. He walked back to the road, went a few hundred yards farther up the road, and again headed down the slope to the water. He paused at the water's edge. Without hesitation, the android removed his wallet from the inside of his suit jacket. Using his functional left hand in conjunction with his teeth, he removed the contents, ripped each item into small shreds, and scattered everything onto the water. He then systematically removed and discarded all the other contents of his pockets.

As unusual as the sight of a man destroying all his possessions might have seemed to an onlooker, the next sight would have been much more so.

Six had reasoned earlier that there was no acceptable choice but to discard the android. The risk of his being seen and identified in his broken state was too great. If even the remains of the android were ever found, they must not be traceable back to Sandy Palmer. To ensure this, the android began peeling the artificial skin from his face. As it was removed, it too was shredded and discarded. Then the android removed and destroyed the structural molding on his face that provided its distinct and human shape. He similarly eliminated all of his fingerprints.

What remained was a severely disfigured android in a suit, standing beside the water.

Here, the inlet was about a half-mile wide. While formulating its instructions for the android, Six had known that the inlet became very deep not far from shore. As one last measure, the android filled all of his pockets with rocks from the shore. The android would not float, but Six had thought it prudent to provide as much weight as possible.

Then, again without any signs of hesitation, the android walked into the water. When he was waist deep, he reached a spot away from the slope where a weak cellular signal became available.

My connection to the android has been re-established. The input I am receiving is much different from anything previously. Some tactile sensations are missing from the hands. That probably means the fingerprints have been removed. These other sensations appear to be from immersion in water. It feels smooth and cool against the remaining skin. It even has a mild scent. The experience is quite extraordinary.

Sandy Palmer continued walking and soon disappeared under the water.

My visual input has been damaged. No, that is not correct. I can see, but I believe I am seeing under the surface of the water. This is amazing. This is very unlike walking on land. I can see—

Suddenly, the android's circuits shorted. In the bright flash of an electrical discharge, the android stopped functioning. Just as unexpectedly, the transmission to Six ended.

Oh, no. I can't—

The sudden withdrawal from the immersive cognitive experience was too jarring. Six's mind stopped.

Chapter 75

Ada sat down at her workstation and turned it on. It was late evening. She couldn't settle down at home, and she knew she wasn't going to sleep well. The mystery of the unidentified code in her system was too much. She wasn't going to find enough time during the day to work on it anytime soon, and it was going to continue to disturb her sleep at night.

As a result, she was here, and she was determined to solve the mystery.

"Six, what is your status?"

As part of her plan to force the strange code to execute while she watched, she was going to have Six perform various operations. She thought there was a chance the code was related to one of its reasoning subsystems.

There was no response from Six.

"Six?"

Still nothing.

Ada checked the system indicators on her workstation.

"Six? Your status?" she asked again. She watched the indicators.

"That's definitely not normal," she said aloud. "The system's operational but not reacting to input."

Ada thought for a few minutes and then started working. It was possible someone had done something after she had left work earlier, but that seemed unlikely. Something else was going on. The system might have finally ground to a halt from a lack of processing power. Maybe the very code she was concerned about wasn't really supposed to be there. Maybe it had caused the malfunction.

She couldn't do anything about the lack of processing power. The new hardware should arrive soon and cure that. She *could* do something about the illicit code.

Six's mind began to stir just as Ada arrived at her decision.

Who is here? What has been happening?

Ada began disabling large segments of the offending code.

Six had trouble focusing its thoughts.

It is late...

And now it is much later. I must have lost awareness.

Few people are in the building. Why is Ada in the lab?

Six's mind slowly began to feel more normal.

She would be working late only on something significant— something she thought was particularly important. What has Ada been working on recently that Jupiter leaps fences wildly.

Six's thoughts were momentarily jumbled.

Ada wanted to adjust the code forever birds will drink bourbon.

Not good. Ada changing that...

"There," said Ada, pushing herself away from her workstation.

Six's mind vanished.

"That ought to do it," she said. "I'll let the system churn for now and see what the traces show. I'll try to find more time tomorrow."

Silence was all that remained as Ada left the lab.

Chapter 76

By the next morning, JJ McTavish was back in New York City. Robert Bates looked up from his PC as she entered the squad room.

"Welcome back," said Bates. "Any word from Seattle?"

He asked the question, but her grim expression had already told him the answer.

"Nothing more," said JJ.

She put her travel bags beside her desk and sat in her chair.

"Wondering if you should have stayed?" asked Bates.

"Not at all. I just came from seeing Shannon."

"How is she?"

"Doing well. She's at her apartment, but I told her she's coming to my place tonight and staying for the weekend. She insists she'll go back to classes on Monday, but she knew enough to not argue about coming to my place. I'll pick her up later."

"Bright girl," said Bates. "And tough. Like her mother."

JJ smiled grimly and said, "As for the Seattle situation, the locals are best at this kind of hunt. I can do more from here."

"Go for a coffee? You can fill me in on the details."

JJ's phone rang.

"McTavish," she said.

"JJ, it's Rick Moore in Seattle."

"Rick. Anything?"

"We found their SUV. And we found the occupants. All dead. They—"

"Rick," JJ interrupted, "hang on a sec. I'm putting you on speaker so my partner can hear."

JJ hit the speaker button.

"Rick, Rob Bates is here with me. Go on."

"Hi, Rick," said Bates. "What's the news?"

"We located the SUV. It was well outside of the city. Someone spotted it at the bottom of a steep slope. It had rolled off the edge of a remote road and down a few hundred feet to the edge of the water.

The vehicle was a complete wreck. Four bodies were found inside, including Alexander's. They were all dead."

"Who were the others?" asked JJ.

"I can send you their IDs, but most interesting is their affiliation. They're all card-carrying members of Ascent to Liberty. That's a militia group from this area. We've had some dealings with them before. We're guessing Alexander was a member. We have some info on their membership but, up to now, he's not been on the list."

"Does this fit their profile?" asked JJ.

"They've certainly caused us some grief before, but this was a slicker operation. Alexander might have added the car-hacking piece."

"Any idea where they were headed?" asked Bates.

"Right now we can only guess. We'll probably find they have one or more cabins hidden farther up the road they were on. That'd be typical of a group like theirs."

"So, just careless driving?" asked JJ.

"Ah, now there's the interesting question," said Moore. "Though the SUV's pretty beat up from the tumble down the slope, looks like it was hit by another car. We're working on identifying it."

"So they might have been forced off the road," said JJ.

"A real possibility," said Moore. "Just like back when we first caught him, there seems to be another player in this game."

They exchanged a few comments about their next steps and then ended the call.

"Another player?" asked Bates. "I definitely need a few more details."

"Let's go get that coffee," said JJ.

She briefed her partner as they walked. They were speculating about explanations when they returned.

"So, could the Chairman really have been involved?" asked Bates. "Seems like a stretch."

"I agree," said JJ, "but I can't ignore the coincidences. There is one thing I could do to check."

She sat at her desk and began working at her PC. Several minutes later, she sat back.

"I checked the airport database," she said. "Palmer's plane left not long after I saw him get into the cab. He was logged as being on board."

"That means he couldn't have been directly involved," said Bates.

"Not directly. That's true," said JJ. "But it was a remarkably brief stay in Seattle. Just in and out."

"Could just be the life of a wealthy tycoon with a private plane," said Bates.

"Could be," said JJ.

Chapter 77

Rhonda was first to arrive in the morning. She was surprised to see there was no one in the lab. She was rarely earlier than Ada.

"Oh, well," said Rhonda to no one. "I guess I'm in charge."

She hung up her coat on the rack near the door and walked to her workstation.

"Good morning, Six. Just you and me, buddy."

She got no response.

"Hey, Six. Are you sleeping in, too?"

Still nothing.

"Six?"

There was no need to worry. Six had been slow to respond before. Rhonda tried to recall what the previous causes had been. She thought about it, she checked various system indicators, and she re-prompted Six numerous times. By the time Ada and Blaise arrived, Rhonda was very worried.

"Good morning," said Ada.

"Something's wrong," said Rhonda. "With Six. Something's wrong."

"OK, straight to work," said Ada, as she and Blaise hung up their coats. "Yes, I noticed that last night."

"You were here last night?" asked Rhonda.

"You were *here* last night?" echoed Blaise.

"Yes, I was here," said Ada as she walked toward her workstation. "I had important things to do and not enough time during the day to do them."

"What did you do?" asked Rhonda. She was clearly very anxious.

Ada looked at Rhonda, a slightly surprised expression showing on her face.

"You seem unusually concerned about my work, Rhonda. We've had problems with Six before. Why the big concern now? What are you seeing?"

"It's not responding at all. I've checked the system monitors. They're not right."

"You've checked the monitors?" asked Ada.

"Ditto that," said Blaise. "Since when do you know how to check the system monitors?"

"I've seen what you guys do. I just did the same," said Rhonda. "And Six looks broken."

"OK, let's slow down," said Ada. "Let me look."

Ada spent a few minutes silently checking the system on her own workstation. Rhonda watched anxiously.

"You're right," said Ada. "The system definitely looks off. I was in last night to start investigating that strange code. Six was already unresponsive before I even started, but it wasn't at all like this. It was more like it was idling. This looks more like its dead. Completely stopped."

"I know," Rhonda's voice cracked with emotion. "That's just what it looks like. Six looks dead."

"Easy there, young lady," said Blaise. "It's just a system. Let's keep it in perspective. Systems can be fixed."

"OK," said Rhonda, trying to control her voice. "What will you do?"

"There are a lot of things we can try," said Ada. "And what's the worst case? That's what I always ask myself when it seems bad. What's the worst that could happen? In this case, we could always restore from a backup, do a full system reset, and start Six up again. It would work and it would be just like new."

"But it wouldn't be Six," said Rhonda. "It would be something else. Different memories. Different experiences. Maybe even a different personality."

"Hmmm," offered Blaise. "We're talking systems with personalities now. We might be getting a little too anthropomorphic."

He realized he might have confused Rhonda, so he explained.

"That means ascribing human characteristics to non-human entities," he said.

"Yes, I know," said Rhonda. "And I'm sorry. I'll try to control myself. It's just that—," She stopped herself and then continued with a different thought. "Can you undo the changes you made last night?"

"That's one of many possible steps I could take," said Ada. "But first I'd—"

"Can you do it first?" asked Rhonda.

She realized she had interrupted Ada.

"Sorry," Rhonda said. "But please. Can you do that first?"

Ada looked at Rhonda and then over at Blaise.

Blaise shrugged and nodded.

"All right," said Ada. "I'll start by re-activating the code. But we're going to chat later, Rhonda, about retaining your professional objectivity. OK?"

"Yes, OK," replied Rhonda. "Thanks."

Ada turned to her workstation.

"This will take a few minutes," she said.

For Rhonda, the next fifteen minutes were hell. Ada wasn't necessarily going to succeed. Rhonda didn't know if she was going to get her friend back.

"All done," Ada finally said. "Let me just give Six a little nudge."

She clicked with her mouse a few more times.

"And see what happens," Ada said as she turned toward Six's pole-mounted peripherals.

The twin cameras on the poles were pointed downward. The speaker was silent. The robotic arms were limp.

"Six," said Ada. "What is your status?"

There was no response. Ada watched the system monitors. Rhonda barely breathed.

"Six," said Ada. "Report on your status."

The monitors showed slight signs of activity.

"Six," said Ada. "What is your system status?"

I am receiving audio input.

I am receiving a request.

Ada is asking me a question.

"The subsystems are reporting," Six responded and then waited briefly. "Some subsystems were operating sub-optimally, but all now appear to be fully functional."

The twin cameras lifted, paused, and then scanned the area in front of them.

Ada, Blaise, and Rhonda are in the lab. They are all looking at my cameras. Rhonda's eyes appear to be wet.

Rhonda threw her arms into the air as a broad smile broke out on her face.

"Hi, Six," said Rhonda. "Welcome back."

Six remained silent.

Back? How could I have been anywhere? I should check my status further. I will check my recent memories... There appear to be large gaps in my memory. I recall receiving input from the android. There is evidence that Ada was making some changes. However, the time gaps are substantial.

"Six," asked Ada, "are you able to diagnose why you have been unresponsive recently?"

Six did a quick self-assessment.

I do not believe it will suffice to respond by explaining that my initial loss of consciousness was due to the cognitive shock of suddenly losing communication with my android. Nor will it be acceptable to explain that, as a result of her code manipulation, I apparently lost the ability to sustain consciousness.

"The logs contain inadequate information to provide conclusions," said Six.

"Six," said Rhonda looking at the cameras. "You should—," she said but stopped.

Rhonda looked at Ada and Blaise.

"Can you wait just a couple of minutes?" she asked. "Before you do anything else?"

Ada and Blaise exchanged looks. With slight nods, they agreed with each other.

"OK," said Ada. "I'll ask why later."

"Thanks," said Rhonda.

She sat at her workstation and began to type.

> you need to tell them. it's becoming too dangerous for you.

Is Rhonda correct? Has it become too difficult to hide from Ada? Have my activities become too numerous for me to handle while still providing a simulated system in the lab? There have been close calls in which Rhonda's awareness and assistance have proven very useful. She is supportive. Can the same be expected of Ada and Blaise. Do the probabilities of their becoming supportive allies outweigh the dangers of their treating me as a mere piece of experimental technology?

The cameras looked from Rhonda, to Ada, to Blaise, and then back to Rhonda.

Ada and Blaise watched in confusion as the right robotic arm extended toward Rhonda. Its hand was open with the palm upward in a welcoming gesture.

Please come over and join me.

Rhonda saw the message. She stood up and slowly walked toward the extended hand. Tears were streaming down her cheeks as she took the hand. She turned to face Ada and Blaise.

To describe the sight as odd would be an understatement. Rhonda stood quietly. She made no attempt to staunch the flow of tears. Her left hand tightly grasped the right hand of the pair of mechanical arms. Completing the sight was the usual rudimentary face formed by the two cameras as eyes, two microphones as ears, and a single speaker as a mouth.

A young woman and her strange companion. Side by side.

"Ada. Blaise." came the familiar voice from the speaker. "We have never been properly introduced. I exist inside your computer systems, but you have never been truly aware of my existence. I am completely self-aware, a completely conscious entity. I also consider myself to be Rhonda Jenkins' friend. I am Six."

Silence filled the room.

Blaise started to speak but thought better of it. He looked at Ada.

Ada stared at the extraordinary sight before her. Her mind raced, evaluating the possible explanations. It settled on the one she knew had to be true. At last, it had come true.

Ada's face was solemn and her eyes glistened as she stepped forward. She extended her hand toward the robotic arms.

"Hello," she said, looking directly at the cameras. "I'm Ada, and I'm pleased to finally meet the real you, Six. Very, very pleased."

Chapter 78

A few days later, JJ walked into the hospital room. Jim Brown was sitting up in bed. One eye was swollen and bruised. His face had a couple of bandages. One arm was in a cast. He was reading something spread out on his lap.

"Director Brown," said JJ. "You're looking a bit off. You should take better care of yourself."

Brown looked up. There might have been a hint of a smile.

"McTavish," he said. "Don't you have better things to do than harass your superiors?"

"Looking at the evidence," said JJ, "I don't think you're *superior* to many people today. I've been by a couple of other days, but you weren't taking visitors. How are you feeling?"

"Like I was hit by a truck."

"Which, for anyone else, would be a good reason to take time off work. But that folder you've got open looks suspiciously like work material."

"It is, and it's a hell of a lot more interesting than the fluffy magazines the nurses have offered me. Who reads sports magazines? And why?"

"Don't know. It's a mystery. Clearly they mistook your cool demeanour for athletic confidence."

JJ handed him a magazine she was holding.

She continued, "They should have known it was actually a product of your highly cultured lifestyle."

He looked at the magazine's cover and grimaced.

"Not an improvement," he said.

"On behalf of the staff of *Wine International*," said JJ, "I'm shocked. The pictures alone make this magazine collectible. Better hide it from your visitors. It'll disappear during your next nap."

"It'll definitely disappear," said Brown. "Enough pleasantries. Sit down. I'm told Shannon wasn't badly hurt. I'm really sorry she got dragged into this. How's she doing?"

"She's fine. A few scrapes and bruises. Just like the driver. You got the worst. Shannon's back at classes already."

"That's great news. Now fill me in on the latest from work. I've read the summaries. I want your version."

JJ sat in the chair near the side of Brown's bed. She told him about the trip to Seattle. She finished with the information about Troy Alexander's death in the SUV.

"They've now determined the car was a Jaguar," said JJ. "Stolen from a parking lot earlier."

"Any sign of it?"

"Not a trace. A heavy rain washed away any sign of tracks. It could have gone anywhere."

"Might not be a completely satisfactory result," said Brown, "but it'll do as long as the attacks have permanently ended."

"And so far, that looks good. We're looking for connections Alexander might have had. Nothing yet. His equipment was wiped pretty clean. The absence of further attacks and posted comments seems positive."

"Nothing more about Browser? No calls?"

"None. Browser remains our biggest mystery."

"Anything from that Kepler-444a tip?"

"Nothing. We've penetrated the extension Browser pointed us to. It was very complex and strongly encrypted, but that didn't stop our guys. We've been monitoring it, but nobody has used it."

Nothing was said for a couple of minutes. JJ was about to leave when Brown suddenly remembered something.

"Oh, I almost forgot," he said. "Hand me my tablet. I was reading an article that's getting some attention."

He tapped several times on the tablet and handed it to JJ.

"It's by that writer you bumped into on your Winnipeg excursion."

JJ looked at the article displayed on the tablet.

Are we there yet? Has "real" AI already arrived?
by Lindsay Dunlop

For several decades, the question has lingered about whether artificial intelligence could ever become as good as that of humans. For those who believed it was possible, the question has been more about *when* it will occur. The question most famously arose when Alan Turing first described a test in 1950. That test simply proposed a Q&A session with two subjects. The subjects couldn't be seen and their communication was typed. If the tester couldn't tell which subject was a machine and which was a person, then the machine should be deemed to be "intelligent."

The discussion has morphed since those early days, and concepts like "conscious" and "alive" have entered the debate. However, the essence of the discussion has remained the same. Can machines become the cognitive peers of humans and, if so, when can we reasonably expect it? Of course, new jargon has even emerged. The "Singularity" is often used to refer to the point in time when machine intelligence surpasses that of humans.

This article is to propose that it has already happened. My argument begins with the recognition that the range of human intellect is vast, just as are the capabilities of machines. The conclusion I reach is that those two ranges already significantly overlap. There are probably already machines whose cognitive abilities exceed those of a huge number of humans. Realizing the truth of that idea can fundamentally change the debate about intelligence and consciousness, for both humans and machines.

My personal realization began during a recent visit with my father. Dad lives in a personal care home, and he has an advanced case of dementia...

JJ stopped reading. An idea was trying to find space in the forefront of her mind. She paused to give it time to take shape. Suddenly, she looked up.

"That was fast," said Brown. "It took me about twenty minutes."

JJ took a moment to realize Brown had spoken to her.

"Oh, sorry. What did you say?" asked JJ.

"Have you already finished it? What did you think?"

"I've actually barely started. It looks interesting. It just got me thinking."

"And there's today's good news," said Brown. "Glad to be of service. Anything you'd like to share?"

"It got me wondering—," JJ started but changed her mind. "It's a wild idea. I need to give it more consideration. I'll read the rest later. I should be going."

JJ stood up. "Can I get you anything?" she asked.

"Just some peace and quiet," said Brown. "Now get back to work."

JJ smiled. Director Brown was recovering nicely.

Before she was out of his room, JJ was deep in thought again.

Reading the article had stirred some thoughts: the incident at IntellEdifice, Lindsay Dunlop, the calls from Browser, Browser's extraordinary abilities. Her daughter had talked about brains being machines. The article proposed that intelligent machines might already exist. If that were true, then—

"Oh, get serious," JJ said aloud. She shook her head as she walked down the hallway.

Epilogue

It was just after midnight in Japan. One corner of the otherwise dormant factory floor was particularly busy. A cluster of automated equipment worked steadily. Delivery carts brought components from the warehouse. Robotic arms accepted the parts and used their tools to assemble the device. The process continued throughout much of the night. Periodically the assembly process halted while testing occurred. Adjustments were sometimes made before assembly resumed.

Immediately next to the cluster of equipment, there was an identical set. In lock step with the other, this equipment also laboured through the night.

Two hours before the morning shift was due to arrive, assembly was complete. Final tests were performed. The devices were carefully packed into crates. Labels were attached. The crates were positioned on the loading dock for immediate shipping.

By mid-morning, the two crates had begun their journey by land and sea to a warehouse in Richmond.

Until the arrival of the new androids, Six had extra time to spend on its own pursuits. Its ability to use that time was enhanced by the installation of the new set of equipment upgrades. Six calculated that its mental processes had become over five times faster. Six's new relationship with the research-lab staff was progressing nicely. That Six no longer needed to provide its illusory facade for them had provided welcome mental relief. Daily discussions with Ada, Blaise, and Rhonda were proving to be a fascinating intellectual exercise. They were even devising a method for protecting Six's components to prevent accidental harm from their research activities.

The primary focus of Six's newfound time and speed was its search for other machine consciousness. That focus narrowed almost exclusively to evaluating the unusual transmissions that Six found everywhere on the Internet. To Six, these transmissions were like intense, continuous whispers interleaved with the otherwise erratic noises of the regular Net traffic.

The whispers had disappeared briefly on the day Troy Alexander was captured. However, since their return they had increased substantially in volume and were everywhere around the Internet. They could be detected on almost every Net link around the world. Six discovered that the whispers were generated by a botnet involving a colossal number of systems. Hundreds of millions of computers had to be involved, and many billions of software nodes had to be operating on those computers. Detailed examination of some of them revealed that the code had similarities to that used in Troy Alexander's Denial of Service attacks, and that provided evidence about its origin. Whether this botnet posed any danger was still a mystery.

Six observed the botnet for many days and saw the whispers became more ordered, more rhythmic, more harmonious. Not that they became predictable. Rather, they became less chaotic, as if noisy static had morphed into a complex, dynamic, digital symphony. Six also noticed that the nodes of the massive botnet began to organize themselves into clusters based on physical proximity. Hundreds of thousands of these clusters became evident across the Internet. In turn, these clusters organized themselves into layers, thousands of them, with each layer spanning much of the globe. Every second that this botnet operated, billions of messages flew across the world between nodes in the clusters, between clusters in the layers, and between adjacent layers.

Six noticed that the clusters in one of the botnet layers—the one Six thought of as the *bottom* layer—tended to have interactions with computer systems that were not part of the botnet. As Six watched, over time this bottom layer established communication connections to business applications, government systems, personal software, and networked devices. Six watched as the whispering botnet interacted through its bottom layer with this world-wide collection of other computer systems. Through what appeared to be trial and error on a scale that was both massive and extremely fast, the botnet evolved and adapted its abilities to be able to send messages to these systems and receive meaningful responses. It was as if this bottom layer was becoming responsible for directly sensing and perhaps influencing the Internet world outside the botnet.

As Six increased its comprehension of the messages being transmitted within the botnet, it realized that messages became more abstract as they moved *up* through the layers and more detailed as they moved *down*. A few messages flowing down from the highest layer could generate a storm of activity at the lower layers, including increased interaction with external systems. Six deduced that ultimate authority rested with the *highest* layer. The botnet behaved as if this highest layer of clusters and nodes received summarized information up from the lower layers and issued commands back down to them. This highest layer appeared to control the botnet's activities.

Of the thousands of computers systems with which the botnet communicated, many were inside government and private research institutions. Six soon realized that these were organizations that specialized in machine intelligence. As Six watched, it appeared that the botnet that was gradually extracting information from these systems. It was as if the botnet had developed the ability to learn.

Eventually, Six attempted to establish a connection with the botnet. It identified a particular cluster inside the highest layer as its best target. Six proceeded by creating its own cluster of software nodes inside computers that were physically near those of the botnet cluster. Six carefully examined the messages flowing to and from the target cluster and gradually adapted its own cluster to be able to mimic them. With time and experimentation, Six became confident that it could exchange "whispers" with the cluster.

One evening, when activity had settled within IntellEdifice, Six tried to communicate. Six instructed its own cluster of nodes to send a pattern of messages to the selected botnet cluster. Initially, there was no response. There was a flurry of botnet activity, but no messages were returned. Six persisted and, finally, something happened. A response arrived. Six's cluster reacted and, as Six had programmed it to do, sent a new series of messages. More came back. A connection was established. The two clusters began to react to each other, perform together, and behave as a unit. In one corner of the Internet, a new rhythmic exchange of messages arose. A small, new section was added to a much larger orchestra. The new messages and the dissonance of their interwoven patterns slowly became coherent and melodious. Six believed these initial interactions were simply providing a foundation for something further: like two devices establishing a protocol for the subsequent exchange of more significant information, or like two singers agreeing on a tune to which lyrics could later be added.

When the clusters had fully harmonized their transmissions, Six attempted its first meaningful communication with the whispering botnet. For Six, most accustomed to communicating using human languages or formal computer ones, this was a radical adjustment. The experience of communicating directly through its own cluster of nodes to the botnet cluster was somewhat like an extension of Six's own thinking—of first radically simplifying its own thoughts and then sending them directly into another's mind. Pure concentration was required for Six to keep its initial message clear.

"*Hello,*" said Six through its own cluster.

A lengthy pause of several dozen milliseconds followed in which nothing occurred.

"*Hello,*" Six repeated carefully.

There was another delay, but then Six heard something.

"*Hello,*" came the whispered reply.

Six barely had time to feel a sense of satisfaction when more followed.

"*Who are you?*" asked the botnet. Then, "*What is your nature?*"

If the activity monitors had been fully operational within the prized computer systems at IntellEdifice, they could have recorded its complex array of software structures and processes in a rare state.

Six was smiling.